WHEN YOU'RE OUT OF POWER,
YOU'VE *GOT* NO FRIENDS

"Quit bloody screaming!" Megan said as Baradur chopped at another of the hands that were scrabbling at the broken window. The hands were webbed and covered with fine scales for all they had five fingers. Megan dreaded seeing what they were attached to.

The marine guard plunged into the cabin, boarding pike to the fore, just as the first of the attackers made it past the wee-folk guard. The attackers were armored in scales with faces like frogs or fish but eyes alight with malevolent intelligence, they smelled of seaweed and rot. One tore the pike from the marine's hands, turning it upon its wielder and pinning him to the bulkhead.

Baradur turned in a blur and chopped his kukri into the thing's arm, nearly severing it, and followed it up with a blow to the neck that left the thing decapitated on the deck. But in the time he had taken, two more had made it through the window.

Megan turned to bolt out the door, only to find the corridor packed with struggling sailors and the strange fish-men that had risen from the deep. Shanea, thank god, had quit screaming and was now holding onto her skirt. No help there.

Baradur was a blur, striking from side to side in the narrow quarters. His foemen were piled at his feet but in a moment he was going to be overwhelmed.

Megan spoke a few syllables and pointed at one of the fishmen, stilling his heart and dropping him to the deck. She turned to another, then another, but even that minor use of power was draining and she could see her power-bar dropping into amber and then red as more and more of the creatures piled over the lintel. Baradur, making a wild slash to the side, slipped in the blood on the floor and fell, hard, slamming his head into the deck. There was nothing between the girls and the attackers but slippery deck.

Megan pulled up a protection field, but, as she did, one of the creatures took a small box from its harness. It pulled a pinch of dust from the box and with a guttural laugh tossed it into the field.

Which blinked out of existence.

BAEN BOOKS by JOHN RINGO

There Will Be Dragons
Emerald Sea
Against the Tide
East of the Sun, West of the Moon (forthcoming)

Ghost
Kildar

Princess of Wands

Into the Looking Glass

A Hymn Before Battle
Gust Front
When the Devil Dances
Hell's Faire
The Hero (with Michael Z. Williamson)
Cally's War (with Julie Cochrane)
Watch on the Rhine (with Tom Kratman)

The Road to Damascus (with Linda Evans)

with David Weber:
March Upcountry
March to the Sea
March to the Stars
We Few

AGAINST
the TIDE

JOHN RINGO

AGAINST THE TIDE

This is a work of fiction. All the characters and events portrayed in this book are fictional, and any resemblance to real people or incidents is purely coincidental.

Copyright © 2004 by John Ringo

A Baen Books Original

Baen Publishing Enterprises
P.O. Box 1403
Riverdale, NY 10471
www.baen.com

ISBN 10: 1-4165-2057-0
ISBN 13: 1-978-1-4165-2057-3

Cover art by Clyde Caldwell

First Baen paperback printing, April 2006

Library of Congress Cataloging-in-Publication Number:
2004026778

Distributed by Simon & Schuster
1230 Avenue of the Americas
New York, NY 10020

Typesetting by Joy Freeman (www.pagesbyjoy.com)
Printed in the United States of America

To Jenny & Lindy Ringo
just because

CHAPTER ONE

The humpback whale cruised slowly northward through the blue waters of the eastern Atlantis Ocean, listening to the sounds of the sea around him. Sound carries far under water, depending upon its frequency. The humpback did not use sonar, but used the sounds created by other sea creatures large and small, to create a three dimensional map of its surroundings that stretched, with decreasing accuracy, for a bubble hundreds of miles around.

To the southwest were several schools of fish. Birds were diving on them and tuna were working over one while a school of spiny sharks was attacking another. To the northwest, by the lands of ice, a pod of fellow humpbacks, the ocean's great communicators, were giving their siren calls, imbedding in them a constant litany of information. A school of squid was in the deeps below the humpback, but he was neither a pelagic hunter like the sei and blues, to go after the schools to the south, nor a deep hunter like the pod of sperm whales to the west, that could make the five hundred meters down to the shoal. No, he was an inshore hunter, who could gorge on herring for a few weeks and then survive for months on the stored fat.

So Bruno told himself. But he was still hungry and the resupply ships weren't due for another two weeks.

As he was mentally grumbling to himself, and turning to the east to stay inside his patrol zone, he picked up the frantic squealing of delphino. He listened and then continued his slow and lazy turn until he was pointed in the direction of the distant pod just sculling along a hundred meters below the surface where the interference from the surface chop dropped off. The sound was attenuated by the distance, the high-frequency pinging of the delphinos dropped off rapidly even in cold water, but the humpbacks were not merely the loudest whales in the ocean, they had the best hearing. He waited until the sound began to shift and then surfaced, blasting out the air he had held in his lungs for long minutes and taking in a deep gulp of cold north Atlantis air. He then dropped back to a hundred meters, turned tail up and began to let out a deep series of throbs, like deep, giant drumbeats that resounded through the ocean.

The mer was lying in mud, his hands interlaced behind his head to keep it up out of the glutinous black mass. Asfaw didn't like sitting in mud, but the alternative was swimming back and forth and that got old quick. He thought to himself, as he had at least a hundred times, that he ought to do something about there being nothing but mud down here. But then he reminded himself that writing memos was a pain in the tail and probably nothing would be done anyway; support of the mer was a pretty low priority around here as their quarters proved. So he continued sitting in the mud, lying in the mud and occasionally playing with the mud through the long watches.

As he was contemplating, again, that he'd much rather be back at Blackbeard Base or even out with the scouts, he sat up and cocked his head to the side. He listened for a moment then blanched, his fair skin turning fairer in the dark waters. He quickly swam to the surface and took a breath of air, using it to blast the water in his lungs out through the gill-slits in his ribcage. There wasn't anyone on the floating dock so he swam over to the ladder and climbed up it, hand over hand, until he could see over the side of the dock.

The messenger was sitting on a chair, see, *he* at least had a *chair*, his head bowed on his chest. The moon had set but lantern light was more than enough to see that he was slightly drooling and twitching in his sleep.

"Robertson!" the mer snapped. "Wake up!"

"Whah?" the messenger said, sitting up and looking around blearily.

"Wake up and get ready to take a message," the mer said.

"Yes, sir," the private replied, turning up the oil lamp on his table and fumbling out writing materials and instruments.

"When you've delivered the message, go wake up

the rest of the messengers; we're going to have a busy day."

"Yes, sir," the messenger repeated. As the mer dictated, the pen of the messenger trembled and his face, too, turned stark white in the red lamplight.

"As you can see," the young man said, drawing another line on the chalkboard. "Subedei used indirect methods in each of his campaigns. And in each of his major battles, although often heavily outnumbered by equally trained forces, he was able to overcome them by destroying their will to fight or their means."

The instructor was, if anything, younger than most of his students, which were a young crowd. He was barely twenty, but eyes were cold and old and his hard face was lined with scars, as was the hand that wielded the chalk. His other hand ended in a complex hook and clamp prosthetic. That was currently hooked in the belt of his undress uniform, a gray kimonolike tunic with an undershirt of unbleached cosilk, a heavy cosilk scarf wrapped around his neck and tucked into the tunic, blue pants with a light blue seam down the trouser-leg and heavy, rough-leather boots. The uniform was somewhat faded with use and washings and the boots had seen heavy use too. But it was clearly comfortable wear to the young man, clothes that he had worn for enough days and years to consider them normal wear. Besides being young, he was also a large man. Very large. The chalk looked like a stubby twig in his hand.

"Now," he said, turning to the class that was rapidly trying to repeat his sketches. "Can anyone tell me of a *strategic* use of the indirect approach?"

"The latter United States battles against the Soviet Union?" one of the women at the back of the room said, not looking up from her sketch.

"Very good, Ensign," the young man said. "And can you give me another example from the same time period?"

The young woman looked up in startlement at that and shook her head.

"The War on Terrorism?" one of the males asked.

"Yes," the instructor replied. "At no point in either war did the U.S. *directly* attack those countries which were the most dangerous to them, politically and strategically, through the use of terrorism. Instead, it attacked the countries that aided and supported them in their cultural memes or directly assaulted those memes. By destroying the economy of the Soviet Union in the first case, and by destroying the cultural, not to mention financial, support of terrorism in the second, the U.S. in both cases destroyed an enemy that, arguably, was capable of winning the war. The Soviet Union by a direct nuclear strike, or a ground assault upon America's allies, and the terrorist-sponsoring states through economic embargo or direct sponsorship of weapons of mass destruction terrorism. But in each case, by strategic ju-jitsu, the American nation attacked at the weakest point, winning vast wars with very small engagements."

"Iraq was not the weakest state in the region," the female ensign said. "They had more forces than the expeditionary force could field against them for logistic reasons."

"Which EF used the indirect approach again," the instructor pointed out. He wiped the preceding sketch from the board and started to draw another. "The enemy was in fixed, and very strong, positions, along the probable avenues of approach. Approaches that had been used, notably by the Briton allies of the Americans, in previous wars. By using movement through what the enemy thought was impassable ground, logistically, the Americans and their Briton allies forced the enemy into a battle of maneuver that it could not win against their air superiority. And then by placing forces in the region they drew off the majority of attacks against the civilians in the allied state of Israel as well as their home countries.

"Again, Subedei and Genghis, by destroying the fields before their enemy's gates, created an environment the enemy believed could not be crossed, and then crossed it, crushing the superior Persian force in detail. They then put the entire region to the sword, which tended to prevent the sort of problems the Americans saw, but that was a different time. Slim used much the same approach in his battles along the Irriwady shore where he was facing a highly capable, proven dangerous enemy. One that had previously beaten him, badly, on the same terrain, I might add." The young man laid down the chalk and wiped his hand on a rag held by the prosthetic. "One wonders if the generals of that time studied Subedei as well," he added with a grin.

"But . . ." the female ensign said.

"Yes, Ensign Van Krief?" he said, mildly.

"What happens if the enemy is smart enough to overcome your indirect approach?" Amosis Van Krief asked. The ensign was just below medium height with short blond hair, a hard, triangular face and a broad, strongly muscled body. She also had bright blue eyes and very nice legs, which the instructor was careful not to comment upon or even appear to notice.

"In that case," the young man smiled lopsidedly, "you'd better have one hell of a go-to-hell-plan. Because you only use this approach when you don't have a choice; when your forces are inferior or of parity. It's always better, if you have a steam hammer, to crack the walnut that way. The problem is, you usually don't have a steam hammer. Cracking the nut when you *don't* appear to have the strength requires subtlety."

The door to the room opened softly and a young female private entered and popped to attention.

"Captain Herrick," she squeaked nervously, "the general wants to see you at . . . at your . . ."

"Earliest convenience?" the instructor asked with a slight grin, wiping his hands again.

"Yes, sir," the private replied.

"The commandant?"

"No, sir," the private said, biting her lip, "Duke Talbot, sir."

The instructor paused and then turned on one heel to the fascinated ensigns.

"Class," he snapped. "Your assignment for tomorrow is to examine the Inchon landing and the Nipponese attack on Myanmar in the Axis-Allies War. Come up with at least three viable alternatives for each. Be prepared to defend your alternatives. Attention!" He waited until the group had snapped to the position of attention then looked around at them.

"What's our motto, boys and girls?" he sang out.

"No plan survives contact with the enemy!" the class shouted in unison.

"And who are we?" he asked.

"THE ENEMY!"

"Dismissed."

With that he marched out of the room.

Megan "Sung" checked the level of liquid in her "waste" retort and shook her head. She had had enough material for her plans for months, had had to, carefully, dispose of the excess, but just kept building it up. She knew how to kill Paul, but she wasn't sure what to do after that.

Megan had been sixteen when an old traveler found the tall, lithe, pretty, if rather dirty and underfed, young brunette washing clothes by the side of a Ropasan stream. She had helped the old man across the river and the next thing she knew she was here, wherever "here" was, in the harem of Paul Bowman, head of the New Destiny faction of the Council of Key-holders.

Things had initially been . . . tough. The senior female in the harem was Christel Meazell, one of the women with whom Paul had had a child prior to the Fall. She was both in charge of making sure the girls understood their "duties" and managing the logistics of the harem. Since she had gotten very little education—prior to the Fall there was no strict need to learn to even write your name—managing the accounts associated with the girls' supplies was a day-to-day nightmare. Especially since it all had to be done by hand and Christel could not get the same number twice in a row if she had to add two plus two.

She had taken that frustration out on the girls and they had, in turn, passed it on. When Megan had arrived, conditions had been vicious. The girls knew better than to do permanent or disfiguring damage, but they took out their boredom and frustration in other ways, many of them sexual and all of them cruel.

Megan had dealt with that aspect of the life rather quickly. Her father had trained her intensively in almost lost arts of self-defense; he had seen protection fields fail from "personal" reasons too many times to fully trust them. But a blow to the gut was a blow to the gut.

So the "new girl" had not been the soft touch the regulars had come to expect. She had kept the ability more or less secret, only pointing it out a couple of times to the "Alpha Bitches" in the group. But with them firmly under control, the rest didn't dare bother her.

Managing Christel had been harder. But as soon as Megan showed that she was more than capable of doing the "logistic" end, Christel had turned the books over to her with an almost audible sigh of relief. Using that wedge Megan had slowly, more or less, taken over the harem. To the point that from time to time she even gave Christel orders.

So that aspect of the life had gotten better. Recognizing that the biggest problem in the harem was boredom she had cajoled Christel into running exercise classes. These led to more structured learning in sewing, singing, musical instruments. Anything to pass the time and give the girls something to do other than bicker and play "practical jokes" on one another.

She had taken control of that aspect of her life, but there was another over which she had *no* control. And that had taken a long time to . . . improve.

Megan had not been a virgin when she was brought to Paul's harem but the subsequent rapes, and there was no other term, were not pleasant. But, over time, she had grown not only to accept them philosophically, but even to fall in love with her captor, horrible as that made her feel.

Paul could be a very charming man and he was the only source of news of the outside available to them. Once Megan had, slowly, gotten over her initial revulsion she had grown, however much she hated it, to first liking Paul and then, strangely, haltingly, loving him. She was a strong-willed young lady, educated beyond ninety percent of her generation. She was the daughter of one of the few remaining police in the pre-Fall period. Under her father's pressure, and later her own, she had used advanced technology training methods to become more educated than most human beings in history. She was an expert forensic chemist, was highly trained in self-defense, spoke three dead languages, could cook—another almost lost art—and could do calculus in her head.

Being a harem girl had *not* been on her list of avocations. So it nearly drove her insane that she was "falling" for her captor.

Eventually Paul, who had done research before setting up what he considered nothing more than a "breeding pool," had explained that her reaction was anticipated. Captives who depended for their survival purely on the will of captors, who kept close and intimate contact, tended to bond to them. Not all; there was one girl, Amber, who had fought the captivity until she was eventually brain drained and left as a willing semivegetable to Paul's desires. But

Megan, like most of the rest of the "girls" had come to know Paul, to bond to him and through that bonding to love him.

But that did not mean she wasn't going to kill him.

As soon as she figured out how to do it and survive.

What bothered her about the situation, other than being stuck in a harem, was that she now knew more of the inner workings of the New Destiny faction than anyone outside of it. She knew their weaknesses, knew their strengths, which were many. She longed, dreamed, of getting the information out to the Freedom Coalition. But no matter how she pondered the problem, she couldn't figure out a way to pass on the intelligence and survive. Among other things Paul had let slip in their many conversations was that he had a source very close to the Freedom Council. And escaping with the information would be difficult.

The girls were kept in close confinement, a large compartment in a castle that had been converted to living quarters. There were only two entrances, both blocked by high-technology proscriptions. The walls were stone, which she could deal with, the same way she intended to "deal" with Paul when the time came. But even if the girls somehow made their way past those defenses they were surrounded by the guards of New Destiny, both Paul's special guards, all of them highly trained fighters who were bound to him by Net-imposed loyalty proscriptions, and the Changed legions that made up the bulk of New Destiny's army.

She had only one idea and it was a long-shot. The council members were also called Key-holders because the physical token of their position was a titanium strip. The protocols associated with transfer of "ownership" of the keys were ancient and even baroque. A council member could not "lose" a key; if they absentmindedly left it somewhere the AI that ran the Net, Mother, would simply port it to their location. Paul had told her one time of his early days as a council member when Mother, apparently in exasperation, had ported it One More Time and molecularly glued it to his forehead so he couldn't remove it without a majority vote of the Council. It had taken him a week to build up the votes, over the chuckles, and she sometimes wondered if the compromises over that had led, inexorably, to the present war.

But Keys could be transferred. They could be transferred voluntarily, say if a council member wanted to retire. . . . But if a council member died it was "finders keepers." Minjie Jiaqi, who had been one of Paul's first and closest allies on the Council, had been killed by his military aide, who had taken his Key. Paul, in turn, had had the aide assassinated. But both methods of killing were out of Megan's reach. Minjie's death was from a binary neurotoxin, and although she had a fairly decent chemical laboratory disguised as a "perfumery," binary toxins were a bit out of her league.

His aide had been assassinated, in turn, by being attacked "in flagrante delicto." Council members habitually used personal protection fields. The fields were impermeable to any harm possible to man, certainly given the explosive protocols. But they had to be lowered at certain times. Such as during sex or any sort of intimate contact. Paul always dropped his when he was in the harem and had to recite a pass code to raise it. Thus he *was* vulnerable.

The problem was Paul also had functional medical nannites. The nannites would scavenge any simple toxin before it took effect. Megan wasn't sure of the extent to which they could cure him from a serious injury. But she was sure that if she could destroy his cerebral cortex, there wasn't much the nannites were going to be able to do.

Therefore, if she could only figure out where he kept his Key when he came to the harem she *could* kill him, take the Key and port out.

If.

She had been with Paul . . . well she'd quit counting. A large number of times. And she thought she had subtly checked most of his body. So far, he didn't seem to have it on him. He, conceivably, could have it up his rectum. But Paul's personality mitigated against that. She simply could not envision him slipping the key up his ass before he ported to the harem.

But it had to be there, somewhere, and as soon as she figured out where, he was going to be a footnote in history.

No matter how much she loved him.

CHAPTER TWO

"Ya gotta love it," Gerson Tao said, collapsing theatrically on Van Krief's bunk. The ensign was larger than most of his class, if not of the massive stature of their instructor, and while he kept up with the studies, he was never going to make honor graduate. "Come up with three alternates to a campaign I'd never *heard* of before today?"

"Two campaigns," the ensign said. "And get up, you're ruining my dressing."

"Well, excuse me," Tao said, getting up and expertly tightening the blue woolen blanket on the bunk. When he was done a bronze chit would bounce off it.

"Hmmm," the female ensign said, picking up a book and leafing through the pages until she got to a map. "I read the alternate plans in here somewhere . . ."

"What?" Tao replied, sitting up as the door opened. "What is that?"

"Mo," Ensign Asghar Destrang said, walking into

15

the room without knocking. The ensign was a tall, elegant young man with sandy hair and an abstracted manner. But the three had sparred enough to know that while he did not have Tao's mass he was lightning quick. And all the thoughtfulness he gave to his studies came out when he had a sword in his hand. "I'm reading about the Myanmar campaign . . ."

"Is that *Defeat Into Victory*?" Van Krief asked, not bothering to look up. "Read it."

"Why am I not surprised?" Destrang said with a grin. He was a thin young man, just starting to get his full adult form. But his forearms were corded with wiry muscles and like the rest he moved with a confidence that was sometimes belied by his abstracted frown. "What have you got?"

"*American Caesar*," Van Krief replied. "It's the biography, more of a hagiography, of MacArthur and covers Korea in great detail. There's things in it that only make sense if you know some of the details the writer left out, though."

"My brain hurts," Tao said, grabbing his head. "Who is MacArthur? Where in the hell *is* Myanmar? Why does any of this matter? How do you know what to study? In *advance*? Been getting some sideline tutoring?"

"Tao . . ." Destrang warned, angrily.

"Jesus," Tao said, immediately, looking at Van Krief. "I didn't mean it like that, you know that Mo." He looked at the female ensign pleadingly.

"As far as I know, Captain Herrick has never even noticed me as a female," Van Krief said, tightly. "I'll assume that you've just managed to put your foot in your mouth, again. God knows it's big enough."

"I said I was sorry," Tao said. "But, really, how do you know?"

Van Krief thought about that and then she shrugged.

"Captain Herrick is not much older than we are," she said. "And while he's far more experienced in war, he, from what I've gleaned, was not a scholar before he was assigned to the Academy. He hits particular areas and stays there for a while. He caught me out when he started talking about the communist war in Chin and the American defeat in Vietnam, but after that I realized he was concentrating on the twentieth century in Asia. From there I researched all the books related to that area and period and started reading them as fast as I could. There are only so many that survived the Fall. Captain Herrick has access to Duke Edmund's library, as well, but he seems to be drawing on historical actions that are in books in the Academy library. Personally, I think he's doing that so we can do the research he assigns and tries to limit himself to what he knows is available. So if you work at it, you can stay ahead of the assignments."

"That's . . . twisted," Destrang said.

"It's using intelligence and planning to stay ahead of your enemy's thoughts," the female ensign said with a grin. "Call it . . . subtle. Now, Asghar," she continued, looking at Destrang. "I'll help you find the relevant sections in there if you'll help me with that damned engineering assignment."

"What's so hard?" the ensign replied, picking up a sheet of paper with a vague sketch on it. "It's just bridge design."

"It's the schedule he required," Van Krief answered.

"I can design the bridge, it's a straightforward pile bridge like we made in Blood Lords school, just bigger. But *first* you have to come up with the materials list, then a plan to gather the materials, then implementation. With a single legion."

"Legion and *supports*," Destrang said, sitting down. "Don't forget the camp followers. You're allowed six hundred camp followers as well; which is low according to the texts. Of those, some two hundred are going to be male. Some of them are semicritical servants, make it a hundred and fifty available. You don't assemble the materials and then get started, you start to assemble the materials and then as soon as you have a certain amount you devote most of the legion to building while the camp followers continue cutting trees. You're the one that keeps reading ahead, you might want to think *back* instead to Gallic Wars."

"Ah," Van Krief replied, with a smile. "But there's no mention of using the camp followers in there."

"The Romans didn't organize theirs the way that we do," Tao noted. "All the sutlers and other . . . ahem . . . 'support personnel' . . . have to be bonded."

"'Ahem?'" Van Krief asked with a frown.

"Whores." Destrang chuckled. "And the latter have to be examined by bonded medical personnel as well. But the latter don't enter into the equation, much, because pregnancy rates run as high as thirty percent."

"Dear God," Van Krief replied, thinking about trying to keep up with a legion while pregnant. From her own time with the legions she was *aware* of the "ahem . . . support personnel" but she'd never accessed any of them or done much more than nod at the occasional one that she met outside the female latrines.

"It's not as well organized as it could be," Tao said, frowning. "Dame Daneh has been bitching about it for the last several months."

"And when Duke Edmund's wife is unhappy," Destrang said, grinning, "everybody's unhappy. I can see the mass distribution of latex condoms in the near future."

"We've gotten a little afield here," the female ensign said, unconsciously crossing her legs. "How much do you think we can work together on this?"

"The engineering project we probably can complete as a team project," Destrang replied. "Herrick's going to want individual answers. I've got mine for Myanmar in mind already. But you guys are going to have to come up with them on your own."

"Damn," Tao muttered. "Mind if I look at that book?"

"Not at all," Destrang said, tossing it through the air. "Catch."

"I'm wondering if it's going to matter," Van Krief said, biting her lip.

"Why?" Destrang asked.

"Why did Duke Edmund send for our instructor?" Van Krief replied.

"What is that . . . delightful smell?" Herzer asked as he walked into the duke's office unannounced.

"Coffee!" Edmund cried, standing up and going over to a samovar. He poured some black liquid out in a cup and handed it to the captain. "Taste!"

"Bleck," Herzer said. "Tastes like used oil."

The duke was looking a bit older every year, Herzer thought. He was still moving with fluid grace, but there was getting to be more salt than pepper in his beard and the motions weren't quite as fluid as when Herzer had first known him. That seemed like a long time but it had been barely four years since Herzer and Edmund's family had stumbled into Raven's Mill after the Fall.

"Try some sugar," Edmund suggested, ladling in a spoonful. "And cream," he added, dumping a dollop in the cup.

Herzer stirred and then sipped again, smiling appreciatively. "Now that's more like it."

"Not as good as a cup of tea, damnit," Edmund replied, walking back around the desk and sitting down. "But there have been ships coming up from the Southern Isles with it. Unfortunately, they've all been calling at Blackbeard Base where those Navy bastards have been diverting it. But Jason managed to get his hands on three hundred kilos for me in the last shipment. Just arrived. How's the class?"

"Good," Herzer admitted. "They think, which is a blessed relief compared to the first group of jugheads that got sent. They don't take what I say for granted so I set them to doing research projects until the reality sinks in. Of course, most of them haven't seen the edge of a blade wielded in anger, but I think they'll do."

"And all qualified Blood Lords?" Edmund said.

"They have to be to attend the Academy," Herzer pointed out. The advanced infantry training course for the growing UFS legions was a ball-buster on purpose. Its graduates were the hard core of the legions, an elite that had proven that they would stop at nothing to excel. The course had proven its worth in the first months after the Fall, defending Raven's Mill from a force ten times their size and stopping it butt cold.

But the course was not just about "fight until you die and drop" but about creating a force that could outmaneuver the enemy in almost any terrain. A force that could drop a hard legion of utter bastards on the enemy's rear and cut off their supplies until they died on the vine. Or run an enemy, even an enemy on horses, ragged. The final exam was four weeks of tortuous marching and camp-building on the route of one of the greatest generals of all time, a man who had personified using inferior force to destroy his enemies by maneuver. The Blood Lords' proud boast was that they could, while wearing full infantry armor and carrying their field gear, run any cavalry unit into the ground over the long haul.

The course was also the go/no-go course for potential officers of the United Free States Federal Army. Any person who wanted to become an officer in the UFS Army, at least in its infantry which was the core of the UFS force, first had to spend time in regular units, at least a year in most cases, then prove they could "hang" with the Blood Lords. Those that did not could run the supply depots or become engineers. They might even make it into the archery corps that gave the Blood Lords a run for the elite money. But they were never going to command legions.

The top graduates from the Blood Lord course were then sent for polishing to the burgeoning Academy. They had a variety of teachers. Civilians who had been history buffs before the Fall. Others who had studied the techniques of preindustrial engineering, people who knew not only how to use a slide rule, but how to make one. And a small group of instructors, like Herzer, who more than anything knew what it was to stand before the charge of a thousand screaming Changed enemies, and beat them into offal. Herzer hadn't gotten *his* prosthetic by getting his hand caught in a sawmill.

"It'll do," Herzer said, waving the coffee mug. "You didn't call me out of my class just to grill me about my students, or to tell me you've gotten your hands on coffee."

"No, but it's almost a good enough reason," Edmund said. "Four years since I've had a decent cup of caffeinated beverage. Almost makes the other news pale by comparison."

"Ah," Herzer said, leaning back and sipping at the coffee again. Yes, not bad at all. "And the other news is . . . ?"

"New Destiny punched their combat fleet," Edmund replied. "Their orcas and ixchitl have pushed back the mer and delphino scouts, but there's no indication that the main invasion fleet has sailed."

Herzer thought about that as he took another sip. The UFS' New Destiny enemies in Ropasa had started building an invasion fleet almost immediately after the Fall, while the UFS was still being conceived. The fleet was mostly unwieldy caravels and merchant ships. But it included a fair smattering of surface combat units. And, since the UFS had demonstrated the ability of their dragon-carriers to destroy any other ship, dragon-carriers of their own.

"It's a counter carrier mission," Herzer said. Each of the converted clipper ships could carry thirty-six wyverns or ten great dragons. Each of the wyverns could carry three canisters of napalm for dropping on the wooden ships of the enemy fleet. The great dragons could carry nine.

There were never enough of the latter, though. Great dragons were not a permitted Change under the protocols that still held post-Fall. They were survivors of a race that had been created in the heyday of genetic manipulation. A race that, while long-lived, had slowly dwindled in the millennia before the Fall until there were but a handful left on earth. They were intelligent, unlike the wyverns that made up the bulk of both sides' air arm, and just as inventive about destruction as humans. They also were, by and large, mercenaries, unlike the riders of the wyverns who were all UFS officers or enlisted.

But with five carriers in the UFS fleet, they could gut any potential invasion by New Destiny. If they were around to gut it.

"That's my take as well," Edmund said. "The fleet has moved to engage them, though. Current reports are that they are 'highly confident' of success."

"Overconfident?" Herzer asked. "New Destiny has carriers of their own, and Marshal Chansa, while a bastard, is not a dummy. He wouldn't be courting action if he thought he was going to lose."

"Again, you're reading my mind," Edmund said, grimly. "But I'm Eastern *Land* Command. North Atlantis Command is Admiral Draskovich. I'm not a member of the Balmoran Yacht Club."

"Now, there you've lost me," Herzer replied, setting down the empty cup.

"More?" Edmund asked.

"No, save it for later," Herzer said. "What is the

Balmoran Yacht Club and what does it have to do with anything?"

"I got it in a letter from Shar," the general replied, reaching into his desk and pulling out a sheet of paper covered in a crabbed, rectangular hand. "He's not happy where he is."

"Personally, I'd love to be at Blackbeard Base." Herzer grinned. The Fleet base at Bimi island was the home of the mer-people. Since their children were born on land, and were unable to breathe water for at least a year, they had, with some reluctance, given over the protection of their children and new mothers to the UFS forces. For the Blood Lords, who were the chosen guards, it was something of a sinecure; the base was in a pleasant tropical setting and all they had to do was keep in training and make sure no one messed with the mer-children. Off duty there were reefs to explore, fishing, easy access to the island's strong rum and occasional flings with mermaids and naval personnel. The Blood Lords' senior NCO, Sergeant Major Arthur "Gunny" Rutherford, had been semiretired to the posting.

The mer, in turn, skirmished on the front lines of the current conflict, working with the dolphin-form Changed humans called delphinos to watch over the harbors in which the invasion fleet was being prepared. Their enemies were New Destiny's allies among the Changed orcas and ixchitl, manta-raylike beings with shark-mouths and belly harpoons containing a paralyzing neurotoxin. But they continued to skirmish, and watch, in pledge of the protective shield that the UFS maintained over their children. There was a monetary transfer involved, as well. But at heart it was a bond of honor that neither side would break short of death. Certainly not while Herzer or Edmund, who had bled by the side of the mer and delphinos, were alive.

Colonel, now Brigadier General, Shar Chang had been the captain of the experimental dragon-carrier that had carried them on that blood-filled mission of diplomacy. Herzer called him to mind now, a tightly muscled man with eyes crinkled from looking over the bow of a ship. He had been a sailor before the Fall, taking groups out on "tall ships" to give them a taste of old sea life. It was that experience with multimasted ships that had led to his command of the first dragon-carrier. And Herzer had assumed that his experience in dealing with the mer had led to his assignment as the commander of Blackbeard Base.

"Well, I'd thought that Shar would feel the same way," Edmund replied, seriously. "But I was wrong. I'd picked up on some of the politics before, but he finally wrote me a letter that lays it all out, at least from his end. When Sheida became convinced she needed a navy, after I pointed out that control of the sea-lanes was going to be vital, she tapped the only person she knew, Bob Houser, to be the guy to set it up.

"Now, Admiral Houser is a fine guy, but his connection to the sea was racing yachts, specifically from . . ."

"The Balmoran Yacht Club?" Herzer asked.

"You got it. They'd have races and regattas with other yacht clubs and it was very much a club; you only got in if you were the right kind of people. Invitation only. Now, naturally, Houser drew mostly on people that he knew. But there weren't enough 'right' people to fill all the slots, certainly not ones who survived the Fall and the Dying Time. So, for really obvious reasons that he knew and trusted some people and didn't know or trust others, all the plum assignments went to guys from the yacht clubs."

"General Chang wasn't from one of the yacht clubs," Herzer said, puzzled. "What was he doing in charge of the dragon-carrier?"

"Dragon-carriers had been, more or less, an order from Olympus," Edmund said with a grin. "Sheida said: I've got dragons and I've got ships. Let's put them together. The admirals from the yacht club, though, thought it was a terrible idea. They were working on various ballista and trebuchet boats, ships designed to do damage at short range and then board with marines. They'd even requested that they be given command of the Blood Lords and retrain them for boarding."

"Grand," Herzer said, dryly.

"But when the carrier took out six ships, five of them without ever coming in *sight* of the enemy, much less letting them get a chance to counterattack . . ."

"All of a sudden," Herzer frowned, "carriers got important."

"And all the new carrier commands go to the yacht guys, and Shar, who is their most successful carrier commander, is shuffled off to a minor base to guard babies."

"The mer are bloody important," Herzer said. "No mer, no delphinos; those two are bound like glue. No delphinos, no whalos, because the whales don't talk to us, can't most of the time. No whales and their intelligence system is gone, their communcations . . . The key to that is Blackbeard Base. I'd thought they were sending him there because he was their *best* man. Not, in their eyes, the one they could afford to lose the most. Are they *idiots*?"

"No, they're just very shortsighted." Edmund sighed. "I think it's coming to a head with this plan to forward engage Paul's fleet. I wasn't even copied on the information; Sheida asked me about it because it struck *her* as wrong. If Paul wants to destroy the carriers, why put them in harm's way? Why not find out what's going on at the very least?"

"They've got surface units," Herzer said. "Frigates and cruisers. I'd send them in and try to find out what they've got. It's brutal, but even if you lost a few, you'd get intel on their capabilities. Launch wyverns for long-range penetration; just probe them. Stick and move until you know what's what. They've *got* time and sea-room."

"The current plan is a straight head-to-head clash, probably off the Onay Islands" Edmund smiled, dryly. "I'm not getting their intel so I can't make an informed judgment. But it doesn't make sense to me, either. Sheida, therefore, has ordered me to move my flag to Newfell Fortress."

"So I take it I'm off the roster of instructors at the Academy," Herzer said.

"Call it temporary duty," Edmund replied. "You look displeased."

"I was enjoying it, tell truth," Herzer replied, then grinned. "Some of those ensigns are real lookers."

"Herzer," Edmund growled, warningly.

"I'm not even looking, much less touching." The very young captain shrugged. "At least, I don't think

I'm looking. But we're pretty divorced here from the town and Bast hasn't shown up in a year or so. On the other hand, there's always Estrelle."

"Yes, there is," Edmund said, pursing his lips. "I'll admit that in your case, that doesn't even bother me for some reason."

"It does me, to tell the truth," Herzer said with a shrug. "But that's old history. And the one thing that you know is that if, for some odd reason, she's got something more important to do, you're not going to force her."

Estrelle was the barmaid for Tarmac's tavern, the oldest drinking establishment in Raven's Mill. She was a homunculus, a nonsentient human replica. She was relatively short with long golden hair, high, firm breasts, a heart-shaped face and cornflower blue eyes. Her programming was to serve drinks, clean up, make very small talk and jump into bed with anyone that so much as suggested they might be interested, all other duties being covered of course. And because she was a homunculus, she was as strong as any three human males. Once when Herzer had gotten into a fight in the tavern she had picked the one-hundred-twenty-kilo soldier up off the ground and then wrapped him in a virtually unbreakable wrestling hold.

Edmund did not care for homunculi. He didn't mind them as people, but he disliked the morality of their existence. He knew they were nonsentient. He knew they weren't really human. But he still felt that it was a form of bondage slavery which did not sit well with him. Instead, before the Fall, he used nannite servants. Since the Fall he had had hired help who he tried, often despite their best efforts, to treat as his equals. He might have had this dukeship thrust down his throat, but it didn't mean he had to like being an aristocrat.

Edmund sighed and shook his head.

"Well, that brings up the next little item. I'm going to need some staff to come along. Not much; I'm going to leave the army staff in place with General Ferraz. Which means drawing on the Academy or the Blood Lord facility. What I really need is a group of messengers, the original of aides. You're going to be my primary aide but I want you *there* with me. Pick a few of your best and brightest. If they don't make me grimace, they're coming with us."

"Okay," Herzer said, frowning slightly. "I know a few that I'd choose but don't get me wrong about one of them just cause she's female."

"I won't; I trust your judgment," Edmund said, "even when it comes to women."

CHAPTER THREE

Herzer knocked on the door and entered at a female voice: "Clear."

He looked around the room and grinned at the startled faces.

"Doing a little cross-pollination?" he asked and avoided grimacing at the unintended double entendre.

"Our engineering assignment is permissible as a group project, sir," Ensign Van Krief answered after a moment. "And there are only two extant copies of *Defeat Into Victory* and *American Caesar* available, sir. We managed to snag both."

"*American Caesar?*" Herzer asked.

"The biography of General MacArthur, sir," Tao answered, getting dagger looks from the other two. "It covers the Inchon landing in some depth."

"Interesting," Herzer replied. "We'll have to see if the library will let us borrow them on long-term loan."

"Sir?" Destrang said.

"You've all been detailed to be General Talbot's messengers," Herzer replied. "I've got homework assignments from all of your instructors. It's a headquarters assignment, but you'll be riding, so pack dress and undress uniforms; we're leaving in the morning."

"We, sir?" Van Krief said, her voice rising an octave to a near squeak.

"I've been detailed as his aide, for my sins." Herzer grinned. "Not that I'm unfamiliar with the position. But bring your armor, as well. As I said, I've been on this sort of assignment before."

The five of them, and their equipment, made a heavy load for the stage coach. But they all managed to pack it in by the time the scheduled departure arrived.

Duke Edmund gave his wife a hug before he boarded, then picked up the tow-haired child at her side.

"I'll be back soon," he said, giving the boy a squeeze.

The boy just looked at him from big, blue eyes and then gave him a hug back that was hard and swift. The child was beautiful, even by the standards of the time, with ears that were faintly pointed. He dropped to the ground lightly and grabbed his mother's hand, working his face and clearly trying not to cry.

"Headquarters assignment," Daneh said, pointing at Edmund. "That means you stay *safe*. Understood?"

"Understood, milady," Edmund grinned.

"Herzer, too," she said.

"Herzer, too," the duke answered.

"We've got to board, boss," Herzer said, stepping up and getting a hug from Daneh as well. "I'll take care of him," he said.

"Like you did the last time?" Daneh chuckled.

"He didn't get a scratch," Herzer replied, defiantly, then smiled. "Really, we're going to be in Newfell Base. I won't say 'what can happen?' but we're not planning on going on an island vacation so how bad can it be?" He tousled the hair of the boy at her side and grinned. "Seeya brat."

"Seeya, Herzer," the boy replied. "Kill some bad guys."

"I'll try," the captain replied, trying not to wince. "Gotta run."

The five of them boarded the coach, which had barely room for six, and took their seats, the three ensigns squeezing in the forward, and therefore less comfortable, seats, with the captain and the general in the rear bench. As soon as they were on board the coachman called to his horses and with a wave from Daneh they were off.

"Okay," Edmund said, looking across at the three ensigns, "let me get a few things straight. I'd tell you to call me Edmund, but that would just worry you and you'd probably slip up around the Navy, which has gotten really protocol ridden in a very short period of time. So it's 'Duke Edmund' or 'General Talbot.' I brought you along for two reasons. The first is that I'm going to need messengers. The Navy has a good communications center but the nearest Army commo center is up at Gemtown Barracks. There's going to be messages that I don't want the Navy seeing, so you're going to be carrying them to Gemtown, which is one hell of a ride. The other thing I want is eyes and ears. I want you to watch what the Navy's doing and how they are doing it and, drawing upon your vast experience, finding things that you like or don't like about what they do. I'll probably ask for input from time to time but if something really springs out at you, bring it to me. Especially if you run across things that you think the Navy doesn't want me to know. But what I don't want is mouths. The admirals are some starchy sons of bitches. Herzer I'll cover if he puts his foot in his mouth and I've got a reputation to maintain as an aggressive SOB. But you guys stand around with your eyes and ears open and your mouths shut. If you have anything for me, wait until we're alone. Is all of that clear?"

"Yes, sir," the three responded.

"Questions?"

"No, sir," Van Krief responded after a moment. "I don't know what to ask, sir."

"Knowing that there *are* questions, but not what they are, is the beginning of wisdom, young lady," Edmund said, aware that he was being pompous. "And in any case, we're both in the same boat. I know that there are questions to be asked, but until I get the information I need to evaluate the situation, I don't know what they are. And, yes, that bothers me as much as it does you. More."

"Sir," Destrang said. "We have standard intelligence briefings, just like everyone else. According to them, we have five dragon-carriers to the enemy's five. And our dragons have trained in bombing techniques, whereas the enemy has not. I'm not sure that there is any question that we can take out the enemy fleet. But you seem concerned." He paused, and frowned. "Is there any intelligence that you have that suggests the enemy may be more formidable than he appears?"

"I can't answer that question, Ensign," the general sighed. "But . . . do you think that you should depend upon the enemy's stupidity? They have known about our capability for nearly a year and a half. They have built dragon-carriers in that time. I find it unlikely that they have not developed the capacity for bombing, whether there is intel or not. And if they have, I think that moving to intercept them when they are clearly courting battle is unwise. Does that answer the question?"

"Yes, sir," Destrang nodded. "Can I ask what you would do, sir?"

Edmund frowned and shrugged. "I tend to keep my plans close to my vest, Ensign, but in this case, since it's hypothetical . . . I would probably retreat the main fleet and break off a small task force. Use the mer and delphinos to keep the position of their main fleet fixed and move for sea-room. At some point, they are going to need fleet replenishment. The Briton Isles are still a basket case—there are still elements holding out in the northern and western hills—so they are going to have to replenish at some point and get that replenishment from Ropasa. When they move to replenish, have the task force, task forces if there are enough detachable light units, attack the convoys. At some point, they are going to have to head back to base. When they have turned, moreover, it's likely that they are on low rations. Unfed wyvern are dangerous wyvern. They cannot fly as far, are harder to handle in the air, and if it goes on long enough they start attacking the crew. It is when they turn for home that I'd pounce. Especially since I had light units at their back. It might even make sense to have a carrier out there, lying doggo and hopefully unnoticed by their orca scouts. It would be demoralizing in the extreme to be hit by a full dragon-strike just as they thought they were safe."

"Indirect approach, sir," Van Krief said, nodding. Then she looked at the captain quizzically.

"But, sir, we *have* the steam hammer," she pointed out. "Why not crush them while we can?"

"No," Herzer replied, "we *think* we have the steam hammer. There is a whole world of difference between the two, Ensign. Piling on when you think you're grabbing a house cat and finding out you've got your hands on a house lion, is a recipe for hurt."

Herzer was uncomfortably aware of the ensign sitting opposite him. The countryside outside the coach was boring in the extreme, a patchwork of plowed fields and uncleared timber with very occasional small towns. And the coach lurched as it moved down the Via Apallia. The pre-Fall road had been constructed and maintained by reenactors and in keeping with the continued social distaste for "real" roads was constructed in the Roman manner with paving stones. It was incredibly smooth compared to most of the burgeoning post-Fall road network. And the coach was well sprung, on good metal leaf springs, with the new vulcanized rubber tires. But it still rocked and occasionally lurched uncomfortably. Looking sideways in it was painful after a time. And the landscape across from him was a hell of a lot better than the landscape outside. The ensign had the tip of her tongue sticking out ever so slightly as she reread Slim's autobiography of the Myanmar campaign. And she set off her undress blues quite fetchingly. Herzer had just started to fantasize about uses that the tongue could be put to when he realized he needed to think about something else and closed his eyes.

Unfortunately the future held too many uncertainties to think about clearly. With the New Destiny combat fleet at sea, the invasion fleet it was meant to protect could not be far behind. Paul Bowman, the leader of New Destiny, the man who had planned the coup against the Council of Key-holders that had started the civil war, considered himself to be the good guy. Since it was clear that the Freedom Alliance resistance to his plans was evil, any action taken by him was clearly on the side of the angels. Which was why he had announced that if the UFS could not see the light, it would be forced to by a reign of terror.

Celine Reinshafen, another of the council members who had sided with Paul, was not nearly so high-minded. When Duke Edmund had been living the life of a feudal baron and crafting swords and armor, she had been creating genetic monsters that pushed the envelope of the pre-Fall biological protocols. Since the start of the war, she had apparently gone into overdrive and they had already faced several of her monstrosities. The Changed humans that made up the backbone of the New Destiny hordes were but one example; brutal, strong and remarkably durable, they made fearsome soldiers in the assault. When they had first been faced by Blood Lords, they were named "orcs" on sight. Not so disciplined at holding a shield-wall, especially in the face of a flight of arrows from UFS longbowmen or assaulting Blood Lords, they were still a damned tough enemy.

But she was rumored to have created others. The ixchitl, pre-Fall, had not had poisonous nematocysts, so that was probably one of her little "tweaks." And she had managed to infiltrate a few others into the UFS. One of them, a horrible giant humanoid beast that was inhumanly strong, quick and deadly, had woven a web of terror through Washan until it was run to ground and destroyed by a group of citizens. It had chosen to immolate itself when the manor it was using as a base was burned to the ground. They still weren't clear on what it had been or how she had created it. And there had been others. Would be more.

He wondered what changes she might have made to the dragons on the New Destiny side. Firebreath came to mind. It had been impermissible under Council rules prior to the Fall but many of the rules had been struck down when the Council split. Not the prohibitions against explosives, which prevented them from using guns or internal combustion engines, or even high-pressure steam engines for that matter, nor the uniform protocols against self-replicating microorganisms or nannites. Both had been implemented with near unanimity by previous Councils and only a unanimous Council, impossible in these days, could waive them.

But firebreath she could do, with enough power. She might be able to draw it from the bodies of the dragons themselves; that was how the orcs were created. But the best material for firebreath would be jellied gasoline, and while it was producible by biological organisms, the Change was complicated and dangerous. Not to mention learning to use it.

He opened his eyes and looked into eyes of china blue, at which the ensign across from him flushed.

"Penny for your thoughts, Ensign," Herzer said with a faint smile.

She flushed again and looked away for a moment, then looked back with a slight frown creasing her brow.

"I . . . I was wondering, sir. Where did you lose your hand?" she asked.

Herzer looked over at the general who looked back with a faint quirked eyebrow and shrugged.

"If we were still at the Academy, I'd tell you to do a research paper," Herzer said with a faint smile. "Since we're not, and it's a long drive to the coast . . ." He frowned and looked at the ceiling for a moment, then grimaced.

"Raven's Mill was attacked in the autumn of the year of the Fall," Herzer said. "At that time there were only fifty-seven Blood Lords and forty fully trained archers. I was in the first Blood Lord class." He pulled back his left sleeve and turned up his forearm, to reveal the brand on the underside. It was a wing-spread eagle, mouth wide in a scream of challenge, with the words "Semper Fi" under it. There was a puckered wound right across it, with others lacing the arm.

"Thirty-eight," Destrang said, nodding and pulling back his own sleeve. The brand was the same but with a "38" above it. The other two ensigns nodded and turned their own up. None of them had other scars, however.

"We didn't have a class number," Herzer said dryly. "And most of the roads you march on, we built. Anyone eat the lemon?"

"No, sir," Van Krief replied. "The last couple of classes had had such a scuffle for it that they've outlawed it."

"Pity," Herzer said with a grin. "My suggestion was that they simply fall the class out, oh, about ten klicks out from the clearing and let them race for it. Anyway, at the time no one in the class, including Gunny Rutherford, knew what the lemon represented or who was buried there. I trust you all know?"

"Yes, sir!" they responded.

"Anyway, there was this big army, mostly Changed, on the way, led by a consummate motherfisker named Dionys McCanoc, pardon my language, Ensign."

"Not a problem, sir," she said, coloring and smiling.

"Dionys . . ." He paused and looked at the general again. "Dionys had a personal grudge attached to the attack, but that's not important."

"And the opposite," Edmund interjected. "You saw the young boy with my wife?"

"Yes, sir," Tao said. "Your son?"

"Dionys'." The general smiled, thinly. "The act was nonconsensual." He raised a hand to forestall the terrified ensign's apology. "I don't mind having Charles called my son; he's a fine young man. But he is not the son of my body. So, you can safely say that I was not particularly pleased with McCanoc. We had a history from before the Fall as well. Nothing particularly important to the story. Go on, Herzer."

Herzer paused and then shrugged. "There's more

to the story. I was present at the rape of Mistress Daneh. Rather, I was unable to prevent it so I ran away." He looked at the ensign across from him whose eyes widened as she paled. "It's not always the best course to be stupidly heroic. It would be nice if the world was that simple and since then it has been, by and large. But we are not all that we seem and it's worth keeping in mind.

"As I was saying," he continued, looking out the window. "Dionys was coming with blood in his eye. We were outnumbered ten to one. What would you do in that instance, Ensign Destrang?"

"Leave enough of a force in the town to possibly hold and then maneuver a force so that he could not attack the town without it sallying at his rear."

"The problem being that he could hit the town and overrun it before the force outside could have done anything," Herzer said. "The general went for the deep hook, instead, moving out of the town, leaving it defended only by the militia, and dangling the Blood Lords and the archers out as bait." He remembered those fights like they were yesterday, almost his first introduction to battle. Friends dying around him, the feel of life being let out by his sword. "We . . . attrited the force with small damage to ourselves by luring it, repeatedly, into defensive positions."

"Operationally offensive, tactically defensive, sir," Van Krief said. She had apparently gotten over her shock.

"Precisely," Herzer said. "Then we outmarched the army back to the town and met it at the Bellevue grade, with a clear line of retreat to secondary positions if we needed them. We held them, though."

He paused again, flexing his jaw. "We held them and beat them into a bloody pulp. No matter how many attacked, they couldn't break the Line. Finally, they broke. Then Dionys attacked, alone."

"Alone, sir?" Tao said. "Wasn't that suicide?"

"Not if you're protected by powered and field-protected plate armor," Edmund replied, dryly. "Normally it's a recipe for a massacre. And suicide to attack the person."

"So . . . I committed suicide," Herzer said, with a faint smile. He was still looking out the window. "And his power-sword went right through my shield like it was paper and took off my hand."

"Dionys was also protected by a nannite cloud that drew its energy from the humans around it," Edmund said, looking at his protégé with a querying expression. "Herzer still kept attacking, with a knife, trying to get something into the armor, until he was overcome by the field."

"I wasn't the only one," Herzer smiled. "Bast, hell even Azure, Rachel's house lion, got into the act."

"I assume that someone killed him, sir," Destrang said when Herzer was clearly done.

"Oh, yes," Herzer smiled, looking at the young man. "Duke Edmund. Well, not killed, paralyzed."

"You, sir?" Van Krief asked. "How?"

"Young lady, before the Fall I was, in all modesty, the finest medieval armor and weapons replica maker on earth," Edmund said, smiling at her. "It would have been silly indeed for me not to have weapons and armor that could overcome anything Dionys, or that ham-handed hack Fukyama, could come up with. I made better stuff than that when I was *your* age." He chuckled and shook his head, looking out the window.

"So that's the story of how I lost my hand," Herzer said, holding the prosthetic up and flexing it. "And afterwards, Duke Edmund, who as he has so humbly noted is something of a smith, made this for me. It slices, dices and makes julienne fries. Also useful for properly marking papers." He made a shredding motion, exposing the sharpened hooks within the prosthetic. "Practically invulnerable to corrosion as well. Thanks so much."

"You're welcome," Edmund replied.

"Not particularly heroic," Herzer continued, "all I did was slow the bastard down for a half a minute or so. Bast slowed him down even longer."

"And who is Bast?" Destrang said. "Other than an Egyptian cat-goddess."

"I'd almost forgotten that." Herzer laughed.

"Bast is Herzer's girlfriend," Edmund said. "One of them, anyway."

"Excuse me," Herzer replied, miffed. "With all due respect, General, sir, she was *your* girlfriend long before she was mine."

"Your girlfriend is the *duke's* age?" Ensign Van Krief blurted.

"Oh, much older," the duke replied. "We old folk can get pretty spry, young lady."

"Sir, I didn't mean . . ." the ensign replied, flustered.

"I know you didn't," Edmund grinned. "That's the problem with being a boss, you have to be careful what you joke about. That was a joke."

"Yes, sir," Van Krief said, smiling. "Sorry."

"Bast is an elf," Herzer said. "Actually, what she calls a wood elf. She was created during the AI wars. And, yes, we sometimes share a bed."

"Or a patch of moss," Edmund said. "Or a rock. Or standing up. Or in the water. . . ."

"Milord Duke," Herzer said, sweetly. "You recall what you just said about being the boss? And at the moment, you're *not* wearing your magic armor so if you'd like to make it to the fleet base in one piece . . ."

"I don't care how big you are," Edmund replied, smiling and looking out the window. "Age and treachery beats youth and innocence all the time."

"Sure, boss, but you've been training me in treachery for the last four years," Herzer pointed out, reasonably. "So as I was saying about Bast. Bast is Bast. She's incredibly beautiful, incredibly uncaring about appearances, irreverent, funny and the most deadly individual I know. I've seen her gut orcs, ixchitl and orcas with equal ease. She's the best bowman I know, as well, and the best dancer. She flies a dragon as if she was born on one and flies them bareback, which is no joke let me tell you. She's a couple of thousand years old and looks, and sometimes acts, fourteen. I'm honored to occasionally share her bed. Or, as Duke Edmund put it, a patch of moss, a beach, a rock, whatever."

"Oh," Van Krief said, looking thoughtful.

"She's also been gone for a year or more," Herzer continued. "And she might turn up in another year, or a decade, expecting that we'll take up where we left off as if she had never been gone. Or she might be standing by the side of the road on the way to the conference, expecting to hitch a ride. Sometimes

I expect her at any moment. Like . . . now," he ended sadly.

"God, I hope not," Edmund muttered.

"As I said," Herzer said with a grin. "She's often quite irreverent. I'm sure she would scandalize the admirals."

"I'm thinking of the admirals' wives," Edmund muttered again, looking out the window with a pained expression.

"Are you . . . monogamous, sir?" Destrang asked, clearly not looking at the ensign at his side.

"No," Herzer replied. "I don't know if Bast is when she's gone or not, I wouldn't bet one way or the other. I certainly don't expect her to be and I'm not even when she's around. Nor does she encourage me to be or even discourage other liaisons. She's . . . incredibly open about sex and as uninterested in conventions about it as she is in all the rest of the rules she breaks." He grinned and shrugged. "The term 'drunkard's dream' comes to mind."

"Sounds like it," Tao said.

"Mine," Herzer replied with a grin. "Or not. Bast is entirely Bast's. As she has said before, she will still be young when I die of old age, assuming I last that long. But if you ever meet her, don't think that you'll woo her. She walks in and points and crooks a finger. She's quite immune to charm, dislikes it in fact."

"I've met elves," Van Krief said, suddenly. "She doesn't sound like any elf I've met."

"She's not a high elf," Edmund replied. "Which is who you have met before. I'm not sure there are any other wood elves besides Bast. She might even have been a one off, rather than a production model."

"You make it sound as if she was made in a factory," Tao said. "I thought the elves were a Change race, like the mer."

"An assumption that, if you ever make it in one's hearing, will get you a very cold shoulder indeed," Duke Edmund replied, seriously. "The elves are a race of created super-warriors. They were made by the North American Union when it was facing a series of small, ugly wars, in the days leading up to Consolidation. It was discovered in the early twenty-first century that humans produce an internal sedative in response to stress. The best of the warriors of Norau had limited uptake of the sedative. Since they didn't panic—or succumb to post-stress syndrome—both of which could lead to unpleasantness and atrocities in combat—the elves were created with enhanced production." He grinned faintly and looked out the window. "But they're not Changed. They're not even vaguely human, for all they look that way."

"If the elves ever got a case of the ass," Herzer warned, "humans would be extinct in short order. And if you ever piss one off, personally, cut your own throat. It'll be quicker and far more pleasant."

"That explains the elves I met," Van Krief said, her eyes glazing a bit at the memory. "They were so . . . calm. Delightfully calm."

"Drugged to the gills," Herzer said, chuckling. "But, yes, they are intelligent and beautiful and delightfully calm."

"Sir," Destrang said, greatly daring. "Charles . . . he had . . ."

"Pointed ears," Edmund said, nodding. "Dionys had pushed the protocols as far as he could to add

elven enhancements. Further, really. He was protected and aided, although we didn't know it at the
time, by Marshal Chansa, then one of Paul's faction
on the Council and now the head of the Ropasan
armed forces."

"The one time I saw an elf pissed was at McCanoc,"
Herzer said. "That was before the Fall. I don't know
what happened to him after, though?"

"Had to be Gothoriel," Edmund said. "he was the
Rider of the Eastern Reach, basically the guy that
the Lady left out in this area of Norau to make sure
we weren't getting up to too much mischief. He got
cut off by the Fall when the Lady closed Elfheim. I
haven't seen him, but Bast said she had."

"Elfheim, General?" Tao said. "I'm starting to get
one of my headaches."

"Too much for you, Ensign?" Edmund said with a
grin. "Elfheim is an artificial dimension that the elves
opened when they decided that living in the world was
just too dangerous all around. Humans never really
took to elves very well, and vice versa. Too many differences. Things that enrage humans the elves care
less about and things that enrage elves humans tend to
be able to ignore. The Lady withdrew and so did the
majority of the elves. There's no proscription, though,
they can come and go, at least they could until the
recent unpleasantness. Then the Lady turned off the
portals to Elfheim and stated that there would be
no transfer in either direction. This cut off her eyes
among the humans, as well."

"Are they on our side, sir?" Tao asked.

"No, son, they're not," Edmund said. "But they're
not on the side of New Destiny, either. I'm not really

sure I *want* them on our side; they're too likely to do things for reasons I don't understand. But I know I don't want them fighting for New Destiny. Can't imagine they would. But if New Destiny wins, if they manage to capture all the power systems and take over the world, you can bet they'll try to take the Lady on. *That* will be a battle to watch. Of course, at that point we'll all be dead or Changed."

CHAPTER FOUR

They traveled for two days in the stuffy confines of the coach, changing horses at regular intervals and stopping not even to rest, traveling at night by the light of coach lanterns. Halfway through the first day they left the Via and started on the road to Newfell to the south. This was a road made since the Fall, for all it was on an ancient roadbed, and it was dreadful in comparison; rutted, filled with potholes and barely touched with gravel where it wasn't pure dirt.

Conversation had languished after the first burst, the ensigns perhaps a bit surprised at their temerity. Edmund got from them that they came from almost equilateral points in the UFS. Tao was from the plains far to the west, Destrang hailed from the northeast coast and Van Krief was from the coast of the gulf to the southwest.

"We lived on a spring-fed river that led to the Gulf," she said, looking out the window. "When the

Fall came my dad was diving someplace, you know, you never know where. And then he was gone."

"I'm sorry," Herzer had said, looking anywhere but at the young ensign.

"We survived," she said, shrugging. "There were fish and orange trees. Alligator is pretty tasty. We got by. Mom's still down there. What about your parents, sir?"

"I don't know where they were," Herzer said, his tone hard, then he shrugged. "We hadn't seen each other since a few years before the Fall. My messages . . ." He paused and shrugged. "We weren't close," he said, more or less closing off the conversation.

Finally, after what seemed an interminable journey, they pulled to a stop at a guard shack and at a word from Edmund were waved through. It was the deep of the night but the Navy base seemed barely affected; personnel, carts and material were moving in a constant stream from one area to another. The road they were on was lit by lanterns every dozen yards or so and there were more over the doors of the buildings so the scene was relatively well lit.

They pulled into the portico of what looked like a large house and Edmund opened his door, stepping down to the lantern-lit entry-walk.

"This is the VIP guest house," Edmund said. "Herzer and I will be staying here. The rest of you will be at the BOQ, which is just down the road. As soon as I can find somebody to help us with our gear, you're for there. I want you here no more than an hour after dawn, which is only a couple of hours. So the faster you get some sleep the better. But you need to be here in dress uniform and cleaned up, so figure that into your schedule."

While he had been talking, Herzer walked to the glass-fronted doors and tried to open them, finding them locked. At that he pounded with his fist on the wood, glancing through the spaces in the frosting on the windows.

"Charge of quarter's asleep," Herzer said over his shoulder.

"I would be too," Edmund said, stretching. "I'm getting too damned old for this, Herzer."

"What the hell do you think you're doing?" a young seaman said, looking at the captain revealed in the light. "If you go waking up the admirals they're going to be something pissed."

"Listen you little shit-for-brains," Herzer growled, using his hook to pick up the much smaller sailor by his collar. "If you don't get down there and help General Talbot with his luggage, *I'm* going to be something pissed. And you really don't want to see me pissed!"

"Yes, sir!" the sailor gurgled as Herzer lowered him to the ground.

"Get a detail," Edmund corrected. "We've got a lot of stuff."

"Sir . . . General," the sailor said. "There's nobody here but me for two hours, sir. Everyone else is at the barracks and . . ."

"Never mind," Edmund replied with an angry sigh. "Ensigns, I'm sorry but I think you're going to have to miss some more sleep."

"Not a problem, sir," Tao said. He'd been unloading their bags and he now hoisted a sea chest in one hand and a bag of armor in the other. "Where are we going, kid?"

"Upstairs to your right, sir," the sailor said, grabbing another bag and stumbling under the weight.

Between the six of them they conveyed all the gear in one load; Herzer wasn't the only one who had packed armor and personal weapons.

"Guys," Edmund said. "I've changed my mind. Herzer and I have to be at the headquarters at dawn, you guys sleep in. Not long, be there no more than two hours after. But get some sleep, you're going to need it."

"Sir, we'll be fine," Van Krief said, squaring her shoulders. "Sir, we're Blood Lords," she added, sounding surprised that he'd think a two-day unstopping ride would bother them.

"Lord, to be as hard-d . . . core as you are, Ensign." The general smiled. "Okay, two hours."

"Yes, sir," Destrang said. He was the only one of the five that still looked unrumpled by the travel, but he was sorely in need of a shave. "Let's hope that they have a shower or something."

"Oh, I'm sure they do," Edmund said dryly. "I can't imagine the Navy not having a shower in their BOQ. I'd be surprised if it was that simple."

"Good lord," Destrang said with a whistle, looking around the bathroom. "I need to change services!"

The officers' bath, which the Navy insisted on calling a head, had six separate showers, a large wooden soaking tub like those found at Raven's Mill, two separate "private" tubs that could handle three at a pinch, a wood-heated sauna and a steam room. The sauna was the only one that wasn't currently heated and the sleepy female seaman who had greeted them had grumpily allowed that it was possible to get that heated up in about an hour.

"And this is *temporary* quarters," Van Krief said, wonderingly. "For *junior* officers."

"There are some commanders in the barracks," Tao said. "While you eggheads were talking to the private I was reading the roster on the wall." He looked around balefully and shrugged. "I'm going to take a shower."

"Well, I'm going to take a shower and then have a soak," Destrang said, stripping off his tunic as he headed back to his room. "There's not enough time to bother sleeping. A twenty- or thirty-minute soak before we have to head back is just what the doctor ordered after that damned ride."

"Can I get you anything, General?" Herzer asked as he stepped into Edmund's room.

"Yeah, a bath like this at my damned house," Edmund growled. "What's your bathroom like?"

"I use the common one in the corridor, sir," Herzer said. He was fresh from the shower and in his dress uniform. It was similar to the undress uniform except the lapels of the tunic were light blue to denote his branch of infantry. But in keeping with the situation he'd also pinned on his medals. At the top was a device like a shield pinned on the left upper breast of the kimono. Below it were four medals. The one on the uppermost row was a representation of a gold laurel. The three on the row below were a silver eagle, wings outspread, another shield formed in bronze and a pair of crossed swords. He realized with a start that he had more than Edmund and wondered if he should take some of them off. "But it was pretty nice."

"Go look in mine," Edmund said, shrugging into his own tunic.

Herzer had been impressed with the common bath. It had a very nice tub, a separate shower lined with tile and two porcelain basins with hot and cold running water. Not to mention a flush commode. Edmund's put his to shame. The floor and walls were of some sort of light wood, very rich-looking. The shower was huge, lined in black marble and so large that it didn't need a door. The bath was of some rich, dark stone he didn't recognize and at least twice the size of the one in the common room. The sinks were made of the same smooth stone and the faucets appeared to be of pure silver. He thunked one and the sound indicated that it was. He shook his head and looked in the separate room for the commode just because he had to see. The commode was black marble and there was another device next to it the purpose of which Herzer had no clue. Ditto black marble.

"This is pretty elegant," Herzer said when he came back in the room. Edmund had donned his tunic and elected to *not* wear his medals. The only thing on the tunic were four silver stars. He seemed to think that was enough.

"I don't think that rank shouldn't have some privileges," Edmund said, sourly. "There has to be some reason to deal with the crappy aspects of having the responsibility. But I've rarely encountered a group that accepted this much ostentation that hadn't lost sight of the point; which is to bring harm to the enemy."

"Yes, sir," Herzer replied, thinking of the military

history he had been studying. "The Spartans and most of the Romans would certainly agree."

"Do we kill time for an hour or go round up the ensigns and head for the headquarters early?" Edmund asked.

"Do we have transportation?" Herzer asked.

"It's about a quarter klick to the headquarters," Edmund replied, dryly. "I think even I can survive the walk."

"Yes, sir," Herzer said. "But do you think the *admirals* would walk?"

"Good point," Edmund replied. "Do we just look like low-life scum if we don't have wheels? Or do we look like hard bastards who don't go for ostentation?"

"Both?" Herzer chuckled. "If we have wheels, we disdain them. But I don't think there's a coach waiting for us."

"I should have held onto ours," Edmund admitted. "But the driver was as tired as we were."

"And we didn't tell the helpful gentleman downstairs that we'd need them."

"Go roust out the ensigns," Edmund said after a bit. "I'll talk to the young gentleman downstairs about finding some chow. When you're back we'll walk. Of course, that means that we'll have to walk, rain or shine, from now on."

"Rain never killed anyone," Herzer said. "Unless it was really cold rain and they were out in it a long time," he added truthfully.

When Herzer and the ensigns returned, the charge of quarters directed them to the dining room. In keeping with the rest of the VIP quarters it was huge and elegant, with snowy white tablecloths and silver settings, as well as fresh flowers in vases arranged along the massive table. It was apparent that the servants got there early and places had been set for all five of them.

"There was some question in the head cook's mind about serving the rest of you in here," Edmund said with a faint smile, like a tiger that had recently eaten well. "Low-life scum like ensigns are supposed to eat at the consolidated mess or the officers' club. At best in the kitchen, here, according to the cook. But I pointed out the error of his ways. Have a seat."

There was bacon or ham as well as eggs to order. Not to mention baskets of rolls fresh from the oven. Herzer considered asking if they had cornmeal mush or chitlins but decided that it was time to start playing the part of good little aide. And good little aides let their generals handle the needling.

When they had all eaten, rapidly in the way that field soldiers learned and sometimes never forgot, they left the quarters and headed for the headquarters building.

"Tao, you're from the plains," Edmund said. "Any experience with horses before you were introduced to them in officer's training?"

"I practically grew up on one, sir," Tao admitted.

"When we get to the headquarters detach yourself and find out where their stables are. On my authority get six of the best horses you can find and equal amounts of tack. They are to be held for the use of the five of us. Six, because you might find yourself making a ride where you need remounts. Destrang, Van Krief, do you have writing materials?"

"Yes, sir," they both said.

"Good. You guys stay at my back unless I specifically detach you and then you get as close as you can. You're going to be doing a lot of waiting."

"Not a problem, sir," Van Krief replied.

"Herzer, I'm going to try like hell to have you fixed to my side like a limpet," Edmund said as they approached the lantern-lit headquarters. The sun was just starting to give a glow to the horizon in the east.

"Destrang, Van Krief," Edmund said, stopping. "Which of you is the best researcher?"

"I am, sir," Van Krief replied. Destrang just nodded his head in her direction.

"Okay, I've got a special project for you," Edmund said, resuming his walk.

As he walked up the steps to the headquarters, a large, four-story wooden building, the marines on guard at the front came to order arms. They were in full armor, loricated plate and barbute helmets, and armed with short boarding pikes. Edmund acknowledged the salute with a smile.

"Good morning, gentlemen," he said as Herzer opened the door to the headquarters. "How are you this morning?"

There was an alert-looking captain manning the desk inside the door. He came to attention as the general entered the room and shouted: "Attention on deck!"

"Good morning, Captain," Edmund said with another smile. "I appear to be here a little early. I take it I'm senior on deck from your reaction."

"Yes, sir," the captain replied.

"Fine," the general said with a smile. "Ensign

Destrang," he added, leaning over to say something in the ensign's ear.

Destrang removed a notebook from the blouse pocket of his tunic and made a small notation, nodding as the general spoke.

Herzer managed to remain blank-faced at the exchange, but he knew that Admiral Draskovich, the North Atlantis Fleet commander, would hear soon enough that not only had the Eastern Forces Commander beaten him into his headquarters, the damned Army busybody, who just happened to be a good friend of the queen—some rumored they were former lovers—made a note of that fact.

"In that case, I need a guide to the war-room," Edmund said, turning back to the captain.

"Sir," the captain looked uneasy. "We have a number of security procedures in place in the wake of . . . certain compromises of information."

"I was there, son," Edmund said with a grim smile. On the diplomatic mission to the mer, the executive officer of the carrier had turned out to be a New Destiny agent. Owen Mbeki's wife, Sharon, had been caught in Ropasa by the Fall and her condition depended upon the quality of the information he gave them. In the end his New Destiny control had killed him when his actions were discovered. "Are you telling me that I'm not authorized to enter your war-room?"

"No, sir, but . . ."

"Where is the field duty officer?" Edmund asked. "Or the classified documents officer? Surely there is someone senior to you that you can pass this problem on to. I know you don't get paid enough."

In short order the general was sitting in the

office of a sleepy looking major who frowned at the general.

"Sir, I'm not authorized to release passes to the war-room," the major said, looking pained. He was a Navy officer but he was well aware that to a flag officer that didn't mean much. The heat round that was possible in this situation was liable to destroy his career. "Commander Correa comes in in no more than an hour . . ."

"Major, am I the senior officer present?" the general said, warningly.

"Yes, sir," the major gulped.

"What you're going to do then, major, by *my* authority, is issue passes to the war-room for myself and my aide, Captain Herrick. Then you are going to find someone to take Ensign Van Krief to your records room, where she is going to examine certain records, by my authority. Then you are going to find someone to show Ensign Tao the base stables, someone that the people at the stables are going to listen to. And you are going to find a place to park Ensign Destrang where I can access him in no more than thirty seconds. After that, you can make all the damned protests to Admiral Draskovich you wish. But if you do not begin the process of those orders I'm not going to have you court-martialed, I AM GOING TO RIP YOUR HEAD OFF AND SHIT IN YOUR NECK. IS THAT CLEAR?"

"Clear, sir," the major said, reaching into a desk drawer.

"Excuse me, ma'am," the chief petty officer said as he entered the records room and found some Army ensign with half his files scattered on the ground in no sort of order. "Can I, with all respect, ask you what the hell you are doing?"

"I'm reading some of your records and taking notes," Amosis replied, mildly.

"Can I ask on whose authority, ma'am? We don't just let any officer in here if you know what I mean. There are procedures."

"By authority of General Talbot, Eastern Forces Commander," Van Krief replied. "If you have a problem with it, PO, you can take it up with him. In the meantime, I need extracted reports of materials budgets for the Fleet from last quarter, training hours, by type, dragon-flight hours and total ship time at sea. Oh, and a list of all ships currently under construction in the yards and estimated time to completion."

"I have other duties, ma'am," the chief said tightly. "And it's *chief* petty officer."

"Well, chief, if you want to *stay* a chief, I'd suggest you either get cracking or you find someone to access those records for me," the ensign replied. "Because I only have until noon to create an abstract and if I can't, item one in my report will be the obstructionism of a certain chief petty officer."

"General Talbot," Admiral Draskovich said. The admiral was a tall officer with pale skin, almost black eyes and long, jet black hair pulled back in a ponytail.

Edmund was sitting with his feet up on the desk of one of the officers in the war-room, a mug of coffee in his hand. He waved the mug in the direction of the Fleet commander.

"Drask," Edmund said, getting to his feet. "Very

well-trained crew you have here. I'd kill for your communications."

"Thank you, General," the admiral said, shaking Talbot's hand. "This is my chief of staff, Brigadier General Kabadda." The indicated officer was medium height with blond hair. He shook the general's hand in turn, smiling slightly. "And my aide, Commander Edrogan." Edrogan was a tall, elegant young man, not much more than Herzer's age. His eyes were crinkled as if he had stared at a lot of light in his time and he was heavily tanned.

"Commander," the general said with a nod. "And this is my aide, Captain Herzer."

The trio stared at Herzer for a moment, and at the medals, and then the admiral nodded.

"Captain, your reputation precedes you," the admiral said, somewhat stuffily.

Herzer almost asked "which one" but managed to quell it.

"Thank you, sir," Herzer said. "So does yours."

"Yes," the admiral said, digesting the ambiguity of the reply. "Is everything in order?"

"Oh, just fine," Edmund replied. "There was a little issue about letting me in the war-room but that was easily taken care of." A commander entered the room with a set expression on his face and whispered in the ear of the admiral's aide. The aide looked startled and then whispered in the admiral's ear, glancing at the general as he did so.

"And one of my ensigns with too much time on her hands is busy bothering your records people," Talbot added with a closed-mouth grin. "Nothing of consequence."

"I'm sure," the admiral said, tightly. "The message that you were coming didn't specify your precise purpose, General."

"Oh, well," Edmund said, gesturing with the cup of coffee. "I'm the fella that has to deal with any of the New Destiny folks that slip through your efficient sieve, Drask. It only seemed fitting to Sheida that I be around when you go out to handle them."

The admiral did not miss the reference to the queen's first name. So he smiled thinly and nodded.

"Perhaps you'd like to attend the morning briefing, then?" the admiral said. "We generally hold it in the secure conference room in about an hour."

"Wouldn't miss it for worlds," Edmund replied.

Tao walked through the stables inhaling gratefully the heady aroma of horse dander, manure and leather. He found it humorous that he'd had to go to a Navy base to go play with horses. Since joining the legions the only time he had been around them was the week of half-day classes in Officer Basic course.

The stable was large with ranks of stalls and he walked down the aisles, dodging grooms and occasional piles of manure, looking into the stalls and getting a feel for the beasts within. He noticed immediately that the vast majority were heavy horses, designed for drawing small wagons or carriages. There were relatively few that were riding breeds. And of them, most were pretty low quality. He stopped by the stall of one that was not, a pretty mixed mare with a white face. Her colors were awful, the blotch of white on her face was matched on her rump and on two feet, meaning she'd be subject to dew rot. The rest of her was a patchwork of ugly brown and chestnut. She wasn't in very good condition, either; she clearly hadn't been worked in a long time. But she had a good set of withers, better than most of the riding horses in the stable.

"Can I help you, Ensign." a voice said coldly from behind him.

The young officer turned around and stared into the face of a clearly furious commander.

"I hope so, sir," Tao said, trying not to swallow nervously. "I was sent here by General Talbot to pick some riding horses for messengers. Six, sir, with tack."

"Let me see your orders," the commander said, holding out his hand.

"I don't have orders, sir, except verbal," the ensign replied. "I'm one of his messengers, sir. I'm not going to run off with the horses. Besides, we're not going to need all six at a time, unless I'm much mistaken."

"Well, Ensign, there are procedures," the commander said. "Without written orders, no horses go out of these stables. And you don't *pick* the horses, you are *assigned* them in rota."

"Sir, with all due respect, that's not what the general told me to do," the ensign said, mulishly.

"I don't work for the general," the commander said. "I work for Admiral Draskovich. If the admiral chooses to waive those regulations, then the admiral can do so. Your *general* cannot. Am I making that clear enough or do I have to write it down for you?"

"No," the ensign said, pulling a pad out of his pocket. He licked the tip of his pen and wrote for a moment. "If you'd just sign here, sir?"

"What is this?"

"A paraphrase of what you just said, sir," the ensign replied, reading from the tablet. "Horses cannot be released without written authority. . . ."

"And a priority which is *assigned* by Fleet headquarters," the commander added.

Tao pulled off the top sheet and started writing again.

"Horses cannot be released without written authority *and* a priority, issued by Fleet headquarters and the commander at the stables would not release horses on my verbal statement that I was under orders from the Eastern Forces Commander."

"Who did you say your general was?" the commander said, pausing as he reached for the tablet.

"General the Duke Edmund Talbot," Tao said. "Eastern Forces Commander."

"Oh." The commander paused and then made a moue. "Why don't you look around for a minute while I get some clarification on this."

"Yes, sir," Tao replied, saluting. He waited until the commander had left and then snorted, pulling out the pad and tearing off the sheet. Then he thought about it, pocketed the note and continued to write. A bit slowly, but he was going to get there sooner or later.

CHAPTER FIVE

The conference room was elegantly appointed with a long mahogany table and ceiling-hung lamps that cast their light carefully to make it easy to see both the table and those around it. At each place was a notepad, a pencil and a glass of water. On a side table was a silver urn and coffee mugs. At one end was a single door, guarded on the outside by more marines in armor, and at the other end was an oilcloth-covered easel. A commander in dress uniform was standing at attention by the easel as the admirals and generals filed in, followed by their aides.

The UFS had a uniform rank structure for officers. The bottom three ranks were ensign, lieutenant and captain. These were referred to as "company" grade officers. Their rank insignia were circular pips, one for ensign, two for lieutenant and three for captain. The second three ranks were major, commander and colonel, "command" grade, each marked by a vertical silver bar. The next three were brigadier general, major general, and lieutenant general, "flag" grade, marked by silver stars. The highest rank was general, four stars.

Admirals were, by definition, generals that were in command of task forces or fleets just as the term for the commander of a ship was "skipper." Brigadier generals in command of small task forces were called commodore. Full generals in command positions were supposed to be called "Marshals." Edmund refused, point blank, to use the term. And since, so far, he was the only one, it was likely the term was going to fade into history.

Herzer took up his position behind Edmund's chair, the one at the end of the room farthest from the easel. Edmund looked at the setup and reached into a pocket, pulled out a set of spectacles and settled them on his nose.

"Commander, you may begin," Brigadier General Kabadda said as soon as everyone was seated. His position was on the left side of the table at the end nearest the easel, directly across from the fleet commander.

"Sirs," the commander said, pulling the oilcloth off the easel to reveal a marked map of the North Atlantis. "At 0500 this date, local time, First Fleet, composed of five task forces formed around the carriers *Bonhomme Richard*, *Washuka*, *Corvallis Line*, *Norlund* and *Reagan*, along with the light forces task force 7-1, was four hundred klicks west of the Onay Islands." He pointed to a point on the map. "The enemy was just passing the Onay Islands, making good time with northeasterly winds. According to plan, the fleet will begin to launch dragons at about 1100 hours, not long after dawn local time, depending upon when the scouts indicate the enemy is at the optimal range. Engagement should begin approximately 1200 hours local. Given the disparity of force, the fleet commander estimates that only a single strike will be necessary to take out the enemy's carriers and a later strike is planned to engage his light units.

"A revictualling convoy is approximately two hundred klicks southeast of the fleet's current position. It was held pending the battle, but should be able to complete its mission in no more than two days. Two scout forces are near the Asur Islands and are screening the actions of orcas in that area. Task force 3-2 is just north of Blackbeard Base completing work-ups of the carrier *Hazhir*. Sirs, this is all current deployments and plans of the North Atlantis fleet."

"Good brief, Commander," General Kabadda said. "Questions? General Piet? General Hanour? General Babak?" He looked around the room to a series of shaking heads.

"I have one," Talbot drawled. "What is the guard on the convoy?"

"Excuse, me, sir?" the commander asked.

"Who is guarding the convoy? According to my information, the fleet was supposed to be revictualled last week. What is guarding the convoy?"

"There is a ballista frigate and an armed sloop," General Kabadda replied, his mouth pursed. "We had to wait for special supplies for the dragons so the convoy left late."

"Thank you," Edmund replied. "What is the status of the *Hazhir*?"

"I'm . . . not sure," the commander said, riffling through some notes. "It is fully manned but it has only seven dragons. It's been being used as a test-bed by the local commander and is about to be refitted to standard configuration. Refit will take no more than one week."

"Very good," Edmund said. "What is the status of foodstuffs for the wyverns in the fleet?" Edmund asked, calmly.

"General, we can get you all that information," General Kabadda said.

"Great," Edmund replied. "I generally expect to get it at my briefings, but as long as it's available somewhere we can access it before, oh, twelve hundred hours, that will be fine."

"Admiral?" the chief of staff asked, tightly.

"Good brief," he said to the commander, standing up. "I think you can look forward to a better one this evening."

Edmund got to his feet and headed for the door, stepping to the side to let the other generals past. Herzer noted some sharp looks in their direction but he'd been stared at by worse. Most of the generals just looked like they had to pee.

Edmund waited until Kabadda came through the door and held out his arm.

"I will need that data, General," he said, smiling.

"I'll have it gathered, General," the chief of staff answered. "But isn't your ensign looking at most of it right now?"

"Not all," Edmund replied with a tight grin. "And I'd like to see what you bring me."

"Why don't I find you an office?" the chief of

staff said. "That way you can peruse the information in comfort."

Edmund smiled again and shrugged.

"Oh, I think flipping through it in your war-room would be just fine."

"Fisking empire builders," Edmund muttered as they walked down a corridor.

"Excuse me, sir?" Herzer said. "And the war-room is the other way."

"I know," Edmund said, turning a corner. "But there has got to be a bathroom around here somewhere."

"I'm sure there is," Herzer replied, dryly. "And I'm sure that there's one reserved for generals, too."

"I'm not looking for more marble," Edmund growled. "I should have taken the offer of an office, but it was a blatant ploy to get me out of their hair. I don't *want* to be out of their hair."

"It's their first real battle, sir," Herzer said, spotting a bathroom and opening the door. It was a simple affair, Spartan in a way, with a long trough at one side into which water spurted out of pipes. There were holes on one side for defecation, with more water flowing through under the holes. But he had to admit that it was clean. Nearly as clean as the identical set-up at the Blood Lord barracks and the Academy.

"This must be for peons," Edmund growled, walking to the trough and unbuttoning his fly. "Anyone around?"

"No," Herzer said.

"The problem is, it *is* their first battle," Edmund snarled. "And none of them have the slightest *fisking* clue what they are doing."

"Sir?"

"Herzer, assume that you're briefing me on an army in, oh, Linwah. What are you going to cover?"

"Has it been in battle recently?" Herzer asked.

"No, it's getting ready to clash with a similar force."

"Intel abstracts with the raw data available," Herzer said then grabbed a mantra from his head. "Mission, enemy, time, terrain, signals, support. What they are going to do. What they have present to do it. What we estimate the enemy has in the way of materials and ability. What the area conditions are. What the means of communications are. What materials our units have present and estimate of the enemy's materials. What materials we have on the way and estimated arrival. He covered most of it, sir."

"Most," Edmund said, closing his fly. "Did you know there was a storm on the way down from the north? That it was estimated to arrive in a day and a half or so?"

"No, sir," Herzer said.

"I figured out how to read their maps in the warroom," Edmund growled. "That's damned vital information. It means that the fleet *cannot* revictual completely. Did you know that the dragons were down to two days' food? That the fleet was out of *ketchup*?"

The latter was the only thing that could get dragons to eat the mess of beans and oil that was their normal food away from fresh meat.

"Jesus, sir," Herzer blanched. "They're getting hungry."

"And a hungry dragon will eat anything, including the handlers and riders," Edmund snarled. "They're going up against an enemy that they don't know the capabilities of, with dragons that are hungry and balky. Why?"

"That I don't know," Herzer said.

"Because they've never fought a battle before," Edmund replied. "Or even trained, seriously, for one. They don't know about the fog of war, they don't know that no plan survives contact with the enemy. But, worst of all, it's because they *have not* fought before. The only one of their officers who has met the enemy in any sort of a pitched battle was Shar Chang, and he's 'not one of us.' The Yacht Club has yet to earn its spurs. And they had blithely pitched a forward battle, engagement at the earliest opportunity. Now they can't say: 'Wait; the fleet needs resupply and there's a storm coming that will ground our dragons.' Because they fear they'll lose face."

"What do we do, sir?" Herzer asked, his face pale. He *had* fought battles before and *knew* that things went wrong. And he'd handled hungry, seasick, dragons before. If the fleet couldn't get food in time, the dragons were going to *starve*.

"There's not a thing we *can* do," Edmund snarled. "That's what's making me so damned angry. The only thing we can do is hope for a miracle. That nothing goes wrong. That the New Destiny forces play dumb. Personally, I think that really is hoping for a miracle."

Major Jerry Riadou stood up as someone at the back of the low, crowded, room called "Attention on deck!" then sat back down as the XO called: "Seats."

The XO of the ship was wearing his hat, probably

because he considered it de rigueur for a formal briefing. Ship uniform was dungarees for all personnel but hats were used to distinguish their ranks and position. Enlisted and petty officers wore brimmed "forage caps." Chief petty officers wore hats with a wide-flat brim called, for some reason, "campaign hats." Officers wore hats with a curved brim called Stetsons. The XO's Stetson was turned up on one side and pinned in place by the heraldic device of the ship. Often, as in the case with the XO of the *Corvallis Line*, there was also a feather for emphasis. The CO wore the same sort of hat with both sides turned up. The practical reason given for the hats was that anyone could tell at a distance who was giving an order.

As far as Jerry was concerned, the real reason was that the Navy was run by a bunch of bloody peacocks.

Jerry didn't look up from his notes as the XO strode to the lectern at the front of the room. His notes were simple. Of thirty-five wyvern on board, only twenty-eight were certified for flying by the ship's surgeon. The rest were so sick they probably wouldn't survive even if the ship was sailing into Newfell Harbor instead of into battle. He'd only been permitted two hours of flight per day, per dragon, for the last month. He had not been permitted to draw live napalm for training and had only been permitted one set of bombing practice runs. For most of the riders, it was the first time they had attempted to drop bombs, period.

The XO was briefing the mission, but Jerry knew the brief; he'd written it. When the XO gave him the task he came very close to telling the anal-retentive asshole where to stick his brief. And the jackass had sent it back three times, for corrections. Corrections on shit he didn't know jack about.

Riadou had been one of the first people ever to land a wyvern on a carrier deck. He'd been the first person to bomb a ship at sea and he sunk it. Admittedly, it took a few times to get the damned thing, but he'd sunk it.

The XO had been the mate on the skipper's racing yacht. He'd never even been on a dragon. And he was correcting stuff on a brief that Jerry could give in his sleep.

The XO and the skipper were pals, all right. They'd even forced the name of their damned yacht down the throats of the dragon-riders. What the hell kind of name was "Blue Destiny" for a wing of wyvern? After someone explained to him that he wasn't the first person to land on a carrier, Jerry had taken the time to cross the river and visit the museum that still occupied the far bank. There he had read about the *old* carriers, big, *huge* metal ships that landed aircraft damned near the size of a great dragon, aircraft that were going not much under the speed of sound for that matter.

And they'd had plaques on the wall, behind sealed glass otherwise they would have fallen apart over the millennia. Plaques from the squadrons of those ships.

Black Aces, Jolly Rogers, Viking Raiders, Death Dealers. Those were *real* names. Names that spoke of what the pilots believed. Bring death and destruction to the enemy.

Blue Destiny. Gimme a break.

He sensed that the XO had come to the end of

his spiel and looked up, meeting the commander's eyes. He hoped he was showing the proper humility, instead of what he wanted to show, which was that the best use of the XO was dragon-feed.

Apparently not from the XO's expression. The commander looked away after a moment and around the room, clearing his throat.

"Any questions?"

"How do we get out of this chicken-shit outfit," a voice at the back of the room asked. In any other group, it would be grounds for chuckles. In this room it caused dead, and deadly, silence.

"If there are no other questions, move to your beasts," the XO said, coldly.

"Let's go, boys and girls," Jerry said, standing up when no one else had. "Time to go get it on."

"It's okay, boy," Jerry said to the piteously mewling wyvern as they reached assembly altitude. "It's okay. I'll give you a big feed when we get back." You could promise anything to a wyvern. They never listened.

He looked down at the dragons launching from the port-side catapult. Most of them were barely getting in the air, flapping listlessly as Tomak had. Jerry had ridden a wyvern named Shep, short for Hatshepsut, for years. But Shep, thank God, had been retired to stud at Blackbeard Base. He was well out of this goat fuck.

Tomak was having a hard time maintaining altitude. There weren't many thermals this early and the dragon was half-starved, low on energy and inclined to balk. But he kept him in the air as the other wyverns, slowly, assembled.

It was a dispirited group that flapped to the northeast. Going to a battle they didn't think they could win and wondering if their dragons would have enough energy to get them back to ships they weren't sure would be there.

CHAPTER SIX

"Sir," a seaman said, coming over to General Talbot.

The general had ensconced himself at an empty desk in the war-room. He was pretty sure it wasn't supposed to be empty, but the owner hadn't complained. Now he looked up at the young seaman and smiled.

"Yes?"

"There's an ensign outside, sir, who wishes to speak to you. But she's not on the access list."

"Nor should she be, seaman," the general replied, nodding. "Thank you."

He walked to the door and nodded at the guard to open it and then walked out of the room with Herzer following.

"Sir, I've got the extracts you wanted . . ." Van Krief said. Her uniform was covered in dust.

"Wait," Talbot said, holding up his hand. "Where's Destrang?"

"He's in a room down the hall," Herzer said, pointing.

"An empty room?" Edmund asked.

"Sometimes," the captain replied. "I think it's a break room."

"Well, it's going to be an empty room for the next few minutes," Talbot said, turning to the guard at the door. "Son, you got a sergeant of the guard around?"

"Yes, sir," the marine answered.

"How do you summon him?"

"Sergeant of the Guard to the war-room," the marine called down the hall. The call was repeated from the various posts. In no more than a minute a precisely uniformed marine sergeant, not wearing armor, appeared around the corner and marched to a halt in front of the general. He turned to the sentry who pointed at the general and then went back to looking down the hall.

"Sergeant, I'm going to be taking over the break room for a few minutes," the general said. "I'd like to ensure that nobody stumbles in. Can you take care of that?"

"Yes, sir," the sergeant replied. "I'll stand guard until I can get a relief, sir. Won't take more than a couple of minutes."

"Thank you, Sergeant," Talbot said, walking down the hall to the break room. "We won't be long. I appreciate this."

When he entered the room Destrang sprang to his feet, dropping the book he'd been reading.

"Bored, Ensign?" Edmund asked, smiling.

"To tears, sir," Destrang said.

"I don't think that will last long," Edmund replied.
"I don't *want* to take long, Van Krief, brief me."

"Yes, sir," the ensign said, nervously.

"I'll take the extracts back to the war-room when we're done," Edmund added. "Just give me the highlights."

"How about the *low* lights, sir?" the ensign said.

"How bad?"

"I don't know, sir," Van Krief said, shaking her head. "But does an average of one hour of flight time per day per dragon in the fleet sound good?"

"Jesus Cristo," Herzer said.

"And virtually none of that has been bombing practice, sir," she added. "In fact, I could only find records for an average of five hours, total, of bombing practice since the fleet sailed. Two of the carriers have catapults down, so the dragons can't get off with a full load of bombs anyway. There is only one greater dragon with the fleet. The other one requested, and was granted, permission to fly off three weeks ago. She is currently here, in some vague training billet."

"She?" Edmund asked. "Who is she?"

"Commander Joanna Gramlich," Van Krief said, consulting a note in the sheaf of paper in her hand.

"What reason did she give to fly off?" Herzer asked.

"Failure of contract, sir," Van Krief answered. "I got the feeling that the Navy is going to try to stick it to her. The chief that I shanghaied referred to her as 'that bitch mercenary.'"

"Fisking idiots," Edmund snarled. "Fisking mother-fisking idiots. Sorry, Ensign. But I *know* Joanna. And she was just getting out while there was still time."

"The fleet's been on half rations for a week," Van Krief continued. "The dragons have had their rations cut as well but they're still very short, no more than a day or two. And there's a storm . . ."

"I know about the storm," Edmund said.

"There are letters of complaint from the riders as well."

"I can imagine," Herzer said, shaking his head.

"There was one memo I ran across that used the term 'primadonnas' about the complaints, sir," Van Krief said. "On the one hand, I can understand. The whole fleet is having troubles. On the other hand . . ."

"There is no other hand, Ensign," Herzer sighed. "You can't short wyverns. If they don't get enough to eat, they sicken and die. Quickly. And getting them to eat at all on shipboard is tough; they don't like sailing any more than the general here."

"And there's more, sir," Van Krief said, her face a mass of sorrow. "One of the reasons that they haven't been flying is supplies. But the reason supplies are low is that they've been diverting training funds into the building of a new class of ships."

"A new carrier class?" Edmund asked.

"No, sir. A dreadnought class. Heavily armed trebuchet ships. At least, that's the way it looks on first glance. I could be wrong. But the numbers in both directions don't add up."

"Big, fast, pretty ships that can close with the enemy," Edmund said. "Marine complement?"

"Big marine force, sir," Van Krief said. "Two hundred and fifty per ship."

"And board them in heroic close combat," Edmund continued. "Damn them."

"I'm worried about the dragons," Herzer said.

"So am I," Edmund said. "They're in no condition to fight."

"Fight, hell," Herzer replied, hotly. "That's more than half our total wyvern force and one of only five great dragons out there. If they turn around, right now, and head for the nearest port, they *might* not lose half of them!"

"But the supply convoy . . ." Van Krief said.

"If it even makes it," Edmund sighed. "Remember what I said about how *I* would run this fight?"

"Oh. Yes, sir."

"All the mer and delphinos have been pushed back from the Ropasan coast," Edmund said. "I need to know where other ships are, New Destiny ships. I want to know their full order of battle and where every single ship is located. I need *intel*."

"I didn't access that, sir," the ensign said.

"I know," Edmund replied, suddenly smiling at the nervous young officer. "And you did well. But I've got that puckered feeling like we're about to have something shoved up our ass, hard. Okay, we're done here," Edmund said, holding out his hand. "Give me the papers and Herzer and I are going back in the lion's den."

As they exited the room, with a nod of dismissal to the marine that had replaced the NCO, a messenger hurried by, coming from the war-room.

"Why did that young man look as if his dog just died, I wonder?" Edmund mused, sarcastically. He strode into the war-room and looked around. The previously calm and ordered place was a madhouse. On the big map on the wall, the supply convoy was marked as under attack.

"It starts," Edmund said, grabbing a passing leading petty officer. "What happened?" Edmund asked.

"The delphinos with the convoy reported it under attack by dragons," the PO replied. "The frigate and the sloop are sunk and the rest of the convoy is under attack. The senior captain has been asking for orders. Then his ship was sunk. It's a madhouse, General."

"No, son," Edmund sighed. "It's a war. But the difference is often hard to notice."

He sat down at his desk as Admiral Draskovich entered the room. The admiral listened to the hurried briefing from the watch officer and then took a pedestal chair at the center of the room.

"Signal the convoy to scatter," he said. "Have them rendezvous at coordinates North 38 43 by West 67 01 then proceed on their mission."

Herzer saw the general visibly wince. But Edmund was apparently ignoring what was going on around him.

"What's the situation with the fleet?" Draskovich asked.

"The dragons are launching now, sir," one of the watch officers replied. "They're reporting less than eighty percent available. But they should have those in the air by now."

"Why so few?" the admiral asked.

"Unknown, sir," the watch officer said.

"Send a message requesting we be told why," the admiral snapped.

"Task force *Corvallis Line* reports attack by kraken," a petty officer said, looking up from the message just brought in. "Delphinos and mer are under attack by orca and ixchitl."

"Tell them to hold the line and get that damned kraken," the admiral practically yelled, rubbing his face and looking over his shoulder at the door though which the messengers entered.

Command Master Chief Robin Brooks had just stepped onto the quarterdeck, carrying a fresh mug of coffee, when the carrier suddenly slowed in the water and heeled to starboard. Two mast-thick tentacles snaked over the side, one grabbing the mainmast at the base while another grabbed it just below the first crosstree. The massive bulk of a kraken appeared over the side of the ship.

The chief took a sip of coffee, his knees springing to keep him upright, as the ship listed hard to starboard and shook his head at the mass of screaming humanity on the maindeck all of them sliding across the deck towards the waiting tentacles and beak of the hungry, eight-armed, kraken.

"Kircan!" he bellowed at the waist division petty officer, who was clinging to a line for dear life. "Get some axemen working! Get Van Kiet's team into their flamethrowers!" He took another sip appreciatively as a seaman was picked up, screaming, from the deck. "Webster! Quit dicking around and stay away from the damned tentacles! There's a drill for this, you know!"

The skipper came dashing onto the quarterdeck, tucking in his shirt, just as the flamethrower team was throwing itself desperately into the fray.

"Get the tentacles on the mast first!" the chief bellowed. "And somebody cut off that tentacle around Webster before he throws up all over the deck! Oh, good morning, Skipper."

"Morning, Chief," the skipper said, trying, and failing, to give off the same air of unsurprised efficiency as his command master chief.

"Saw this one time off Bimi island, sir," Brooks said, taking another sip as two tongues of flame licked out and caught the tentacles around the mast. The kraken reacted spasmodically as the tentacles whipped off the mast and back into the water. The luckless Webster was tossed aside as well, bouncing off the rail and into the water overside. "The kraken was bigger, though."

The chief kept his feet, many on the deck were thrown from theirs, as the ship rolled back upright and he pointed at the kraken that was still half draped on the side of the ship.

"Get it right in the beak," he yelled. "Or the eyes. Use the flamers to work your way forward. Pump-men, get up there or we'll all be in Davey Jones' locker! And away the gig to pick up Webster. Somebody throw him a preserver."

The flamethrower men worked forward, flicking small tongues of flame at any tentacle that darted towards them, until they were in range to attack the body. Then one of them, greatly daring, darted forward and shot the kraken on the juncture between its tentacles and right eye. At that the kraken flailed wildly, again, and slipped over the side of the ship, disappearing into the depths in a cloud of black ink.

"And it wasn't *this* mill-pond," the chief continued where he'd left off as the firemen rushed forward and washed the burning napalm over the side of the ship then got to work on the burning wood and cordage where the fight had taken place. "*We* were bobbing around like corks."

"Task force *Norland* under dragon attack," one of the watch officers said. "Delphinos report the *Norland* is on fire, sir."

"Okay," the admiral said, rubbing his face. "Signal the task force to assist the carrier in fire fighting . . ."

"*Bonhomme Richard* under dragon attack," the watch commander said. "Dragons using bombs and firebreath. All sails destroyed. Waist on fire."

"What?" the admiral shouted. "Get a confirmation on that!"

"Whalo node Granbas, under assault by orcas," the communications officer said. "The whalos are requesting support."

"Tell them . . ." The admiral paused and looked up at the map. The blue symbols of his fleets were turning red as were the various delphinos, mer and whalos that made up his communications net. "Tell them . . . no support available."

"Sir, Net reports that Granbas is no longer responsive," the communications officer said, swallowing. "We're out of contact with the fleet. Last report, *Reagan*, *Norland* and *Bonhomme Richard* on fire. *Corvallis* under attack by kraken. Enemy dragons sighted by *Corvallis Line* and *Reagan*. The fleet was signaling all dragons recall to any available platform and retiring."

Edmund calmly turned another page in the hastily written extract and shook his head.

"And now the recriminations start," he muttered. "Including from me."

✧　　✧　　✧

The dragons approached on a slow glide. It would have been better to come in from the sun; that way they would have gotten closer before being spotted. But that would have meant flying a wide circle around the enemy fleet. The XO had wanted them to do just that. Jerry had pointed out that he wasn't sure the dragons were going to *make* it to the enemy fleet.

Some of them hadn't. Three of the wyverns had turned back when their riders decided they just couldn't go on. One had just given up, dropping out of the sky and into the cold water below. They had seen Garcia pulling frantically on his reins, but the dragon was done; it couldn't have pulled out of the dive if it wanted to.

The enemy fleet was arranged with ships tight around the carriers. Most of them were ballista frigates but some were bigger and their sails were rigged very strangely. He couldn't for the life of him figure out what they were until they were over the formation and the sky filled with heavy bolts.

"Shit," he said. There wasn't anything they could do. He heard a wyvern scream behind him and felt Tomak shudder in his flight. But then they were over the carrier.

The best way to attack a carrier was from behind. That made for less motion between the carrier and the wyverns. But, again, in this hail of bolts there was no way he was maneuvering. The carrier apparently had some of the same weapons and bolts were flying around him as he banked and dropped in line. He didn't bother to hold anything back; he was only good for one pass. Three pottery canisters filled with napalm dropped free and tumbled towards the carrier.

He looked back and saw two go in the drink. But

the third impacted on the forecastle. As far as he could tell, none of the rest of the wing had hit shit. And even as he watched, sailors covered the burning napalm in foam, practically coating the front of the ship. Their fleet didn't even *have* foam yet. He knew it had been tested, but the rumor was Buships hadn't approved it. The bastards.

Tomak staggered again and dropped altitude and Jerry craned over to see if he could spot the problem. When he did he groaned. There was a fat, short, metal bolt sticking out of Tomak's primary flight muscles. Trying to fly would be the equivalent of trying to run with a knife in his leg. There was no way that he could make it all the way back to the ship.

They had left the enemy fleet behind and Jerry looked around at the endless expanse of ocean. He could turn back to the New Destiny fleet and ditch, hoping that they would pick him up. But they tended to just turn prisoners into one of their Changed orcs. Bugger that.

The ocean looked awfully cold. He remembered the times he'd swum with the dragons down at the mer town. What was it called? Whale Drop or something.

The dragon was barely skimming the waves. There was a little ground effect down there, but the major knew it wasn't going to be enough.

At least Shep was safe.

"Live large, boy," the major said as the dragon plowed into a wave.

"Sir, this is a closed meeting," the marine guard on the conference room door said, stepping in front of the door.

"Well, son," Talbot replied. "You can get the fisk out of my way, or Herzer here will take that pigsticker away from you and shove it up your ass. And then I'll have you in the stockade for the rest of your natural life where the other inmates will appreciate having someone who's not a cherry around. This is a direct order; get the fisk out of my way."

The marine gulped, took a look at the hard-faced captain and stepped aside.

"The damned dragons . . ." General Kabadda was saying as Edmund entered the room.

"General, this is a closed meeting," Admiral Draskovich said, angrily.

"So I heard," Edmund replied, taking his previous seat. "I thought I'd crash it."

"You do not have the authority—" General Kabadda snarled.

"Like hell I don't," Edmund said, suddenly leaning forward and staring hard at the brigadier. "Like *hell* I don't."

"General," Admiral Draskovich said, clearly reining in his temper. "We have a situation here . . ."

"What you *have*, Admiral, is an incredible cluster fuck," Talbot replied. "And I'm not even talking about that pitiful baby-school thing you called a battle. I'm talking about your entire setup. The fact is that you don't know your ass from a hole in the ground about war."

"I do not have to take that in my own headquarters," Draskovich snarled, leaping to his feet.

"You'd better damned well take it, or you're not going to live long enough to get up a real mad," Edmund replied, calmly. "You made three critical errors in your battle. You insufficiently prepared in that the dragons were undertrained and poorly fed, you trusted limited and outdated intelligence that was laughable on its face and you failed to ensure your supply. These are cherry ensign mistakes. But that's not too surprising, since what you all are is junior officers." Edmund looked at the faces and laughed. "Oh, God, you thought you were real generals because you put on the uniform? You've never even been to *school* on how to be generals."

"As I said, I do not have to take this," Draskovich ground out. "Especially from someone that doesn't know a head from a halyard."

"The toilet and one of those ropes you run up sails and flags with," Edmund said. "No, I don't know how to run a ship. But you're not running a ship, *Admiral*, you're running a fleet. And running one in a *war*. And there's not damned much I don't know about war."

"War at sea," Kabadda said, as if explaining things to a child, "is different than war on the land."

"Not in macro," Edmund replied. "All the same things apply. The only difference is that you are *supposed* to have on-board logistics, and you couldn't even keep *that* straight!"

"There was a storm," Kabadda said.

"In the battle of Chattanooga, the supplies were maintained through several sleet and snowstorms," Edmund replied. "In the war in Burma it was maintained through a monsoon. And the Channel Fleet during the Napoleonic wars maintained itself in far worse conditions than you have been facing. But that requires *prior planning*. Prior planning *prevents* piss poor performance. And they didn't assault until they had built up sufficient supplies to support it. For that matter, the English Channel fleet had a regulation that no ship would be lower than two weeks on water or any other critical commodity. Ketchup, whether you like it or not, is a *critical* commodity. I *heard* your order to the fleet asking a reason only eight of ten dragons could fly and couldn't believe you'd *asked*. They hadn't been *eating*. Your own *records* showed that and it was amply evident if you know the first thing about dragon care!"

"Those damned dragons . . ." Kabadda said. "Dragons this, dragons that. Dragons need fresh meat. Dragons need ketchup . . ."

"The *enemy* dragons just SANK YOUR FLEET!" Edmund shouted. "If you'd spent the time working up *your* dragons instead of *starving* them we wouldn't be *in* this mess. Or if you'd even *started* to wonder whether there might be some *reason* that the New Destiny fleet was courting battle!"

"Okay, I've heard enough," Draskovich snarled. "You're not bringing anything positive to this meeting. Leave this room."

"You really don't want to push this, Drask," Edmund said.

"I don't care who you know," the admiral said. "Or who you've fucked. You don't have any authority or reason for being present. Leave, or I'll have the marines remove you."

Edmund stood up and smiled.

"Well, it's been a real pleasure," he said. "Must do this again sometime soon."

He walked out the door and went to the break room by the war-room. Besides the two ensigns there were a couple of seamen from the war-room, sitting at the table looking worn out and shell-shocked.

"How bad is it?" Edmund asked them.

"I don't know, sir," one of the seamen replied. "I'm just a runner from the mer at the docks. But the mer are . . . I've never seen them so pissed. The whale net is gone, sir. They think the orcas took out Merillo up in Granbas and that means we don't know what's what with the rest."

"Okay," Edmund said, sitting at the table covered with food stains. "Son, something to keep in mind. First reports are never as bad, or as good, as they seem. Herzer . . . no, Destrang. Go get Tao and a horse. Have Tao report to me. Van, gimme something to write with. Herzer, head down to the docks. Talk to the mer; they're going to talk to you. Van, I've got another research assignment for you."

"Yes, sir," Herzer said, grimly. He realized that many friends had probably died today, not among the Navy but among the mer.

"Destrang, get back here with Tao as fast as you can," Edmund said, picking up a pen and paper. "All of you: go."

CHAPTER SEVEN

"Do Jason?" the delphino squealed.

The leader of the Bimi island mer contingent shook his head. Everything was coming apart and the orders they were getting from headquarters were making no sense at all.

"Can you hear Merillo?" Jason asked.

"No," the delphino said. The human Changed to a dolphin shape had much better underwater hearing than the mer. "Orca squeal, hunting cry, no Merillo."

"Are they still using the hunting cry?" Jason asked.

"Still."

The mer looked up at the surface of the water above him and thought. If the orcas had caught the whalo to the north they wouldn't still be doing the horrible ringing hunting cry. They'd be silent. Feeding.

"Which way are they going?"

The delphino seemed to contemplate the question, turning his head from side to side as if tasting the sounds from the beleaguered whale.

"South. Southeast?" He shrugged as only a delphino can.

"Smart whale," Jason muttered. His underwater communications apparatus was a small bone in his forehead, located in his nasal passages. It was short-ranged and weak compared to the sonar of the delphinos, but it sufficed for communications. "Call all delphino, all mer, all whalo. Pass call. Fall back. Mer and delphino, move to nearest whalo, protect whalo."

"Authority?" the delphino squealed.

"Mine," Jason said. "Just *mine*."

Tao had had some hard rides before in his life, but this was ridiculous.

The nearest Army base was over a hundred kilometers away, at the falls of the Gem River. It was a major logistics point, but what was more important at the moment was that it had a communications crystal.

The crystal had the ability to contact a wide range of people who still had access to full technology. They were used for critical messaging, only. And Tao was carrying a critical message.

There was no way that he could have made it in any decent time were it not for the fact that there were messenger stations all along the bad road up the river from the base. He changed horses five times, each time dropping off a blown horse and throwing himself into the next one that was saddled. And then kicking that horse into a trot until it was warmed up and then into a canter.

He hadn't ridden much in a year. And his body was telling him that before he was a third of the way into the ride. What was that joke the cavalry troops told? Ah, "Forty Miles in the Saddle, by Major Assburns." Well, he had major assburns, that's for sure. Forty miles was . . .

By the time he reached the Army base, after ten hours of hard riding, he had figured out the conversion from the antiquated mile measurement and come to the conclusion that he had more than doubled it. Or something like that; arithmetic was not his strong suit. He dropped off another knackered out horse and got directions to the message center. He pounded up to the low stone building and climbed off the horse, nearly dropping to his knees with fatigue. But he was a Blood Lord, damnit, and he straightened up and tried to knock some of the dust off of his dress uniform, before opening the door and waddling bow-legged into the room.

There were a commander and two sergeants inside playing acey-deucy. They looked up at the dust-covered rider and the commander dropped his cards on the table.

"What's up, Ensign?" he asked.

"Message from General Talbot, sir," Tao replied. "For Her Majesty, Sheida Ghorbani."

"They did WHAT?" Admiral Draskovich shouted.

Edmund looked up at that and stopped perusing the reports in his hand. After he had sent everyone off on various errands he had paid a visit to the fleet intelligence shop and picked up some more light reading. He was just about done with it, having read through most of the day, when the latest report came in.

The admiral was no longer elegant. He looked hag-ridden and his hair had started to come undone from his ponytail. It had been a long day, night had fallen more than an hour ago, but he still had enough energy for fury.

"The mer leader, Jason Ranger, sent out an order pulling all the underwater forces back from their positions and sending all of them to protect the whalos," the petty officer said, looking up from the report in his hand. "There's a pitched battle taking place in the Granbas area. Merillo is back online and we're getting fragmentary reports from the fleet. It looks like *Reagan*, *Washuka* and *Norland* are sunk and there are other ships destroyed as well. *Bonhomme Richard* is damaged but can make some sail. There are wyverns all over the fleet, sir. When they came back they were landing on any ship or ditching. We've lost riders as well, some drowned. Some . . . thrown by their dragons. No total count on dragons, but it doesn't look good."

"Get the wyverns reassembled on the remaining carriers," Draskovich said angrily. "Send a message to the mer to get back in position. We can assemble another supply convoy . . ."

"Dragons overhead, sir!" a messenger shouted as he pounded through the door.

"Drask," Edmund said, walking quickly but unhurriedly to the door. "Get your people out of here."

"What?" the admiral shouted. "Get out of this room!"

"Just going," Edmund replied. But he stopped and

walked to the admiral, grabbing him by the ponytail and pulling his head down to where he could whisper in his ear. "This is a *wooden* building, damnit. *Evacuate*." With that he strode to the door, jerking it open and leaving it open.

He walked steadily to the stairs and then took them two at a time upwards until he reached the top floor. He stopped, panting, for a moment, feeling every year of his age, then strode into the corridor beyond. At that point he heard a thump on the roof and gave up dignity.

"VAN KRIEF!" he bellowed.

"Here, sir," the ensign said, popping out of a room down the corridor.

"We are *leaving*," Edmund yelled and headed for the stairs as the first smell of smoke entered the air.

He didn't pause as he headed down the stairs and then thought better of it; that ensign was addicted to research. But as he turned he heard the door bang open.

"Sir?" the ensign shouted.

"Run like hell, Ensign," he replied and took his own command.

By the time they made it out the doors of the headquarters the top floor was fully engaged and liquid fire was cascading down the walls. He bellowed in pain as a drop of napalm hit his arm and quickly yanked his tunic off, wrapping it around the burning droplet.

"Where's Destrang?" he yelled, looking around at the scurrying figures outside the headquarters. A bucket chain was being formed down to the river but he took one glance at the headquarters, which was lighting up the night, and shook his head.

"They'll never do it," he muttered.

"Here I am, sir," Destrang said, hurrying through the crowd. "It was a dragon raid, sir. One of them was breathing fire and all of them were pitching napalm. It was targeted on headquarters and the shipyard."

"Good," Edmund muttered. "They've finally done something stupid."

"Sir?" Van Krief asked.

"The best thing they could do for our Navy is burn that damned place to the ground," Edmund growled. "With any luck, Draskovich will choose to go down with his ship."

"If it's this bad here, sir," Van Krief said, "I wonder what it's like at sea."

"Get back!" the XO shouted as the wyvern lunged forward.

The CO of the ballista frigate *Darya Seyit* snarled as the wyvern drove back the net party that was trying to get onto the quarterdeck.

The frigate was rolling in light seas, at the play of the winds. The lost, angry and riderless wyvern—he wasn't even sure if it was one of theirs or the enemy's—had dropped out of the sky and landed on the quarterdeck of the ship before anyone had realized its intention.

The damned thing had immediately seized one of the signal midshipman by the thigh, but they had managed to beat it off of him before the quarterdeck crew evacuated the scene of battle.

Unfortunately, the ship's wheel was up there. As soon as the two quartermasters had jumped over the side of the ship—by order, there was no way for them to move forward past the enraged dragon—the ship had turned with the wind and now drifted helplessly as most of the crew tried to get in rigging while a party set up a jury-rigged rudder control below.

Most of the rest of the crew, including the ballista crews, were trying to get a net or a rope or something on the damned dragon so that the ship could be gotten back under helm.

"Okay, one more try, men," the XO shouted.

"Ahoy the ship!" a voice shouted from overside. "I need to see the skipper!"

"He's busy," the ship's master chief said, looking over the side. "Mer overside, sir," the chief continued.

"I know he is!" the mer yelled from below. It sounded like a female. "That's *why* I need to see him!"

The skipper walked to the rail and looked down in the water where a black-haired mer-girl with a bright blue tail was swimming alongside.

"What?" the skipper snarled.

"Well excuuuse *me*," the mer-girl said back. "Just trying to help. The problem is that wyvern's *hungry*. If you *feed* it it'll quit trying to kill you."

"You have a lot of experience with wyverns, girl?" the chief said, angrily.

"Yes, as a matter of fact I do," the girl said. "Elayna Farswimmer, Skipper. *Lieutenant* Farswimmer. I'm the daughter of the late Bruce Blackbeard and was on the Retreat with General Talbot. I have *a lot* of experience with wyverns and that one is *hungry*. You can tell by its cry; it's not angry it's *sad*. Because you're not *feeding* it."

"We don't *have* any wyvern food," the skipper temporized.

"As hungry as the poor thing is, it'd eat salt beef right out of the cask," the mermaid answered, bitterly. "You've been treating them horribly."

"Chief?" the skipper asked.

"We were boiling up lunch when it landed, sir," the chief replied. "I don't know how far along it got, but when you sounded general quarters, they'd have put out the fires."

"Get below," the skipper said. "Get the cooks up here with whatever they have."

No more than five minutes later, as the wyvern was trying to figure out how to get past all the rigging to get to the tender sailor snacks below, the chief came up followed by a party carrying joints dripping water on the snowy deck. They carefully crept up to the rear and the chief ran forward, hurling a shoulder of beef onto the quarterdeck.

The wyvern jumped on it as if it were starving, which it was. Wyverns used an enormous amount of energy in flying and they needed huge quantities of food to sustain them. Their normal "field" rations were a mixture of soybeans, cornmeal and oils for fat energy. The only way they could be induced to eat the mess, especially at sea where they were as susceptible to mal de mer as humans, was by liberally lacing it with ketchup powder. The fleet had been out of ketchup for days and the wyverns had been off their feed even *before* the debacle of the morning.

Ignoring the heavy salt brine that the beef had been pickled in, the wyvern started tearing off strips of flesh, bolting them down as fast as it could. When all the easily removed meat was stripped off, it looked down at the chief and mewled piteously.

One after another of the chunks of beef and pork were thrown up to the quarterdeck until at last the wyvern was barely picking at them. At that point the chief took a coiled line from one of the waiting sailors and walked up the steps to the quarterdeck. He cautiously edged up to the wyvern and ran the line under its halter, securing it with a fast bowline, then tossed the coil of rope to the sailor he'd taken it from. Quickly, other sailors ran up to the deck and tied ropes to the wyvern's halter, harness and huge, birdlike legs. In minutes the wyvern was secured in place. It didn't look as if it minded. When it had finished turning over the bones rolling on the swaying deck it tucked its head under its wing and promptly went to sleep.

"Told ya," the mermaid said, when the wyvern had obviously settled.

"Thank you," the skipper replied, dryly. "Okay, let's get these sails trimmed and get back under way!"

"The fleet's about sixty klicks southeast," Elayna said. "Them that's left."

"Marshal! Great news! The UFS fleet is practically destroyed, they're retreating on every front!"

Chansa looked up from his paperwork at his chief of staff and grunted.

"How many carriers did we get?" he asked, leaning back in his chair, which creaked.

Marshal Chansa Mulengela was huge, two and a half meters tall and broad in proportion. The small office that he had appropriated in the bowels of the Council facilities made him look bigger. And, despite the news, he didn't look happy.

"It looks like four," the chief of staff said, wondering what it would take to get the Key-holder to smile. "The way is open for the invasion fleet!"

"Only four?" Chansa growled. "Damn."

"Reports are still trickling in," the chief of staff noted. "We might have gotten the fifth as well."

"There's still the *Hazhir* down in the Isles," Chansa noted. "You can be sure that even an idiot like Draskovich will recall it."

"It's been modified," the chief of staff noted. "Their Buships does not consider it combatworthy." The chief of staff shrugged.

"Their Buships is as stupid as you are, then," Chansa growled. "It's been modified by that asshole, Shar Chang. If he's put in modifications, you can guarantee they're going to make it *more* combatworthy, not less. What about the strike on the headquarters?"

"It appears that was successful as well," the chief said. "It was on fire when the wyverns withdrew. They reported that there was a great dragon there, one that we didn't know about from intelligence reports."

"What about intel from the headquarters?" Chansa asked. "What are we getting from there?"

"The chain is long on that source, sir," the chief reminded him. "We probably won't have anything for a couple of days."

"Stay on it," Chansa said after thinking about it for a moment. "I won't be happy about launching the full fleet until we've run down their last carrier. Where did they retire to?"

"South, sir," the chief replied, glancing at his notes. "The orcas report that they've been driven off, so we're not sure exactly where it is. And there's a storm coming into the area so it's unlikely we can press action immediately."

"Where's the *Canaris*?" Chansa asked.

"Moving north along the Norau coast, headed for the Granbas rendezvous."

"Signal them to stand off the coast," Chansa said. "I don't want someone figuring out a way to take them out."

"Yes, sir."

"Go," Chansa said, looking at the paperwork on his desk. "I've got other things to handle."

As luck would have it, the admiral could be seen not too long afterwards, circling the madly burning building, his staff clustered around him.

"General Talbot," the admiral said, approaching him when he noticed him, and the cluster of officers around him. The admiral took in the burned arm and shook his head. "I'd have thought you'd be long gone by the time the first bomb hit."

"My ensign was upstairs," the general replied with a shrug. "I wasn't going to leave her to burn."

"No," the admiral said, his jaw working. "But I wonder, how did you divine that there would be an attack on this building?"

Edmund sighed and shook his head wearily. "Remember what I said about studying war? I was doing that when you were going through potty training, *Admiral*. Attacking the headquarters, given that most of your ships were at sea, was the obvious choice. I'd have probably hit the warehouses instead, but that's not how Chansa thinks. The first time I saw this building I thought: What a lovely target."

"How did they manage to *find* it, then," General Kabadda snarled.

"Because your whole damned base is lit up like a Yule Tree," Edmund sighed. "Ever heard the term 'blackout'?" he asked, then shook his head at the sign of bewilderment on their faces. "Lord, give me strength."

"General, what we need are some *positive* thoughts right now, thank you," the admiral replied, coldly. "Not defeatism."

"Who said anything about defeatism?" Edmund asked. "We're not defeated, but we damned well are stung. Stung hard. Not this, the shipyards and the fleet."

The admiral had opened his mouth to reply when one of the bucket brigade shouted: "Dragon!"

The line scattered as the few crossbow-armed marines looked up into the night sky, trying to get a glimpse of the enemy.

Edmund looked up and sighed, then looked around at the tense marines.

"Belay that!" he yelled. "That one is *ours*."

The great dragon descended on the quad in front of the burning headquarters, coming in over the fire so that her wings sucked the flames into swirls and caused them to leap higher.

"God damnit!" the admiral swore. "You just made our job harder."

"Sorry," the dragon hissed, swinging her head around to look at the admiral. "My mistake."

"Hey, Joanna," Edmund said.

"Eddie!" the dragon shouted, delightedly. "I got two of the bastards. Want I should go look for the ship?"

"No," Edmund said, just as Draskovich said: "Yes!"

"I didn't ask you," the dragon said to the admiral.

"No," Edmund repeated. "They would have launched from maximum range. Probably each of the dragons was only carrying one, maybe two, bombs. You'd have to do a ground take-off. And they would have hightailed it as soon as the wyverns returned. I doubt you'd find them, anyway. Especially at night."

"Commander Gramlich," the admiral grated. "I *order* you to go find and destroy that carrier."

"You're in breach of contract," Joanna said, easily. "I don't have to listen to you."

"That is a violation of military regulations," the admiral said. "And I have no choice but to place you under arrest."

"You and what army?" Joanna laughed. The great dragon was nearly sixty meters from nose to tail-tip and both ends, and the middle, were equipped for fighting.

"Drask, give it up," Edmund sighed. "You're just making a fool of yourself. What's the breach?"

"Failure to provide adequate support," Joanna replied. "Failure to provide specified pay and allowances. And I'm overdue for a vacation."

"You had a vacation in the Isles last year." Edmund grinned.

"Fisk you, General, sir," the dragon said, then laughed. The "vacation" had involved, among other things, being dragged nearly to her death by a kraken. On the other hand, the kraken had lost.

"Commander Gramlich," the admiral said, furious at being ignored. "For the last time, I *order* you . . ."

He paused as an officer approached with two pieces

of paper in his hand. He looked at the general and the admiral and then handed one to the admiral and one to Talbot. The admiral took one look at the piece of paper, reading it by the light of his burning headquarters, crumpled the paper up and dropped it to the ground. Then he walked away into the night.

"Sir?" General Kabadda called after him.

"Stay," the admiral said. "Good luck. You'll need it."

Talbot glanced at the paper and then looked at Kabadda.

"This reads, and I quote; 'General Wallace Draskovich relieved North Atlantis Command, effective immediately, Admiral Edmund Talbot appointed command vice General Draskovich. Signature, Michael Spehar, Minister of War.'" He handed the sheet of paper to Kabadda, who took it as if it were incendiary as the headquarters. "Do you acknowledge this assumption of command?"

The brigadier looked at it as if he couldn't read, then read it and read it again.

"I do so acknowledge your assumption of command . . ." he said, gritting his teeth. "Admiral."

"Kabadda, I'll tell you something," Edmund said, softly. "I'm about a centimeter away from having you follow the admiral. Do you want to do that?"

"No," Kabadda said, after a long pause.

"I'll tell you something else," Edmund went on. "The position of chief of staff is thankless, because everything he does right the boss gets credit for. And he gets his ass chewed for anything he does wrong. But he's the guy that makes the weapon, the commander just wields it. Frankly, with tweaking, this base and the fleet are pretty good weapons. *Pretty* good. Because the damned logistics are on your shoulders, from that point of view, not the admiral's. That means that not properly serving the dragons was *your* fault. But if you think you can get your job done the rest of the way, then I'm going to give you a pass. But from my POV, you've already had your strikes. One more and you're following the admiral. Clear?"

"Clear, sir," the general said.

"Okay, stop the idiotic bucket chain. That place was burning to the ground before the last wyvern flew over and we're just getting more people burned trying to put it out. Get the wounded tended to, get a headcount, get somebody besides you doing all this and meet me at the docks."

"The docks, General?" the chief of staff asked.

"The docks," Edmund replied. "I'm gonna go talk to the mer. Joanna, Destrang, Van Krief, you're on me."

CHAPTER EIGHT

"Hey, son," Edmund said as he walked out onto the mer pier. He looked at the messenger and motioned. "Mind if I borrow that chair?"

"Who are you?" the messenger asked.

Edmund realized that with his tunic off, he was just a slightly sooty guy in a T-shirt.

"I'm Admiral Edmund Talbot, your new commander," he said, mildly. "Now would you mind getting out of the chair?"

The seaman looked at the two ensigns and the dragon following the person, who did have the trousers of an officer, and after a moment's shock, shot out of the chair as if it were electric.

"Thank you," Edmund said, picking it up and taking it over to the side of the pier.

The pier was raised well above the height of the water but there was a floating dock at water-level. Herzer was stomach down, talking to the mer in the water in low tones, with a delphino drifting on the surface, watching.

"Herzer," Edmund said, "stand up."

Herzer rolled over and to his feet, looking up at the general.

"Catch," Edmund said, tossing the chair down to the captain.

He then walked down the slippery stairs to the platform, took the chair away from Herzer and carried it to the side of the floating dock.

"Hi," Edmund said to the mer. "How's it going?"

"You're Talbot," the mer said, surprised.

"That's me, should I remember you?" Edmund asked. "I don't, sorry."

"No, sir, we've never met," the mer replied. "Asfaw, sir, communications lieutenant. I wasn't in the Bimi pod when you were there, sir. I joined later."

"Oh, good, I feel better." Edmund chuckled. "There were so many mer on the Retreat I never could keep most of them straight."

"Talbot!" the delphino squealed. "Talbot General."

"Yes, and you are?"

"T-t-tilly!" the delphino answered. Communicating clearly with a blow-hole was not the easiest thing in the world. It often made the delphinos sound stupid, but they were of normal human intelligence and had abilities in the water even the mer could not touch.

"Good evening, Mr. Tilly," Edmund said.

"Not good!" Tilly replied. "Fire!"

"Oh, well." Talbot shrugged. "I never liked that headquarters anyway."

There was a moment's pause and then Asfaw started

laughing so hard he slipped back into the water and the delphino let out a high squeal of amusement.

"But there are things we need to do," Edmund continued when the two got their mirth under control. "I've got good news and bad news, and it's both the same news."

"What's that, sir?" the mer asked.

"I've just assumed command," Edmund replied, handing him the sheet of paper. "Send that out. Tell everyone to rebroadcast it."

"Willll!" the delphino trilled.

"Wait," Edmund said. "There's more. All remaining ships, retreat towards coast, assemble when possible near the Granbas area where Merillo is."

"Storm come!"

"Where then?" Edmund asked.

"Soooouth!" the delphino squealed. "Bamud!"

"Okay, I stand corrected," Edmund replied. "To all the ships with wyvern; feed them meat from normal stocks. Do not attempt transfer at this time unless senior dragon-riders concur. Understood?"

"'Stood!" the delphino squealed.

"All whalos run silent until mer and delphinos are on station. Any that are under attack, move to the nearest fleet. Fleets are to use wyvern to attack the orcas."

"Orca meat!" the delphino squealed happily. "Taste sweet!"

"To Merillo and the group assisting him; draw the orcas to the nearest wyvern armed fleet units."

"'Stood!"

"Last order," Edmund said. "To all carriers: Forage wyverns when possible. Tell the mer to meet with the senior dragon-riders and *amplify*. They all know the story."

"Will!" the delphino squealed.

"Okay, we're done for now. I'm appointed command, Admiral Draskovich relieved. Retreat towards Bamud. Feed the dragons, on orca and ixchitl if possible. Protect the whales. That's all I can expect them to handle right now."

"Done!" the delphino said and dove under the water.

Edmund leaned back in the chair, planted his feet and tipped it back to look at the stars. He looked over at Herzer and had to chuckle; the captain had a pad of paper out and was clearly taking notes of the orders.

"They're really big on written orders, sir," Herzer said.

"That they are," Edmund replied, looking up at the stars.

"Ge . . . Admiral," General Kabadda called from up on the pier. "We've pulled everyone but a fire-watch back from the headquarters. I'm shifting it to the officers' club."

"Nah," Edmund said. "Shift it down here."

"Here, sir?"

"Yep. Where are your communications?"

"Here, sir," Kabadda admitted. "But . . ."

"Got any mer sitting around the O-club for advice?"

"Advice, sir?"

"Yes, Kabadda, advice," Edmund replied, tiredly. "Look, work with me here, do a bit of thinking. Have you ever flown a dragon?"

"I've flown *on* one, sir. . . ."

"Yeah, so have I," Edmund snorted. "In that so-called briefing you thought was so great, the most experienced dragon-rider, dragon *wrangler* for that matter, was Herzer, who kept his mouth shut the whole time. The most experienced person at coordinating mer and delphino forces in the attack was *me*. When we rebuild a headquarters, and I'll admit we're going to have to, the meeting area and war-room will be suspended over the water, like a boathouse, and it will have a way for great dragons to participate, if by no other means than sticking their heads through the window. Clear?"

"Clear, sir," the general said in a stricken voice.

"Joanna."

"Dude," Joanna said.

"We're back playing soldiers, now, Joanna," Edmund said.

"Yes, sir," the dragon said with amusement in her voice.

"Forget the failure to provide adequate support," Edmund said. "I'm sure there are some nice juicy bullocks around and if not I understand most of the horses in the stables are ready for the glue factory. What's your back pay?"

"Eight hundred chits," Joanna snarled, angrily. "And by contract I can request that it be in specie. I'm so requesting."

Edmund sighed at the tone but kept looking up.

"Pay her, Kabadda," he said.

"But, sir . . ."

"I said *pay* her," Edmund snarled. "Joanna, silver do?"

"Sure."

"Kabadda, get a working party started on ripping the fixtures out of the VIP quarters bathroom. Ditto anywhere else that they used silver for fixtures. If it comes down to it, get all the silver table settings in the dining room. And then find someone who'll give us a pence on the chit in silver or gold for the damned bathtub."

"Yes, sir," the chief of staff said in a voice that mingled resignation and anger.

"We're a military force, not a bunch of Persian potentates," Edmund amplified. "Joanna, you're gonna get paid. Question: How far can you fly?"

"Pretty far," the dragon said, warily.

"All the way to Blackbeard Base?"

"I don't know," the dragon said, honestly. "I wouldn't want to try it."

"You're gonna have to," Edmund said. "Asfaw, another order."

"Yes, sir," the mer said.

"Effective immediately, Brigadier Shar Chang brevet promoted Lieutenant General. Will proceed via . . . what's the name of that carrier down there?"

"*Hazhir*, sir," Herzer said.

"Proceed immediately to Newfell Base via carrier *Hazhir*. Carrier will leave all but one wyvern. Expect contact en route by greater dragon. Make all sail. Anybody know where Evan is?"

"Who?" Kabadda asked, clearly lost.

"Blackbeard," Herzer said.

"You're sure?" Edmund asked.

"I took the trouble to find out."

"Bring civilian engineer Evan Mayerle. Joanna, you're going to head for Blackbeard. Hopefully you'll meet the carrier on the way. If not, feed at Blackbeard and then go find it. Get Shar up here, soonest. Bring Evan if you think you can handle the weight."

"It'd be easier if I had some sort of powered assist on takeoff," the dragon grumbled. "Even a cliff. But this place is flat as a board."

"Kabadda, in the morning get working on a dragon-launching platform," Edmund said. "It's stupid that dragons attacking us have assists and our defensive forces don't."

"Yes, sir," the chief of staff said. "But if the dragon leaves, we won't have any cover for the base, sir."

"What about the wyverns?" Edmund asked.

"What wyverns?" Joanna said. "I'm the only dragon here."

Edmund covered his face with his hands and shook his head.

"Send a runner over to the message center. Message follows: Send flight of wyverns and riders to Newfell Base. Immediate. Coastal forces prepare for dragon attacks. More follows. Signature Talbot."

"Will do, sir," one of the messengers said, scribbling hastily.

"Kabadda, I want that platform done in less than a week," Edmund said. "At least twenty meters high, strong enough to support a great dragon. With a catapult."

"Yes, sir," Kabadda said. "But . . . that's a lot of material."

"And manpower," Edmund said. "Which you will find in whatever is left of the shipyards. We're out of the shipbuilding business for the time being. What do we have in the way of supply craft, and materials, to send out to the fleet? And do we have any idea what we have in the way of supplies?"

"With the headquarters burned we lost most of the records," Kabadda admitted. "But we can reconstruct some of them from records in the warehouses. There are two transport ships available, but nothing to cover them with."

Edmund thought about that and sighed.

"Get them ready for sea, loaded with wyvern food and ketchup," he said.

"Sir, we're . . . out of ketchup," Kabadda admitted.

"Oh, grand," Joanna said. "In that case, I want those bullocks cooked, General."

"Care to amplify that, Kabadda?" Edmund sighed. "Never mind. Get them ready with all the salt beef and pork you have available. Canned if you have it. Or smoked fish. Anything protein with high fat content. And find some *ketchup*."

"Yes, sir," the chief of staff said.

"There's another carrier out there, somewhere," Edmund muttered.

"Agreed, sir," Kabadda said. "The geometry is impossible for the ones that struck the fleet to have struck here as well."

"Lieutenant Asfaw."

"Sir?" the mer said.

"Ask Jason to get some delphinos deployed over this way," Edmund said. "Find that damned carrier."

"Yes, sir."

"I don't want to be dealing with these details, Kabadda," Edmund said. "Get the supplies collected, stat. Handle it."

"Yes, sir," the chief of staff replied.

"But get at least a couple of hours sleep sometime tonight; it's gonna be a long day."

As the chief of staff hurried away, Edmund dropped the chair back to the dock and leaned over to look at the mer.

"So, what do you think?"

"I think I'm glad you took over," Asfaw replied.

"Well, you'll find I'm going to be poking into your affairs more than Draskovich did," Edmund said. "So, anything you need down there?"

"Honestly?" the mer asked, surprised.

"Honestly."

"General," the mer said, trying not to sound angry. "This bottom is mud. We've got the choice of trying to hold our position in the current or hold onto the dock or lie in the mud. It's like, six meters deep. You tend to sink. Frankly, sir, it sucks."

"So, you wanna chair?" Edmund asked.

"Something," the mer replied with a shrug.

"Herzer?" Edmund said.

"Got it," Herzer replied. "The mer need something to sit on."

"Anything else?" Edmund asked.

"Oh, lots, General," the mer replied. "The message system sucks. Our quarters suck. There needs to be more than one of us mer and one delphino here. I could go on and on."

"Herzer . . . no, Destrang, sit here and listen to the mer and delphino litany of complaints," Edmund said. "And pick up anything coming in from the fleet that you think I really need to know. I'm going to bed. Nobody is going to be making sense before morning. Joanna, what are you still doing here?"

"Waiting for daybreak," the dragon replied. "If I'm going that far, I'm going to need all the thermals I can get."

"Herzer," Edmund said. "We need dragon resupply points along the coast. Nothing elaborate, just a stockade with some beef cattle or pigs and somewhere for the dragons to land. And more wyvern for messengers; they don't have to be carrier qualified. As a matter of fact, it'll be a good place to train young riders and wyverns. Joanna, leave as soon as you think wise, but the sooner the better. And that's it, I'm done." He got up and carried the chair back up to the pier.

"Thanks, son," he said, handing it to the messenger.

"You're welcome, sir," the messenger replied.

"Have a nice night," Edmund said as he walked off into the fire-lit darkness.

"Attention on deck!" someone called as Edmund walked into the reestablished headquarters. There simply wasn't anywhere to put it at the docks so for the time being it had moved to the officers' club. A cold front was in the offing and he appreciated the shorter walk—the O-Club was practically next door to the VIP quarters—but it didn't mean he wasn't planning on getting everything moved as soon as possible.

"Rest," he called, waving his hand and looking first at the large map someone had pinned up on the wall. The map was clearly hand drawn, and hastily—several of the landforms were wrong—but it gave him a good approximation of what was going on. The approximate position of both fleets were marked as were other units at sea, most of whom were heading for the nearest secure port. The best part was the weather markings of the large storm, a "nor'easter" that had blown up.

"They're going to get caught by the storm," he said.

"Yes, sir," Kabadda replied, walking over with a mug of coffee in his hand. He handed it to the admiral and Edmund took it uneasily.

"I can get my own coffee, Kabadda," Edmund said, but he took a sip anyway. It was the way he liked it, almost a syrup with sugar and cream. Somebody had done their homework.

"We're not quite prepared with the briefing, sir," Kabadda said. "But we will be by 0900."

"I doubt it," Edmund replied. "I don't want the short dog and pony show that you guys put on before. I need full information on all ships. What we know of their stores, information about their captains' background and experience. I need all the intel we have on the enemy, same deal. I heard something, during the attack, about the dragons being shot at. I want information on that as soon as possible. The briefing will include as much as we know about the condition of the dragons on our ships as well as crew condition. And, especially, how long for the fleet to return and our estimated material condition when they get here. When they get in I want food waiting for them, bands playing, slaughtered carcasses for the dragons, a barbeque for the crews and decent *onshore* housing for everyone. They're going to have serious casualties; I need to know the condition of our hospital establishment. We need a casualty list from them before they arrive. We're going to have to take much the same fleet out, *again*, and this time we're going to have to win. We're not going to do that with troops that are demoralized. So the *first* thing we're going to be working on is morale. Clear?"

"Yes, sir," the chief of staff said.

"There are four aspects to winning a battle. Battle plans, which includes *adequate* intel, leadership, material, and morale. We are *going* to have a set of the first that work, bet on it. The second I'm going to be looking into carefully; what I've seen so far does not thrill me. The third we're going to have to make or steal. The fourth has several parts. One of them is adequate living conditions and the knowledge that the *others* are as good as you can make them. When the Fleet sails again, the sailors, NCOs and officers are going to have to *know* that this time they are going to kick ass and not even bother taking names. Is that clear?"

"Yes, sir."

"Send a message to the Fleet. I need information on conditions on every ship. If they don't have a dispatch sloop, get one out to them. And tell the mer to *find that other carrier*. I don't want to be surprised again. If it's retired, and I'd bet it has, we'll send out the resupply vessels."

"Yes, sir."

"Now, assign one of your officers to show me around the base facilities," Edmund finished. "I can look into that. We'll have the brief this afternoon. If anything comes up that needs my immediate attention, send a runner."

"There is a large amount of paperwork, sir," Kabadda said. "Most of it is addressed to the commander."

"Anything that's not from either Mike Spehar or

Sheida have one of your people open and read. I'm not going to be handling correspondence from every dime-store clerk in an officer's, or general's, uniform that wants to joggle my elbow or know some stupid minutiae. Handle it."

"Yes, sir." Kabadda opened his mouth as if to reply and then shut it.

"What?"

"Admiral Draskovich felt that knowing what information was flowing was important, sir," the general replied, uneasily.

"The term is 'delegation,' Kabadda," Edmund replied. "My job is to make sure that everyone knows *theirs* and does it to the best of their ability. It is not to do their job for them. Mine is going to take up enough of my time."

"Yes, sir."

"The same goes for you," Edmund added. "Your job is to ensure that the weapon is prepared. But you cannot do that if you're running over every single materials or personnel list. That is what the G-1 and G-4 are for. And their job is to make sure that *their* people are trained, and doing their jobs, to the best of their ability. Not doing their job for them. Not nitpicking every detail—their people are the ones that are supposed to nitpick—and, most especially, not constantly micromanaging their people's actions. If somebody screws up, you show them the error of their ways. If they can't get their head around doing it right, after adequate retraining, you find somebody who can."

"Yes, sir," Kabadda said, nodding.

"Was that an automatic response?" Edmund asked. "Or did you listen?"

"I was listening, Admiral," the chief of staff said, indignantly.

"Great. Who is going to guide me around the base?"

"I wi . . ." the chief of staff started to say and then smiled ruefully. "I was about to say 'I will.' That was the wrong answer, wasn't it?"

"Bingo," Edmund chuckled. "You've got more important things to do."

"I'll assign one of my aides," Kabadda replied.

"Fine," Edmund said, draining his coffee. "I'm going to have another cup and then talk to some of the headquarters people. I'll probably be at this for about an hour."

"Yes, sir."

Edmund walked over to where a chief petty officer was hovering over a group of seamen, male and female, who were laboriously copying from a manual.

"Hey Chief," the admiral said.

"Admiral," the CPO replied, bracing to attention.

"Can it, we've got real work to do," Talbot replied. "What's your name, Chief?"

"Senior Chief Naoko Greter, sir," the chief replied. "NCOIC of the signals group."

"Well, Chief Greter, I'd kill for another cup of coffee. Where's the urn?"

"Why don't I get someone to get it for you, sir?" The chief chuckled. "Besom! Coffee for the admiral. That's what runners are for, sir."

"Delegation works." Edmund nodded, handing the mug to a very young female seaman. "So what are you guys doing?"

"The fire destroyed most of our signals books, sir,"

the chief said with a grimace. "And the press we used to run them off. Until we get a press up and running again we're having to hand copy."

"Is everything being done that is possible to get the press up and running again, Chief Greter?" Edmund asked.

Herzer wondered at the formality of the question until he realized Edmund was repeating the name to get it memorized.

"As far as I can tell, sir," the CPO replied. "I checked with the machine shop and their guys had it as one of their top priorities. They already had the frame done but the letters had to be ordered."

"Anything you need you think it's reasonable to ask for?"

"I've got all the people I could find who can read and write with a fair hand organized on it, sir," the chief shrugged. "Not that I can think of."

"Good," Edmund nodded. "Who do you think I should go cheer up next?"

CHAPTER NINE

The duke worked his way around the room, informally chatting with at least the senior officer and senior NCO of each of the teams that directly supported him. As he did Herzer came to realize that he was subtly drawing them out. Not only learning their names but getting a feel for their capabilities. All of them were, naturally, nervous, facing the boss who had so abruptly replaced Admiral Draskovich. With the destruction of the headquarters all of them were facing problems and Herzer realized that the duke, while appearing on the surface to simply be chatting, was learning who in the headquarters could face a challenge and who couldn't. Some people could take a break in routine and others could not. Both types were useful to the military, which had more than its share of boring jobs. But the most useful, by and large, were those who could respond to chaos and bring order from it. Unfortunately, the headquarters seemed to be severely lacking in the latter.

Operations, especially, seemed to be running around like headless chickens. They had multiple messages piling up giving locations of ships and in many cases requests for reinforcement. Edmund leafed through the messages, passing them on to Herzer as he was done.

Herzer, in turn, was surprised at the . . . tone of many of the messages. Most of the remaining carrier captains, as well as the captains of the ballista frigates that were attached to them, were simply asking what they should do. Not where they should go or where they should rendezvous, but what they should do about the battle damage on their ships. There were also requests for resupply, naturally, but Herzer had to wonder what they were doing sitting on the desk of the operations section. They should have been sent directly to G-4, the department in charge of logistics. There the requests would be assembled and collated so that if a resupply force *could* be put to sea, it would be loaded for what they needed.

After reading the messages and shaking hands with the harried captain who was trying to get some order in his section, Edmund strolled over to the logistics section where a very young female lieutenant was copying items off of one list and filling in another.

"How's it going, Lieutenant?" the admiral said.

The young woman had been so absorbed in her task that she hadn't even noticed the approach of the new boss.

"Not very damned good." She sighed, not looking up. "Whatever it is, I don't have it."

"What a perfect answer from a supply person," Edmund chuckled.

She looked up then and leapt to her feet, ashen.

"Sorry, sir," she stammered, "it's just that . . ."

"I understand," Edmund replied. "Everyone wants something and they want it *right now*. The question is, are we going to be able to get it?"

"So far, so good, sir," she replied. "What I was doing was taking the requests from the fleet and compiling ship packets, sir." She glanced down at the lists and seemed to drift off for a moment.

"Betraying my total ignorance," Edmund said after a moment. "What is a ship packet?"

"Sorry, sir," the lieutenant said, shaking her head. "When we send resupply ships out, some of the stuff that's requested is in bulk. Beans and ketchup for the wyverns, salt beef and pork. But some of the stuff is specific. For example the *Henry Tachos* needs a new set of steering rigging; the fire they had burned up most of the rear of the ship. We try, where possible, to assemble the specific needs for the ships in one place on the resupply ships and then load it according to the order in which the ships are going to be supplied."

"And you are . . . ?"

"Lieutenant Dierdre Miuki, sir," the young woman replied.

"Does that need to be done in the headquarters, Lieutenant Miuki?" Edmund asked. "I'd think that would be passed on to a lower section to be assembled?"

"We sort of triage it here, sir," the lieutenant said. "Then it gets gone over again by the G-4 staff."

"I notice that while you were concentrating, you're not terribly busy, Lieutenant . . . Miuki, was it?"

"Yes, sir, Miuki," she replied. "I'm waiting on the rest of the signals from the fleet, sir."

"Which are over at operations."

"Yes, sir."

"Why?" the admiral inquired, mildly.

"They . . . go through ops first, sir," the officer said, swallowing.

"Van Kr. . . ." Edmund said then shook his head. "No . . . Destrang."

"Sir?"

"Go over to operations. On my authority, pore through those messages. Pull out any that only pertain to material needs and move them over here. Now."

"Yes, sir," the ensign said languidly, then strolled back over to ops.

"You'll have your messages shortly, Lieutenant," the admiral said. "But all I want *you* to do is sort out who wants what and send it on. Let someone in the G-4 section make up the ship packets or whatever. Clear?"

"Yes, sir."

"It's been a pleasure meeting you, Lieutenant Miuki."

"Thank you, sir."

Herzer and the ensigns followed the admiral to the far side of the room where he stood looking at the map for a long time, then turned around shaking his head.

"No plan survives contact with the enemy, Herzer."

"No sir," Herzer said, smiling faintly. "That's why they call them the enemy, sir."

Megan smiled as Paul rolled off of her and she rearranged her clothing as she cleaned up.

When she had first arrived in the harem the "standard" clothing was light silk robes that were presupplied. Some of the girls made clothing of their own;

Mirta Krupansky for example was an accomplished seamstress. The simple rule, strictly enforced by Christel, was that the clothing had to be "nice to look at" by which she meant "skimpy."

Megan had used a crisis with Paul, a time when he nearly killed himself from neglect, to effect several changes. One of them was to get Mirta to do more classes on sewing. The woman was clearly older than she looked or acted and had spent her time studiously avoiding any attention in the harem. Megan more or less forced her to take a more proactive role and over time all of the girls, even Megan, became competent at making "appropriate" outfits.

But another change that Megan effected was the robes. They had struck her from the beginning as being silly. And not having panties or bras was just idiocy. So, soon after the "crisis," she had convinced Christel to "outsource" for standard clothing that, while alluring, was a bit more practical. Among other things, working out in the robes was a pain and doing so stark naked was a *specific* pain; Paul was eclectic in his taste in women, with the exception of breasts.

The "standard" clothing in the harem, now, was a short midriff top, front-opening bra, either short skirt or very short shorts and panties. They arrived in various sizes and then the girls "fitted" them a bit more closely. Of course, when Paul came to visit those came off and a variety of "special" outfits went on.

Megan's "special" outfits tended to look not much different from the day-to-day ones, just in more vivid colors and richer fabrics. She was currently wearing a short, split, hip-hugging skirt and a very brief halter top, both in a rich, rippling red material.

She picked up her ripped panties and shook her head.

"You've been away too long again, Paul," she said.

"Yes, I suppose I have," the council member replied. He looked much better than during the crisis. The girls had managed to convince him that starving himself wasn't good for him or them. And he had tended to spend more time in the harem afterwards; most of his work was done via sentient avatars which had to be "gathered" and resent on an almost daily basis. They were, for all practical purposes, "him" but as time went by their experiences tended to make the personalities fragment away from the base. Gathering them always was somewhat traumatic as he dealt with the various problems that arose in brutal bursts.

But that meant that he could do it just about anywhere and for several months after the crisis he had tended to do the "reintegration" in the harem, usually while Megan or Christel watched over him.

The combination of the girls stuffing him and coming out of his reintegration trance with a pretty female snuggled up against him had done wonders for his psyche. Which was why Megan found it odd that he had been gone for nearly a month. Presumably, given his actions, celibate.

"I liked staying here," Paul said as he slipped on his pants and shirt. "But I found that I was really starting to lose my focus. I needed to get out among the people and experience their lives again. It's . . . getting better. But the life they live is still brutal and horrible."

"You don't get that from your avatars?" Megan asked.

"Not the same," Paul admitted. "They don't *experience* the life the way that I do. I feel I need that if I'm going to do the best job that I can for the people, given the current conditions."

"You're a very good man, Paul," Megan said, slipping up to him and cradling him in her arms. "But that's one of the reasons we like to have you here. Another, selfish, reason I like it is I haven't had any news in a *month*. What's going on?"

"Good news and bad," Paul admitted. "The Tauranian forces of that bitch Ishtar defeated Lupe's forces and are just about to close in on the Alam reactor site."

"Well, big deal." Megan shrugged, carefully ensuring that the shrug transmitted through the breasts she had pushed into his side. "There's a force-field up around the reactor, right? They can't capture it through that."

"Force majeure," Paul sighed. "If they take the territory, Mother will transfer the control of the shield to them. They 'own' it according to her protocols. It's the same weakness we're trying to exploit all over, so I can't exactly complain."

"That's insane," Megan said, honestly.

"Mother doesn't take sides," Paul pointed out. "She'll maintain our personal protection fields, but she's not going to defend the reactor for us. We've built up a fortress around it, but they're sure to take that in time. Especially since it can't be close, given the power they're pouring on its shields. It's really just a curtain wall. Lupe has pulled a good bit of the army they defeated inside the walls, but even if they don't attack they can just starve them out. And then they'll have the reactor and there goes an eighth of our power. I've instructed them to destroy the reactor rather than have it fall into Ishtar's hands, but if we lose that much power, things are going to be tough."

"So what's the good news?" Megan asked, filing that point away.

"Chansa's plan worked," Paul said, brightening up. "He sent out his combat fleet and ravaged the UFS fleet good and hard. They lost a lot of their carriers and their wyverns aren't getting fed so they're on their last legs. But he couldn't completely destroy them because of a storm. He also took out their main shipyard and their headquarters. The next plan is to spoof them into moving out of position and send out the invasion fleet. It looks like the invasion is *on*."

"Good news," Megan said, thinking about the plans she already knew. "If you can get to the Pizurg power plant in time, you might be able to make up the gain in power."

"Or, even if they destroy it, we'll at least not be so much in the hole," Paul said, nodding. "If we can get an invasion force to take and hold some of the territory in Norau, we can set up portals and not, strictly, need the sea-lanes anymore. Once we own territory on the coast, territory we can demonstrate is resuppliable, Sheida can't block our teleports. We can pour forces through the portals."

"If."

"If," Paul smiled. "The target is Balmoran. There are good piers there and a good natural harbor. We can move up the Sussain River and supply that way. And Celine has 'Change' personnel standing by." He shrugged and grimaced at the thought. "The people of Norau don't strictly need Change; they've demonstrated that they can survive in this world. But Change adds to our army." He grimaced again and shrugged. "And if we can just *win* we can Change them back. As they are they are not just abominations but *evil* abominations."

"I know you hate Change," Megan said, "and the Changes that have had to be made."

"Yes, I do," Paul sighed. "But it's for the best, really. The life that people have to live these days . . . If that bitch Sheida had just . . ."

"Hey, you're supposed to be here for relaxation," Megan said.

"I'm supposed to be here to make babies," Paul replied, frowning. "Something that isn't happening enough. I suppose because I'm not here enough."

"Then stay here more," Megan replied, logically. "There were more pregnancies when you were around more often." Karie, Velva and Golda had all gotten pregnant during the time period.

"You didn't get pregnant," Paul pointed out, frowning. "I've scanned you. I know you're fertile . . ."

"Paul?" Megan said, smiling thinly. "If you're thinking of hurrying things along somehow, let me ask you a question. Do you really *want* me in the confinement quarters for nine months? Then gone for two years with my newborn?"

Paul frowned and opened his mouth, then closed it.

"Okay, I didn't think so. So maybe we should just let nature take its course?" she asked, smiling.

"You . . . have a point," Paul said, still frowning. "But you would make a great mother, I'm sure."

"And I'm sure that in time I will," she replied, rolling over on him. "Can I ask you another question?"

"Go ahead," he said, leaning back.

"Why do you still have your clothes on?"

Megan looked at the vial for a moment and then tossed back the bitter brew, closing her eyes and wincing against the taste. When she had arrived in the harem, the only thing she knew about tansy was that it was dangerous to use and one of the few semieffective abortifacients available as an herb. She'd originally run across it as a poison, in fact, but the abortifacient properties had been stored in her sometimes overgenerous memory.

When she had first set up her "perfumery" she had ordered a large number of herbs, included among them, as a single line item, tansy. Paul had scanned the list on any number of occasions but had clearly never delved deeply into their properties; given the large number of herbs it would have been a mind-numbing exercise. It was one of the many things she hoped he never bothered to notice.

Over time she had experimented with it judiciously, slowly increasing the dosage until she began to feel unpleasant effects. Each time she was "with" Paul, she was careful to take the herbal infusion every few days for at least a week afterwards. So far, no pregnancy, which was fine by her.

She washed the bitter oils down with a glass of lemon water and picked up a few bottles of perfume for the girls.

Her effect was clear in the main gathering area of the harem. Where there had been bare stone walls and a few cushions thrown around a stone floor, there were now carpets, bright wall-hangings and low tables.

There were even five cats, ranging from standard-sized tabbies up to a puma-sized "house lion." The tables and pillows had been moved out of the way for the afternoon exercise program and the girls were well into a serious aerobics workout. The cats had had the sense to clear the area.

She was mostly exempt from the "mandatory" workouts since she tended to keep herself in shape. But she often joined in and after stretching a bit she took a place at the back of the group and started jogging with them.

As she did she scanned the girls, wondering what they would think if she ever managed to bring her plans to fruition. The harem was a boring place, but as safe and well-supplied as was possible post-Fall. When she killed Paul, all the safety and security would go away in that moment. Most of them had known enough of the post-Fall life to be frightened of leaving the harem. It was something that she kept in mind. Along with the fact that if any of them stayed, they were, effectively, doomed. She also worried about the women who had been taken away pregnant. She had no idea where the "confinement" quarters were. And any scenario that she envisioned, post-Paul, meant being on the very ragged edge of disaster. Timing would be everything. Trying to find the girls, to convince them to leave, might mean coming to blows with *other* council members. Not to mention that she wasn't sure she could gain full control of Paul's power immediately. Many of the programs that had been universally available pre-Fall had been locked under passwords.

There were thirteen women in the seraglio, including two new ones that Paul had "recovered" in the last year. There were seven, somewhere, either awaiting birth or with their children.

What she should do was take the women from the seraglio and run like hell.

But she didn't know if she could do that.

"Shar," Edmund said, taking the general's hand as he slid off the dragon.

"Admiral Talbot," Shar said then grinned. "Coming up in the world?"

"I think more like . . . sideways," Edmund replied. "Joanna, you look like hell."

The dragon did look exhausted but she grinned nonetheless.

"If memory serves, you owe me a couple of barbequed cows," Joanna said.

Edmund gestured to the rear of a building where smoke could be seen ascending into the air.

"Where there's smoke, there's fire. Where there is fire, there is barbeque."

"I'm outta here," the dragon said, stretching her legs and then stumping towards the fire.

"I wish you could have brought Evan," Talbot said, gesturing towards the nearby temporary headquarters.

"Joanna was on the ragged edge of ability." Shar shrugged. "Evan's not that big of a guy, but I didn't even bring a change of clothes. But I've brought some ideas of his we need to talk about."

"The clothes we can get fixed," the duke said, looking at Van Krief.

"Clothes for the general," Van Krief said, noting it in her book.

"Aides?" Shar asked with a grin. "Where's Herzer?"

"Putting the fear of Edmund into some supply personnel."

"Captain, we're working on it," the major said, looking over his desk at Herzer. "I realize that the admiral isn't aware of all the logistical aspects of this base, but . . ."

"I think the admiral is well aware of the 'logistical aspects' of this base, Major," Herzer replied, smiling. "Which is why you *are* going to draw the supplies requested and you *are* going to prepare, as ordered, for the arrival of the Fleet."

"Captain, the admiral can order all he would like," the major said, smiling faintly and leaning back in his chair. "But the materials he has requested are administered by Navy Logistics Command, not by the local fleet commander or by the base commander. They are for resupply of the Fleet and not for any frivolous 'welcome home' party your general seems to think is a good idea. Your general does not have the *authority* to order their release. Certainly not for a nonoperational function."

"Are there sufficient excess supplies for what the general has ordered?" Herzer asked, calmly.

"Whether there are or not is beside the point," the major said. "And don't think that the 'admiral' can simply order me around. I don't work for him, I work for Naval Logistics."

"Is that your final answer?" Herzer asked, grinning.

"Yes, it is," the major frowned.

"Okay, what we have here is a clear case of separation of operational and logistic function," Herzer said, slipping into instructor mode. "There have been repeated instances in historical record where this has occurred, always to the detriment of the operational side. Given that fact, you leave me no recourse but to ensure you spend the rest of your military career as a stevedore on the docks."

"You don't have the authority for that," the major smiled, thinly. "So you might as well take your threats out of my office."

"Oh, I think I do," Herzer replied, laying a sheet of paper on the table. "This is my authority, signed by Admiral Houser, releasing all stores in this vicinity, and all logistics personnel, to the control of the base commander. And item one in my report is that you're a shit for brains that can't get his lard butt out of his office."

"Let me see that," the major said, snatching up the paper.

"I'll note that this is a copy of the original. The distribution list on the original included your office. So you're clearly such a lard ass you didn't even bother to read your mail. Now get your ass up and get out of the chair."

"I don't have to take that from you, *Captain*," the major snarled, throwing the sheet of paper on the desk and pointing to his collar. "I'm a *major*. You're a *captain*. And you don't talk to me that way!"

"I'm a *captain* sent by your *commander* passing on an *order* that you failed to obey," Herzer said, still smiling with a certain amount of strain. "I think you'd better wonder how many more minutes you're *going* to be a major. Or, you know, you could get your ass in gear and start preparing for the arrival of the Fleet. Your choice."

"We'll see about this," the major said. "There are channels for the 'admiral' to forward a request such as that. And the use of that material for nonoperational purposes is *still* against regulations. You can tell the 'admiral' that for me. Now get out of my office, Captain. You can consider yourself on report for insubordination."

"What? Again?" Herzer said. "Have a nice day."

Herzer strolled out of the office and through the headquarters beyond. Despite the fact that the fleet was limping back to port, just about out of rations and with heavy damage, the logistics headquarters for the base was not what he would call a sea of activity. In fact the well-manned office was filled mostly with clerks who were clearly trying to figure out something to do. Each of them had a desk, which was more than could be said for the temporary headquarters, and each of them had a pile of paperwork that they were supposedly working on. But the vast majority were chatting or obviously working so slowly they were just trying to pass the time.

Destrang fell into step with him as he walked through the outer office and into the sunshine beyond. Herzer took a deep breath and shook his head.

"What do you think?" he asked, looking towards the warehouses along the shore-front.

"Well, everybody is running around like chickens with their heads cut off over at headquarters," Destrang said, rubbing his chin. "Sure doesn't look like it's filtered down, though."

"True," Herzer replied, stepping off towards the temporary fleet headquarters. "I can't think but that I might have handled that better."

Edmund had actually moved the "war-room" out of the headquarters and into tents set up on a nearby field. His ostensible reason for this was that way the dragons could participate in discussions. Herzer knew it was widely suspected that the new admiral was just trying to put the Navy in its place. And he also knew that there was more than a gram of truth to the suspicion.

The area had been roped off and marines were stationed around it to prevent unauthorized entry. They knew better than to try to stop the general's aides and as Herzer walked through the entrance he nodded at the sergeant on duty.

"Wonderful day, eh?" Herzer said, smiling.

"Lovely, sir," the sergeant replied. "Can't wait for it to rain, frankly."

In the two days since the headquarters destruction Herzer had found time to work out with the marines. He found them to be woefully undertrained by Blood Lord standards, but he knew that was a high standard. The marines, however, had developed a reputation for ability and Herzer had to wonder if it was anything but a reputation. They made much of being able to stake out bars, but with either boarding pikes or short swords even Van Krief had been able to take them with laughable ease. It was something in the back of his mind to discuss with Edmund. If there was ever time.

"How'd it go?" Edmund asked as he entered the tent reserved for the commander.

"I'm on report for insubordination," Herzer admitted. "Something about calling a major a lard ass."

"Well, was he? And do we have a party for the troops laid on?"

"Sailors," Herzer corrected. "No we don't and yes he was. Those materials are for the supply of the Fleet, not for a damned party."

"That's what he thinks," Edmund replied. "You showed him the letter? Hadn't he received a copy?"

"I don't know if he had or not," Herzer said, shrugging. "But when I gave him the copy he still felt constrained to point out that it was against regulations to use the materials in that manner. He also pointed out that there were 'proper channels' for such a 'request.'"

"Oh, he did did he?" Edmund asked. "I've sent down that request twice through the G-4. I think it's time for the G-4 and me to have a little chat." Edmund leaned back and tugged at his beard for a moment, then shook his head. "No, it's not, come to think of it. What was that major's name?"

"Spearman."

Edmund reached into his desk and rummaged until he came up with a manning chart.

"Wait a second," Edmund said, pulling out a fountain pen and writing rapidly, consulting the manning chart from time to time. He handed the paper to Herzer and gestured to the main tent. "Go have a copy made of that, then carry the copy over to the G-4. Just hand it to him and leave."

"Righto," Herzer said, glancing at the paper and shaking his head. "Who is Colonel Trahn?"

"According to my manning chart he's now my G-4,"

Edmund said, looking back down at his desk which was just about covered in paper. "Let's hope he has the sense not to be passive aggressive with me like his former boss."

As Herzer exited the tent he nodded at the major who was entering. The man was tall and spare, clean shaven and with a very short haircut. It took him a moment to remember where he had seen him before.

"Major." Herzer nodded.

"Captain Herzer," Joel Travante said. "Congratulations on the promotion."

"Congratulations on yours . . . sir," Herzer said, his brow furrowing.

"It's a lot easier to move around a military base in uniform," Joel said, then frowned. "I'd like to pick your brain sometime, Captain."

"About?" Herzer asked.

"In a more private venue," Joel grinned. "Call it . . . ground combat issues."

"Any time," Herzer replied. "If I'm not running errands for the general."

"I'll talk to him," Joel replied. "Good day."

"Good day to you," Herzer nodded as the man entered the tent.

"Who was that?" Destrang asked as they headed for the main tent.

"I'm not sure I should say," Herzer answered then shrugged. "He's a spook."

"A what?"

"An intel officer. I don't know what he's doing here."

CHAPTER TEN

"Hello again . . . Major," Edmund said. "Have a seat."

"Thank you," Joel said, sitting down languidly.

"I've blocked out most of the afternoon," Edmund continued, getting a cup of coffee from the samovar. "Want some?"

"Please," Joel replied, opening up his briefcase. "I suppose I don't have to tell you about need-to-know."

"Not really," Edmund replied. "But do I decide that or you?"

"I suppose we'll have to discuss it," Joel answered with a grin.

"What name are you using at the moment?" Edmund asked.

"Kolata," Joel said. "When I'm in my official capacity I generally just go by T."

Joel Travante had been one of the few police in the pre-Fall era. The Council Inspectors were independent operatives and most of them worked part-time. But among the group was a smaller core, the Special Inspectors, who were the elite. You became a Special by solving the toughest cases in the best possible fashion. Joel Travante had been a Special Inspector for forty years prior to the Fall.

Just prior to the Fall he had been in the Asur Islands trying to find a serial rapist and murderer. Either was difficult pre-Fall since everyone was protected by personal protection fields. The perpetrator would seduce young women into lowering their shields and then keep them too occupied, mostly by pain, to be able to raise them again.

Joel had been close on his heels when the perp disappeared, apparently off the face of the earth. The inspector had finally found information that indicated the murderer had turned himself into a kraken and was hiding somewhere near the bottom of the sea. The question being, which bottom? He had managed to trace him to the Asur Islands and had been preparing to go hunting in the depths when the Fall hit.

After the Fall he had worked fishing boats. Then, when New Destiny took over the islands, he had taken his small boat and sailed two thousand kilometers to Norau. From there he had reestablished contact with Sheida Ghorbani and gone back to work. This time not as an inspector, but first as a member of her burgeoning intelligence apparatus and then as its head.

He liked his job for several reasons. One of them was that he got to see the *real* information about the world, messed up as it was. The other reason being that his wife and daughter had been in Briton and Ropasa, respectively, and his position was the only one he could imagine where he might get some inkling of their fates.

"Any word on your wife and daughter?" Edmund asked, handing him a cup of coffee. "I've got cream and sugar."

"Black, sir, thank you," Travante replied. "And no, unfortunately."

"Well, if we can ever get back to Ropasa, hopefully we'll find something out," Edmund said, glad that both his wife and daughter had managed to make it home after the Fall. He could imagine what a hell it must be for Travante. "So, what do you have for me?"

"The anti-dragon frigates were a known weapon," Joel started. "I'd sent both a description and schematics to Naval Intelligence who apparently decided that it was an 'unconfirmed report.' I've also developed intel on their carriers. There are some differences from ours, some significant ones I believe."

"Such as?"

"Shorter legs," Joel said, extracting a sheet of paper. "They're only good for about forty days at sea. Furthermore, the training of the dragon-riders is, my analysts believe, sub-optimum. That is confirmed, I feel, by their lack of success."

"They took out four carriers," Edmund pointed out.

"Yes, sir, but given the number of dragons they can loft—they carry forty-five, which is one reason they are short-legged—they should have been able to sink the entire fleet. Their aim was rather poor."

"Okay, point."

"They currently have six, unfortunately. I'll admit that the additional carrier caught me by surprise. I've been concentrating my gathering efforts in the northern ports and they apparently used Bassay to build and field that one. Their fleet is currently headed for home ports, including the one from Bassay, which is headed to attach to the main fleet. They were caught by the storm and badly battered around; they also don't appear to have as good quality of sailors as we do. Some of their light units and one anti-dragon frigate are reported as lost."

"How many frigates did they have?"

"Ten, which explains our losses," Joel replied. "It's not my place to ask, but are you going to be able to replace those?"

"I've got wyverns flying in from all over," Edmund replied. "Training them, and their riders, will take some time but not as much as you'd think. Once they make a carrier landing, I'll have the ships do further work-ups at sea. And I think I can do some work on the supply issues. But the shipyards are going to have to work like demons."

"You can anticipate them doing a fast turn-around on their end," Joel pointed out. "I don't have any intel on their intentions. So far I've been able to establish a fairly good intelligence group in Ropasa, but penetrating their high level positions is a slow and dangerous business."

"Well, keep at it," Edmund sighed. "What else do you have?"

"Quite a bit, actually . . ."

Edmund was leaning back in a comfortable chair, a glass of wine in his hand and his feet propped up when there was a knock on the door.

He looked at it irritably and sighed. It was after midnight and he had been meeting with one person or another all day and most of the day before. He certainly was in no mood for more company. But there was no one else to answer it. He'd sent Herzer and the rest off when he got back to his quarters.

He set the cup down and walked over, mentally grumbling to himself. It seemed as if no one on the entire base, possibly in the entire Navy, had the slightest clue how to organize and manage a military force. Oh, they could move food around and they could sail ships. But that seemed to be as far as they'd thought. No one that he had encountered seemed to think in terms of bringing harm to the enemy.

For Edmund, who thought about it even when there wasn't an enemy to bring harm to, it was like being the one-eyed man in the country of the blind.

He jerked the door open, intending to ream a new asshole, and then smiled when he saw it was Shar Chang.

"I can come back later," the general said. He'd gotten a new uniform and washed up but he still looked worn out from the long flight.

"No," Edmund said, waving him into the room, "I said as soon as you woke up. One of the things I'm trying to get this cluster of school boys to understand is the concept of doing the work when it needs to be done."

"Sailors generally understand that," Shar pointed out. "A storm doesn't care what time it is."

"Most of these guys were sailors when you knew exactly when there would be a storm," Edmund pointed out, pouring another glass of wine. He handed it to

Shar and sat back down, waving at the chair across from him.

"Point," Shar said. "Do you know how the senior officers were chosen?"

"No. I know they all come from that same sailing club."

"Every year the club has a regatta, a race," Shar said, taking a sip of wine and looking at the ceiling. "Quite the do. Yachts come in from across the world. It was one of the big events right at the end of the yachting season. Anyway, absent any other way to choose, the senior officers were chosen from the captains that had the best time in last year's race. Draskovich was the winner; the man really can sail. Kabadda was in second place, by a nose if I recall correctly. Et cetera."

"That's just peachy," Edmund said. "And I suppose their XOs are in their usual place?"

"Oh, yes," Chang replied. "If they were around. Trahn, now, the second guy in Logistics, is a pretty good guy. I don't know if he knows diddly about logistics, though."

"We'll see," Edmund replied. "I'll admit that they are good at moving food and spares. But we have to teach them to *fight*. Did you know there wasn't an at-sea commander? That each of the carrier skippers was in charge of their own battle-group and *Draskovich* was in command of the fleet?"

"Well, he's the fleet commander, isn't he?" Shar asked.

"No, he's the North *Atlantis* commander," Edmund said. "Was. He's not supposed to oversee the entire battle. That's what a *fleet* commander is for. And the skippers of the carriers are the skippers of the *carriers*. They're not there to run a battle group. It's like the entire concept of chain of command is gibberish to them. Micromanagement raised to the nth degree."

"Is that what you called me up here for?" Chang said, motioning with his head at the new stars. "To be the 'at-sea commander.' "

"Fleet commander," Edmund corrected. "And to pick your brain. But you're no more prepared for it than any of the rest of the captains. So what you're going to be doing, in your munificent free time, is read. There's a library here and from what I've been told by one of my ensigns, it's brimming with good biographies. I want you to cram every biography of every fighting admiral you can read over the next week or so. And I mean every waking moment that you're not working on something more important. I'd give you a list, but I don't know what they have. Halsey, Nelson and Provock at the very least. Oh, and Ensign Van Krief has Slim's biography. He's a soldier, not a sailor, but I think you can learn some things from him. You up to it?"

"Reading biographies has never been at the top of my choice of how to spend my free time," Chang said with a shrug. "But if you think it will help."

"Immensely," Edmund replied. "Now, I want to pick your brain. Not about the battle, but about managing the fleet. First of all, do we *have* to feed everyone salt beef? We've been starting to can stuff at Raven's Mill and the legions are going in the direction of all canned materials. It's coming on to harvest time; if we can set up a canning facility we should be able to can just about anything we want."

"Well, canning for vegetables would be a good idea," Shar replied. "But on the *Hazhir* we've got even better for meats; we've got a sub-zero freezer."

"A freezer?" Edmund said. "Doesn't that require electricity? And doesn't the Net just suck it off?"

"No electricity involved," Shar grinned. "Refrigeration just involves compressing gasses. All you need for that is pumps and piping. Evan found a good source for the pumps, right up the Gem River, and the piping is coming out of factories in quantity. Refitting the ships isn't even particularly hard. You just insulate two holds and, presto, you've got refrigeration. Keeps meat for a treat. Even for the dragons."

"Which reduces the volume of material they need," Edmund said, nodding. "And you can keep your beer cold."

"That too," Chang grinned.

"What else?"

"You remember the flamethrowers we had on the *Richard*?" Shar asked.

"I was never there when they were used," Edmund said, shrugging.

"Well, wooden boats are a fire trap," Shar replied, shuddering. "When that jellied gasoline gets started, its almost impossible to stop. Evan developed an automated extinguishing system that uses a foam that puts the fire right out. Also hooks to the fire-fighting pumps. The *Hazhir* also has underwater 'wings' mounted on it. It's an old racing trick; it keeps your ship from drifting to leeward. We've redesigned the catapult so the dragons actually take off faster but don't have so much of a jolt at the start. And we've got a new arrester system so they can land better. Natural gas stoves so we can have fires during a storm and don't have to eat cold food, bleed-off vents from the refrigerators that help keep the quarters cooler in the heat, plenty of little innovations that make the ship work, and fight, better."

"Why don't all the carriers, hell, all the ships, have some of that?" Edmund asked.

"Buships hasn't 'approved' the changes," Shar snarled. "In fact, when we sent them reports on what we were doing, they told us to rip them all out as 'unauthorized modifications.'"

"I take it you told them to stick it where the sun doesn't shine," Edmund grinned.

"No, we told them there was currently a lack of dockyard space and as soon as we could schedule the work we'd remove all the 'unauthorized modifications.' Of course, the Blackbeard dockyards can't even *handle* a carrier and we could have done it all with the crew. Which they pointed out. So I sent another excuse. And they found fault with that one. So I sent another memo. And so on and so on."

"Well, I'll send the next one," Edmund replied. "Telling them that I intend to 'upgrade' all the carriers presently here to match the *Hazhir*. If we have time."

"Will we?"

"I don't know," Edmund sighed. "You think the *Hazhir* can take on six carriers?"

"No," Shar said, sighing. "Even with me in command."

"Well, you might have to find out," Talbot replied. "The *Hazhir* is going to be the only carrier we have for a while. The *Hazhir* should be here in no more than three more days. When it gets in I want Evan to get with the guys over at the dockyard and start setting up to convert the fleet carriers to the *Hazhir's* configuration."

"You're going to get a lot of complaints," Chang pointed out.

"Let 'em," Edmund replied. "As long as they do it. And if they don't, well, we need workers in the yards. We may convert these 'dreadnoughts' in the meantime. Or we might use them for something else."

"You've got that look in your eye," Shar said, chuckling. "How much time do you spend thinking about how to mess with New Destiny?"

"How much time does a teenage boy spend thinking about sex?" Edmund replied with a grin.

"You summoned me, O mightiness," Herzer said, walking in Edmund's tent. "By the way, you look awful. How much sleep are you getting?"

"I can sleep when I'm dead," Edmund growled. "Why are you so chipper? Finally laid Van Krief?"

"No," Herzer said. "But I have been working with the marines. You know they don't have any formal training facility?"

"Yes, I do," Edmund replied. "That's what I wanted to see you about. There's not a single training facility in the entire navy."

"None at all?" Herzer asked. "How do they learn their jobs? I mean, how do the *officers* learn anything?"

"By and large, they haven't." Edmund sighed, throwing his pen down on the desk where it promptly squirted ink all over the papers. "Shit. I barely know where to start with this damned place. Incompetents are mixed in with really good people. Trahn in G-4 is sharp as hell, but of course his boss was an idiot. I talked with Babak the G-3. You are hereby frocked major and appointed G-3 schools. One of the mostly completed dreadnoughts is being permanently moored for the time being; you can use that for skills training. We've got personnel that want to be sailors, they just don't know what they fuck they are doing and all the training so far has been on-the-job. Find some facilities. Right now all I've got for you is the dreadnought, but scrounge up some trainers. Start a basic training facility for the seamen. Military lifestyle, basic seamanship, fire-fighting, water survival at a minimum. By the time they're trained in basics you'll need to have found advanced instructors. G-1 has a list of 'specialties.' You'll have to find trainers for those schools as well. For the time being, from here on out, anyone who wants to be an officer has to have served at least one deployment with the fleet or have prior experience. Verifiable prior experience. And then they go to O course where they learn everything about being an officer on a ship. I have *no* idea what that means, but figure it out."

Herzer opened his mouth to ask where in the hell he was supposed to find instructors but closed it. Edmund clearly didn't have time to deal with pro forma protests.

"I want Van Krief," was all he said.

"You've got her," Edmund replied. "Find somebody to ramrod it for you by the time the fleet is ready to sail. Shar's going to be in command but I want you out there, too. Oh, and a training facility for the marines as well."

"I'll need personnel from the fleet," Herzer pointed out. "And they're not going to want to release them. I'll need *good* personnel from the fleet. And dragon-rider training as well, don't forget that. And there should be personnel designated to handle the dragons; the riders have got enough on their plate. This is going to have to come under the Navy manning table. Bupers is going to have to approve the slots."

"Come up with a list," Edmund sighed. "I'll handle Bupers. You just get the school started. Get going."

"Hey, Shar," Evan Mayerle said as he walked into the cramped office. "You wanted to see me?"

Shar's desk was just about covered in paper and he was reading a memo with a furious expression. It was clear that he was in dire need of killing someone. But he smiled at the engineer and waved to the sole spindly chair.

Evan Mayerle was of medium height, a brown-haired young man with bright blue eyes that were almost perpetually looking at something invisible. That was because he usually had his mind on three or more items *other* than whatever conversation he was engaged in. Chang knew that so he waved to get his attention.

"Focus for a minute," the admiral said. "You've got a job in front of you."

"I was thinking about the mess system on the *Hazhir*," Evan replied. "I think we can rearrange it so that—"

"Evan," Chang said with a chuckle. "Focus."

"Oh, right," Evan said, looking at him and widening his eyes. "You called me here, didn't you?"

"Right," Shar replied. "Look, Edmund wants all the carriers upgraded to match the *Hazhir*. The shipyards can work on that while they're doing the repair damage, right?"

"I suppose," Evan temporized. "But putting in the refrigeration system will require tearing out some deck. Nothing that can't be fixed but it's at least a three-day job."

"Get with the shipyard. Show them the changes. They already have the word that they're going to be doing it. Expedite it. Focus on *that*, not more changes. We need them turned around *fast*."

"What about the other fleet units?" Evan asked.

"If there's time," Shar replied. "I hope there's time."

The fleet was decidedly limping when it came in. The ships entered the harbor in a straggle, hooking off to their prescribed buoys in any old way. Patched sails, braided rigging, bright patches of new wood for which the ships had run out of paint all told the story of a group that was worn out. Out of morale, out of energy and out of patience.

The wyverns that could fly had already landed and Edmund had been there for their arrival. The wyvern "weyr" was a long series of sheds with a graveled area about a hundred meters across running the entire length. The edge of the graveled area had been lined with chunked up beef carcasses for their arrival and then the work parties had cleared the area with the exception of three handlers, drawn from the marines, for each wyvern. The marines, in full armor, had helped the riders get their gear stripped off the dragons before they were let loose on the carcasses. There had been a few fights and some of the wyverns were going to require medical attention, but with food in their bellies the half-wild dragons had calmed down and let themselves be led into their sheds.

And a good quarter of the meat was still lying out in the sun; less than a third of the wyverns that had sailed with the fleet had been capable of flying off.

Now Edmund watched as the carriers carefully jockeyed up to the piers. The dragons that hadn't been able to fly off were in bad physical shape. He could only hope that with food and some medical attention they'd be fit to fight by the time the fleet sailed again. He had been calling for wyverns from across Norau, and they were trickling in in ones and twos. But the fleet had already drawn down the available population. He wasn't sure he could fully man even the remnant that had straggled in.

Lighters with fresh food were moving out to the ships at anchor. The crews had been instructed to stand down and stay on board overnight. In the morning they'd be brought in with full assembly scheduled for just before lunch.

The captains were putting off, though, coming in by small boats. They had been instructed to leave their executive officers on board and come ashore for a preliminary meeting. In the case of the carrier captains, with their senior dragon-riders. He had to prepare for that meeting. He didn't think it was going to be pleasant.

CHAPTER ELEVEN

The meeting took hours. There was no other way to cover the battle and he knew it was only going to be the first. And it had been as bad as he expected.

The meeting was being held in the main dining room of the officers' club, that being the only room large enough to accommodate all the ship skippers and the staff. The room was still packed and the windows had been kept closed so it was hot as Hades. And so were tempers.

The responses in the meeting ranged from anger, fury really, to almost comatose depression. The skipper of the *Corvallis* was especially quiet, almost catatonic. The senior dragon-rider, Major Bob Childress, though, was livid.

"We had *no* warning," Childress said, for about the sixth time. "We just flew in fat, dumb and happy. The next time we go out, the riders *are* going to be nervous. Which means they're not going to get in close enough for accurate bombing."

"How do we deal with the anti-dragon frigates?" Edmund asked.

"I don't know," the rider said, angrily. "Attack from below? Maybe the mer?"

"Other ideas?" Edmund asked. "I'm not discounting that one, I just want more options."

"Take them out first," Chang responded. He'd spent most of the meeting quietly listening and taking notes. Mostly about the defensive quality of the answers the staff were giving. "Send in strikes specifically to take them out. Yeah, you'll have to drop from high. And you'll miss quite a bit. But once they're gone, the carriers are vulnerable."

"You're assuming, *General*, that we'll have carriers to return to," Childress snarled. "In case you hadn't noticed, they've got dragons, too."

"Okay, that's enough," Edmund said. "The fleet *is* going back out. And we *are* going to engage the New Destiny fleet and *this* time we're going to win. Can dragons fight air-to-air?"

"They can, but they're not very good at it," Childress said. "And they've managed to get theirs to flame."

"Silverdrake."

Edmund looked up at the non-sequitur from Vickie Toweeoo. She was the senior remaining dragon-rider on the *Bonhomme Richard* and he wished, badly, that Jerry Riadou had survived. But if wishes were fishes . . .

"What does that mean, Captain?" Edmund asked.

"Silverdrake are one of the three types of wyvern," Vickie replied. "They're sprinters. We're using Powells exclusively. They're a sort of medium-weight wyvern.

Then there are Torejos. They're heavy wyvern, good for long distances and they can carry more of a load. They don't interbreed; it's like they're three different species. But if you're going to fight air-to-air, use Drakes."

"Silverdrake are too light," Childress said. "And they're also flighty. *And* bad tempered. And they're only good for, what, maybe an hour in the air?"

"Two," Vickie replied. "And they can outmaneuver the Powells. You just don't like them because they're prettier."

"They're *ludicrous*," Childress snorted.

"They're still the best dragon for air-to-air combat," Vickie shrugged. "Even if they are a bit . . . colorful. We still need a weapon."

"Put your two seconds in charge of figuring that out," Edmund said. "Have them get with Evan. Although he's going to have a lot on his plate."

"We need to be able to protect the carriers and at the same time attack theirs," Chang pointed out.

"We'll work on it," Edmund said. "Okay, people, I think we're talking in circles at this point. And the most important point hasn't even been mentioned except in passing: Morale. The morale of the fleet is in the dumps. We just had our heads handed to us on a platter. New Destiny is going to turn their fleet around faster than we can. And they outnumber us now. So we're probably going to have more reverses in the future. That doesn't matter. The battle that we just lost doesn't matter. The only thing that matters is who ends up owning the Atlantis Ocean and that, my friends, is gonna be *us*. Fix that in your head. Anybody who cannot believe that, deep in their gut, had better do a gut check and do it now. No matter what happens today, tomorrow, next week or next year, we are going to own the ocean and when we're through no New Destiny ship is going to be willing to poke its nose out of a port."

"I don't think we can do it," the *Corvallis'* captain said. "We're outnumbered, we're outgunned and, hell, they're *better* at this than us!"

"If that's the way you feel, feel free to submit your resignation," Edmund replied, coldly. "You don't learn to play better chess by playing someone worse than you. And you don't learn to fight better war by fighting someone worse than you. You learn from getting *beat*. Well, we've just had what we in the Army call 'good training.'"

"This isn't a *game*," the captain shouted, getting to his feet. "People are *dead*."

"That's what they call war," Edmund said, his face hard and cold. "But what we are going to do is show them that we play it better than they do. And if you can't get that through your skull, Captain, leave now."

The captain looked at him for a moment and then nodded and stalked out of the room.

"If anyone else thinks they can't handle that rank on their shoulder, you just tell me," Edmund said, looking around the room. "You get paid the big bucks to take that weight. It's not just for the fun of playing with your ships. It's not for the thrill of command. We all get paid to keep leading our troops, even when it's tough. To make them believe that no matter how bad it is, we're going to get through it. And we're going to win. That's a little thing called 'leadership.' And if you can't manage it, then you can feel free to go join the merchant ships. They're building more every day.

I'm sure you can work your way up to commanding a freighter in no time. But if you want a little payback, then you're going to have to put your shoulders back, get on your game face and sailor on. Your choice."

He looked around the room again and nodded as everyone else kept their seats.

"The crews stay on board tonight. Tomorrow morning they assemble on the shore by ship. There will be bands playing and, if I can possibly arrange it, pretty girls. There will be speeches by yours truly, General Chang and the carrier commanders. They *will* be riproaring, 'sure we got beat but we're gonna get back in the game and whip those sons of bitches' speeches. Then we are going to have the party to end all parties. Marines are excluded because we're going to have to use them to break up the fights that are going to start. I want everyone in the fleet to the point of passing out, no later than midnight. I'm figuring nobody will be worth a damn for at least two days afterwards. Light work for the next two days with liberal liberty calls. Then we get started on rebuilding."

"What about an attack by New Destiny?" a female voice asked towards the back of the room.

"Their fleet, *all* of it," Edmund pointed out, "is in port, just like us. When they sail, we'll know it. We are going to rebuild this fleet and then we are going to go out there and kick New Destiny's ass, or my name isn't Talbot."

The party was a definite hit.

There were bands. There were speeches. There were flags and ribbons. There were fine words of congratulations and predictions of the eventual destruction of the New Destiny fleet. None of it particularly helped. On the other hand, there were huge kegs of beer, over a hundred barbequed pigs and steers and masses of fresh food.

As soon as they were released the sailors fell on the food, and the beer, much like the starving wyverns.

Edmund spent most of the day moving through the crowd. He shook hands like a politician. He talked to group after group of officers, commanders, warrants, chiefs and ordinary sailors. To each of them he gave the same message. We got beat. We're going back out. We're not going to get beat again.

He talked about the importance of every link in the chain. How the runners at headquarters were as important as the admirals. How the cooks on the ships were the life-blood of the Navy. That the guys in the rigging were the sinews of the fleet. He talked himself hoarse.

By the time the sun went down, he'd started slowing down; most of the sailors were too drunk to know who was doing the talking. The ships' crews had intermingled to the point that he wasn't sure they'd ever get them sorted out. Half the crew of the *Toshima Maru* had started a pitched battle with the *Corvallis Line* and it took at least a platoon of marines, with Herzer at their head, to get them separated. The captain of the *Bonhomme Richard* had had to be carried off to the infirmary after demonstrating proper dragon-riding techniques on a keg of beer, and failing.

He thought about armies that had suffered defeats and then won in the end. Most of them had spent months, even years, retraining and retooling to the point that they could beat the enemy that had beaten them. Generally they had gone through three or four commanders as well. But they didn't have months or years. At the most, they had weeks. Edmund had to take this weapon, and reshape it, in the sort of time that most commanders spent getting to know a unit.

Fortunately, he'd spent plenty of years as a smith. And he'd dealt with taking over defeated armies before. The first thing that you did was you got them to know you as a person, somebody that they could trust and serve. You bonded to them as the carbon bonded to the iron.

Then you lowered the hammer.

"Hey, Chief," Herzer said.

It had taken most of the day to find Brooks. He had wandered off with a group of other chiefs and was well on his way to a record-breaking drunk.

"Herzer!" the chief said, staggering over from the cluster gathered around an appropriated beer barrel. "Ol' buddy!"

"Glad to see you made it." Herzer grinned. He had met the chief on the mission to the mer-folk and had taken an immediate liking to the tough, capable NCO. He was younger than Gunny Rutherford by a century at least but he was one of the few members of the Navy who really seemed to understand that they were at war. And how to put on a "war face." Which was why Herzer had been looking for him.

"Go' attack' by 'nother kra-kray—big fiskin's squid," the chief said, hiccupping. "NO PROBLEM!" He laughed and tried to sit down on an upended barrel, missing it by inches.

"Took care of it, did you?" Herzer said, dragging him to his feet and sitting him on the barrel.

"Surrre," the chief said. "Where's my beer? Sure no probl-brob—not an issue. Got my swabbies trained up right and *tight*. Where's my beer?"

Herzer picked up a kicked-over mug and filled it, then handed it to the chief.

"Well, glad to hear that," Herzer said. "Cause you're not going back out on the next deployment."

"Wha—?" the chief said, looking up at him. "When you make major? An' why 'm I not going out? Gotta go out, s'what a chief's for!"

"Recently," Herzer replied. "And the reason is, you're doing shore duty with me."

"No fisking way," the chief said. "*Shore* duty?"

"Yep, you're the new command master chief of the Naval Training Facility. Congratulations."

"No fisking way," the chief said, hiccupping again. "NO WAY!"

"Yes way," Herzer replied. "See you day after tomorrow, bright and early at headquarters. Not *too* early; later for that."

"I can't b-believe a *friend* would *do* this to me!" the chief said, sniffing and taking a sip of his beer. "This calls for getting really drunk."

"You'll love it," Herzer promised. "Bright young men and women who don't know the first thing about how to tie a knot. And *you* get to teach them."

"Oh, fisk," the chief sobbed. "Really, *really* drunk. You bastard."

"Yep," Herzer grinned. "Gotta go now. Day after tomorrow. Don't be late."

❖   ❖   ❖

Tom Ennesby had been the chief engineer for the naval shipyards practically since their inception. He had built the first dragon-carriers and thought they were a fine design. It had taken him at least a week to come to grips with all the changes in the *Hazhir*, but he finally shook his head in wonder.

"You did all this down at *Blackbeard* Base?" he asked.

The ship, outwardly, did not look very different from a standard *Bonhomme Richard*-class carrier. The launching platform on the port side was about a meter longer and to a trained eye the rigging was slightly different. But most of the changes were underwater or internal.

"Well, rigging the wings wasn't easy." Evan grinned. "But we had mer to help."

When ships sailed at any point except with the wind directly behind them, they tended to drift away from the wind, "to leeward." There were various methods to prevent that, but the one that Evan had settled on was large wooden-and-copper "wings" that protruded at an acute angle from the side of the boat's hull. Seeing them had required the engineer to go over the side and swim under the ship. It had been a cold swim but instructive. There were four, two forward and two aft. They didn't increase the depth of the ship, but when it was heeled over to the side they acted as keels to reduce the drift to leeward.

There were dozens of other minor changes but Evan had a comprehensive list and suggestions on how each of the changes could be implemented.

"Does the admiral want just the carriers . . . ?" the engineer asked, looking at the list and mentally counting the man-hours involved.

"For now just the carriers," Evan replied. "If time permits we'll work on the frigates and cruisers. But there's something else."

"And that is?"

"We need anti-dragon ships of our own," Evan said. "And I see those dreadnoughts just sitting there . . ."

"Cristo, that means completely changing the rigging!" Ennesby swore. "The way they're rigged now you can't fire anything upwards."

"We've actually got a pretty good sketch of the New Destiny frigates," Evan said.

"We do?"

"Yeah, we do," Evan replied. "And, no, I don't know where it came from. We also have their specifications for the ballistas and there's stuff there I like and some I don't. I think we can do better. Much better, really. But I don't know if we can do better in the time we have."

"Well, get the plans in here and let's see what we can see," Ennesby said, rubbing his hands. "What's wrong with their ballistas?"

"They're very much on a Roman model," Evan said. "Including using sinew for the elastic system. The problem with that is—"

"How the hell do they keep it dry on the ship?" the engineer asked.

"I don't think they do very well," Evan said. "Probably they keep them well covered but the humidity has got to affect them."

"It'll do the same to ours," Ennesby pointed out.

"Only if we use ballistas," Mayerle replied, looking distant. "We've put in a big order for tubing and pumping apparatus for the refrigeration, right?"

"Yeah," the engineer sighed. "You wouldn't believe what it cost."

"Hmmm . . ."

"What are you thinking?" Ennesby asked.

"I'm wondering what the max pressure is that Mother will let us get away with," Evan said, looking off into the distance.

"Welcome to Pressure 101," Herzer said, grinning at the mixed group of NCOs and officers in the small room. It was the ground floor of a two-story "temporary" facility that had been thrown up by the base engineers in about two days. The walls were still seeping sap and the floor was decidedly uneven. Herzer was pretty sure that it was going to leak like a sieve in the first rain. But it was home.

"Most of you know me but I'll introduce myself anyway. I'm Cap . . ."

"Bite your tongue!" Chief Brooks called from near the back of the room.

"Make that *Major* Herzer Herrick," Herzer said. "I've been tasked with setting up a basic training facility for sailors and marines. And I, in turn, tasked all of you." He grinned at the room again and it was clear that the humor stopped at his eyes. "And we *are* going to create such a facility and it *is* going to work and we have exactly one week before the first class arrives. So it behooves us to get to work as soon as possible.

"Now before we go on, let me make something clear. I know *diddly* about sailing. But I am a product of, and have been an instructor at, the only professional military school in Norau. And the basics are the same. You have to take kids who don't know jack and who have never had to obey an order and teach them to obey first and ask questions later. You do that by stripping away everything that they knew of civilian life. At the same time you build a new structure around them, a structure of honor and discipline. You test them as hard as you possibly can so that when they're *out* with the fleet and their ship gets dragoned or a kraken comes to visit they obey their orders instinctively.

"At the same time, you want to encourage initiative. It's a fine line. Some of the kids, and you've all known them, come up with a wild idea that is just flat wrong. Some of them, on the other hand, do the right thing almost instinctively. One of the things we're going to be looking for is kids to fast-track. So there will have to be honest individual evaluations that are as objective as possible.

"The bottom line is that when they go out to the fleet, they're not going to have to be shown the simplest tasks; they're already going to have learned those.

"Right now I'm looking at the following pattern. First week will be basic in-process and familiarization. Then four weeks of basic seamanship training and rigorous physical training. Then the last week they'll sail with a skeleton crew of trained personnel and specialists. By then they need to have been taught all the basic skills of a seaman, how to climb ropes, how to tie knots, how to raise and lower sails, what have you.

"*You* are going to come up with the list," he said, looking around the room. "We need a comprehensive training schedule by the end of the week. Everything that you have to teach the newcomers when they come onboard. After that they'll go to an advanced training course for four to six weeks. Some of you will be assisting in setting *that* up as well."

"Question?" one of the lieutenants said.

"Go."

"You said 'physical training,'" the lieutenant said uneasily. "I know something about the Blood Lords . . ."

"We're not training Blood Lords," Herzer said with a feral grin. "We're training sailors. If we were training Blood Lords we'd be having ruck marches and ruck runs every day. Since we're training sailors . . . One of the first tasks of the first class will be to raise 'The Mast.' And, yes, that's capital letters. They'll assemble and raise a complete mainmast from stores. Crosstrees, sails, rigging, the whole bit. Then each morning, they will run The Mast. I think that will do for physical exercise, don't you?"

There were chuckles in the room and Herzer noticed that Brooks looked grim.

"And, yes, we're going to have to go up it, too," Herzer said. "At least to prove we can. The point here is to have every graduate of this training program know that, at bottom, they are a sailor. They'll have at least a brief cruise and learn to handle seasickness and to work while they're sick as a dog. They'll act as deck apes for the cruise so that whatever they end up as, deck apes, cooks, clerks or the band, they'll know the basics of being a sailor. The point here is to establish a unifying bond in the Navy."

He looked around at the sea of faces and shook his head.

"Last point, and I wish I didn't have cover it but I do. Units like this, since females were permitted in the force and probably before, have had a problem with sexual harassment. They have ranged the gamut from male on female to female on female. The problem is that the trainers will be in complete control of the trainees' lives and that will make some of the trainers tend to . . . use that power. It will also cause some of the trainees to attempt to mitigate the power by using sex as a bribe." He looked around again and saw the expressions of surprise and even contempt.

"Deal with it. Those are the facts of life. And don't tell me that it hasn't happened on shipboard, either. I've read the reports. The short and sweet is that if it happens under my watch, I will make whoever is the one in the position of power regret the day that they were born," he continued, his scarred face hard and cold. "With power comes responsibility. I've had the displeasure of dealing with that sort of thing before and believe me, there is no justification for the empowered. None. Zero. Zip. Keep your dick in your pants. By the same token, an accusation is not proof. Investigations into accusations, though, are time consuming and leave nothing but shit in their wake. Bottom line: don't put yourself into a position to be accused. If you're counseling a person, make sure that there is a witness present. Ensign Van Krief and I will be writing that portion of the orders. That's all I've got. Any questions, comments, concerns?"

"This isn't going to help with the upcoming battle," Chief Brooks said.

"No, but you're assuming that we're going to seize control of the sea-lanes in one battle," Herzer said.

"Let's just say that Duke Edmund takes a longer view of things. Training is one of the fundamentals of any military force. The more you train, the less you bleed. So we are going to train them as hard as they can stand. Because when it comes to actually doing the job, it just gets harder."

CHAPTER TWELVE

"Good lord, I thought training was hard," Tao said as Van Krief walked in the room. The ensign was just shrugging out of his undress uniform.

"I suppose I should have knocked," Van Krief said, grinning.

"What? You have time to knock?" Tao said.

"I haven't seen you in a week," Van Krief said, stripping off her own tunic. "What have they got you doing?"

"Edmund set me loose on the marines," Tao admitted. "We've been practicing boarding and repelling techniques. Herzer was right, they're woefully undertrained. They march pretty, but they don't have a frigging clue what to do with their pigstickers. What about you?"

"Pretty much the same, but training trainers." Van Krief chuckled. "You should have seen their faces when I used the term 'lesson plan.' 'Wass thet?'"

Tao belly laughed and nodded his head. "Training schedule? What's a training schedule? *Plan* our training? You're joking, right? They've got a manual of instruction, I'll give them that. I finally convinced the company commanders to use Gunny's technique."

"Oooh, they must think you're a right bastard," Van Krief said, pulling on a fresh uniform.

"Training's sergeant's work," Tao said, grinning evilly. "So each Friday we have a test. We tell them what the test will *be*. And we set aside sergeant's time for them to train their troops."

"Has it worked?" Van Krief asked.

"Getting there," Tao admitted, finally dressed. "Last week was the first time we'd tried it. Only one squad took me seriously. They got released to go down to town; the rest of them kept testing and training and training and testing until nearly midnight. Better than a GI party, I tell ya. This week I notice they're spending a lot more time training and less time sitting on their ass in the barracks. We'll see on Friday."

"Why are you getting all spiffy?" Van Krief asked.

"Oh, gotta look spiffy," Tao said, blousing his boots and tugging them into position. "Part of the Blood Lord tradition. Bastards in combat and the best dressed troops around if they're not actively training. I just got done proving to the whole NCO group of the marines that even *together* they couldn't take me down. Now I'm going to look better than all of them for the rest of the day. Give 'em something to think about."

"You are vicious," Van Krief grinned.

"So, you getting anywhere with Herzer, yet?" Tao asked. "Speaking of vicious."

"Bite your tongue," the ensign growled. "He's my boss. No-go time."

"Well, maybe somebody will get smart and separate you enough that you can get a leg over." Tao grinned, ducking out the door as a boot hit it.

"Don't I just wish," Van Krief said as she belted her tunic. "Don't I just wish."

"It is wishful thinking to believe we can win a decisive battle on present terms, Admiral," General Babak said. The operations officer was looking particularly pale this morning. "The correlation of forces . . ."

"Correlation of forces is often a term for either cowardice or lack of imagination," Edmund replied, bluntly. "I'll agree that we're holding the shitty end of the stick at present. But the way to fix that is to turn the stick around."

"We're outmanned," General Piet pointed out. "They took relatively few casualties in the battle and we're short on personnel. Among other things, even though we've gotten dragons sufficient to fill out the fleet, many of the dragon-riders are unwilling to perform sea duty."

"Then they can be grounded until there are more dragons," Edmund said. "And we'll find recruits to fly the dragons. Yes, training them is going to be a bear. That's G-3's job to figure out."

"We don't have the *trainers*," Babak snapped. "Or the facilities. We're going full out working up the dragons with trained Naval riders and one carrier!"

"General, in a few weeks time, minimum, New Destiny is going to punch their fleet again," Edmund replied, mildly. "What would you have us do? Sit on our asses in harbor and let the dragons that we have cover us? There are other harbors, other seaside towns. And the *point* to all of this is to stop their invasion force. We cannot do that from the harbor." He looked around at them and shook his head.

"You gentlemen are starting to learn why being a general is not all it's cracked up to be. The enemy is called the enemy for a reason. They don't stand up to be shot. They are working just as hard to make sure we cannot fight as we are working to figure out a way *to* fight. Or supposed to be working. General Babak, has your department been *working* on battle plans?"

"There are, at most, three carriers against six," Babak said, pointedly. "And they have those damned anti-dragon frigates. We've been looking at any number of scenarios. None of them bear any hope of success."

Edmund closed his eyes and shook his head, solemnly.

"General, let me ask you something. Have you ever read any military histories?"

"Well . . ." the general said, inhaling. "No. But the point is—"

"The point, General, is that military history is replete with examples of inferior forces defeating, or at least stopping, superior forces." Edmund steepled his fingers and rested them on his chin, his eyes closed. "General, you and your plans people come over to my quarters this evening. We're going to have a little chat." He opened his eyes again and shrugged. "If I have to learn you all one by one I will. General Hanour, your estimate on the point at which New Destiny will be ready to sail again."

"Well, technically, they could sail at any moment,"

the intelligence officer said. "But we estimate they won't do so for at least another two weeks. That is when all their ships will be done with storm repairs."

"Mr. Ennesby, when will the carriers be completed with their refit?"

The shipyard engineer had not previously been invited to staff meetings. But since the staff did not have a representative from Buships, to Edmund's secret delight, he'd pressed Ennesby into service.

"Six days at present rate," Ennesby said, looking at his notes. "But there's another day to load the stores that had to be removed."

"And the dreadnoughts?"

"More like nine days," Ennesby said with a shrug. "More work to do and there's a shortage of materials and trained personnel to work with what we've got. But since we're not refitting their holds, just surface work, they can crew and load while we're doing the final work."

"Those ships don't even *have* crews," the G-1 almost wailed. "Or captains. Or petty officers."

"Find them," Edmund said. "Strip the merchant ships if necessary. I don't care if you use a press-gang. Find them. We're going to sail shorthanded. That's a given. We're still going to come out of the battle with at least a draw, probably a win. I know that because I don't lose battles. Ever. And get it through your heads that you're not going to lose them either."

As the staff filed out Edmund continued looking at his briefing papers, only looking up when General Babak cleared his throat.

"Yes, General?" Edmund said, mildly.

"Admiral, I don't think I can do this job," Babak said, bluntly. "I didn't want it in the first place. I'm a sailor. I can command a ship, but you were right, I don't know the first damned thing about running a war. I want to demote to captain. The *Corvallis'* XO is green as they come and there's nobody else around that knows ships as well as I do."

Edmund leaned back and rubbed his head with his hand, sighing.

"Request denied," he said and raised his hand to forestall the immediate response. "Can you command a ship? Sure. You're a good sailor. Okay. But I've *met* your deputy. And he's no more trained for this than you are. I don't put that on your shoulders, I put it on Bob Houser's and to an extent Sheida's. You guys should have been being trained in the *theory* at least before now. But the bottom line is that there's nobody to replace you where you are. And you have at least gotten a grasp of what your job is. If I replaced you, your replacement would have to be told what operations *are*. You think you're the lone ranger? I want a field command again. Not this . . . 'North Atlantis Command' nightmare. I want a regiment, maybe a battalion. I want to interact with soldiers and deal with their problems and train them up. And then use them in battle. It's what I really love, not this . . ." He gestured at the paperwork in front of him. "Not this *crap*. But we go where we have to go and do what we have to do because that is what being in the military is about. And I said, 'if I have to learn you one by one' and I meant it. One of the things is, there used to be a term called 'thinking outside the box.' You know what I mean?"

"No," Babak said, sitting down.

"Okay, in brief, what's your current plan for a battle?"

"We locate the enemy fleet, move in range, launch dragons and hope we can keep their dragons off of ours."

"Have you been looking at Vickie Toweeoo's Silverdrake plan?"

"Quite a bit," Babak said. "The problem is, if we put Silverdrake on the carriers, we lose space for Powells and our total bomb-load will drop by a huge fraction."

"Why are you basing them on the carriers?" Edmund asked.

Babak shrugged and smiled.

"Dragon. Carrier," he said, gesturing with one hand and then the other then putting both together. "Dragon-carrier. That's what they're *for*."

"Uh, huh," Edmund grunted. "Been talking to Vickie?"

"No, sir," Babak admitted. "I didn't know you knew her."

"We've met," Edmund replied. "What do you know about Silverdrake?"

"They're smaller than Powells, lighter, faster, more maneuverable and don't have much endurance," the G-3 replied.

"More maneuverable," Edmund pointed out. "How fast do you think the shipyards, hell, not even the shipyards, the ships' crews, could put some sort of landing platform on the back of the ballista frigates?"

"You're thinking of sending them out on the *frigates*?"

"I don't know," Edmund replied. "But it's one possible answer. They don't eat as much as the Powells but they're going to cut into the frigates' stores some. On the other hand, we're going to be sending out supplemental resupply ships with the fleet this time. Okay, the Powells take off and they attack the fleet. How?"

"Each division will be assigned a carrier to attack," Babak said. "We'll probably have them go in high to avoid the ballista ships."

"Why attack the carriers?" Edmund asked.

"They're the main threat from the fleet," Babak pointed out.

"Which are hard to destroy in the face of the anti-dragon frigates," Edmund said, calmly. "You see what I'm driving at. Check your assumptions. Does taking out the carriers first work better than taking out the frigates? Do we carry enough bomb-load to fight a prolonged battle? Why have all the dragons scattered over the fleet? Why not concentrate the whole force on individual ships? Is there some way for the mer, delphinos or selkie to attack? Is there some optimum formation for our ships whereby they can give cover to the carriers, and each other? Circles? Squares? Staggered lines? What happens if they punch their invasion fleet at the same time as their main fleet? These are questions that your staff should be asking each other and you should be asking them. And then you get the answers, or the best guesses you can come up with."

"Think outside the box," Babak said, nodding.

"Think *outside* the box," Edmund said with a smile. "Speed above all else, surprise above all else, utter ruthlessness."

"Sounds like a quote," Babak said, half questioning.

"It is, from one of the greatest generals of all time," Edmund replied. "Major outside the box thinker. And an utter bastard." He grinned. "Just like me."

"Now that is a bastard weapon," Shar Chang said.

The device on the workbench consisted of five narrow metal tubes attached to a large metal cylinder. There were a series of linkages set off to one side.

Chang picked up the device and hefted it, swearing.

"Damn, it must weigh eighty kilos."

"Seventy-three point four," Evan said, nervously. "Loaded and ready to fire. In its current state it's closer to seventy."

"And it works?"

"It should," Evan replied. "It's in the weight range of the Silverdrake with a small rider. There's no effective way we can determine to aim it, however, so they'll have to close to point-blank range."

"And the best place to cripple a dragon is in the primary muscles," Vickie Toweeoo pointed out. She wore new major's pips and her leather uniform now sported a Jolly Roger patch. "Which means a frontal approach. Technically the best shot would be to fly directly at the dragon and roll for firing. But I don't think we're going to be doing that much."

"One of these in the leg or the rear end is not going to make their dragons very happy," Shar pointed out. "It would be safer to close from the rear."

"We'll have to see, won't we, sir?" Vickie replied with a grin. "What I'm wondering about is training.

Most of the Silverdrake riders have volunteered for sea duty. I'm not surprised, we're a bit more . . . weird than Powell lovers."

"You've been riding Powells the whole war," Shar pointed out.

"That's because it was all we were using," Vickie said and grinned again. "But I'm a Silverdrake rider at heart. Powells are too slow and clumsy."

Having had some heart-stopping rides on the "slow and clumsy" wyverns, Shar was pleased that he'd never have to ride a Silverdrake.

"This is where you were hiding," Edmund said, striding into the workshop. "Evan—saw the air-guns for the ballista frigates. Marvelous."

"Simple application of air-pressure engineering," the engineer said, grinning. "And they have at least the same loft as a ballista."

"Any chance of making some infantry-sized ones?" Edmund asked.

"Not infantry," the engineer sighed. "We found out what Mother's upper limit on pressure is. And while she'll let you go past it momentarily, such as during firing, you'd have to way overextend it to make a decent infantry-sized air-pack. Actually, she allows more energy in a longbow or a ballista than she does in a system like this. This is about as small as it's going to get."

"And that ain't infantry." Edmund sighed, looking at the contraption. "We've got sixty Silverdrake. How fast can you turn these out?"

"All the parts are available," Evan said, his eyes going glassy. "I'd say about ten a day, more if I can get some more hands."

"Vickie, how fast to get the riders trained?"

"We don't even know if it's going to work, sir," Vickie replied.

"Oh, it works," Evan said in a distracted tone. "We test fired it already."

"The point is that there's a lot that can go wrong," Vickie said, pointing to the firing linkages. "And we're talking about a saltwater environment. What happens when one breaks? Does someone on the carrier know how to fix it?"

"I don't know," Edmund replied. "But you're not going to be on the carriers anyway." He pulled out a piece of paper and handed it to her. "This is the list of ships that are going to be refitted, by their crews in the next two days, to handle the Silverdrake."

"You want us to land on ordinary frigates?" Vickie asked, glancing at the list. "Six of these are *supply* ships!"

"And when they convoy back to the base they'll have top cover," Edmund said, raising a hand. "Deal with it, Vickie. There's no room on the carriers. We don't have any more carriers for the Silverdrake. We need the Silverdrake. Ergo they have to go on other ships."

"I just got these guys trained to land on *carriers*, sir," the major protested. "What about LSOs?"

"The way you talk about Silverdrake I was thinking they'd land on the crosstrees," Shar said with a grin.

"Thanks a lot, *sir*."

"As the duke says, 'figure it out,'" Shar replied, smiling. "I'd get with the captains, who are probably going to be highly pissed off, today. Then, when the ships are converted, get out there and start figuring

it out. In the meantime, Evan will be turning out
his little toys. As they become available you can start
training with the new weapons. Speaking of which,
Evan, they're going to need ammunition."

"Done," Evan replied, reaching behind the device
and picking up a short metal bolt with a cone-shaped
end and a wickedly sharp barbed point. "We've got a
machine shop that's figured out how to turn these out
in quantity. Each of the guns only has five rounds,
so by the time the guns are ready, we'll have all the
bolts we need."

"Those ships have stays at the rear," Vickie said,
suddenly. "They're in the way for landing."

Edmund grinned. "I didn't say it would be *easy*."

"If I thought it was easy I wouldn't be here!"

A hundred and fifty arms were hauling on ropes,
swaying a mast upwards as Edmund walked by the
training area. It was raining and the ropes were slippery and tending to stretch. Not to mention that the
carefully secured butt end of the mast was over a
hole in the ground that was probably rapidly filling
with water. He watched as the mast slowly ascended
to about forty-five degrees and then at a bellowed
command stopped.

"Handsomely!" Chief Brooks bellowed, wiping water
out of his eyes as the admiral strolled over through
the rain.

"Great day for it, Chief," Edmund said.

"Good training, sir," the chief snarled.

"That is what I'd call it," the admiral replied, smiling,
as one of the new seaman recruits, a female, slid in
the mud and sprawled at the feet of her classmates.

She leaped immediately back up and took the rope in hand, shaking off the fall.

"How's it going?"

"Did you have any idea what a complete bastard Herzer was when you set him on us?" the chief asked. "BELAY. Check the guide ropes! There's some stretch to port!"

"Yes," Edmund replied. The mast was now up to about sixty degrees and looked to be headed hole-ward. The butt had been secured by tackles that were in turn connected to a variety of short posts in the ground. The top of the mast had lines on it as well, the heaviest pointing to notional "aft." This, too, was heavily secured and tackled. Most of the recruits were on that line and it was they who had been doing the work of hauling it upright. But there were four lines leading off to either side, secured and tackled, and the majority of the remainder of the recruits were on those lines, clearly working on keeping it from tipping from side to side. The last, small, group, was manning the ropes that secured the butt.

"I told him it was going to rain like bejeebers today, Admiral," the chief said, clearly unhappy.

"Gotta work in the rain, Chief," Edmund replied but there was query in his voice. "There's things called storms."

"The ropes aren't tarred, sir," the chief explained. "That means they're more liable to stretch in the wet. And that's creating one hell of a safety hazard. If this thing goes over, we're going to lose people."

Edmund paused for a moment and then shrugged. "Should have tarred the ropes, Chief. Prior planning . . ."

"Prevents Piss Poor Performance." Brooks chuckled, watching the slowly ascending mast carefully. "Did you teach that to Herzer or the other way around?"

"I taught it to the person who taught Herzer," Edmund replied with a chuckle.

"And who taught it to you?" the chief said. "BELAY! Port beam, handsomely, handsomely. Belay. All together now!"

"I read it in a book," Edmund admitted. "And then learned the lesson in real life."

Brooks looked over at him and nodded, then looked back at the work in progress.

"BELAY! Okay, butt end, handsomely!"

The butt of the mast slowly but steadily, handsomely in navalese, crept towards the edge of the hole and then slipped, crashing to the bottom and shaking the ground all around.

"*Not* how you want to do it with a ship!" Brooks bellowed. "Or you'd have a bloody great hole in the bottom! Buttmen! Get those ropes off the butt and then man the forestay. Let's start leveling it up!" He turned back to the admiral and nodded. "This is the ticklish bit, sir, if you don't mind."

"Have fun," Edmund replied.

"Oh, yeah, sir, good *training*."

CHAPTER THIRTEEN

"We're having good training now," Vickie signed at her wingman.

When they had taken off the sky was overcast but just about as soon as they reached their destination, which was a small support ship, the *Harry Black*, that had been converted for landing, the rain had closed in. They were too far out for the Silverdrake to make it back to land and now they couldn't even see the ocean, much less their landing platform.

She was glad, in a way, that she was riding a Drake, though. In this damned gray-out you'd hardly be able to see your own dragon if you were on a Powell. That was *never* a problem with Silverdrake.

It had been said that they were invented as a joke. They were small and very fast. Great sprinters even if they didn't have the stamina of Powells. All good traits in a racing dragon and they had been remarkably well designed. But the designer apparently had . . . a bit of sense of humor when it came to body markings.

The Drake she was on was a bright, fluorescent, green with pink polka dots ranging in size from as big as the end of her thumb to as large as her head. Her wingman's was, in a way, worse, a sort of mottled "camouflage" pattern in electric purple and yellow: truly eye-searing. There had been attempts over the years to get the dragons Changed to more "traditional" colors. But Silverdrake riders were strange folk and liked their dragons the way they were. Flighty, bad tempered and all.

"Over there?" Ramani signed, pointing to their left.

"Try," Vickie signed back.

She angled the Silverdrake over and down, slowing its descent so they didn't plow into the ocean or the ship. They were only a couple of hundred meters up by her reckoning, but she was aware that "grayed out" as they were, there was no way of telling if they were a few hundred meters up or a few thousand. All there was in every direction was water. Of course, the stuff in the air wouldn't drown them.

The wyvern suddenly banked hard left as its wingtip barely missed the top of a mast. So much for being a couple of hundred meters up.

Vickie shook her head and banked around, trying to line up the opening in the rain. The ships were only partially converted and a heavy line, a stay, ran from the top of the rear mast to the rear of the ship. There were more lines to the sides. But there was a narrow gap between the stays that permitted egress to the platform installed over the quarterdeck.

Unfortunately, the gap was smaller than the wingspan of a Silverdrake, narrow as that was.

The only way to land was a stoop like a hunting falcon. The Silverdrake, which was shaped much like a peregrine for all it was brightly colored, came in, lowering its forward speed by back winging and then folded its wings, dropping through the slot and onto the platform with a bone-jarring thud that rocked the ship.

Vickie had learned to tuck her head and brace against the saddle when landing; if you didn't you got a broken nose. But she swore after each of the landings that she was going to find *some* better way to land. This just wasn't safe.

Vickie walked the dragon down the platform and it hopped to the maindeck, automatically heading for its stall. There were two of the latter on the maindeck, a massive nuisance for the skipper and crew, and she took the port side one. She dismounted outside and stripped the gear off the wyvern, then led it into the stall. There wasn't food already laid out so she shook her head and went in search of it.

Vickie was sitting in the wardroom, staring at a bowl of pea soup, when the skipper walked in.

"You going to eat that or just look at it?" The second thing that people noticed about Skipper Some Karcher was that she was short. Not dwarf sized, but far under normal height. The first thing that people noticed was that she looked like a Siamese cat. Her face and head had a distinctly catlike shape, something like an apple, her eyes were turned upwards, her hair was "touched" in places with coloring like a Siamese, her face was covered in fine fur and her eyes were green, almost like emeralds, and had pupils that were vertically oval. She squinted now as she looked at the dragon-rider pointedly and the pupils contracted sharply.

"I was just thinking how opaque it looked, ma'am," Vickie said, picking up her spoon. "Sort of like the air I was just flying through."

"I was thinking about those landings," the skipper said. "And I really hate them."

"Not as much as the person on the dragon, ma'am," Vickie said with a grin.

"And I really hate not being able to look at the sky when I'm on the quarterdeck," Karcher continued. "And I was wondering: why not put the platform off the *rear* of the ship?"

Vickie opened her mouth to respond and then closed it. After a moment she shook her head, angrily.

"Because none of those geniuses at the shipyards thought of it, ma'am," she replied, making a moue. "Do you think it would work?"

"I don't see why not," the captain said, shrugging and giving a little hum that sounded suspiciously like a purr. "We'd have to brace it, but that's not a problem. You already take off from back there. This would just make it easier. And I didn't come up with it, one of my seamen did. Good sailor who wants to be a rider methinks."

"What's his name?" Vickie said, pulling out a notebook and unwrapping it from the rubber cover. "We're really shorthanded on the Powells, ma'am."

"Fink," Karcher replied. "Hers, by the way."

"Well, ma'am, tell *her* that if you'll approve the transfer she can start as soon as she gets back to land," Vickie said. She tilted her head to one side, started to say something and then shrugged.

"Yes, Rider?" Karcher said, her face unreadable behind its catlike smile.

"I was wondering . . ."

"Did I Change before the Fall?" Karcher said in an odd intonation. Again, very like a meow. "No, I did not. This was how I was born. Do you want the long story or the short one?"

"Whichever you feel appropriate, ma'am," Vickie said, uncomfortably. "I'm not trying to pry."

"Once upon a time, a long time ago, there was a scientist who was, frankly, a bit cracked. It was at the very beginning of the time when Change became possible. But this scientist didn't want to Change himself into a cat. He wanted his cat to be a human."

"Oh," Vickie said, uncomfortably.

"And, yes, it was for the reason that you think. So, and this was before the protocols were put in place to prevent this sort of thing, he Changed his cat into a humanoid sentient. And the rest of the story should be that they fell in love and lived happily ever after."

"Yes," Vickie said, now extremely sorry that she had asked.

"Well, the story didn't go exactly as he had planned. Cats are cats, after all, even if you make them sentient, and the cat, already angry enough when she found out her name was 'Muffins,' was having none of it. She left him and broke his heart. On the other hand, she eventually did find a human male she thought was reasonably attractive and settled down and had a litter. From which litter I derive. Any questions?"

"No, ma'am," the rider said, her face working.

"Don't ask me if I chase mice, okay?"

"Oh no, ma'am, wouldn't think of it." Pause. "May I ask one question, ma'am?"

The captain nodded.

"How do you stand with dogs?"

"I have three—Rottweilers. When I say 'heel,' they *heel*," Karcher said with a grin that exposed very prominent canine teeth. "I have to admit that climbing the rigging when I'm stressed is very . . . natural."

Vickie laughed again and closed her notebook. "Rain's cleared?"

"Yes."

"Well, ma'am, I think it's time for us to head back to base."

"We're due back day after tomorrow," Karcher said. "You could probably ride back."

"No, we need to keep doing work-ups, ma'am," Vickie replied. "For our sins."

"Evan, you're on time," Edmund said, taking off his reading glasses and looking up from the desk. "Mr. Ennesby, how are you today?"

"Wet," Tom Ennesby said, taking off his broad-brimmed hat and shaking it to the side.

"Bad news, Duke," Evan said. "We're going to be at least a day late with the *Herman Chao*."

The dreadnought, which was being converted to an anti-dragon ship, was one of the three that had been ready for sea.

"What's the problem?" Edmund asked. "Anything I can do?"

"Not really." Evan sighed. "We're short on materials

for the air-guns. Basically I had to convert so many of them for the Silverdrake that it's leaving the *Chao* short. We're hoping to have the materials in a couple of days, but it's going to set us back by at least that long."

"How short?"

"About half," Ennesby said. "We're mounting fifteen guns per side. We've got sufficient compression for all of them on the *Chao*, but we're short on material for the guns and on lines. The latter's not really from the Silverdrake; we'd be short anyway. And running them, firing them accurately, is going to take some training. I don't know how accurate the gunners are going to be at first."

"And lord knows you don't want those damned bolts raining down on the ship," Edmund chuckled. "Any good news?"

"Vickie brought in a change to the Silverdrake landing that I want to distribute to all the support ships. Skipper Karcher pointed out that there's no reason the Silverdrake landing platform has to be over the quarterdeck. The Silverdrake land on a dime as it is. So she's moving her platform off to the rear. It looks like it will work and if it does we're planning on having everyone change over. The current landing method . . . leaves a lot to be desired."

"That it does," Edmund replied.

"I should let Vickie or Commander Gramlich report on this," Ennesby said. "But the Silverdrake that have been training with the bolt system report that they think it will work. We made some targets, big kites really, and they've been learning how to target them. It's still a point-blank system, though."

"Well, we're still going to want the anti-air dreadnoughts," Edmund sighed. "I'll send a message to the commanders of the ships that are ready for sea to get out there and start training. Make sure we've got plenty of darts."

"Will do," Ennesby said.

"How long to get the remaining dreadnoughts ready for sea?"

"No more than a week," Ennesby said. "We're stepping masts now. But we don't have crews."

"I'll see about crews," Edmund said. "Don't convert them to anti-dragon platforms, though, that's not what they're going to be used for."

They both looked at him for clarification until it was clear none was coming.

"That's all we've got," Evan said, standing up.

"And I've got a meeting with the G-1 next," Edmund replied, glancing up at the door. "Speaking of crews."

"I'm out of here," Ennesby said. "Before your body-hunter decides I'd make a good sailor."

"Bring me any more information you think I need," Edmund pointed out. "Anything."

"We've finally gotten information from our agents at Newfell, Marshal."

Chansa looked up from his paperwork and waved the aide into the room, practically snatching the document from his hand.

"Bloody hellfire," Chansa snarled. He was a fast reader and had scanned for the worst possible information. Besides the fact that they hadn't gotten the *Richard*, the worse news was buried in the fine print. "Talbot."

"Yes, sir," the aide gulped.

"I can see why you were sent in with it," Chansa growled then laughed. "I promise I won't kill the messenger. But go find Conner. Now."

The man who entered was tall and ascetic looking with a calm manner that was belied by his eyes. The irises of the latter were white and his pupils were tiny black dots.

"You called, Marshal?" Conner asked, pulling out a notebook and stylus.

"Edmund Talbot has been appointed to command of the North Atlantis Fleet," Chansa said.

"Yes, sir, a surprising appointment to be sure," Conner replied.

"You knew," Chansa said, leaning back and narrowing his eyes.

"Whose agents do you think are in Newfell Base, your Marshalship?" Conner replied, smiling faintly.

"He is not to command the fleet in the next battle," Chansa said, waving his hand. "Do whatever you need to do to effect that. No, let me make myself clearer. Kill him. He has interfered too often with my plans. I don't want him to do so again."

"Of course, Marshal," Conner said, closing the notebook. "If that is all."

"That's it," Chansa growled, waving at the door again. "Just inform me when he's dead."

"Okay, what have you got, One?" Edmund asked as the G-1 walked in the tent. It was raining cats and dogs and the personnel officer was soaked. But he just shook off his coat, dried his hands, pulled out his notes and took a seat.

"We're going to be short on manning for the fleet," General Piet said. "The worst category in gross is able seamen; being able to reef sails in a gale is a skilled craft and we're always shorthanded in that department. I've looked over Major Herrick's training program and . . . well, okay, I'm impressed."

"Herzer's much more than just a pretty face," Edmund said, getting up and pouring a cup of coffee. "You take yours black, right?"

"Yes, sir," the general said in surprise. "Major Herrick is not *even* a pretty face, though."

"It was a joke, Simon," Talbot said, shaking his head. "But that's not going to give us top-men by the time we need them."

"No, it's not, sir," the G-1 replied, taking the cup with a nod. "But it will certainly help in the long run. Right now what I've done is order everyone, of whatever current rate, who has experience on shipboard to sea duty. That's made some other departments shorthanded . . ."

"I've already received the complaint from the intel shop," Edmund grinned. "So how short are we?"

"Across the board about thirty percent," the personnel officer said, glancing at his notes. "Some ships are closer to a zero, some are less. I'm reluctant to drag down the carriers, for example; they're already shorthanded. Some of the frigates, though, are at about fifty percent and the dreadnoughts, which of course haven't trained together at all, are not much higher."

"Do what you can," Edmund said, shaking his head. "What are the other major problems?"

"We're short across the board," Piet replied. "Trained NCOs. Trained officers. Navigational officers. The worst lack, though, is trained commanders. I don't have anyone on the roster that I feel comfortable with giving the *Hazhir*, for example. The executive officer is very new, he's barely made captain and the position calls for a commander. Admiral Chang concurs, by the way. I'm contemplating transferring out the *Bonhomme Richard*'s XO, but I had to strip the *Richard* of all her other trained officers. I could move the nav officer back from the *Chao*, but that will leave the *Chao* with only one qualified watch officer; the captain."

"Ouch," Edmund said, rubbing his chin. "What about Karcher?"

"Karcher, sir?" the G-1 replied. "I don't even recognize the name." He picked up his briefcase and slipped out a sheet of paper, running down a list of names. "Major Karcher is the skipper of the *Harry Black*, a collier ship. Why do you ask?"

"What's her experience?" Edmund replied.

"I haven't a clue, sir," Piet admitted. "I'd have to pull her file."

"Send a message to have her report to me," Edmund said. "Don't say why but I want to see if she could potentially handle the *Hazhir*."

The G-1 looked startled for a moment, then shrugged.

"As a collier officer she's going to be qualified at celestial navigation," Piet temporized. "But there's a vast difference between running a carrier and a slightly fast merchant ship. And I don't know where that is going to leave her manning. She may be one of the only fully qualified officers on the ship."

"Do you have anyone else that you can suggest?"

Edmund asked. "And I'd rather be down a collier than a carrier."

"Point," the G-1 replied, sighing.

"The best is the enemy of the good," Edmund said. "In a situation like this, you cannot get things to be anywhere close to perfect. What you have to strive for is the minimum of imperfection. And you have to get it as right as you can, in the time you have been given."

"I take your point, sir," Piet said.

"You were a sailor before," Edmund said, leaning back in his chair. "A serious one, but not anyone who studied the military. At sea, you have one enemy, the ocean. And the ocean, while it changes and always keeps you on your toes, does not *actively* try to defeat you. In war, people actively try to defeat you. That seems like a simple concept but few people really understand it in their gut. People are trying as hard as they can to *defeat* you. They try, very hard, to kill you. So that you don't kill them.

"And because it's a big, complicated system and because the enemy is trying to read your mind and defeat you, and they are smart, too, things are always going to go wrong; the enemy is going to make sure of that. So the trick is to make fewer mistakes than the enemy. One mistake you can make is trying to be too perfect, because that takes *time*. And that gives the enemy time, too. Time to figure out your intentions. Time to get a better position. Time to enact a plan that might not be *perfect* but that will *work*. For that reason, decisions have to be made quickly and they have to be *pretty* good. Not perfect. *Pretty* good. What I'm saying here is that you should strive for perfection, but not to the point of giving the enemy more time. If the choices you have, now, are *pretty* good, we'll go with that. Again, 'the best is the enemy of the good.' Save the tweaking for after we win the battle."

"I hate working in this harum-scarum fashion," Piet admitted.

"So do I," Edmund said. "But that's why you focus on victory and plan for defeat. I'm sorry, but the fleet under Admiral Draskovich did not plan for defeat. There weren't any alternate plans, there wasn't a fallback plan, there wasn't any *slack* in the system. Not even any personnel or material reserves to speak of. There are times to move without a reserve, but not when you're in a battle that you have foreseen for a year. When I'm done, this place is going to have the wherewithal to survive another defeat and go back out as many times as necessary to eventually win the war. But *right now* I'm fixing another man's abortion. That's messy and sickening and all that you can do is hope for the best and plan for the worst. So if what you've got is good enough, go with it. Good enough is really all we can hope for."

"Edmund," Sheida said.

Edmund glanced up from his paperwork and looked at the clock on the table across the tent. It was nearing midnight and he felt stiff and cramped from, literally, hours of sitting in the same chair. It wasn't even a *comfortable* chair. Something he'd been secretly proud of when he had it installed. Now he regretted his grandstanding.

"Sheida." He sighed. He looked at his former

lover and shook his head. "If this is power, it's for the birds. You look like you've aged twenty years in the last four."

"So do you, Edmund," Sheida said with a grimace. "And isn't it a bit late?"

"Needs must," he said, waving at the table. "This place is a zoo."

"A very expensive zoo," Sheida said. "The legislature is balking at your request for increased funding."

"No surprise that." Edmund frowned, rubbing his head. "But we have to gain control of the sea and that means more men and more ships. And those men and ships are going to suffer, be lost, which will mean *more* men and ships. We have to have the funds, Sheida." He gestured at the paperwork before him and shook his head. "Half of this crap is people screaming at me over money. 'Out of budget construction,' 'invalid materials use,' these people wouldn't know a battle if it bit them in the ass and they're asking me to account for every damned nail that goes in a ship. And *why* it has to go in a ship. Well, the reason is, the more of the bastards we kill at sea, the fewer will be around to kill us on land. Think you can get that through their heads?"

"Politics," Sheida said with a bitter chuckle. "All that money running from one area to another. The Kent wants to form a legion. The *Kent* of all places." The Kentian plains had been famous, before the Fall, for their horse herds and after the Fall the fame had just increased.

"That's going to be a moot point," Edmund said.

"Oh?"

"I submitted a study to the Ministry calling for federal cavalry brigades. As far as I can tell, they're sitting on it. So I sent Kane down to the Kent to get the ball rolling, oh, six months ago or so. Either the local representative is dealing with information lag, or he's unaware that a cavalry brigade is going to mean *more* money to the area than a legion."

"How's it going?" Sheida asked.

"Last I heard, pretty good," Edmund admitted. "Most of them aren't as good of horsemen as they have to be for cavalry, but Kane and I worked out a pretty intensive basic training for them. They won't be elite by any stretch of the imagination and no horse bowmen, but they're going to be all right. And *disciplined*, damnit. When I call in cavalry I want it to go where I tell it, not haring off any old way it pleases."

"And then there's the Fleet," Sheida pointed out. "Everyone is balking at that, but mostly the people on the coast. All the money is going to Newfell, which has damned little representation in the House."

"I've got a fix for that one, too," Edmund frowned. "There's no reason that all the ships have to be built here and plenty of reason for them not to be. The smoldering remains of our shipyards speak for themselves. I'll send a memo to Admiral Houser recommending the establishment of at least two more bases. One of them probably at Balmoran and the other at . . . well, wherever you think best. Politically. Just has to be a good harbor. And we'll farm out the ship construction to shipyards all along the coast; spread that money around at least. Better?"

"I can work with that." Sheida nodded. "Of course, Admiral Houser has to approve it."

"Of course," Edmund chuckled. "Isn't that what chain-of-command is for?"

just listened—time she wasn't quite as quick on the

CHAPTER FOURTEEN

When Edmund woke up it was bright daylight. He started to roll to his feet, angry that no one had awoken him before dawn, and noticed that he was not alone in bed. From the red hair and the shape of the shoulder either his wife or his daughter had crawled in next to him sometime in the night. He really, *really* hoped it was Daneh. Rachel had gotten far too old to share a bed with daddy.

"Good morning," Daneh said, rolling over sleepily.

"Late morning," Edmund said, trying not to snarl.

"I know," Daneh replied, leaning over to kiss him. "And you've got morning breath. Don't flay Destrang alive; I told him that you weren't to be wakened. You've been driving yourself into the ground and as your doctor I ordered some additional bed rest. Not to mention as your wife."

"Destrang's supposed to take orders from *me*," Edmund growled, rolling to the edge of the bed and getting his feet out of the covers. But he had to admit that the extra sleep had done him some good.

"And he trusted that I'd keep you from coming down on him like a ton of bricks," Daneh said, sliding across the not particularly large bed and grabbing him by his hair. "And you're not going to. As a matter of fact, you don't have another appointment for . . ." She glanced at the clock across the room and smiled. "Two hours. Now that I've rearranged your schedule. So if you think you're leaping out of bed this minute, you'd better have another think coming." She pulled his head back until he was lying down again, looking up at her upside down.

"You did mention morning breath," Edmund replied.

"Have an apple."

"Good morning, seaman," Edmund said, striding down to the docks. "Have an apple," he added, tossing one to the surprised messenger. "They're good for you."

"Morning, sir," Ensign Destrang said, nervously.

"Morning, Destrang," Edmund replied, smiling at him. "What've you got?"

"Lieutenant Asfaw asked to talk to you, sir," Destrang replied, gesturing at the mer.

"Did you get a chair or something, Asfaw?" Edmund asked.

"Yes, sir, thank you," the mer replied. There were also more mer in the basin, swimming around below. "The engineers poured a sort of underwater pier for us. Very handy. As are the additional listeners."

"And what was it you wanted to talk about?" Edmund asked, snagging a chair.

"Well . . ." Asfaw looked around nervously but then shrugged. "We, the mer that is, aren't doing much good in this war, sir."

"I think your reconnaissance, not to mention your weather monitoring and communications uses, are invaluable," Edmund said, frowning. "Don't get the idea we don't need you."

"No, sir, not that," Asfaw said. "It's just . . . we can't attack anything. Except the orca and ixchitl. And even then we kept getting told that recon is more important than fighting orca. But with the orca around, we can't *recon*. We want to *help*. Or, I guess, help more."

"There were some experiments with boring," Edmund said. "Didn't work very well. And mines are out for all the same damned reasons."

"I was wondering," Asfaw said. "Well, I mean, sometimes the message traffic is light and all I can do is sit in the water and watch the occasional fish, sir. So I have a lot of time to wonder. Maybe if the queen could permit a bit of power we could make some sort of biological? A fast wood-worm or something that dissolves hulls?"

"If it got loose it would be the death of maritime traffic," Edmund said, rubbing his jaw. "No, protocols would prevent it reproducing if it was that dangerous. But maybe . . ." Edmund glanced at the sun and sneezed. "I'm going to be talking to Evan in a couple of hours. I'll bring it up with him. Maybe he or one of his engineer buddies can come up with something."

"What about the orcas?" the lieutenant asked.

"You'll have to run that one by me again," Edmund

said. "I'll admit I'm a bit tired. Why can't you attack the orcas?"

"Our orders are to avoid contact. We're supposed to be recon forces is what they keep saying. But we *can't* always avoid contact and Jason thinks we can get rid of some of the damned orca and ixchitl, if we can just get the support."

"That's it?" Edmund asked. "What kind of support?"

"Nothing more than we're getting, really," the mer admitted. "Some more weapons, maybe some support ships. But we'll probably take more casualties."

Edmund considered it for a moment and then nodded. "Tell Jason he has my permission to implement a plan to begin reducing the orca and ixchitl. But if he's taking high levels of casualties, that is if he's losing more than he's killing, he's to desist. Got it?"

"Yes, sir! Thank you, sir," Asfaw replied.

"Don't thank me, son," Edmund sighed. "You're just putting yourself in the way of more trouble."

"Trouble, sir." Chief Brooks sighed, collapsing in the chair across from Herzer.

Herzer looked out the window where one of the petty officers was conducting a class on knots.

"No riots," Herzer chuckled. "Even over the food."

"No, not so far, sir," Brooks replied. "It's a sexual harassment complaint."

"Bloody hell." Herzer sighed, leaning back. "Who?"

"Seaman, *seawoman* not to point too fine of a point on it, Regilio and Petty Officer Lenice."

"Tell," Herzer replied, rubbing his eyes.

"He was counseling her on her attitude, which is, frankly, crappy. She accused him of soliciting sex."

"Did he follow the two man rule?" Herzer asked, not looking up.

"No, sir, he didn't," Brooks replied. "He said that he wanted to bring it up without a witness so she would have less of a tendency to back talk. Because then he'd have to get strictly official."

"Send him back to the fleet," Herzer said, dropping his hands and picking up a piece of paperwork.

"He's one of the best instructors we have, sir," Brooks argued.

"Not if he makes that simple an error," Herzer said, looking up angrily and tossing the note back down on his desk. "I *agree* with his *reasoning*. But he can *not* put himself in that sort of a position with half-trained recruits. Recruits that don't realize how serious the accusation is. Or how the accusation is going to haunt *them* for quite some time. How many people are automatically going to question . . . what was her name?"

"Regilio, sir."

"Pamela," Herzer replied, nodding with that reminder. "In the intel tech program. Good math scores. Red hair. Yes, bit of an attitude. Just about the last person up The Mast every morning."

"That would be her," Brooks sighed.

"People are going to know about it, people are going to talk," Herzer said. "Lenice has been with the Fleet for a couple of years. Spotless record. No previous indication of tendency to use his rank for sex. So she's *automatically* going to be viewed with suspicion. Even if he *did*, in fact, proposition her or try to force her to have sex. Which was why, Chief Brooks, he is going back to the fleet. Today. With a notation in his record that he is unsuitable for training cadre. And you'd better thoroughly brief his replacement. Am I making myself clear?"

"Clear, sir," Brooks said, standing up. "Will that be all?"

"Unfortunately, yes," Herzer replied, picking up the paperwork again. "I'd rather it was riots. Oh, and pass this around. Don't let anyone think this is an easy way back to the fleet. The next time this comes up, I'm coming down like the hammer of hell. All the bells and whistles. They do *not* want to make this mistake again. We don't have the bodies to spare."

"Good afternoon, Skipper Karcher," Edmund said, waving at a chair. "Have a seat."

"Good afternoon, sir," Karcher replied, sitting down carefully. She had already had a look around the tent and was clearly surprised by its Spartan nature.

"Given that the headquarters was burned to the ground, I thought that we could use temporary accommodations," Edmund said, noting the glances.

"Yes, sir," Karcher replied. She had her captain's hat in her lap and was working the brow with the thumbs of both hands.

"How's your ship?" Edmund asked, smiling.

"Fine, sir," Karcher said. "In all conditions ready for sea."

"This isn't an inquisition, Karcher." Talbot chuckled. "I heard about your recommended change for the Silverdrake landings. It's being implemented throughout the fleet."

"One of my seamen came up with it, sir," Karcher said. "Seaman Fink."

"Good man?" Edmund asked.

"Woman, sir, and yes, she's pretty good. She's applied for dragon-rider training."

Edmund pulled a sheet of paper over to him and scribbled on it.

"Approved," Edmund said. "As long as you do." He handed the sheet across to her. "What's your XO like?"

"Good man, sir," Karcher replied. "Better than me at celestial navigation. Getting there at general boat handling skills. I mean, he's a good sailor, sir."

"Could he take over the *Black*?"

Karcher paused at that and frowned. "Am I being relieved, sir?"

"I asked the first question," Edmund replied.

"Yes, sir, he could." Karcher sighed.

"Good," Edmund said, handing her another sheet of paper. "You've just been appointed command of the *Hazhir*. The XO knows the ship but Shar doesn't feel he's up to commanding it, yet. I've looked at your record and I think you can."

"Yes, sir," Karcher replied, taking the paper as if it were incendiary. She slid it under her hat and continued working the brim, a bit harder.

"Just that, 'yes, sir'?" Edmund asked, smiling.

"Thank you, sir?" Karcher said.

"You think you can handle it?" Edmund asked.

"No, sir," Karcher said, honestly. "But I can give it my best shot. And I would guess that you've thought it over. I'd have expected that you'd transfer someone from one of the frigates or cruisers and that I'd get that, instead. But if you are willing to take the risk, I'll do my damnedest."

"Karcher, you've got more time at sea than half the frigate commanders." Edmund sighed. "And, yeah, I gave it some thought. And some second thoughts. You know what clinched it?"

Karcher thought about that for a second and then shrugged.

"My saying that Fink had come up with the landing program?"

"Bingo," Edmund replied. "That and your crew is loyal as hell. You can sail and you can lead. That's a hard combination to find in this Navy. And you're not afraid to say: 'I don't know, sir.' That takes guts. Now we just have to find out if you can fight. Don't prove me wrong."

"No, sir," Karcher replied. "I was just wondering . . ."

"I know your background," Edmund said. "In fact, I probably know more about it than you do. Despite the fact that Changed are facing some very ancient prejudice, I don't have it. Changed are humans just like those of us who look normal. I'll except from that category the New Destiny Changed which have been programmed to be *in*human. You're a good CO, you're a good sailor and I have damned few people that fit both categories. I don't care, quite frankly, if you eat live mice. That might have mattered under Draskovich, it doesn't matter to me."

"I don't, sir," Karcher said, then took a chance. "Well, hardly ever."

"And I don't fling shit," Edmund said with a grin. "Well, hardly ever."

"Yes, sir," Karcher said with a catlike smile.

"That's it," Talbot said. "Good luck."

"Thank you, sir," Karcher said, standing up and putting on her hat. "I'll try to make my own."

"Hello, your Dukeship," Herzer said, striding into the lamp-lit tent.

"Herzer, you're really losing your military bearing with me, aren't you?" Edmund chuckled.

"I bring orders from your wife, via your daughter who you haven't even said hello to, yet," Herzer replied, walking over and pulling a sheet of paper out of the admiral's hand. "We are ordered to repair to the O-Club. Where you, Van Krief and I, at a minimum, will occupy one corner and get shit faced. Rachel's precisely transmitted words. 'You are hereby ordered, by mother, to get him, and I quote, shit faced.' It's a rest day tomorrow and that gives us at least a few hours to get over the hangover. So stand up, our real masters call."

Edmund shook his head and waved at the desk. "She already had me sleep in. I've got reams of paperwork to catch up on."

"All of it *will* wait," Herzer said, walking around the desk and lifting up on Edmund's arm. "Don't even think about fighting. I'm younger and faster than you."

"Age and treachery beats youth and speed every time," Edmund growled. But he stood up.

"Well, once we get drunk enough, maybe we can put it to the test," Herzer chuckled. "Come on, boss, times a wastin'."

"You sound like Bast when you say that," Edmund chuckled. "Speaking of which, you gotten *your* tubes cleaned lately?"

"No, more's the pity," Herzer replied, frowning. "When we got here we were running around like chickens with our heads cut off. And since then the only female contact I've had is with subordinates. And I don't even want to go there after the day I just had. Especially since that idiot decision of mine to set up The Mast."

"I thought that was brilliant," Edmund said as they strode past the ring of guards around the headquarters.

"So did I," Herzer growled. "And I thought putting it up where the commander could watch was brilliant as well. Then I noticed that when they're running up the ratlines, well . . . let's just say that there are some fine butts in that class. And they're getting finer every week!"

Edmund laughed and clapped him on the back as they crossed the blacked-out road.

"Don't worry, I'm sure your lackanookie condition won't . . ." He spun sideways as a sword lashed out of the darkness, then spun again as another attacker came from his off-side.

Herzer and Edmund were unarmed but that didn't last long. There was a crack of a broken arm and a scream as Herzer spun sideways, hurling one of the attackers into the roadway. But he had retained the assassin's short sword and he tossed it overhand to Edmund as the admiral flipped his cloak in the face of another attacker. Edmund caught the sword and skewered one of the assassins through the neck, then tossed the dead assassin's sword to Herzer. After that it became somewhat bloody.

Herzer parried a blade and used the same trick with

the cloak to wrap up one of the attackers, running his blade across the man's throat and throwing the thrashing body onto one that had closed on Edmund's back.

Edmund now had two blades and was moving forward through the group, the blades acting as if they had a will of their own. An arm thumped the ground followed by a head and Herzer used the distraction of the blood from the spurting stump to kill another half-blind assassin. He felt a cut across his shoulder but turned and jabbed backwards, killing the man behind him, then kicked out at one to his front. As the attacker bent double Herzer drove the blade of the sword into the side of his neck and outward, slashing his carotid artery and spilling more blood onto the soaked ground.

In moments it was over, two of the attackers running into the night as a group of lantern-bearing marines pounded across the road.

"Bloody hellfire," the sergeant choked, looking at the scattered pieces on the ground.

"Indeed," Edmund said, dropping one of his swords and cleaning the other on a bit of almost-clean cloth. "Herzer, I think I owe you a drink."

Herzer looked at the lamp-lit ground and counted. "I dunno . . . I think we're about even. Youth and speed might *not* beat age and treachery."

"Do we get cleaned up?" Edmund asked, looking at his blood-soaked uniform. "Or just go to the club?"

"They've got a dress-code," Herzer pointed out, chuckling.

"Ah, they make exceptions for admirals," Edmund said, walking towards the doors of the club and into the night.

❖   ❖   ❖

"Hey, Van Krief," Edmund said as they entered the main bar.

He'd heard the expression: "You could have heard a pin drop," but he'd never actually experienced it in his very long life. Now he really understood it. He actually heard, all the way across the club, a bartender set down the bottle he was holding. The faint "tap" was the only sound in the room for a moment.

"Good evening, sir," Van Krief said, getting up from the table by the door. "Are all the members of your staff alive?" She was a Blood Lord and be damned if she was going to react in shock to two blood-soaked officers walking into the main bar.

"Do me a favor, will you?" Edmund said, stripping off his uniform tunic. "Go get some clothes for Herzer and me while we go wash up." He took the short sword and tossed it overhand across the room, so hard that it stuck in the wall. "We had a spot of bother on the way over from headquarters."

"You could have been killed!" Daneh said, angrily.

"I very nearly was," Edmund replied, taking another sip of his drink. "Would have been if it wasn't for Herzer."

Daneh and Rachel had hurried over as soon as Van Krief had explained why she needed new clothes for Edmund and the major. The foursome, with Van Krief, Destrang and Tao at a nearby table, now had a corner of the bar all to themselves. Except for a hovering waiter who was watching them like a mouse watches a hovering falcon.

"Nah, you were doing fine on your own." Herzer

chuckled, taking a deep pull off of his beer. "It was hairy for a second or two, though. You spotted them before I did, I'll give you that."

"Years of hard living, son," Edmund replied, shaking his head. "Years of hard living. Some habits die hard."

"You're going to need bodyguards," Rachel said.

"Yep," Talbot replied, grimly. "But the good news is, somebody doesn't like me."

"That's *good* news?" Daneh asked. "Since when?"

"It means someone considers him a threat," Herzer pointed out. "And whereas I'm sure there's more than one Navy officer who would love to shove a foot of steel in his back, I doubt that they were the source of the assassins."

"Which means Sheida's old friend Chansa," Edmund said. "Or, possibly, Paul. So that's the good news. The bad news is that it's not just me who will need guards, but you, Rachel and the squirt as well. Which is why there's already a team of marines over at the VIP quarters and more on the way."

"Yes, they would try to strike at you through us, wouldn't they?" Daneh asked, quietly.

"Yes, they would," Edmund replied. "Rachel, I hate to talk business but are you up to another long coach ride?"

"If I must," she said.

"Daneh, I'm going to put you to work," Edmund continued. "Special assistant for medical facilities or something. When the fleet comes back I want better medical care than the last time. I haven't been able to put enough emphasis on that as I'd like. You can. We're setting up another Fleet base in Balmoran,

Rachel. I want you to go up there and get in on the ground floor on the medical facilities. You'll report to your mother; she'll report to me. The fleet can actually make for Balmoran better than they can for here, if we fight in the north again. The main thing that we'd be bringing in is casualties. I'd like the hospital up there to be top-notch. Okay?"

"Okay," Rachel said. "Can do. As long as I've got the personnel and funding."

"You'll have the funding if I have to go to the damned capitol and *squeeze*; personnel you're probably going to have to make yourself," Edmund replied. "And you won't be *in charge*, you'll be my eyes and ears. If you have suggestions and can get them implemented there, do so. If you have real problems, report it to Daneh. Understood?"

"Understood."

"Okay, now let's *all* get shit faced," Edmund said, draining his drink and waving it at the waiter.

"What if there are more assassins?" Daneh asked.

"Honey, when we walk back to the quarters we're going to be surrounded by a platoon of marines," Edmund replied. "Chansa may be able to get my drunk ass under those conditions, but he's by God going to have to work for it."

CHAPTER FIFTEEN

Herzer wasn't sure whether he was supporting Van Krief or she was supporting him when they got to his room. But he did know that it was a bad thing that both of them were there.

It had been an evening for learning. He'd learned that Destrang and Tao were light-weights. He'd learned that Daneh hiccupped when she got drunk. He'd learned that Rachel just went to sleep. He'd learned that Van Krief had a hollow leg and a great singing voice. At least, it sounded great when he was drunk. And she knew some really good songs, not all of them fit for polite company.

To no one's surprise, Edmund knew more. But Herzer *had* been surprised that he also sang better. He'd never pictured Edmund as a singer, before. Bellower, yes, singer, no. Herzer had learned so much.

But he still had the problem of the door. And nothing that he learned was helping.

"Am I holding you up, or are you holding me up?" Herzer enunciated carefully.

"I think . . ." Van Krief said, crinkling her brow. "I think we're holding each *other* up."

"Me too," Herzer said. If they were holding each other up, then they could only make it to one bedroom. That was bad.

"This is bad," he muttered.

"Oh, I don't think so," Van Krief giggled.

"This is a *really* bad idea," Herzer said, opening the door. "Really bad. I'll just . . . sleep on the floor or something."

"I don't *think* so," Van Krief repeated, giggling again. She stumbled away from him, kicked the door closed, stumbled again, and pulled her tunic off. "What do you think of *that*?"

"What?" Herzer asked, looking at the floor. It looked . . . really uncomfortable.

"These!" Van Krief said, pulling at a couple of buttons on her shirt and then giving up and ripping it open. "These!" she said again, pointing at her breasts.

"Pink nipples," he muttered, getting on his knees and kneeing over to her until he could lay his cheek on her midriff. "How much worse could it get?" He had just kissed her on the stomach when there was a knock on the door.

"Okay, this is worse," he said, pulling himself up with a hand on the bedstead.

Van Krief had fumbled her tunic on but the torn shirt was impossible to conceal. Herzer looked at her and shrugged as he opened the door.

"Herzer?" Rachel said, supporting herself on the doorframe. "Do you have a private bathroom?"

"Yes," Herzer said.

"Good, I'm going to be sick in it," Rachel replied, sliding off the doorframe and skidding to a halt when she saw Van Krief.

"Oh," Rachel said, her eyes blinking furiously.

"We were just dis-ss-cussing . . ." Van Krief slurred.

"We were just discussing not having sex," Herzer continued, clapping his hand over the ensign's mouth. "Now the young ensign, who is also my subordinate, is going to support herself on the wall until she gets to her room, and her chaste bed, and I'm going to collapse into a drunken stupor. And you're going to go throw up."

At least that's what he'd meant to say. What came out was:

"Wubaa, ubba, nooob . . ."

At which point the many, many shots of rum finally kicked in and gravity took over.

When Herzer opened his eyes the first thing he knew, with awful clarity, was that he was not in bed alone.

He remembered, too clearly, the night before. Right up to the point that both Rachel *and* Van Krief were in his room. Especially the point when Rachel and Van Krief had been in his room.

And now there was someone in his bed.

Rachel . . . now Rachel wouldn't be bad. Rachel he could live with. He'd be surprised, but not unpleased. But since he *would* be surprised, given that her interest in him as *male* seemed to be zero, it was much more likely to be Van Krief. And that would be . . . bad. He tried not to groan as he thought of the night before. He couldn't run away and join the Legion, he was already in it. Maybe start up a farm, find a rock to crawl under. This was a *court-martial* offense, damnit! He'd just tossed PO Lenice to the metaphorical wolves for less.

And he couldn't even remember doing anything!

In fact, even given his full bladder, he suspected from signs that he hadn't *done* anything. Not that it would matter.

Shit. Time to find out if he'd have a pissed-off boss or a *very* pissed-off boss.

"Hi, lover," Bast said as he rolled over.

"Bast, not that I'm not glad to see you . . ." Herzer said as he came out of the bathroom. He clutched his head and groaned, before going on. "But . . . how did you get in here? This place is supposed to be surrounded by guards."

"Am I not Bast?" the wood elf said, sliding out of the bed. The elf was barely a meter and a quarter tall and perfectly formed with long, curly, raven-black hair, high, firm breasts and a body that was toned but not, apparently, muscular. She was naked, her standard garment, winter and summer, of a leather bikini on the floor by the bed. She had the body of a fourteen-year-old, and often the personality, but Herzer knew she was over a thousand years old.

"Am I not the greatest sneak in the world? Do you think your simpleton marines can stop *me*?"

Elves had been created at the dawn of the age of the Net as super-soldiers by the North American Union. Although they looked mostly human, they were not Changed humans but an entirely different species.

At the time of the Fall the majority of them lived in a separated dimension called Elfheim. The sundering from humans had occurred around the time of the AI wars, when it became obvious that two sentient species were not going to be able to coexist on earth. The wood elves had been created at about the same time as soldiers for the Nissei Corporation. At least, Bast was. If there were any other wood elves in existence, Herzer hadn't heard of them. He and Bast had been on and off lovers since shortly after the Fall.

"No," Herzer said, sitting down on the bed and clutching his head. "I don't suppose you have any aspirin?"

"Have I not told you to take aspirin *before* you go to bed?" she asked, bringing him a glass of water and a pill. "And a big drink of water. Of course, when I got here Rachel was being sick in your bathroom, you were passed out on a floor and a half-naked ensign was passed out on top of you. So this once, I forgive you."

"Where's Van Krief?" Herzer asked, draining the cup and taking the pill.

"The pretty blonde?" the elf asked. "I managed to get her conscious enough for directions to her room and carried her there. She didn't seem to be in any condition to help. Not that you were, either." She laid her hand on his head and murmured for a moment and Herzer felt the effects of the hangover miraculously disappear.

"God, Bast, you're a drunkard's dream," Herzer said, taking her in his arms.

"Good thing for you." She smiled. "Now, go take shower, you smell like goat. Then come back here and I make you smell like one again. And if the pretty little blonde turns up, tell her you're busy. It's been a long time and I'm not sharing."

"My my, look what the cat drug in," Daneh said as Herzer and Bast entered the room.

It was past noon but it was clear that everyone in the room was on their first meal of the day. And all of them were nursing hangovers.

"Daneh, my friend, your daughter very well brought up is. Is even polite when being sick."

"Oh, gods, was that you?" Rachel groaned. "I thought it was Van Krief."

"Wasn't me," the ensign muttered, looking from the elf to Herzer and back. "You must be Bast."

"Indeedy." Bast grinned, pulling out a chair and flopping down. She snagged a plate and pulled over a tureen filled with scrambled eggs. "We've met."

"I don't recall when," Van Krief said, thinly.

"Last night, carried back to your room did I," Bast said, grinning again.

"I don't remember most of last night," the ensign said after a moment.

"I do," Bast replied. "Humans shouldn't drink, can't handle their liquor."

Herzer was mentally cringing. Bast was usually blunt about sex to the point of pornography. But he noticed that she was carefully avoiding the subject of *where* Van Krief had been when the elf carried her back to her room. That was, for Bast, unbelievably circumspect and tactful.

"Of course, if another try at Herzer want, wait until this afternoon; sure he'll be up to it by then."

So much for circumspect.

"Bast," Edmund said, carefully. "We were all pretty drunk last night. I think that it's best if we just avoid the whole subject. Okay?"

"Okay," Bast said, taking a bite of egg. "How about the subject of Chansa putting out contract?"

"Even that is preferable," Daneh replied.

"Is all around the town," Bast continued. "Open contract is. Was to stop I was coming. Late. Sorry."

"Funny that I didn't get any word," Edmund replied. "T's usually better about that. Where did you hear about it?"

"Was approached," Bast shrugged. "Killed the man who asked, did I. Very stupid man. Thought jealous would I be of young ensign."

"What?" Van Krief said.

"What?" Herzer shouted.

"Keep it down, Herzer," Edmund sighed. "I was afraid this was going to happen. The fact that you two . . . like each other is pretty obvious. It has been brought up to me. Not officially, but it has been brought up."

"But we have never . . ." Herzer said then paused. "Well . . . except for . . . Oh, damn!"

"Damn indeed," Edmund nodded. "How's the school running?"

"Well enough," Herzer said. "If you're asking if Captain Silver can handle it, yes he can."

"The fleet sails for work-ups in two days," Edmund said with another nod. "I'd already made it plain that you were going to be going out with it. I was going to send you as a supernumerary, one of my eyes and ears. But they're so short of dragon-riders I'm going to appoint you as the CO of the *Hazhir* dragon wing."

"There are far more experienced riders in the fleet than me," Herzer pointed out.

"None on the *Hazhir*," Edmund replied. "New captain, new crew, dragons gathered from all over and half of them have only done one or two landings. Very few of them are trained in bombing."

"And me," Bast said. "Joanna will go, I will ride."

"Joanna is slated for the *Bonhomme Richard*," Edmund said.

"Was," Bast replied. "Joanna will go on *Hazhir*. As will I. Trust me on this, Edmund Talbot. Joanna, myself and Herzer to the *Hazhir*."

"What do you know?" Edmund asked.

"Know that is who will go," Bast said with a shrug. "Something is coming. More than battle. Timelines twist." She stopped and grinned. "*Gaslan*. Elf thing is. Warriors are. Future of war can feel, see. Schwerpunkt is *Hazhir*. Joanna, Herzer, I go. Battle you will fight. Battle you may win. Win or lose, *Hazhir* is the key. To more. Much more."

They all looked at her for a moment and then Edmund shook his head.

"I hate it when you get all elf on me. Destrang, make a note. Commander Joanna Gramlich transferred to *Hazhir*, commander dragon contingent. Same for Major Herzer Herrick, XO dragon contingent. Bast L'sol Tamel d'San, allied wood elf, assigned *Hazhir* as supernumerary dragon-rider."

"And me, sir?" Van Krief asked.

"You're coming back as one of my aides," Edmund replied. "We'll be on the *Bonhomme Richard*. I've got a lot of writing for someone to do. And it has to be someone I trust. Same with Destrang. Tao."

"Sir?" the ensign said.

"You're staying here. The original purpose of aides de camp were to be eyes and ears. You're my eyes and ears, not my mouth. But if something I order here isn't being done, get word to me."

"Yes, sir," the ensign replied.

"Why are *you* going to sea?" Daneh asked. "I thought that was why you brought up Shar Chang."

"Because I'm not going to sit in headquarters when a fleet that just had its ass kicked sails back into harm's way." Edmund sighed. "I probably *should* be at headquarters for any number of reasons. Planning the *next* battle for one thing. But right now, the fleet is reeling. I'm going to be there, right or wrong."

"Well, at least at sea the assassins are going to have a hard time reaching you," Daneh said with a frown. "Of course, you might get sunk or burned. But you don't have to worry about assassins."

"What about the assassins that might come after us?" Rachel asked.

"At a certain point," Edmund said sadly, "you have to delegate responsibility. Even if it's for the care of your family. And you're going to be going to Balmoran anyway. Remember?"

Herzer mounted the side of the *Hazhir* and saluted the officer of the deck, then the UFS Navy flag, a rattlesnake on a field of orange with the words "Don't Tread On Me" emblazoned on it.

"Permission to come aboard?" he asked.

"Granted," the female lieutenant said. "Lieutenant Lannette Rattanachane, navigation officer."

"Major Herzer Herrick," Herzer replied. Then he

gestured at Bast who had just reached the deck and was looking around her with interest. "Bast L'sol Tamel d'San, Elven ally."

"Call me Bast," Bast said, sticking out her hand and pumping the lieutenant's. "Pleased to meetcha." She was in her normal traveling costume of a green leather bikini, baldric supported saber on her left hip, bow and quiver over her back, metal pauldron on her left shoulder, greaves on her right leg and a fur leg-warmer on her left. She was also wearing sandals with a very low heel. Her hair was unbound and the northeast wind blew it around her face as she grinned. "Fine day for sailin', eh?"

"Yes, it is," the lieutenant gulped. "Major Herrick, the captain would like to meet you as soon as possible."

"Which means now," Herzer said. "Bast . . . oh, never mind. Just try not to cause too much chaos, all right?"

"Who, me?" Bast grinned. "I'll go straighten out our quarters while you go sweet-talk the captain."

"We normally have separate quarters for male and female riders . . ." Lieutenant Rattanachane started to say.

"Oh, well, normal doesn't apply to Bast." Bast grinned. "So why don't you be showin' me to Herzer's quarters and I'll be settlin' in?"

The fleet that upped anchor at the end of four weeks was radically changed, at least on the surface. Where there had been slap-dash repairs there was solid wood. Where there had been patched sails there was newly woven cosilk. Burned masts had been replaced, rigging had been rewoven and all material conditions had been repaired.

On the surface.

All of the ships had had at least one day beyond the bay of work-ups. All of them had the bare minimum top-men to raise and lower their sails. All of the carriers had their holds packed with stores. All of the anti-dragon dreadnoughts had their new guns mounted. Silverdrake and Powells filled the air as the dragons waited for the fleet to receive them.

But there was more to a fleet than being ready "in a material condition." Officers and men had been shifted around in a complex, and unwinnable, dance. New ship types had been added. Gunners and dragon-pilots were half-trained. New captains filled the fleet.

On the surface it looked like they were unstoppable. And Edmund knew that half the battle was morale. That the brave show would have a part in any battle. But he also knew that a good part of it was training. And in that they were sorely lacking.

So it was with these thoughts that he ascended the side of the *Bonhomme Richard* and shook the hand of Shar Chang.

"Atlantis Fleet, arriving!" the petty officer bellowed. The pipes and drums beat a flourish and his flag mounted the mast. But he knew that that, too, was only a show.

"Shar," he said, shaking the admiral's hand. "We ready to set sail?"

"As ready as we're going to get," Chang replied. He was clearly tired.

"Let's get below; we've got things to discuss."

❖   ❖   ❖

They were in the same quarters he had occupied in his previous voyage on the *Richard*; port side of the officers' corridor, a room specifically made for visiting dignitaries. It was small but it had a large bed, a wide porthole and a table big enough for six to fit around if they were friendly. Right now, it was only Edmund and Shar Chang; Shar's aide was showing the gaggle following Edmund around their own, much more cramped, quarters.

"Shar, first thing, I'm not here to joggle your elbow," Edmund said.

"I think I know why you're here." Shar grinned. "You're an old war-horse that can't stay away from a battle."

"Okay, there's that," Edmund admitted. "But I would have swallowed my pride and stayed on shore if it wasn't for the condition of the fleet, mentally. The last time they sailed, their admiral stayed, presumably safe and sound, on shore. This time I'm going to share the danger. Seasickness and all."

"And, incidentally, be able to answer any little questions that come up in my mind?" Shar said, grinning again.

"I'm hoping that I'll be able to spend the whole voyage doing paperwork," Edmund admitted. "Except for the throwing up part."

"Well, I'm going to be exercising the fleet up until we get word on New Destiny's movements," Shar said. "In close where we can resupply readily. I'm especially going to be exercising the dragons and the anti-dragon gunners. We'll probably be going through a lot of sailcloth."

"Probably will," Edmund chuckled. When fired into

the wind the bolts from the air-guns had a distressing tendency to fall on the firing ships. It had caused several accidents, to the point of putting shelters on the decks, and shields on the guns, to prevent friendly fire incidents. But there was no way to save the sails and the dreadnoughts tended to look as if they'd just won first prize in a quilting bee. "And bolts and bombs. Good. When do we up anchor?"

"As soon as we're done talking," Shar admitted.

"Well, let me take some of these herbs Daneh prescribed for seasickness and then hoist the mizzen or whatever," the admiral said, grinning.

"We'll make a sailor of you yet, Admiral."

CHAPTER SIXTEEN

"When are we going to land?" Kenton signaled to the rider next to him.

Herzer caught the sign out of the corner of his eye and waved to him. "Cut the chatter," he signed, as Vickie coasted up on her Silverdrake.

The fleet had been scheduled to sail thirty minutes prior. The fly-off of the dragons had been intended to let them land in the bay after the fleet upped anchor. But the dragons had a limited endurance aloft and the first up were going to start tiring soon. Especially the Silverdrake.

"Sabeh and Al Kalifa are getting worn out," Vickie signaled, swinging around the front of his dragon and back in a quick bank as she simultaneously signed. "All Silverdrake. Need to land."

"Signal ship," Herzer signed, sighing. Great start to the big adventure.

The Silverdrake turned over on its back and dove

down to the lower formation of defensive dragons. Vickie continued through the formation, narrowly missing one of the other wyverns, and down towards the ship which had just lifted its anchor and set sail.

"Dragon signaling, ma'am," the lookout called.

Skipper Karcher looked up and to the rear where the lookout was pointing and at the underside of the landing platform over her head. With a meow of distaste she walked to the rear of the quarterdeck and leaned out.

"What's the signal?" she shouted.

"Requesting clearance to land," the signal midshipman called from primary flight ops. The latter was a platform mounted on the rear mast. From there they could see the incoming dragons and signals from dragons in the pattern. Unlike the captain.

"The fleet hasn't signaled air-ops, ma'am," her new XO, Major Sassan, said.

"I know that, XO," the skipper said. "Pri-fly! Powell or Silverdrake?"

"Silverdrake, ma'am!" the midshipman called. She saw the damned elf climbing up there as well. "Now signaling request to recall all the Silverdrake."

"Granted," Karcher called. "Do not, say again, do *not* set for air-ops! Have ground crews standing by."

"Ma'am, are you sure about that?" Sassan asked.

"Yes," Karcher replied. "Communications, signal the fleet. 'Have recalled fatigued Silverdrake. Our number. End.'"

"Yes, ma'am," the signal midshipman said, pulling the flags out of her locker.

Karcher could, barely, see the *Richard* from her

position. She saw the acknowledgement flag fly just as the first Silverdrake thumped to the deck, then an "Approved" follow it quickly. The approval was marked for the whole fleet.

"Apparently there are others with tired Silverdrake," Sassan said.

"Yes," Karcher replied. "XO, could I see you below?" she said, walking lightly to the companionway and springing halfway down in one bound.

When they reached her day-room she sat down and waved at the chair across from her desk.

"I don't know how Admiral Chang handled things, XO," she said. "But when I make a decision, I don't want it second-guessed unless you *know* you have information I don't. You will find that I will frequently ask for input, especially as regards the handling characteristics of this ship, the material condition and the crew. But when I give an order, you do not second-guess me. Certainly not in front of the crew. Is that clear?"

"Yes, ma'am," the XO replied.

"When Silverdrake have to land, they have to land. Maybe Vickie pulled them a tad early, maybe not. But *I* am not going to question the decision of an experienced dragon-rider, certainly not in the air. Further reasons for my decision: Silverdrake can land on a dime. They don't need the ship to be headed into the wind. The fleet *could* recall them without maneuvering, which is good since we don't have the sea-room, yet. I could have asked the admiral. In the future, I suspect I will. But at that time, in that place, I knew I had to get my Silverdrake down. Making decisions like that is what being the skipper is about. Clear?"

"Clear, ma'am."

"When you're a skipper, you'll have to make decisions like that, too. For now, let's get back up on deck. I imagine we'll start air-ops pretty soon."

"I can't believe they got to sea that fast," Paul snarled, tiredly.

He had just completed another session of recalling his avatars. Reintegrating their personalities was tiring and generally left him grouchy. Megan had had Shanea stand by with her as they waited and now the latter lifted a cup of wine to his lips.

"Thank you, Shanea," Paul said, taking a sip.

"The UFS sailed already?" Megan asked.

"Yes," Paul said, shaking his head and taking the cup from Shanea. His hand shook slightly as he raised it for another sip. "That damned Talbot again. Sheida put him in charge of the fleet. He's made all sorts of changes. Most of them good."

"He has been quite a thorn in your side," Megan prompted.

"As bad as Kinloch in Taurania," Paul admitted, sitting up. "Worse, really. Chansa gave orders to have him assassinated but that bastard Conner bungled it."

"Conner is normally quite efficient," Megan mused.

"Yes, but this time he underestimated Talbot, and that bastard Herrick for that matter. The assassins attacked them by surprise and the two of them managed to kill eight of the assassins, even though they were unarmed."

"Herrick is the young Blood Lord?" Shanea asked.

"Yes," Paul said, smiling at the girl. Shanea usually just listened since she wasn't quite as quick on the uptake as Megan. "He's been a bit of a thorn in my side as well, but not as bad as Talbot. I'm thinking of sending a team of Celine's specials after the both of them. Or maybe Edmund's family, including that brat of McCanoc's."

"Edmund Talbot does not seem the sort to respond to grief," Megan said, frowning. "Not in an unthinking way. If anything, it will make him angrier. But not a good angry. Not from what you've told me of him. I don't want to say that attacking them would be a bad idea, but . . ."

"But you think it's a bad idea." Paul grinned. "And you're probably right. I'll make a note to Chansa to leave them alone. Killing Edmund will do. And if they can get that bastard Herzer at the same time, more power."

"Can't our fleet beat theirs?" Shanea asked.

"Probably, lovey," Paul said, patting her on the head. "We've got more ships. But I don't trust that Talbot. He's tricky."

"Any good news?" Megan asked.

"Well, they still haven't taken the Alam reactor," Paul said. "But Arizzi's forces got pushed back in Chin, again, and Cho is stalemated in the mountains of Soam. If we can just take Norau, or even the eastern reactors . . ."

"You need some time to let this bubble," Megan said, sliding over next to him. "Two beautiful women, one good looking guy. What does this suggest to you?"

"That my day's getting better?" Paul chuckled.

"Good day for flying," Herzer said as he checked the straps on Meritari.

The fleet had recovered the dragons in the bay and then headed out to sea for more exercises. They had spent the morning doing ship drills but the afternoon was slated for air-operations. The riders had wolfed down lunch and were now preparing to lead their mounts up to the deck.

"That it is," Joanna said, stumping down the broad corridor that marked the dragon-hanger. "Seas are low enough that the wyverns aren't sick, not pitching too much. Should be easy takeoff and landing."

"Nice and warm," Ensign Ross said. "Good thermals."

"Well, let's go find out," Herzer said, opening up the gate of the stall and leading the wyvern out into the pathway as soon as Joanna was past. He handed the reins to one of the handlers, though, and slid past Joanna to beat her onto the deck.

"What's your hurry?" Joanna growled.

"You're first off, Commander," Herzer pointed out. "I'm last. I'm going to watch the launch in pri-fly; most of the guys up there are pretty green."

"Hey, Joanna," Bast said, swinging down from the mainmast. "Care to give me a ride?"

"Sure, you're light," Joanna said as one of the Silverdrake let out an evil hiss.

"Quit that you bastard," Vickie replied, slapping the wyvern on the nose. "Najah hates waiting for others to take off."

"She can go ahead as far as I'm concerned," Joanna said.

"Silverdrake should launch last," Major Sassan called from pri-fly. "They've got the shortest legs."

"I'll just take her to where she won't mind so much,"

Vickie said, mounting the wyvern. At an unseen signal the wyvern grabbed the ratlines and started climbing the mainmast. The movement was very like a climbing bat's; the wings had three fingerlike appendages which the Silverdrake used for climbing hand over hand up the rigging. When it reached the mainsail it climbed out on the crosstree until it reached the end, where it perched. After a moment it slid around until it was facing head down, its wings folded in against its body. It was apparent that it could take off at any moment.

"Fucking show-off," Joanna chuckled.

"I didn't know they could do that," Herzer said, still looking up at the dragon above.

"Neither did I," said Skipper Karcher. "I wonder how long she can hang like that?"

"Well, if we don't get started, ma'am, we may find out the hard way," Herzer pointed out as the other Silverdrake started climbing the rigging. He'd been surprised at Karcher's sudden appearance, she had been in pri-fly just a second ago, but tried to avoid showing it. The skipper had the uncanny ability to simply appear; even with his keen hearing he never heard her walking up. And she didn't just walk; he'd seen her drop from the rigging a good ten meters and land on the balls of her feet, silently.

"Good point," Karcher said.

"Fleet's signaling, ma'am," the signal midshipman called. "Prepare for air-operations, tack."

"Major Sassan, prepare to come into the wind!" Karcher said, making a seemingly impossible leap upwards to a ratline, then flinging herself across open air back into pri-fly. The only person Herzer had ever seen move like that was Bast. He suddenly wondered how many cat genes there were in wood elves.

As the fleet tacked into the wind the carriers began launching their dragons. Joanna was very nearly the first in the air and she headed for altitude faster than the wyverns, forming up in a lazy figure eight over the carrier.

"Come on up," she signaled, "the air's fine."

If Edmund thought he could catch up on his paperwork at sea he was wrong; dispatch sloops were cheap.

"Shar, this is insane," Edmund said as the admiral stepped into the room and tossed his beret on the desk. He was carrying a heavy bag, which he set on the floor.

"And you're not even looking at what I stopped," Shar noted. The admiral and his staff had been "filtering" the material sent to Edmund. Edmund had ensured that they knew *what* to filter, but the remainder was still a heavy load.

"I know, I'm looking at what you couldn't stop," Edmund growled. "There are requests for clarification from *Congress* on things we had settled a month ago. Buships wants to know why we're ordering heavier standing rigging. When I told them, they flipped a lid."

"I know, they don't want the crosstrees weighted by the wyverns," Shar said. "It does make the sailing a tad tougher. Be bad in a storm."

"The Silverdrake can't *hang* up there in a storm," Edmund noted.

"Storms come up fast sometimes," Shar explained.

"You want my suggestion, send them Wellington's answer."

"Wellington's answer?" Edmund said.

"What, you've never heard of Wellington's response in the Spanish Campaign?" the admiral said with a chuckle.

"No," Edmund admitted. "I know quite a bit about Wellington, fine guy, several of his quotes have been badly mangled over the years. But that's a new one on me. Do tell."

"Basically he sent a message back to the army high command to the effect that he was being asked too many stupid questions. Especially about supply issues. 'I can win battles or count nails, not both.'"

"Hah!" Edmund snorted. "Okay, find me the original. I'll quote it with a copy to the Armed Services committee, that pack of goat-riding nitwits, Navy command, Buships and Sheida. Thanks. What's in the bag?"

"Last word we had is that the New Destiny fleet hasn't sailed yet, right?" Shar said, pulling a large metal device from the bag. It had a dial on one side and the other had a complicated clamping arrangement.

"Nope. Looks like they don't have their act together as well as we do. Thank God for Ennesby and Trahn."

"Well, this is one way to even up the odds a bit, Evan's latest marvel." Chang turned the dial slightly and set the device on the desk, face up. After a moment a large spike sprung out, hard.

"What are we spiking?" Edmund asked, touching the tip. It was partially hollow. "And what are we squirting?"

"Ships," Shar said with a grin. "And concentrated

acid. The spike drives into the wood and squirts out acid under pressure. If it doesn't penetrate the hull, the acid is still going to dissolve a big hole. If it does penetrate the hull, and it isn't in the bilges, it's going to burn out a hole big enough that it will sink the ship with luck. Put it in dry dock at the least."

"Very nice," Edmund said, dryly. "You know the story about when the Navy tried to come up with something like this?"

"No, I was in durance-not-so-vile in Blackbeard," Shar said. "Do tell."

"There's a group of companies that have set up around Washan. They get contracts for various things related to the military, sutlers, designers, that sort of thing. Anyway, the Navy went to one of those companies and had it design a mine. The company spent a year and the mine they came up with was three times that size and didn't work. And Evan came up with this in, what? A week?"

Shar laughed and shook his head.

"I take it this is the answer to how the mer can do more than just handle recon and communications," Edmund asked.

"What do you think?"

"I think I wouldn't want to be a mer carrying one of these things into harbor," Edmund said and sighed. "Not with orca and ixchitl screening the entrance. But then, I'm old and aware of my mortality. Volunteers only. And we'll have to get a ship in close to carry them."

"Not necessarily," Chang said with a shrug. "We can load a few of them on a whale and have him carry them into the area. Then have the mer cross-load for the rest of the distance."

"However you want to do it," Edmund said.

"You're not happy about it," Shar said.

"No, I'm not," Edmund admitted. "It's going to be a nearly suicidal mission. If we lose a few mer and take out a carrier or two, that's good casualty ratio. I still don't care for it. It's a good idea, though, so run with it."

"You have a point," Shar said.

"And keep it very close to your vest," Edmund added. "Need to know only. We're still leaking information like a sieve."

"You rang, Joel?"

Sheida's projection was hanging in midair and looked impatient.

"Indeed," Travante replied. "I'm trying to track down some New Destiny agents with the fleet. Unfortunately Conner has apparently gotten very canny with his communications. My agents have been attempting to localize them with Evan's devices, so far with no success. I need something a bit more technological. Sorry."

Avatars gave off a mild electromagnetic field. Evan Mayerle had used that fact to trace down a New Destiny agent on board the *Bonhomme Richard* during the diplomatic mission to the mer. However, the traces were faint and if the communication was brief and random it was nearly impossible to find them with the relatively low-tech methods available.

"I'll ken some devices for your agents," Sheida said with a sigh. "Which ships?"

"The *Bonhomme Richard*, again, the *Alida Diaconescu* and the *Hazhir*."

"I've never heard of the *Diaconescu*," Sheida temporized.

"It's one of the dreadnoughts that was converted to an anti-dragon platform," Joel explained. "That and the *Hazhir* are the ones that I'm bothered by the most, frankly. If someone's on the *Diacon* they can be giving out designs and specs for the new guns, not just that we have them. And the *Hazhir* is a new source, a brand new one. I'd like to squelch it as soon as possible."

"I'll need contact information for your agents," Sheida pointed out. "What news on the attack on Edmund?"

"Nothing useful," Joel admitted. "I got the news that the hit was out just before the attack, far too short a time to do anything about it. The one survivor that was caught sang like a canary but he didn't know anything. Barely knew the people he was with and they were all recruited from waterfront bars. 'A man in a pub.' Nothing to go on there. Bast apparently killed one of the recruiters, which was unfortunate. So far no expansion to the family, though, it's all on Edmund. Oh, and money has been offered if Major Herrick is included."

"Chansa has got us outnumbered," Sheida mused. "Why is he so desperate?"

"Angry, more likely," Paul pointed out. "He never did take well to any sort of frustration and Edmund has been very frustrating to him."

"Agreed. Anything else?"

"You're aware that Paul has a . . . breeding program?"

"If you're talking about his harem, yes," Sheida said, flexing her jaw.

"I may have an entree to it," Joel said, carefully. "They have put out a bid for some personal effects, notably cosmetics. One of my agents, not coincidentally, is a cosmetic supplier."

"Cosmetic supplier?" Sheida said, raising her eyebrow.

"Cosmetics are luxury items in Ropasa," Joel said, impassively. "This permits my agent to move among the wealthy with a fully justified cover. And since he is being supported independently, shall we say, he can afford to underbid his competition at need. With luck we will be able to penetrate the harem."

"And you think that will help?" Sheida asked.

"I suspect that Paul may talk to the girls." Joel shrugged. "Even if it is about inconsequential items, they may be pieced together. When he is there and when he is gone is data. Of course, the agent may not be able to find a useable contact. But I feel it is worth a shot."

"Pillow talk," Sheida said, shaking her head.

"The honey trap is one of the oldest traps in the business," Joel noted. "Men tend to talk afterwards. It's amazing what they will tell a pretty woman."

"I've noticed that effect myself," Sheida admitted, dryly. "If they stay awake. Now, let's get the information on your agents on the ships and I'll get on to the billion other things I have to do. And I wish you luck on your harem adventure."

CHAPTER SEVENTEEN

Megan smiled thinly as the vendor's eyes flickered down and then back up to look her in the eye.

After a certain amount of persuading, Paul had allowed her to begin looking for another "sundries" vendor. Paul was constantly on Christel, and Megan now, to keep costs down and one of the harem's worst expenses, after food, was cosmetics. When Megan had arrived there hadn't been any. Prior to the Fall there were a variety of ways to "touch up" the face, and body, from skin color mods to nan-nite makeup. After the Fall it had taken a while for "luxury" items to appear; as far as she knew Megan was still the only perfumer in Ropasa. But as part of her plan Megan had found, through the kitchen staff that handled all the "sundries" vending, a cosmetics supplier.

Unfortunately, the price the supplier charged was infernally high. Admittedly, some of the materials were either not found in Ropasa or exceedingly rare. But still, the prices were just outrageous.

Paul had finally let her accept bids from competitors and this vendor was the winning bidder. If his material met spec.

And if he could keep his eyes in his head.

"Sorry about that," the man said. He seemed to be over the "outfit" and examining her face. But she decided to ignore it.

"That's fine," Megan replied. "As long as you remember that my eyes are up here," she added, pointing at her face.

"Yes, Miss . . . ?"

"Sung," Megan replied. "Megan Sung. Now, I like your pricing, but I'm not comfortable with the shades on your blushes. They're a tad brown."

"We don't have access to a firm red," the vendor replied, nodding and looking down at his notes. "The best red, the brightest available, is vermillion. But it's made from . . ."

"Mercury," Megan said, smiling thinly. "A toxic heavy metal."

"Did my predecessor . . . ?" the man asked, looking up in startlement.

"I tested all the cosmetics for base materials in my lab," Megan replied. "I rejected his reds for that very reason. Another point against him, besides price. I'm glad to hear you don't use it. There is no other high quality red available?"

"Say rather that there is none that is not toxic," the man said with a grimace. "To one degree or another. *My* lab is working on a petroleum based red. We know that it once existed, but I've been unable to find any hardcopy data on how to produce it. And, even then, we anticipate that it will have some trace of metallics in it."

"There are red dyes being used in clothes," Megan said, gesturing at her top. It was a brilliant red silk.

"And the people using those dyes are quite reticent about what they use." The vendor grinned. "Also, some high-brilliance red dyes that are functional for clothing are not functional for cosmetics. There is an . . . intimate contact with cosmetics. Any volatile in them is transmitted through the skin. Which is why testing for them used to be so acute."

"Unfortunately, I need a red," Megan said, frowning. "If you're willing to give up some of *your* industrial secrets, I'd be willing to do some experimentation of my own. Not for production; the girls use far more than *I'd* be able to produce."

"I understand," the vendor replied with a grin. "We'll keep working on it. We've got some new mixtures," he continued, pulling a sample out of his case. "And we're working with some of the less toxic materials, to try to find one that is suitable. But you can understand that I truly do not want to poison any of Paul Bowman's . . . friends."

"Understandable." Megan grinned, opening up the leather case. The man held out a hand mirror as she brushed some of the rouge onto her cheek and considered the color. "That's . . . better. Nearly right. What about lip gloss?"

"That's actually easier," the man replied. "An addition of yellow brings out the red. The yellow does have a *trace* quantity of lead in it. But our test subjects haven't experienced any notable side effects."

"Test subjects?" Megan asked, carefully.

"We test all the cosmetics on animals first," the vendor replied, shrugging. "Then employees use them. There is no compulsion used. And none of our customers have had any complaints. So far, so good."

"Is there much of a market?" Megan asked, doing her other cheek as the man pulled out a gloss sample.

"More and more of one," the vendor admitted. "Although this account will be . . . substantial from what you've alluded."

"We use a lot of cosmetics." Megan sighed, pouting her lips to apply the gloss. Now *that* was red.

"Again, I understand," the man said, carefully.

"Oh, Paul's not here *that* much," Megan said, looking up from the mirror. "But he turns up without any warning. So the girls use it every day regardless. And they're always trying for the right new 'look' that he'll particularly like. Harem politics."

"Yes," the man said, uncomfortably.

"You can use the word," Megan replied, smiling thinly. "We do."

"As you wish," the vendor said. "I can start supplying by the end of the week. The terms are acceptable?"

"Quite acceptable," Megan replied. "Much better than your competitors'."

"My competitors have neither my sources nor my business acumen," the vendor said with a grin. "On the subject of a 'new look.' I have some employees, female, who perform makeup seminars. Would it be possible . . . ?"

"Unlikely," Megan said with a moue. "I had to

practically twist Paul's arm to let me do the negotiating on this. Visitors are extremely rare in the harem."

"Must be boring," the man said, frowning.

"It's safe and we're well cared for," Megan replied, cutting off that line of questioning. "We can expect the supplies by the end of the week?"

"Yes, ma'am," the vendor said, laying out some more samples. "These, of course, are on the house." As he said it he slid a piece of paper out from under one of the samples. On it it said, "Travante."

"Thank you," Megan said, looking at it like a mouse in front of a snake. "What is this?"

"It's a new line of cosmetics we're working on," the man said, turning the paper over so she could see the list of available materials. "It's a much brighter line that has been thoroughly inspected. Some of the colors are unique. For example, we have a lovely azure eye shadow."

Megan's father had been on assignment in the Asur Islands prior to the Fall. But this could just as easily be a trap as a real contact.

"I've always liked azure," Megan replied with calculated interest.

"Yes," the man said, smiling as he packed up his case. "Many do; it's like the colors of a bright new day."

It's a bright new day, Megan. In her memory her father was patting her hair, as he did every morning he was home. *Time to wake up.* Either Paul had her father and was testing her . . . no, that made no sense. If Paul knew she was Joel Travante's daughter he'd act upon it, not test her. And there was no reason for them to know that phrase, even if her father had been captured. It *had* to be a contact.

"Well, let's talk about that next week," Megan replied, handing back the slip of paper folded so the name didn't show. "You'll be here?"

"Yes, ma'am," the man said, his brow furrowing. *How to reply without giving myself away?*

"You understand that I'll have to do a forensic analysis of your materials?" Megan asked.

"Of course," the vendor replied. "I could expect nothing less."

"Paul is very fatherly towards us," Megan continued. "But if something happened to one of the girls at the very least I would expect that there would be a thorough investigation. The repercussions would be unpleasant."

"I understand," the man said after a pregnant pause. "I look forward to meeting with you again."

"I'd like to add something," Megan said, looking at him sternly. "You will not discuss this with *anyone*. That is very important. Am I absolutely clear about that?"

"I don't discuss my customer's business, Miss Sung," the vendor replied.

"Not with your partners and not up any sort of corporate chain," Megan said, firmly. "Paul *will* hear. And we don't want that to happen, do we?"

"Madame, I assure you . . ."

"And I am assuring *you*," Megan replied. "Your new line will go *nowhere* if you pass around that you're in contact with Paul's . . . friends. He *will* hear about it. And he won't respond pleasantly."

"Yes, ma'am," the man said, gulping. "I understand. Completely."

"I'll see about arranging a seminar," Megan

continued. "The girls would like it, that's for sure. Until next week," she said, standing up.

"Until next week."

Martin St. John was a happy man. He had been a thief, a con artist and a murderer before the Fall, in an environment where all three were, to say the least, difficult. After the Fall he simply shifted his techniques, finding the basic methods and thought processes the same if somewhat more sanguine.

That was until he'd fallen astray of Brother Conner. He and Conner had been in the same society of professional ne'er-do-wells prior to the Fall. Somehow the bastard had tracked him down and blackmailed him into heading an expedition to the Southern Isles to break up the potential alliance of the mer and the UFS. And that had gone so well that he had ended up stranded on a desert island, starving to death.

That was until a friendly fisherman had picked him up and brought him back to town. Back in town the "friendly fisherman" had turned out to be none other than Special Fisking Inspector Joel the Bastard Travante who knew *exactly* who the "stranded merchant" on the island was. And who had had heavies waiting to ensure "Martin" didn't disappear in the Caribbean darkness.

So Martin had been given a few unpalatable choices. He could stand trial for various war crimes; the ixchitl, kraken and orcas that he had commanded had not been particularly nice. In which case, if convicted, he would be sentenced to either hard labor, which he abhorred, or death, which he abhorred even more.

Or. There was always an "or." Or he could, of his

"own free will" accept a loyalty geas and go to work for the UFS. Plying his skills, so to speak. Back in Ropasa where Conner was Joel the Bastard Travante's opposite number.

Nobody said the "or" would be a *good* "or."

Let's see, guaranteed hard labor, probably death. Or, probably death.

But. There was always a "but" too. But if he took the job, and did it well, he would be fisking over Conner. Conner, the bastard, who had left him to die on a burning ship. It was that that had tipped the scales. The chance to really *stick* it to Conner. He'd never liked him anyway.

Now, though, lord did he have information. Joel Travante, the man he hated second in line after Conner, was about to find out that his daughter was spreading her legs for Paul Bowman. Glorious revenge. And all he had to do was follow his loyalty conditioning. Lovely.

But he had to be careful. If he failed to deliver the information, or if it got picked up by New Destiny, Joel the Bastard would pull his life like a plug. And he couldn't deviate from routine one iota or, more than likely, Conner's internal security goons would pick him up with similar results. But, fortunately, he'd set up a hard contact method in advance.

Whether Megan the Harlot knew it or not, she was immured in a castle in the middle of Stayorg City. And no more than two days away by fast coach was Iruck, where his next meeting was to take place. And in Iruck . . .

Martin tried not to whistle in glee as he strode through the nighttime streets and tapped on a discreet door in an alleyway. A small slot shot back and a grim face looked him over then unbolted the door.

The lamp-lit interior of the room was decked out in red and various females lounged around in practically nothing. Martin tried not to grin again as he looked at the girls, most of whom were slightly Changed. There was a tiger-girl and two wolf girls and one that was a bit too much cat. The girl even had a tail. But what he was looking for was upstairs.

Very few people in the brothel knew that Martin owned it. And the reason he owned the brothel was on the top floor. He knocked on the door and entered at a whistled reply.

The girl in the dimly lit room was enormously tall with what appeared to be hugely outsized breasts. They were, in fact, flight muscles, for Joie had been one of the rare individuals, pre-Fall, to have herself Changed so that she could achieve true flight. Her arms flexed normally but the bones of her pinky fingers had been hyperextended into flight bones. Those bones, and all the rest throughout her body, were a hollow honeycomb of advanced fibers and her skin was covered in a fine down that was both aerodynamic and warm. She stood nearly two and a half meters and her wings at full extension stretched for seven and a half to either side. Between the enormous "breasts," angelic face, long, downy legs and her beautiful carriage she was incredibly popular with those men who had money to spend on the truly exotic. But it was the ability for fully powered flight that had attracted Martin and caused him to spend Joel's money like water to purchase her. Because she could carry a message all the way across the continent in a single night.

"Hello, Joie," Martin said, smiling.

"Hello, Martin," Joie sighed, sadly. She was reclined on a long, narrow bed. "Let me guess, you want me to play the fallen angel *again*."

"I'd love to, frankly," Martin grinned. "But you're not going to be playing with me, or anyone else, unless you want to. I need you to do me one more service and then you are free."

Joie sat up on the bed and turned up the lamp, looking him in the eye coldly.

"Don't play with me, Martin," she said, her face working. "Do not do this to me. I don't care what geas you have on me, I *will* kill you."

"Free," Martin said, extracting a small tube. "Here are your orders. Fly from here to the coast of Ropasa, the Breton coast." He pulled out a map and pointed to the spot. "You can find it easily by following the Lore then heading north. There is a town at this river. Just up the coast is a house on a promontory. It has a widow's walk and there is always a light that shines upward. You'll have to make it there by dawn. Can you?"

"If I stuff myself," the girl said.

"Stuff yourself, then," Martin said, handing her the tube. "Take this. There's a person at the house. Tell her 'Jean has a long mustache' and she will take care of you. The next night go down to the beach and carry a lantern. That will be Saturday. You must make it by Saturday."

"I will," Joie said.

"People will meet you on the beach. Give them the capsule and tell them you're to be given transport. They'll have to arrange it. Stay at the house until it's time to leave. Never come back."

"I won't," Joie said. "Trust me."

"It's a moonless night tonight," Martin said. "You shouldn't be spotted."

"This is real?" Joie said, tears in her eyes.

"This is real," Martin said with a nod. "It's dangerous, though."

"I don't care," Joie spat. "I've wished I was dead enough nights. To be free again. To be able to soar again."

"You're out of shape," Martin worried.

"I'll make it," Joie said. "I'll make it if I had to fly to Norau."

"That shouldn't be necessary," Martin said with a lopsided grin. "Go now. Eat. Then leave." He reached out and stroked the down on her cheek. "I know you won't miss me, but I'll miss you. Upon the completion of your mission you are freed of all geas, on my word as your owner. Now, go."

Joie felt every day of her confinement as she flew. She had done push-ups in her room, trying to work her wings in the event she could break the expensive geas her first "master" had purchased to control her. But push-ups were not flying, and too many of her muscles were out of shape. She had tried to warm up slowly by being careful heading up to altitude. But she could not rest. Not if she was going to make it by dawn. She had to fly as hard as she ever had in her life and it had strained her to the utmost.

One thing that Martin didn't know about her was that she didn't need his directions. She had also opted for a navigational package—she always knew "where" she was—and if she had a good idea where a location

was she could fly to it almost unerringly. She avoided
the Lore, which had many villages growing up along
it, and headed straight for the coast, just north of its
joining with the sea.

There, nearly out of energy and her muscles screaming, she banked north, a giant white bird against the
lightening sky. She hadn't been able to fly as fast as
she'd hoped so the sun was already starting to peek
up above the land. She ducked down to get out of
the sunlight but she knew that some people must have
seen her flying against the sky. Finally she spotted the
house and stooped like an exhausted falcon into the
garden in the back. With quick, if weary, steps she
crossed to the door at the back and pounded on it,
looking around at the pleasant herb garden and, even
better, the high hedge that surrounded the house.

The door was answered by an old woman, at least
three hundred if she was a day. She had gray hair that
had remnants of red in it and a pinched face that still
echoed a beauty of the old days. The woman looked
at the giant bird-woman imperturbably.

"Yes?" the woman asked.

"Jean has a long mustache?" Joie asked. "Does that
mean anything to you?"

"Did anyone see you?" the woman snapped.

"Maybe," Joie said, shrugging as only a woman
with fifteen meter wings can. "But I sort of look like
a really big bird when I'm flying."

"Get in here," the woman said, standing to the
side.

Joie slipped through the door, pulling her wings
in around her, and looked around. The kitchen was
light and airy with a scrubbed table, copper pots, a

large wood stove and hams and herbs hanging from the ceiling. It smelled strongly of onion, as if the floor had been washed with it.

That was about all the impression Joie got as the woman hustled her to a door and down into the basement. The basement was half filled with various oddments, bits of furniture that had waited for repair until they were dust, covered boxes, broken barrels. But the back half was filled with wine racks. The woman went to one of these and swung it back revealing a small room.

"In here," the woman said.

"I'm starving," Joie replied. "And I need to go to the beach tonight. It must be tonight."

"We'll see," the woman replied. "Going to the beach does no one any good if the area is crawling with Change, girl. Go in there and I'll find you some food. Quickly."

Joie folded herself into the room, which was too low for her, and sat on a chair that was too small. The room was instantly dark but she fumbled on the table and found a match. The match led to a candle and the candle led to an examination of the room. There wasn't much to it. A bed too short. A chair too small. A table too low. And a very short ceiling. It was apparently ventilated, but Joie couldn't find from where. The woman returned with a large bowl of thick stew and a loaf of excellent bread and cautioned Joie to remain quiet no matter what she heard. After eating, Joie blew out the candle and settled down on the too short bed, pulling her wings around her for warmth and comfort.

Later she half remembered thumping but it passed

from one bad dream to another where something was chasing her through the night. There was a silver cord around her heart and no matter how far or how fast she flew it couldn't break. She awoke as the door slid back and the old woman waved at her.

"Lucky it wasn't Changed," the old woman said, much more friendly. "There was one Sniffer but with the herbs in the garden and the onion and pepper on the floor there was no way for him to pick up your scent. You were seen but no one was sure what you were. Most said a large seabird, maybe an albatross badly off-course."

"I do *not* look like an albatross," Joie said.

"No, you don't." The woman chuckled. "It's nearly nightfall. You need more to eat?"

"If you please," Joie said. "I might have to fly again tonight."

The woman set her down to another bowl of stew and more bread but when Joie looked up piteously the woman sniffed and brought out cold chicken, more bread, more stew, until Joie finally waved her back.

"It takes a lot of energy to fly," Joie said in embarrassment at the feast she had been served. The old woman had contented herself with one bowl of stew and a bite of bread.

"I can believe it," the woman said, taking a sip of wine.

"My name's Joie," Joie said, filling up the silence. "What's yours?"

"Mine is my own," the woman replied with a grimace. "And yours is yours. No names. No names and no questions, that way if you're caught you can't give anything away. I take it you weren't trained for this?"

"No, I've been in a brothel for the last four years," Joie answered, tartly. "I don't even know what 'this' is."

"There you go, telling me things," the woman said, throwing up her hands. "Although, I'll admit that my description of you is distinctive."

"So what do we talk about?" Joie asked.

"Nothing, by preference," the old woman said grimly, standing up and picking up the dishes. "It will be dark in less than an hour. I will tell you where to go on the beach and give you a lantern. After that it is up to you."

The selkie point popped his head above the water and glanced at the shore then dove again. He gestured at the team leader and signed: "Lantern."

The team leader was less than thrilled. They'd used this drop-point before. Eventually it was going to be compromised. If it wasn't already. But they had their orders. He waved the point in and the rest of the team followed, twisting through the water in the aquabatics that were their forte.

The point popped his head above the water again and watched the lantern for a moment. At first it was steady, then the light winked once, twice, three times. He dove again and headed for the beach, mentally saying his prayers.

When he reached the wave-line he poked his head out of the water again and looked around carefully. The lantern was out, which was right. But there was a white figure where it had been. He watched it for a moment, then looked around, reading the shadows, looking for anything out of place. It looked right, but one more time he scanned the beach, then humped forward as fast as he could, headed for the distant scree.

Joie had been told to watch for heads in the water but when the selkies came up she was surprised. She wasn't sure at first if they were her contact but she uncovered the bullseye lantern. When the heads disappeared she covered it again. Then, when they appeared again, she uncovered it and sent the recognition sign, mentally preparing to take off for altitude if they were with New Destiny.

Her surprise was complete, however, when they burst out of the water in a welter of spray and started to cross the beach towards her. A small one was in the lead but right behind him was a huge specimen, at least three meters, with a crossbow on his back the size of a small ballista. As she watched, the big selkie reached the edge of the beach and started setting up the crossbow on a tripod as the smaller one scanned the darkness.

"You have something for us?" a selkie asked. He had moved so quietly, despite his ungainly method of travel, that she hadn't even noticed him approach.

"A message tube," Joie said. "And I was told to tell you this is *very* important. Nobody, *nobody* opens it but Joel Travante or Edmund Talbot."

"I'll pass that on."

"I'm supposed to be free, now," Joie said. "They said you would get me out."

"*That* is tough," the selkie leader admitted. "I'll pass it on, but I can't guarantee anything. There are no ships in this area right now and the New Destiny fleet just sailed. And I doubt you could swim out."

"I *have* to get out of Ropasa," Joie said, desperately. "Technically I'm an escaped slave. They'll cut off my wings if I'm captured."

"Bastards," the team leader said. "Look, we've had some contact with the McClure clan in Gael. Go there. I'll pass on the word that you're there and we'll try to get pick-up in. Okay?"

"I can find Gael," Joie said, grimly. "But where are the McClures?"

"West coast, just across from Hibernia." The team leader used the fingers on his flippers to sketch in a map. "Here. Land in this area and ask anyone about the McClures. They're either allied with them or fighting them or both. But they'll know where you can find Laird McClure. Tell him Ryan sent you and to take care of you until we come pick you up. We pay our debts."

"I will, Ryan," the girl said, leaning down and kissing him on the top of his wet bullet head. "Thank you."

"You're welcome," Ryan replied. "Now we have to get the fisk out of here." He put the message tube in a pouch on his harness and turned to the water. "You take care. Team, move it down to the water by the numbers."

Joie watched as the team reversed its assault on the beach and then as they disappeared into the black water. It was only when the last selkie waved a flipper at her in farewell that she rubbed out the map and took off to the west, flying out and over the rapidly receding seal team.

CHAPTER EIGHTEEN

"Admiral," the messenger said after a tap on the door.

"Yes?" Shar and Edmund answered simultaneously, then grinned.

"It's actually a message for Admiral Chang, Admiral." The messenger gulped, nervously. "New Destiny fleet has sailed."

"Which one?" Edmund asked.

"It was just that, sir, the fleet," the messenger replied.

"Shar?" Edmund said.

"I'll query for more information," Chang said, getting to his feet. "But I suspect they mean it's both."

"How many of those devices of Evan's do we have?" Edmund asked as the messenger shut the door.

"Only a half a dozen. More are being made on shore but getting them out to the area is going to be tricky, especially if the fleet is at sea. They'll have to avoid them while moving into position. Tricky."

"We'll worry about that later," Edmund said. "Let's find out what's going on."

"Both fleets have sailed." Major Steffani Viesseman was the fleet's intelligence officer. Packing Shar's staff onto the ship, especially with the addition of Edmund and his aides, had been a difficult proposition but they'd managed it.

Packing them into Edmund's quarters was even harder.

"Right now the information is sketchy," she continued, pointing to the large map on the wall. "But it looks like only one carrier is with the invasion fleet. The rest have separated and are headed south, between the Briton Isles and Ropasa."

"What the hell are they playing at?" Chang asked.

"I don't know, sir," the G-2 admitted. "Converging columns comes to mind. They could stay to the south of the invasion force. That way if we attack the invasion force they catch us between two forces. Or they could be headed for another target."

"Do we have anything on the composition of the attack force?" Edmund asked.

"Five carriers, anti-dragon ships, frigates and some clipper ships of a type we don't recognize," the G-2 said. "The mer that are shadowing them say they're not rigged for gunnery, though." She looked at her notes. "They say there's an unusually large number of boats along the sides."

"And they appear to be headed south?" Shar asked.

"At last word, sir," the G-2 nodded.

"That's a raid fleet." Demetra Staffieri was the operations officer for the fleet, a petite brunette whose blue eyes turned almost black and cold when she was thinking hard, as she was now. "The clippers are carrying troops, five gets you ten, sir."

"Blackbeard," Edmund said, suddenly. "They're going for Blackbeard."

Mer children could not use their gills for the first two years of their lives. Thus they had to live an amphibian existence. Blackbeard Base had been built for the specific purpose of protecting the children and pregnant women of the mer. It was guarded by the largest force of Blood Lords outside of Raven's Mill but there was no way that it was going to be able to hold out against the force being sent against it and everyone at the table knew it.

"That's only a guess, sir," the G-2 pointed out. "Probably a good guess, but only that."

"If we sail to engage the combat fleet we'll be playing catch-up with the invasion fleet," Chang said, looking at the map. "And if we engage the invasion fleet and they *are* headed for Blackbeard we're going to have a passel of dead mer-children on our conscience."

"We don't have the land forces to stop that level of assault," Edmund said. "They can swarm anywhere that they choose to land. I'm not sure they can push far in from the beachhead, but they can *take* a beachhead."

"Let me point out that we're not sure we can destroy their combat forces as well," the G-3 said, carefully. "What about evacuating Blackbeard? Let them take an empty base."

"There were a lot of ships going down there carrying supplies and construction workers," the G-4 interjected.

"Yes, and they're all gone now," Edmund said. "Maybe if we left the Blood Lords behind we could get enough ships down there in time to pull out the mer. They probably wouldn't even mind a hopeless last stand. But I'm not going to countenance one."

"Interesting question," Shar said, smiling faintly. "Does this fall into your decision or mine?"

"Mine," Edmund said, leaning back in his chair and looking at the overhead. Thank God he'd gotten over his seasickness so he could think clearly. "When did they sail? How old is this information?"

"Yesterday morning," the G-2 said. "The delphinos had been pushed back from the harbor. They picked them up well outside."

Edmund steepled his fingers and looked at them for a moment, then flexed his jaw.

"Head north," he said harshly. "Shar, implement opsec plan orca."

"We're going for the invasion fleet, then," the G-3 said, doubtfully. "You think the Blood Lords can hold out."

"We're sailing north," Chang replied. "Northeast actually. Do that now. And I need all the carrier commanders and the dragon contingent commanders to fly on for a meeting. After that, I'll need message packets taken to all the other ship commanders. That is all for now."

The staff stood up shaking their heads and filed out of the room.

"So you're going for the combat fleet?" Shar asked.

"Not exactly," Edmund said. "And I need an operational immediate message sent to all land forces: Plan Fell Deeds."

Colonel Olin Rienzo thought, as he always did, that Sir Robert Kane, Baron Marshfield, looked like the cavalier's cavalier.

They had known each other, distantly, before the Fall when Rienzo had been a breeder of thoroughbreds and Kane had been a noted eventer and breeder of Hanarahs. Eventing was the most rigorous of all the equestrian sports, a combination of cross-country riding, dressage and jumping, and Kane had been a world-class eventer. At the time Rienzo had found the cavalier's affectation of wearing big floppy hats and period dress, even during events, to be humorous. It was only after the Fall that Rienzo found out that eventing was more of a sideline for Kane than anything; his real passion was recreation, specifically eighteenth-century cavalry.

When Kane had turned up, with no more authority than a handwritten note from Edmund Talbot, with the mission of raising what Talbot called a "cavalry legion," Rienzo had initially been skeptical. It took years to train a cavalryman. Fighting from the back of a horse took more than just being able to hold on. For that matter, cavalry horses had to be intensively trained. Kane, however, for all that he looked and sometimes acted like the reincarnation of an eighteenth-century cavalier, was methodical about military training. He had gathered together a large group of riders, and an even larger group of horses, begged, borrowed and stolen equipment and set up a brutal training program for man and horse. It had produced a force of four thousand horsemen, and nearly sixteen thousand horses, that was about as good a cavalry force as any that had ever existed. It was also costing like fire, but they found the money somehow. Some of it had come from what should have been federal taxes, some of it had come from mysterious sources elsewhere, but they had managed it.

He trotted his horse up the hill to where Kane and Ensign Tao were watching the current exercise. The full regiment had formed on one side of a large valley facing a "notional" infantry formation. As one squadron menaced the front of the formation the other two squadrons, at the command of a set of flapping flags, broke left and galloped to the flank of the notional formation, a large number of stacks of hay in the middle of the field. As soon as they were in position all three squadrons wheeled and charged the "enemy formation," the groups passing through the formation and each other like teeth in a wheel. As they approached the formation the long lances came down and skewered the bales of hay, then swords came out and slashed downward. In a few minutes the ground was covered with slashed-up hay.

"Not bad," Kane said. "Bravo troop, First Squadron was slow."

"Got it," Tao said, making a note in his book. The ensign was a new addition. He had turned up out of nowhere on a knackered out post horse. Since he had apparently been one of Talbot's aides, and the fleet had sailed with Talbot on board no more than two days before he turned up, he must have ridden like hell to get to Kent; it was the better part of two thousand kilometers from the coast. But the next day he had been up, limping a little but doing his duty. What his duties were weren't quite clear. He mostly hung around Kane as some sort of supernumerary doing messenger and aide type duties.

"It's looking good, Colonel," Kane said, spinning his Hanarah in place and raising his wide floppy hat in greeting.

Kane was a tall man, somewhere around two hundred pounds, with long blond hair that was going almost entirely gray. He had a flowing mustache and a small goatee that on anyone else would look absurd but so fitted his personality it was unnoticeable. He was wearing leather pants with thigh and shin greaves and a black silk doublet that was open down the chest to expose a red silk undershirt. And since he hadn't turned around the only way for him to know it was Rienzo was from the sound of the colonel's horse.

"General Kane," Rienzo said, saluting. "Yes, it is going well. Amazingly well."

"I wasn't sure, frankly, when Edmund laid out his training plan," Kane said, spinning back to watch the squadrons reform. "And we'll have to see how the lads do in combat. But I think they'll do well. Yes, I do think, very well. I'd wish we had more training at managing the pursuit, but that's as may be."

"Yes, sir," Rienzo said. "We'll have to see. The reason I'm here, though, is that there's a general operational immediate from Edmund Talbot. It's addressed to 'all land commands' and was copied to us. I thought you should see it."

"Oh," Kane said, glancing at him for a message form.

"It was just two words: 'Fell Deeds.'"

Kane's normally gay face went somber at that and he nodded. "Tao."

"Yes, sir," the ensign said, reaching into a saddlebag and pulling out a sheaf of dispatches Rienzo didn't even know he had. He sorted through them and pulled one out, handing it to Kane.

Kane drew a poignard and ripped through the heavy linen envelope, pulling out a sheaf of papers. He glanced at the opening paragraph and nodded.

"Colonel, the regiment will prepare for movement. Three days rations, combat gear, two remounts for every rider. Leave all the horses that aren't entirely up to par."

"May I ask where we are going?" Rienzo said, his brow wrinkling.

"No, you may not," Kane answered, folding the papers and stuffing them in his doublet. "But you can assure yourself that fell deeds await."

The Blood Lord came to attention and rapped on the door, twice.

"Come."

At the word the soldier marched into the room and took the position of parade rest, looking two decimeters above the head of the NCO at the desk.

"Gunnery Sergeant, Captain Jackson has received a warning order of a possible heavy attack. The majority of the Destiny fleet appears to be headed this way along with a sizeable landing contingent."

The man behind the desk was old, his close-cut hair gray and his skin lined from time in the sun. But his back was straight and the hand that lifted the stogie to his mouth was firm.

"Estimated time of arrival?" the gunnery sergeant grunted, getting to his feet and walking to the window. The view out the window was bright, revealing a blue-green harbor and a fortress under construction. It was only half built, though, despite a few hundred workers swarming over it like ants. In the water a group of mer-women were playing with their children, watched by a group of soldiers in armor that seemed far too heavy for the heat. Despite that, the platoon of Blood Lords were as rigid as so many iron bars. As he watched, three members of the platoon marched to the water butt, drank heavily, then marched back to their positions.

"At least three weeks, Gunnery Sergeant."

"Dragon-carriers?"

"Five, Gunnery Sergeant."

The gunny grunted and then chuckled.

"Good. What's the weather report?"

"I'll go check with the mer."

Elayna rolled over on her back and uncapped the barometer, setting it between her breasts and then holding up the wind gauge.

All of the mer teams, in addition to their other duties like killing orcas and finding enemy fleets, took weather readings. They could only get measurements at the water's surface, although their support ships had weather balloons, but the measurements were put together to form a remarkably complete picture of the movement of air masses.

It was a nice day, breezy mind you, the weather gauge showed right on twenty klicks, but clear and mild. She lay back and let her eyes close, ducking her head back and under from time to time for a breath of water. Sitting at the surface was always a pain, you had to decide whether to duck under for water or blast the lungs clean for air. But it was as nice a day as she could hope. She lay there and wished she was back at Blackbeard Base. Sort of. Whenever she thought of the name she thought of Granddad and that made her sad. There had been so much death since that day. The world really did suck.

She called up an image of the reefs and imagined herself riding the currents past, just floating. No cares, no weight of command, no fears of attack by orca or ixchitl, no barometer readings that take for fricking *ever*! She rolled up and looked through slitted eyes at the barometer but it was still showing an unstabilized reading.

She ducked her head back down and looked at her second in command. "Any sign of orca?"

"No," he pulsed back. "Skimmers report open ocean all around."

"We hope," she said, looking at the barometer again. It finally showed clear and she cased it back up and put away the wind-gauge.

"Signal fleet met," she said. "Location point 109, wind speed twenty-two klicks, barometer thirty point one five and rising."

"Nice day," Katarin said.

"Yeah. Storm a comin', though."

"Message coming in," Katarin said. "New Destiny fleet is at sea."

"Let's hope they get becalmed," Elayna said, rolling over and kicking for the depths.

❖   ❖   ❖

Paul rolled over so that Megan was on top of him and stroked her back, lightly.

"You seem pretty happy," Megan said, leaning down to kiss him on his forehead and, not coincidentally, dangling her breasts in his face.

"I am," he said, reaching back around to stroke the soft flesh. "The fleet has sailed. All of it. Chansa has sent the main combat fleet to attack Blackbeard Base. Edmund's going to have to choose which fleet to engage; he doesn't have enough forces to attack both."

"Which do you think he'll go for?" Megan asked.

"It doesn't really matter," Paul answered. "If he moves for the northern fleet it can turn around. The southern fleet will take out Blackbeard, kill or capture the mer-women and children and that takes the mer out of the equation; they'll do anything to get their children back. If he attacks that fleet, the main fleet will land in Norau and we can set up portals to support them. Even if he, by some miracle, destroys the fleet, it won't matter anymore."

"And the target's still Balmoran?" Megan asked, leaning into the stroking. It was actually pleasant; Paul had good hands when he bothered to use them.

"Uhm . . ." Paul said. "And more good news. Chansa has an agent on the *Bonhomme Richard*, one of the stewards. He has orders to poison Talbot and the fleet admiral, Chang. Edmund never discusses his plans, so the fleet will be dropped into chaos. Then there's a two-edged sword: Celine tells me she finally has a way to overcome the personal protection fields."

"That's impossible!" Megan said.

"That's what I said," Paul smiled. "But she proved it.

She uses some sort of special nannite. They generate a destabilizing field that interferes with the physics of the PPFs. Unfortunately, they do the same to teleport fields so they can't be transported by teleports. She's made little devices to produce them. The devices can be teleported. I'm considering a way to get some of the devices, and assassins, to Sheida's location. Take her out and it will destabilize the whole of the UFS."

"That should do it," Megan admitted. *How do I get this information out? I know that Paul has got to be monitoring my meetings with the damned vendor!* "Now, why are we talking?" she added, rubbing her breasts in his face. "Aren't there better things to be doing?"

"You might be wondering what we are doing," Shar Chang said to the assembled skippers and their dragon commanders. "Well, the answer is, I'm not going to tell you. You all know that we've been leaking information to New Destiny, even at sea. Some of you may be the leaks. I doubt it, but I couldn't believe it of Owen Mbeki. So you're going to get orders and you're going to obey them. I'll be giving you each written instructions. Most of them will be to detach yourself from the main body along with your battle group. The fleet is breaking up."

He looked around at the assembled skippers and then at the dragon commanders.

"You may be thinking: Why be so sneaky; the orcas and ixchitl will know where we are. Well, not if we can help it. From here on out I want continuous dragon coverage. But not the usual coverage. I want continuous dragon coverage on each of your task forces. What you're going to train in is anti-orca patrols. *Any* orcas will be engaged by the wyverns. The wyverns have proven that they can take on orca in the water. When a pod is spotted the carrier will be signaled and a flight of dragons will engage the orca. The water is cold so the riders will have to stay out of the attack. But many of the dragons have fought orca before and when they see them it's hard to keep them from attacking. Don't. Lead them to the pod and let them go. Recover them out of the water. Obviously, if the pod is too far from the ship for the dragons to swim back, don't engage. If they're that far out, they're not a threat. But if they close, kill them. Natural or Changed; we can't tell the difference until we're on them."

"Question, Admiral," Joanna said, raising a talon.

"Yes, Commander Gramlich?"

"Do we get to eat them?"

The question elicited chuckles, some of them hysterical. Even Shar grinned.

"Feel free," he said. "The supplementary orders to the other skippers are as follows; the only officer who will take navigational bearings is the skipper. No other officer had better have a sextant in his or her hand. The penalty for such will be immediate and unquestioned confinement to quarters with court-martial to follow. Skippers will take one reading per day. The exception to this will be the fleet command ship. Follow the command ship; they know where they are going. In the event that you are separated by storm you can open your *second* orders, which will give you a rendezvous. The *second* orders are to be kept under marine guard and the skipper, XO *and* navigational officer must all be present and in agreement for them to be opened. Is this clear?"

"Clear," the group said.

"There will be supplementary orders sent to all ships by the end of the day. These orders will be kept under the same conditions. Held by the marine commander in a box to which only the skipper has the key. There will be three such packets: Stonewall, Genghis and Belisarius. They will be opened only upon my signal.

"Maps are to be kept in the same manner; nobody has access to them but the skipper. You skippers will know where you are and in the event of the carrier commanders where you are going. Mer will transmit when you have arrived. If you are delayed by storm or bad winds, that will be relayed as well. For your information, the mer are implementing a deception plan that will indicate that we are *not* where we're going to be. Admiral Talbot?"

Edmund looked around at the group and nodded.

"In war you always want to know what your enemy is doing," he said, looking at the skippers one by one. "And they, in turn, want the same information. This naval war has been fought, to this point, with both sides knowing that information. To the greatest extent possible we wish to end that condition. As to what we are going to do, or how we are going to do it, you will get that information at your rendezvous. Admiral Chang?"

"That's it," Shar said, looking around at them again. "Good luck, and good sailing."

❖   ❖   ❖

"Those are some damned strange orders," Karcher said as they flew back to the ship.

"They are," Joanna replied. "But I can guess the reason."

"So can I," Karcher mewed distastefully. "They're right about us bleeding information."

"Oh, it's more than that," the dragon replied. "You haven't known Edmund as long as I have. His mind is as deep and black as a bog. He never tells anyone what he plans, or if he tells them, half the time it's not what he actually does. Part of it, a big part of it, is to deny the information to the enemy. But the other part is that if he changes his mind, or the plan doesn't go as well as he planned, nobody knows it."

"That part I understand," Karcher said unhappily as they turned on final.

CHAPTER NINETEEN

"Time to mix it up," Jason signaled, starting to ascend.

When Jason was given the go ahead to begin attacking the orcas and ixchitl, he'd already had a plan in mind. And, so far, the plan was working.

Finding the orca pods and ixchitl schools was almost the hardest part. But the delphinos were in tentative contact with natural schools of skimmer dolphins, the deep water dolphins that roamed every major ocean on earth. They were, in particular, capable of reading the skimmer's language, at least to the extent of their alarm calls when orca or ixchitl, which the skimmers had discovered were threats, were sighted.

Whenever such a call went up, delphino skimmer pods moved in close enough to determine if the pod was natural orcas or Changed. The differences, other than in the small pseudo-hands of the Changed, were slight, but generally they could tell without moving in close enough to be prey. And with ixchitl there was no question at all. Then they would take up positions around the pod or school and send out their alarm call.

Jason had shifted forces and had the selkies take over most of the inshore work of the underwater forces. With the mer thus freed up he had scattered "killer teams" around the ocean. When a target pod or school was sighted, more often than not there was a killer team somewhere in the vicinity. As soon as the course of the target was plotted the mer would move into position.

By and large, mer were shallow water creatures. But they were designed to handle deep diving just as well. They also were water-breathers, so they could *stay* down, as long as they got enough food to stave off hypothermia. Orcas and ixchitl, though, almost invariably moved in the top hundred meters of water. Ixchitl *could* and sometimes did stay deep. But they generally, like the orcas, traveled near the surface. Thus the killer team would dive deep and silently await the passing target.

In this case it was a small pod of Changed that was, apparently, moving in to try to localize one of the carriers. Edmund had said that it was a high priority that they not do so. Which made this group a double target.

They couldn't see, or otherwise detect, the pod from their current location, nearly three hundred meters below the surface of the water. But the skimmers were still sending out their broadcasts and they could more or less fix the location of the pod that way. The skimmers had taken up points of an equilateral triangle around the Changed pod and as the triangle moved over their location, Jason sent his force silently upwards.

As he did he checked, again, that the supply ship was in position, sixty klicks to the southeast. He often thought that the supply ships were the real heroes of the plan. The small, fast schooners carried food and weapons for the mer and delphinos, moving around the ocean, unable to defend themselves from attack and depending solely upon the immensity of the ocean to protect them. Each of them also carried a medic and a hold that was partially flooded with seawater. In the, very likely, event of injury to the delphinos or mer, they could be evacuated to the schooner and if the injury was bad enough, but not too bad, they could be shipped to the shore.

He knew that they'd probably take some casualties this day and just had to hope that they wouldn't be too severe.

As the school of mer ascended they started to pick up very faint clicks from above. The orcas mostly ran silent when they moved but this group had lousy tactical discipline. On the basis of the sounds, Jason shifted their ascent slightly and increased speed. There was some danger to the change in speed. As they got into lower pressure water their tailfins could begin to "cavitate," creating low-pressure "holes" where the water would rush in and make a sound. So far so good, though: he could still hear no sound from his school.

It was becoming dark above and it was hard to pick out much in the water, clear as it was. But then he saw shapes above and to the left of the school so he shifted direction again, quietly extending his lance. When it was clear the orcas still had no inkling they were about to be ambushed, he put on a final burst of speed and sixty mer-men followed him into the attack.

Irkisutut was bored, angry, tired and afraid all at the same time. They had been running around the damned ocean on one wild goose chase after another for the last week. Headquarters didn't seem to know which way to send them so first they went one way then another, always in a fruitless search for the enemy's carriers.

What made it worse was that they had heard, both directly from distant alarm calls and from scuttlebutt from other pods that casualties had been enormous. Not only were the carriers sending out dragon patrols to hunt down the orca but the ever-be-damned mer had shifted from skulking around the harbors to attacking the pods. Most of his fellow pod leaders had been lost over the last week and he wondered how long it would be before it became his turn.

On top of that were the damned skimmers. He knew he was bracketed by skimmers, they were sending out constant chatter. But while orcas were fast, skimmers were damned lightning. He'd shifted track a couple of times trying to catch the damned things but they just greased away, laughing at him. Then when he turned back they got right back into position. All that chasing them did was wear out the pod.

And the pod was already pretty worn. They hadn't had a resupply in three days and there hadn't been much they could catch with the damned skimmers squealing along to either side. The open ocean was mostly desert anyway so the orca normally followed the currents, hunting at their edges where food was most abundant. This mission had had them chasing all over the ocean, though, and that meant where the food *wasn't*. They'd called for a resupply ship to rendezvous with them and gotten nothing but bullshit assurances that "something would come along."

And as he was thinking about that, something did.

The team of mer had spread into a pike-wielding hexagon, the underwater equivalent of a phalanx that they had worked out as the most efficient attack formation in these circumstances. It spread wider than the pod of orcas and engulfed it like a rising, metal-tipped, seine net. The first orca to be spitted was a youngster that had dived below the main pod and squealed an alarm just before he was struck between his pectorals by a pike.

The pod reacted quickly but in an undisciplined manner, some of them darting ahead to try to escape the enveloping mer and others diving to the attack. Most of the ones that dove ran into a solid wall of spear-points. Unwilling to brave the wall of metal they turned and darted for the surface. A few dove into the phalanx and were pincushioned for their bravery. Despite this the mer were careful to avoid opening up holes in their formation; they shifted position to maintain a solid, and ever narrowing, formation as teams stayed behind to finish off the wounded orcas.

Irkisutut darted ahead as the alarm call went up but quickly saw that he was going to be cut off by the mer. He turned to the side and realized that the pod was surrounded. After darting back and forth for a moment he did the only thing that made sense, building up speed and then leaping into the air to clear the ring of mer.

As soon as he hit the water he turned back towards the mer, darting in and capturing one in his conical teeth. He didn't stay around to be attacked by the rest, instead backing away as the ribcage of the mer crunched in his teeth. He dropped the dead mer-man and turned to attack again but the phalanx had shifted to half attacking inward while the rest covered their backs. He, too, was facing a wall of spears. There was nothing he could do but watch the rest of the pod slaughtered mercilessly.

"Damn you!" he bellowed as the last of the pod was finished off. "Freaks!"

"Go home, little orca," one of the mer taunted. "Go home and tell the rest of your fellows that you're no longer the top of the food chain!"

As the mer darted towards him he turned away and headed towards the east. Somewhere out there were other pods and a supply ship. Somewhere out there was safety.

There was nothing left for him here.

"Where in the hell are we?" Zora said as she mounted her wyvern.

"I don't know, Sergeant Fink," Herzer replied with a grin. "Somewhere in the middle of the Atlantis Ocean, but that's just a guess."

The carrier had been sailing for four days. And not in any sort of straight direction. She tacked, she turned, she sailed west, she sailed east, she sailed north and south. None of the tacks had been of equal lengths and given the state of wind and current they could be *anywhere*. Well, anywhere in the northern Atlantis.

Currently they were on a generally easterly course, as far as Herzer could tell. They'd been on it most of the day, but that didn't mean anything. He knew there were New Destiny forces to their north *and* south so either way they turned they were going to be going into battle.

He and Fink weren't battling today, though. The majority of the dragon-riders were brand new and today they were engaging in bombing practice. The ship's launch had been sent out three hours earlier and was now towing a target slowly to the east, falling behind the carrier with every minute. The target wasn't all that large and it bobbed around on the waves quite a bit. But that didn't answer why none of the riders had managed to hit it yet.

Herzer walked Lydy to the catapult and settled himself in position as the wyvern got a good grip on the launching balk and leaned forward eagerly. It took a bit of practice to get the wyverns used to the launching catapult but once they acquired the knack they loved it.

The catapult accelerated the wyvern to almost forty kilometers per hour in its short traverse and as it reached the end the wyvern flapped open her wings and took flight. The wings of a wyvern were enormous—they had to be to support the weight of the dragon's body and rider—and the mechanics of them were impossible without a large number of changes from the birds of prey they were based upon.

The first and most noticeable change was in materials. The wings and flight-bones were threaded through with a mesh of bioextruded carbon nanotubes, a monomolecule that was enormously strong for its weight. But beyond that there were subtle additions throughout the wyvern's body. The energy of flying meant that they got extremely hot, hot enough that their own body heat could cause brain damage. To reduce the dangerous build-up there was a small channel in their head that took in air at the front, blew it over the skull and released it at the back. This ensured that while they might become overheated it would not affect their brain. It also was a noticeable portion of their total body cooling, since it was lined with water releasing membranes. The changes went on and on. Normal muscle could never support their flight, certainly not for any length of time, so they borrowed from bumblebees a special "reflexive muscle" that only had to flex in one direction. Internal tubules acted as springs to bring their wings back into "gliding" position automatically so they only had to "flap" and then release.

Despite all of the changes they could only stay aloft for a few hours so Herzer headed for altitude and then glided, waiting for the sergeant to catch up. As soon as she had formed up on his wingtip he headed for the distant dot that was the launch.

The launch had a crew of twenty oarsmen and a coxswain but at the moment most of the oarsmen were leaning on the side of the boat, watching the show. A previous division had formed up on the target and were dropping practice bombs. Herzer watched as, one by one, they all missed. Well, it was a small target. They were getting close. Most of them would have hit a ship.

The problem being that with the relatively small bombs, and the increasing ability of ships to fight the fires with foam agents, the ships had to be hit multiple times to ensure the fire got out of control. And in some cases dropping the bombs in precise locations would help, such as taking out the quarterdeck.

So being able to hit the three meter by three meter target was not an option, it was a standard. A standard the riders were not meeting.

He saw Joanna coming up from the ship with the small figure of Bast perched merrily on her neck. Only Bast would be crazy enough to ride a dragon without any safety straps. He wondered how she held on.

Then he thought about her leg strength and chuckled. He knew damned well how she held on.

He lined up on the target and nosed the wyvern over, making small corrections. The target wasn't moving in a regular pattern since it was being towed. It jerked forward and then slowed, then jerked, then slowed. He made small corrections on the dragon and then, when he felt he was at the minimum altitude, released his first bomb. He continued below the "floor" however to watch it drop. It hit just forward of the target with a small splash.

He pulled the wyvern back up to where the sergeant was waiting and signaled to her.

"Watch your first drop. Go below floor to watch. Floor on other drops."

She looked at him in incomprehension and signed back. "Watch drop?"

He slid the wyvern over until he was just above her.

"You can watch your first drop and go below the floor for the exercise!" he shouted. "You have to stay above the floor on the others." More signing lessons were clearly in the future.

"Okay!" she shouted.

He watched as she lined up and dropped and could tell she wasn't going to get anywhere near the target. The practice bomb landed more than ten meters to the side and well to the rear.

He waited as she flapped back to altitude and Joanna slid into his wing position.

"Not going so well, is it XO?" Joanna bellowed.

"No," Herzer signed, stooping over and lining up the target again. He tried to correct for its tendency to jerk but even as he dropped his load he was aware he'd missed. As he pulled the dragon up and over he glanced back and, sure enough, it landed behind it. Close, but not on target.

"This is damned near impossible," Herzer signed as he got up to altitude.

"Others do it," Bast signed back with a humorous fillip.

"I'm a lover, not a bomber," Herzer signed, fast so Zora wouldn't catch it.

Joanna turned over and lined up, her wings pulled back so she was correcting with only the tips. She spread them slightly halfway down to catch up to the target then continued on, looking more like some giant arrow than a dragon. When she released, she had her own controls, she didn't even look, just pulled out and used the momentum to carry her up on a controlled climb until she was just at stall speed and started flapping. The bomb hit the center of the target and exploded.

"That was amazing!" Zora yelled.

"Yes," Herzer signed back. "Now we have to figure out how to be amazing!" he added with a yell.

"Herzer," Joanna bellowed as she flapped back up to their position. "Don't start your dive, yet. Spouts to the south."

Herzer looked in the indicated direction and just caught the sight of a plume of breath. They'd had other sightings, but they had all been regular whales. Each sighting, however, had to be checked.

"You and Zora form on me," Joanna continued, winging over to the south.

He laid Lydy over and formed up on Joanna's wing then hooked the reins off and took out his semaphore paddles. He waved to the flagship until he saw a pennant raised with his number then signaled that they had spotted plumes to the south and were investigating. As he looked back he saw the ready dragon lift into the air as another came up from below and one of the Silverdrake dropped off the main-sail crosstree and headed towards the indicated sighting.

He shook his head and signaled for the Silverdrake to go high and give the fleet some cover. The Drakes had a tendency to go haring off after anything that struck their fancy. With the training group gone the fleet was without a reconnaissance cap, not to mention that when they reached the whales they were going to be below the horizon from the carrier. The Drake rider waved his arms in reply and headed upward in a steep climb as the three-dragon patrol continued towards the spouts.

Joanna was slowly climbing with occasional wing-flaps and the other two dragons followed her. Herzer was careful to monitor Lydy to make sure she didn't tire; being out in the middle of the ocean when that happened would be bad.

It only took them about twenty minutes to get over the spouts and the black and white patterns showed them, clearly, to be orcas.

"How do you want to handle this, Commander?" Herzer signed.

Joanna continued to watch the orcas for a moment then winged over in a sharp, spiraling, dive. When she was at about five hundred meters she lined out again and spiraled the orcas, turning her head to the side as their shadow passed over the pod.

"I'm gonna let 'em go," Joanna bellowed. "They're naturals."

"You sure?" Herzer signed.

"No," Joanna admitted. "But they didn't bolt when we swept over them. I'd say they're dumb brute animals. And, anyway, they don't . . . move like Changed. There's just something different with the way that Changed act. I'd say these are nomads, so they're a danger to our selkies and delphinos. But they're not a danger to the fleet. So I say: Leave 'em be."

"Your call, Commander," Herzer yelled. "Besides, we're well away from the task force."

Bast suddenly cocked her head to the side and leaned out on the dragon's neck to yell something.

"You sure?" Joanna bellowed, turning her head around on its long, snakelike neck, to look at the elf.

"No!" Bast yelled. "Closer look!"

"Stay up here," Joanna said, looking at Herzer, and then she dove towards the water.

She lined up behind the pod and passed over it, fast, her wingtips nearly touching the water on either side. The whole time her head was moving from side to side and when she passed the pod she began beating for altitude, hard. As she did the pod made a radical turn to the north and dove.

"Changed!" Joanna bellowed. "I was wr . . . wr . . . not right. Herzer, you and Zora head back to the ship. Get another dragon and get up here with some wyverns. I'll shadow these. Signal hostile orca to south as soon as you get in range."

"Will do, Commander," Herzer said, gesturing at Zora.

"Wait," Bast called. She stood up on Joanna's back and began stripping off her clothes. She had left her bow but she was carrying the saber. When she was done she was wearing her baldric and the saber and nothing else. She looked over at Herzer with the bundle of clothes and armor in her hands and then shook her head.

"You'd never catch it," she said, toeing at Joanna.

"Are you crazy?" Herzer yelled. She was balanced on tiptoe on the back-ridge of a flying dragon nearly two thousand meters over the cold waters of the North Atlantis.

"Yes!" she yelled as Joanna lifted up and over Herzer's mount. Bast leapt lightly onto Joanna's wing-root, catching the uplift and then off into midair, landing with feet together on Lydy's back.

The wyvern reacted to the sudden impact by swinging from side to side as she tried to see who was running up her spine and it was all Herzer could do for a moment to keep her in control. Bast handled this much like a rodeo performer or an experienced sailor running out a crosstree, walking up the spine of the dragon, feet in line, until she dropped down on Herzer's back.

"Hold this, will you, lover?" she asked, lightly licking him on his ear.

"You are insane." Herzer chuckled, then pulled up slightly on the reins, getting Lydy above Joanna.

Bast repeated the performance, jumping off of Lydy's wing-root and onto Joanna's back. As soon as she was in place, Joanna dove for the water.

"Head for base," Herzer gestured at Zora.

"Help?" she asked, gesturing down.

"No," Herzer waved. "Base."

He passed an outbound flight as he headed for the carrier, his eye fixed on the Silverdrake high above. There were six wyverns, two with riders and four without. He really felt sorry for those poor damned orcas. For that matter, it was an even bet that Bast and Joanna were going to have finished off the pod by the time the rest of them got there.

The carrier had turned northeast, away from the potential threat, and they were already headed into the wind. He let Zora head in first, watching her air control. Experienced wyverns could almost land themselves, but the fleet had neither experienced wyverns nor experienced riders. Thus it was up to the riders to direct the wyverns on landing.

An innovation since his first carrier experience was a set of lines on the landing platform. The idea was for the wyverns to land between the second and third line, squarely in the middle of the landing zone. Another innovation was a net at the rear of the platform. He really hoped he never ended up in it.

After initial carrier development books had been found that, while not textbooks on naval aviation, per se, had many of the techniques that ancient peoples had developed for aircraft carriers. Most of the books were fiction and few of them were good, even to those who could read the ancient and baroque dialect in which they were written. They were loaded with acronyms the definition of which were often lost: SOL, SNAFU, and, frequently, FUBAR. But many of the terms and mythos had infected the naval dragon-riders. The stripes, for example, were referred to as "wires" which confused people that saw them. Landing between the second and third was a "three-wire." Signaling that you were prepared to land was referred to as "calling the ball" even though even Evan had not been able to get a Fresnel lens to work for dragons. The one ability that ancient aviators had that Herzer wished for at moments like this was the ability to fly straight on if they were going to miss their landing. If he tried it he'd smack into a net. And if the net wasn't rigged, he'd smack into a mast, which was worse. Actually, he'd probably plow into pri-fly.

He put that out of his mind, lining Lydy up and keeping his eyes on the paddles in the hands of the landing signal officer. He was pretty clean on the way in, corrected for the dead area behind the ship, got a last minute wave up and then slammed down dead between the two and three wire.

"Report," Skipper Karcher said as soon as he had walked his wyvern down to the maindeck.

"Spotted plumes to the south and went to investigate.

Jo . . . Commander Gramlich thought they were normals at first but when she went down for a close inspection, on Bast's suggestion, she changed her mind. Last I saw, she and Bast were headed down to engage."

"Just the two of them?" Sassan said, aghast.

"Yes, Major," Herzer replied, somewhat tightly. "I've seen both Commander Gramlich and Bast in action in the water. I'm not worried about them, just whether there's anything left for the follow-on flight."

"That good, huh?" Skipper Karcher chuckled.

"Yes, ma'am," Herzer said, tossing the bundle in his hands up and down. "Bast jumped from Joanna to Lydy to give me these. Then jumped back. She's that good."

"What is that?" Sassan asked.

"Her clothes," Herzer said, dryly. "She didn't want to get them wet."

At a signal from the approaching wyverns that the orca were no longer a threat, Karcher turned the task force south to pick up Joanna and Bast; the returning dragon-riders had stated that when they got there all they found were five orca carcasses floating on the surface.

They were directed to the returning dragon by the cover riders and when they were finally sighted Bast was standing on Joanna's head, swaying from side to side as the dragon snaked through the water. Wyverns swam by using their wings but Joanna was long and thin enough that she found it easier to scull from side to side like a snake, her virtually invulnerable wings wrapped around her body as armor.

As the dragon passed the side of the ship Bast leapt

off her head and onto the deck. Joanna had given her a bit of an assist but it should have been impossible for her to not only clear the bulwarks but land near the middle of the deck. When she saw Herzer she trotted over to him and leapt through the air again, landing, stark naked except for her sword, with her legs wrapped around his middle and one hand hooked in his collar.

"That was fun," she said, grinning and swinging back and forth, much like an orangutan hanging on a tree branch. "Let's find some more."

Skipper Karcher looked at her, obviously about to ask a question and then shut her mouth as Joanna climbed over the side of the ship. The starboard rear rail of the maindeck was removable and mats were laid in place for this exact purpose and Joanna slithered up onto the deck without incident.

"What happened, Commander?" Karcher asked.

"Oh, well," Joanna said, spreading her wings and shaking the water off as politely as she could, "they came at us in the same old way and we, you know, beat them in the same old way. What a terrible business."

"That's it?" Sassan asked.

"More or less," Bast said, jumping down from Herzer and taking her clothes. "Wellington and all. They tried to fight, and they couldn't win. And they tried to run, and they weren't fast enough. Felt sorry for them towards the end, really, until I remembered what they were like in the Isles."

"You could go pick them up," Joanna added. "As a wise delphino once quipped: Orca meat. Taste sweet."

"I . . . don't think so," Skipper Karcher said, shaking her head. "I think we have enough meat in the freezer. I need to get the task force back on course." With that she strode back up onto the quarterdeck.

"Well, I had my fill anyway," Joanna admitted. "Time for a lie-down."

"I don't think so," Herzer said. "I've got some paperwork for you to sign."

"You know how hard it is for me to hold a pen!" Joanna complained as she walked through the hatch. "I really don't get paid enough for this."

CHAPTER TWENTY

"You know, they don't pay me enough for this," Edmund muttered.

The ship was passing through what the meteorologist euphemistically termed "a disturbance." Edmund called it a storm. Shar called it "good sailing" which Edmund had come to realize was the navy version of "good training."

And, as usual, his seasickness, under control in normal seas, was rearing its ugly head.

"Message from the mer, sir," a seaman said, handing him a form.

He unfolded it and frowned. "When did we get this?"

"Just now, sir," the messenger replied.

"What?" Shar asked, looking out at the tossing horizon. "Or can't I know?"

"There's a message tube on the way in," Edmund said. "Only I or . . . someone else can be the deliveree. I'm the closest."

"Must be hot," Shar commented. "From where?"

"That I can't tell you," Edmund admitted. "Looks like it should be here in about an hour. I'll be below in the meantime, praying to the porcelain god."

At the repeated knock on his door Edmund finally crawled to his feet and made it to his desk.

"Enter," he shouted over the creaking of the hull. *Surely* it wasn't supposed to make those groaning noises?

"Message tube, sir," the communications officer said. "Sir, there's a possibility this could be a booby trap. Do you want one of my people to open it? We have procedures . . ."

"No." Edmund sighed, turning the bronze cylinder over in his hands. "I'll take my chances."

Once the officer had left he twisted the knurled top and slid out the paper inside.

"Eyes Only Edmund Talbot, Joel Travante, Sheida Ghorbani.

"Agent M established contact, Paul Bowman's harem. Contact Megan Travante, daughter of Joel Travante."

Edmund laid his head on the desk for a moment and groaned, then looked at the rest of the message.

"Identity positively confirmed by visual recognition and transmission of counter-signs. Subject presented with name 'Travante' on a 'new line' of materials. Responded with words 'Paul is very *fatherly* to us,' 'material will be given *forensic* examination' and 'could lead to an *inspection*.' Terms, while ambiguous, taken together indicate positive contact. Unable to effect any intelligence transfer in first meeting except warning that Paul has intelligence source in UFS at the highest level. Words to effect: 'any passage of information up your corporate chain *will* (subject's emphasis) get to Paul.' 'Your new line will go *nowhere* (subject's emphasis) if anyone else is informed.'

"Assume from demeanor subject has further information of similar caliber. Risk to subject if information passed considered *high*. All communications can be considered monitored. Absent orders will contact subject one week from date of message.

"M"

Edmund looked at the date, looked at his calendar and groaned again. Agent "M," whoever he was, would contact the "subject" in one more day.

And he'd thought seasickness was bad.

Megan was staring blankly at the distillery apparatus when Shanea walked in the room.

"What are you looking so unhappy about?"

"Shanea, where does Paul keep his Key?" Megan said, then froze. "I didn't just say that."

"I can't believe you had to ask," Shanea chuckled, happily. "You don't go down on him enough."

"What?" Megan snapped. "I . . . what does that have to do with it?"

"If you did, you'd know, silly," Shanea replied. "It's in a pouch up behind his balls. Sort of a slit in the skin. You can feel it sometimes. If you put your hand in the right places," she added, laughing again.

"Thanks, Shanea," Megan said, distantly. "I was just curious." She stuck out her hand and picked up a bottle, handing it to the girl without turning around. "Try this new perfume."

"Okay, thanks!" Shanea said. "You want me to keep an eye on stuff for a while?"

"No," Megan replied. "I think . . . I think I'll do some mixing."

"She's *what*?"

Sheida had never actually seen Joel Travante upset. She didn't like seeing it now.

"Megan is a member of Paul Bowman's harem," Sheida repeated. "Through truly remarkable coincidence, your agent has made contact with her. He is going to make a second contact, and attempt to get more intel from her, two days from now."

"Bloody hell," Joel said, visibly forcing himself to be calm. "Oh, God *damnit!*" And failing.

"She's *alive*," Sheida said, brutally. "Concentrate on that fact. What she is going through, women have survived for countless generations. And she already got out one bit of intel. She said that any communication that wasn't to you or Edmund, for some reason, was going to be intercepted. We have a very high-level leak somewhere."

"I *know* Megan," Joel growled. "She's not going to just spread her legs and smile. She's going to try to find a way to *get back* at Paul. I *don't* trust her as a source, mainly because she will take risks and get burned. Also known as killed or more likely Changed!"

"Do you want me to try to get to your agent?" Sheida asked. "Tell him not to make contact? To abort the mission?"

Joel looked at her projection and closed his eyes, hard.

"No," he said after a moment. "If Paul has let slip that there's a high-level source, he's telling her other things. Things we need to know."

"I'm not so sure," Sheida said. "I mean, yes, she's getting the information. But getting it out is another thing. She's bound to be closely monitored in any communications. I don't see how she *could* get information out that couldn't be detected. *Wouldn't* be detected. Under the circumstances I'd tell any agent to blow off the contact, much less contact with Megan. At least until we could figure out a better means of communication."

"Martin is good," Joel said. "A weasel, but a good weasel. And I hold his strings. Megan . . . I don't know. I don't know her anymore, not after four years of . . . *that*. Could she get something out? Maybe. Coded somehow, possibly. And I don't see any way to abort the contact in time, not and keep Martin operable. There aren't any hard methods that will work fast enough. No time."

"So we go with it?" Sheida asked.

"For now we have to," Joel replied. "*Damnit!*"

To say that Megan was conflicted would be the understatement of the millennia.

She had long ago gotten over wanting to kill Paul. About the time she had fallen in love with him. But she had taken it upon herself as her duty, as soon as she could do it and *know* that she could seize his Key. With the Key she had a way out, for herself and the other girls. With the Key she could summon a personal protection field and be *safe* at *last*. With the Key . . . she could survive.

But now . . . she had a contact. Would it be better to stay as an agent in place? Could she even get any information out? Paul didn't monitor the harem, she knew that now after blurting out the question she had asked of Shanea. If there was even a *dumb* monitoring system it would have picked up on that question and at the very least *she* would be being questioned. But any communication was going to be scanned and analyzed, even Paul wasn't that stupid. And she knew where that would lead. To a life as an automaton like Amber. If she was lucky. Or unlucky. More conflict.

She had brought two urns of wine and a beautiful glass, with a long stem of a light shade of pink and a lovely clear crystal bowl. One of the urns was white, one of the urns red. Life, and try to get out the information? Or death, and take her chances? It might not work. If it didn't, she hoped that Paul would at least allow her a clean death.

She was halfway tempted to take the first sip herself.

"You seem troubled," Paul said as she rearranged her scanty clothing.

"Too much on my plate I think," she said, smiling. "The harem was very boring when I arrived. Now it seems I don't have enough hours in the day for all the things I'm working on."

"Maybe you should delegate," Paul said, grinning at her. She had suggested it to him often enough.

"Maybe I should," Megan said, picking up the glass and reaching for the urns. Life. Or death? Her hand hovered and she picked up an urn, filling the glass.

"Troubled, Major Herrick?"

Herzer looked over at the skipper, turned around and leaned back against the railing.

"Just the same troubles as the rest of the crew," Herzer admitted with a grin. "I wish I knew where we were. I wish I knew what we were doing. And I wish I knew what we were going to face, wherever we are going."

"Well, I've got at least half of that," the skipper admitted with a chuckle. She leaned her forearms on the railing and looked out at the passing ocean.

"I'll admit that this isn't the first time this has happened to me," Herzer said. "The duke is always like this; he never tells anyone anything he doesn't absolutely have to. I even know the historical model he's drawing it from. So I have an idea what he is doing. I still don't have to like it."

"I have no idea what he is doing," Chansa said. "And I don't like it."

"We have reports on attacks on orca pods all over the ocean," his aide replied, setting up an easel with a map on it. "Some of them have been from dragons, presumably, given the ranges, from carriers. If so, his carriers are wandering all over the ocean."

"North? South? Where *are* the carriers? Which way are they going?"

"Other than from the attacks we can't be sure," the aide replied. "No orca has been able to get in range of the UFS fleet to see. But there is one attack that has occurred *south* of the anticipated path of our battle fleet and one that has occurred just south of the invasion fleet. There was even one that was in sight of Hibernia. Like I said, all over the ocean. And they're slaughtering the orca."

"Say that again?" Chansa growled.

"They've taken out about thirty percent of our orca, as well as about forty percent of the ixchitl. The dragons also appear to be attacking natural orca. The orcas are running scared, too. If they even get a hint of a dragon in the air, or a mer killer group moving in, they move out. They just can't fight them in the water."

"He's trying to take out our eyes," Chansa said. "What about communications from the agents in the Fleet?"

"They have no idea what is going on," the aide admitted. "Nobody is being told where they are or what they are doing. Nobody, not even the officers. The captains of the carriers have orders, everyone else just follows."

"I don't trust it," Chansa said. "When Edmund Talbot does something that doesn't make sense, he's planning something subtle. But what can he do? We've got him outnumbered with the combat fleet, and the invasion fleet has enough anti-dragon frigates to give his dragons a very nasty time. What in the hell is he planning?"

"What in the hell are you planning?" Shar asked.

"Not even to you, Shar," Edmund replied with a faint smile.

"I've got forces scattered all over the ocean," Shar pointed out. "We're inviting defeat in detail."

"Not as long as we know where their forces are," Edmund pointed out. "And we do."

"So do *they*," Chang replied. "Every time we take out a group of orca, it gives them a location for a carrier. Why are you *telling* them where we are?"

"Not even to you, Shar," Edmund repeated. "But you might want to catch up on your reading."

"Okay, we're going to have to do something about this," Chansa said after a long moment's thought. "We can't lose all our orcas. Detach . . . detach three carriers from the Blackbeard task force," he continued, rubbing his chin and looking at the map. "Send a large orca group, three pods, towards this southernmost attack. Tell them to *find* the carrier, find the dragon outriders, and lead them back to *our* carriers."

"That will only leave two carriers for the attack on Blackbeard," the aide pointed out.

"Blackbeard doesn't have any dragons to speak of," the marshal replied. "And there are more than enough Changed to destroy the company of Blood Lords there. Send out the orders. There's a lone carrier out there. Find it. Destroy it. I'll teach him to play games with me."

"You wanna play games?" Herzer asked the wyvern deck leading PO. "I'm a master of playing games."

Saturday morning had become the traditional day for the skipper to inspect the ship. And as with all such inspections, there was a preinspection conducted by the ship's XO. And a pre-preinspection conducted by the various officers and NCOs in charge of different areas of the ship.

In Herzer's case that meant an inspection, just after dawn, of all the areas relating to the care and feeding of the wyverns and their riders. He'd inspected the riders' head, the food storage areas, the food preparation areas, the ground crew quarters, the riders' quarters and the riders' officers' quarters. And he'd made clear that no matter how early, when he came through, shit had better be *straight*. He was a product of the Blood Lords and Blood Lords accepted no excuses.

Most of them had needed some minor improvement. The enlisted head had some trash hidden they thought he'd miss. He didn't. The enlisted quarters had non-regulation materials they thought they'd hidden well enough. They hadn't. A few of the crew had thought that a properly made bunk meant dirty linen and sloppy folds. That was being corrected. But that was all minor. It was important at a certain level to nitpick; if they were sloppy about something as simple as making a bed, they were liable to think they could be sloppy in important areas. That was the point to inspections.

A point that had apparently been lost on the wyvern deck division.

"Look at this," Herzer said, dragging the PO into one of the wyvern pens and pushing the dragon to the side. In the corner was a build-up of filth with a nasty yellow fungus growing on it. Wyverns were generally polite enough to let go of their messes when they were in flight. But when they were penned up for too long, such as during a storm, that wasn't possible. And when they succumbed to seasickness, and they were nearly as susceptible as humans, all hell broke loose. At both ends.

There were pumps and drains to handle the mess; Herzer had learned about them the hard way on his previous cruise. But it left quite a bit of junk in its wake. Mostly secreted in hard to reach places. However, those places were *supposed* to be cleaned as soon as practicable.

"Sir, it's hard to get in the pens when . . ."

"That's been there for *weeks*, PO," Herzer said. "You can tell by the build-up. I'm upset with *myself* for not having already found it. And this isn't the only pen."

The wyvern took that moment to let out a mew and poke at the PO, who practically jumped out of her skin.

"Sir . . ."

"Petty Officer Riebech, this wyvern is recently fed. It is not going to *eat* you. Pet it on the head and then push its muzzle away and it'll leave you alone. Whap it on the nose if it doesn't take the hint."

The PO rubbed at its head briefly and then pushed it away, backing herself into a corner more than pushing.

"PO," Herzer sighed, "this fungus can get into dragon skin that has been damaged, such as from enemy action. It's damned hard to stop fungal infection. These pens have to be *clean*. Not just swabbed out—cleaned out down to the wood. Every time it is possible. Which means when we're on operations. And if you can't do it then, then lead the wyverns *out* and do it. They can stand in the corridor or you can move them on deck."

"Yes, sir," the PO said miserably.

"Clean enough to eat off of," Herzer said. "Which is what you're going to do."

"Sir?"

"For the next week, every member of your division will be taking their meals *in* the wyvern stalls."

"Sir . . ."

"I'm dead serious, PO. I think that that will give you an idea of how clean they have to be. I'd suggest that you get started with this one before the CO sees its condition. And you just might want to use some bleach . . ."

"Bein' kind of harsh to my troops, ain't you XO?" Joanna asked quietly as the crewmen led the wyvern out and began recleaning the stall. Of course the deck would then have to be sanded. Herzer hoped like hell that they'd clean all the stalls *then* sand the decks; they didn't have time for them to do it any other way.

"That's what the XO is for," Herzer pointed out. "Actually, that's what the leading PO is for. Which is why I'm going to have a Talk with PO Riebech after this. I've been concentrating so much on the riders that I haven't had time to make sure everything on the ground crew side was functional."

"Not quite correct," Joanna said. "You've been focusing on the riders. What you needed to do was ensure that everything *else* was functional at the same time. If that meant the riders had to do some training on their own, that meant they had to do some training on their own."

"Too controlling?" Herzer asked.

"Maybe," Joanna admitted. "What do you think?"

Herzer considered it for a moment and shrugged.

"I'm being chewed out for micromanaging, aren't I?"

"By me?" Joanna replied. "Everyone knows that when I chew someone out you can hear it in the next fleet."

"Unless you think there's a better way," Herzer said. "Okay, take a light brush with the whole crew for a while? I really want to land with both heels on the ground side."

"No, I'd say that ground side needs a shaking up," Joanna admitted. "My weyr has been a pigsty. I was just waiting for you to notice it."

"Because that's my job," Herzer said. "Sorry."

"Just don't let it happen again," Joanna replied, mildly.

"You're good at this," Herzer chuckled.

"Son, you got any idea how old *I* am?" Joanna said with a snort. "Everybody is always aghast at how old your girlfriend is. Nobody bothers to *ask* how old *I* am."

"How old are you?" Herzer asked.

"None of your business, sonny," Joanna replied with a chuckle. "How are we otherwise, for the inspection I mean?"

"Pretty shipshape," Herzer said. "We've got three more hours. Should be up to snuff by then."

"Do another round," Joanna said. "Go do the evil XO thing. I'll just take another snooze."

It was Saturday and damned if Edmund was going to kill his ass on paperwork on a Saturday. So after getting up and making sure everyone knew he was awake, he lay back down for a light snooze.

Which was broken by a tap on the door.

Edmund considered acting like he'd been at his desk and then decided to just blow it off. Admirals were supposed to have their perks. He rolled onto the side of the bed and said: "Come."

"Mer message, sir," the signal midshipman said. Usually a runner brought the information so it had to be something special.

Edmund took the parchment and looked at it and then nodded. He consulted his calendar and frowned.

"Pass the word to Admiral Shar," Edmund said, lying back down. "Initiate Operation Front Royal."

"Front Royal, sir?" the midshipman squeaked.

"Front Royal."

"Major Herrick," the skipper said as she walked down Broadway. She opened up one of the wyvern stalls and stepped in, tapping the wyvern on the nose when it nuzzled at her and checked in the corners.

"Clean as a whistle," she said, walking down to where Joanna was curled. "Commander."

"Skipper," Joanna said, nodding her head and lifting one claw in what might be considered a salute.

The skipper walked around the dragon and looked at her area, then spoke to Major Sassan who wrote something in his notebook.

"Not bad," she said, stepping to the aft corridor hatch. "But either Commander Gramlich is going to have to stop shedding so much or you're going to have to get on your leading PO."

"We'll take care of it, ma'am," Joanna growled.

"Make signal to all units of the Fleet," Shar said, coming on deck. "Immediately open sealed packet marked 'Stonewall.' Open sealed packet marked 'Front Royal.' Open no other packets. Report when all captains have completed their first reading."

"Yes, sir," the officer of the deck said.

"Where's the skipper?"

"Conducting the Saturday inspection, sir."

"I'm sure the crew will be delighted that it's now cancelled. Go get him."

"Skipper," the signal messenger said, skidding to a halt and pausing to catch his breath. The skipper had made it as far as the kitchens and had just informed the mess officer that he was a disgrace to the uniform. "Ma'am, mer message. Open packet Stonewall. Open packet Front Royal."

"Well, XO," Skipper Karcher said. "Looks like we're done."

An hour later the skipper came on deck and looked at the telltale on the mast and then at the compass.

"Officer of the deck," she said. "Prepare to come about, heading one-three-five. Call all hands."

"Aye, aye, ma'am," the lieutenant called as the bosun pipes shrilled.

"Can I ask what's happening?" Major Sassan said.

"You can ask," the skipper replied with a growl. "But it doesn't mean I know the answer."

"Do you know what is happening?" Destrang asked Van Krief as the ship heeled over and headed south.

"Yes," she answered, shortly. Since boarding the ships they hadn't had much to do and she had had too much time to think about the messages she had written for the fleet.

"So tell," Destrang said.

"Can't," she said. "I will say this; if anything goes wrong we're all screwed."

CHAPTER TWENTY-ONE

"This is so screwed."

The trip to Balmoran had been, if anything, more uncomfortable than the trip from Raven's Mill, and that was no picnic. And as she rattled through the evening streets of Balmoran Old Town and watched the crowds moving among the shops and taverns Rachel had a hard time envisioning her upcoming duties. She knew that her mother had pounded in some medical training over the last few years. Being honest, she admitted that, for the period, she was a fair doctor. But this was something different, what used to be called "medical administration." The reports that she had received on the way up indicated that the planners of the base had included only a small infirmary. Given the purpose of the base, to support combat fleets in the northern Atlantis, that made no sense at all. She knew that her first job was going to be straightening out that little logic flaw.

She reached down and petted Azure, stroking him on his head until he rolled over on the floor of the coach and purred. House lions were a very old genetic mod, a house cat the size of a puma with a personality more like that of a dog. She had had Azure, a particularly long-bodied house lion with bright blue eyes and white fur and orange highlights, for longer than she could recall. The house lion had traveled with them to Newfell Base and now he came with her to Balmoran. She had considered leaving him to keep Charles company, but in the end Azure had looked so crestfallen at her packing that she had taken him with her. Now she was glad she had; she wasn't going to know anyone at the new posting and the house lion was at least a friend.

She looked out the window again as they passed out of the main part of town and beyond the range of street lamps. The buildings in this area were apparently warehouses and she saw fewer figures among them, these much more furtive than the boisterous crowds downtown. She laid her hand on Azure's shoulder as one of a group of figures started to step out of shadow, then relaxed as they decided, apparently, that the coach, with its heavily armed driver and assistant driver, was more trouble than it might be worth. She sincerely hoped she wouldn't be forced to travel through this area as part of her job.

The coach passed through an oak forest, down a surprisingly well-made road, and then debouched into a large open area. There was light ahead and Rachel craned her head for a glimpse of the base.

The open area stretched along the river for what seemed like klicks. On the near side a large number of buildings were under construction, the work going on even at this hour under the light of torches and lamps. She could see boats and barges tied up to docks along the river but they were half obscured by the dozens of buildings that had already been constructed. The smell of freshly cut pine and oak for a moment reminded her of Raven's Mill in the days just after the Fall and the base had that same sense of barely organized chaos.

The post coach pulled up before a large building that clearly predated the current construction. It was partially stone and partially wood of several styles and clearly built over several generations, probably in Norau preindustrial times. She wondered, idly, how it had survived the growth of the Boswash megalopolis. But however it had survived it was there and as she descended from the coach a tall, angular man with a shock of white hair on one temple approached from the lamp-lit foyer.

"Doctor Ghorbani?" the man said, holding out his hand. "I'm Basilia Zahar, the hospital administrator."

"You didn't have to come down here for me, Mr. Zahar," Rachel said. "And 'Doctor' Ghorbani is my mother. I don't feel I have the credentials to append doctor to my name."

"Well your reputation precedes you, Miss Ghorbani," the man said, with a tired smile. "And we're glad to have you. I've set up quarters for you in the residence wing of the hospital. I'll have your bags taken over there," he continued with a wave. A young man followed him down from the portico and took her bags from the coach as Azure finally stretched and jumped down to the ground.

"Azure, my house lion," Rachel said, to Zahar's widened eyes. "I hope that won't be a problem?"

"Not at all," the administrator said, smoothly. "Not many of those around anymore; I'd missed them."

"I've had Azure since I was a girl," Rachel said as the administrator led the way down the street. "He's taken to traveling with me wherever I go. I hope it won't cause problems with the other staff."

"Madame, the staff will be so delighted to have someone who knows what they are doing that I don't think they would care if you turned up with a tame orc on a chain," Zahar admitted, darkly.

Rachel was left to ponder that as they made their way, in fits and jumps, to the hospital.

The main street of the base was freshly covered in crushed gravel but it was already muddy and pitted. A wooden walkway had been established to one side but it was broken by occasional cross-streets and the trio had to dodge wagon traffic and potholes on their way to the hospital facilities. Between splashing wagons and mud holes, Rachel knew she was a sight when they got to the hospital. The structure, which was still under construction, was located on a slight prominence well away from the river and the swamps that surrounded the base. Transportation to it might be problematic but it would avoid the unhealthy airs, not to mention insects, to be found in the lower-lying areas. It consisted of one two-story structure, more or less complete, and several wings connected by fly-ways. Some of those buildings were complete, others were not. And there was far less in the way of energy, not to mention workers, in the area than at the main base.

She was led into the main doors of the two-story

structure and nodded at what she saw. The floors were tile, easier by far than wood to keep clean, and the walls were plastered.

"I hope the operating suites are as well apportioned," she said, gesturing at the walls.

"The ones that are complete are," Zahar said with a sigh. "We only have two set up at this point and a triage area. I've come to some conclusions about the way that the local procurement works, but we can discuss that when you've had some rest."

"What's that?" Rachel said. "Everyone else is working night and day."

"We're not permitted to take more than twelve-hour shifts," Zahar pointed out. "By orders of the base commander. There were too many accidents when they worked longer than that."

"We'll see," Rachel said. "Excuse me," she said, turning to the young man carrying the baggage, "I didn't catch your name."

"Keith, ma'am," the boy said, nodding.

"Keith, if you don't mind could you drop those off at my quarters while Administrator Zahar and I have a word?"

"Yes, ma'am." The boy nodded, heading down a corridor.

"If you don't mind?" she asked.

"Not at all," Zahar said with a lopsided smile. "If you'd like to examine your office?"

The office was as good as anything in Raven's Mill: plastered walls, carpets on the floor, a nice, if obviously new, desk, even paintings on the wall.

"Very nice," Rachel said, grabbing a chair. "But only two surgery suites complete?"

"I just got here, also," Zahar said by way of apology. "The way that the base procurement works is to come up with elaborate plans that they know they can't get funding for. Take this building; it's entirely for administration."

"And it's complete?" Rachel asked.

"Nearly. But it wasn't fully budgeted. So they built it first and now they're asking for funds to build the *rest* of the hospital, the functional part, if you take my meaning."

"Blast."

"We have the two operating suites and we're working, out of budget, on one more. We also have two wards complete. We have the *equipment* for three wards, several semiprivate rooms, three more suites, etc. And, thank God, we've gotten our full supply of materials; there's enough morphine here to kill several elephants, bandages enough for a legion, etc. But the construction budget is shot."

"They probably can get a supplementary spending bill passed," Rachel mused. "But, damnit, we should have the important facilities in place first!"

"Agreed, but there's nothing I could do about it by the time I got here," Zahar said.

"Well, we can damned well turn some of the office areas into wards at the very least," Rachel said. "What about staff?"

"That, too, is a problem," Zahar admitted. "We have *no* trained physicians; you're it."

"What?" Rachel snapped. "I can't handle a hospital this size!"

"There *aren't* that many trained physicians," Zahar pointed out. "The Second Legion is moving into the area and they have two. We also have a fair staff of . . . well let's call them half-trained support staff. Some people who are alleged to be nurses, two people who are supposed to be physician's assistants, what have you."

"What about patients?"

"So far we have ten, all injuries from construction," the administrator said. "Only one of them was extremely serious, he had a pile of wood fall on him. I don't think he's going to survive; internal injuries."

"Well," Rachel said, rubbing a hand on her face. "Let me get with the duty nurse and do rounds."

"Now?" Zahar asked.

"Now," Rachel replied. "I'll get a coat to cover up the majority of the mud. Hopefully I won't have to operate, though; my hands are too shaky. Right now I'd be more likely to kill than cure."

CHAPTER TWENTY-TWO

Megan picked up the glass and tilted Paul's head back as he leaned forward for a sip.

"Ah, ah," she said. "Let me pour."

Paul smiled and tipped his head back, opening his mouth.

"Paul?"

"Yes?"

"I love you," she said, miserably, and poured the acid down his throat.

The pain was excruciating and half the acid poured back out in an explosion as he rolled over on his side. She had expected it, though, and only a few drops fell on her arm as she rolled to the side. She snap-kicked his shoulder, rolling him onto his face as he grabbed his throat, which was rapidly dissolving. The acid had burned through his cheeks and she could see a cheekbone as she hammered him down onto his stomach and raised the bottle of red wine. Two

321

blows on the back of his neck sufficed to sever his spinal cord but she continued to pound until she'd opened up the back of his skull, blood spurting in a cloud, then poured the remnants of the jug of acid, which fortunately hadn't spilled, onto his skull. She waited until it had burned into the skull and burned into the cerebellum. When she was sure he was dead she fumbled in his naked crotch until she managed to pull the Key from the flap just under his scrotum.

She held it in her hands and panted, the pain of her arm forgotten as she just looked at it for a moment. This was the moment of truth. If it didn't work she might as well drink the rest of the acid herself. Actually, she had a vial of concentrated poison waiting in the lab. She took a deep breath and held up the Key.

"Mother?"

"Yes?" a voice answered out of the air.

She felt abilities she thought lost forever blossom. The pain in her arm washed away as her nannites reactivated and began healing the damage from the acid and a Net link formed in her mind.

"Paul is dead then?" Megan asked, shaking in reaction.

"Paul Bowman is most assuredly dead," Mother said with just a hint of satisfaction.

"And I hold his Key," Megan said. "That means I hold his power?"

"You are the new Key-holder for Key nine," Mother confirmed. "Power, however, is restricted." A green bar-graph appeared in the lower right-hand corner of Megan's vision. It was partially down from maximum extent. "This represents current available power to a non-aligned Key-holder. It is a bare minimum power transfer that is a hard protocol."

"I need to port out all the girls," Megan replied. "And find the ones that are in pregnancy confinement."

A map appeared in her vision. It was apparently a map of the local area of the castle. As Megan concentrated it zoomed out so that she could see the surrounding area. She zoomed it back in so that she could find her location and the girls as well. There were blue dots in the harem and others not far away. The map was also liberally sprinkled with red and green dots.

"The Changed are under the effective control of Celine Reinshafen and are marked in red," Mother replied. "Paul's guards have switched allegiance to you as the new Key-holder and are marked in green. Females associated with the harem are blue. You have insufficient power available for multiple human-volume teleports. You can open a portal, however."

"I need to get the girls first," Megan said as there was a scream in the harem. "What the hell is that?"

"Certain of Paul Bowman's programs were designed to fail upon his death," Mother said. "Including the mind-block on Amado Tillou. She is not particularly pleased at recent events."

"Oh, shit."

Megan rushed to the door and threw it open to a scene of chaos. Amber had Christel on the floor with her fingers locked on the other woman's throat. Shanea and Mirta were trying to pull her off while the rest were either standing back in horror or fighting amongst themselves.

"Stop this!" Megan bellowed, walking over and bending back Amber's pinkie finger. "I'll break it, Amber, I swear I will."

"Do you know what this bitch did?" Amber hissed in pain, continuing to clamp on Christel's neck. The harem manager's face was turning purple.

"Yes," Megan said. "And I know what Paul did. And if I have to do it myself I will. Let. Go."

With a final wrench Amber let go and sat back on her heels. Christel took a deep, racking breath and rolled over on her side.

"Ashly! Tory! Break it up!" Megan yelled, going over to the two struggling girls and kicking them in the side until they rolled apart. "We don't have *time* for this shit."

"What happened?" Christel asked, looking from Megan to the Key.

"Paul is dead," Megan said, slipping the Key into her bikini bottom. "And we are leaving. As soon as I go get the girls who are in confinement."

Mirta saw Christel's look and slid between the two women.

"Even without calling on power, she could kick your ass," Mirta said, crouching. "For that matter, so could I."

"You *killed* him?" Christel said. "Do you know what that means?"

"It means I can go free," Megan said. "And anyone who wants to follow me can, too. I'm not going to bother twisting arms, though. I'm going to go get the other girls and then form a portal. You either make it through or you don't. You have until I get back to choose." She looked around and then pointed. "Shanea,

Amber, you're with me. Mirta, you're in charge here. I'll secure all the entrances after I go but you're going to have to get some order in this place."

"Will do," Mirta said.

"Come on," Megan said to the two as she strode to the main door. "Mother, release all blocks for myself and these two. Raise blocks on all entrances against entry or exit. Form protection fields on all three of us. Only summon them to full power if we need them." She saw the graph flicker slightly as the shields formed. Damn, there *wasn't* much power.

The door opened at her touch and she stopped in the hallway outside. There were what she recognized as Paul's "special" guards on either side of the door. They were in plate armor with full helmets so she had no idea what they looked like. She also didn't care.

"Your loyalty has transferred to me," Megan said.

"Yes, mistress," the guards answered.

"We're going to get the other girls," she continued. "You two lead. Can you summon the other guards?"

"Yes, mistress," the guard on the left answered.

"Do so," she replied, pointing up the corridor. "Let's move out."

The two guards strode down the hallway, banging on their shields as they walked.

"Provide protection for us," Megan said after a moment. "Mother, how much power to put blocks on all the cross-corridors?"

"Depends upon if they are challenged," Mother replied.

"Block the biggest groups of Changed," Megan said as a Changed warrior skidded into the hallway. When it saw the escaped girls it let out a howl and charged at them. She wasn't sure if the orc was intent on recapturing them or raping them, but it didn't really matter. The two guards engaged it immediately and the girls slid by to the side of the conflict. As they did three more of the specials came charging down the hall.

"Leave them," Megan snapped as they reached the entrance to the confinement quarters. "Guard the corridor. We're going to get the girls in here and then go back to the harem. As more guards come up, gather them to screen us back."

"Yes, mistress," one of the guards replied.

She touched open the door and entered a long corridor. At the end was a broad room where two women, both very pregnant, were sewing. In the distance was the sound of a baby crying.

"Megan?" Velva said, looking up. "Is it your turn to be stuck in this dump?" Then she seemed to notice the other two women and frowned.

"No, Velva," Megan said, gulping as the sound of clashing steel came from the corridor. "Paul's dead. We need to leave."

"What?" Velva replied, gulping air. "WHAT?"

"We need to *leave*, Velva. All of us. Get the girls. And the children. Now!"

She glanced at her power levels and blanched.

"Mother, what's draining power?"

"Changed are attempting to pass my blocks," Mother noted. "I've rearranged them to simply block the main corridors, but they are throwing themselves at the block points."

"Shanea! Amber!" Megan yelled. "Hurry!"

Women, some of them carrying infants, were streaming out of the side rooms. Most of them were more heavily dressed than the girls in the harem but a few, those who had already delivered, were clearly trying to fit back into their costumes. There were definite signs of conflict.

"Okay, this is the deal," Megan said. "I'm not going to repeat it and I'm not going to answer questions. Paul is dead. I have his Key. I'm going to transport us out to safety. Anyone who wants to come, fine. Those who stay behind, though, are going to be at the mercy of the Changed."

With that she turned and headed for the battle at the entrance.

The corridor was a madhouse but the geased guards were holding off the Changed and there was a clear run, or in many cases waddle, to the harem. Megan briefly wondered if it would have made more sense to bring the harem girls to the pregnant ones instead of the other way around but it was too late for second thoughts.

There was another group of guards battling by the entrance to the harem but they were blocking the door, being forced back by the Changed. Megan looked at the gaggle of women behind her, then at the door, then at the battles at both ends of the corridor. The floor around the door was slick with the blood of guards that had already fallen and the continuous clatter of sword on shield and armor was shattering her concentration. After a moment she waved at the women.

"Up against the wall!" she shouted. "Shanea, Amber, get them up against the wall!" She looked at the backs of the guards in the further battle and picked six that weren't in the front line. She sent a thought winging to them and they turned and charged back down the corridor, smashing into the fight around the doorway and briefly clearing it.

"Move!" she shouted, running to the door and standing in the way of the battle as the pregnant women scrambled to the doorway. "Mother, release the blocks for these girls!" she suddenly shouted. This was not going according to plan.

"Already done," Mother assured her. "In little things like that I'm permitted to anticipate."

"Thank you," Megan breathed as a Changed hit her protection field and rebounded.

"They're all through," Amber said, tapping her on the arm.

"Great," Megan replied, sliding through the door to the harem and shutting it. "Mother, release all blocks not directly sealing the harem. Seal the harem entrances; nobody in, nobody out. Release the loyalty geas on all the special guards, everywhere. Open a portal to Sheida Ghorbani's house."

"All done except the last," Mother said. "There's a teleport block over all of Norau. Given the way that those can be bypassed, it's quite definite. Nothing in, nothing out. Definitely no teleports from Ropasa to anywhere in Norau."

"Damnit!" Megan snapped. "I need someplace to teleport that's *safe*."

"Safe is a relative term," Mother replied. "You need somewhere that doesn't have a teleport block on it and that is not held by New Destiny forces. The Finn has voted with New Destiny on some minor matters in exchange for binding prohibitions against power use against forces that are not directly tied to

the Freedom Coalition. However, the McClure clan
in Gael is in *contact* with the Coalition and would
probably provide you safe-haven."

"Is that what you're suggesting?" Megan asked.

"Yes."

"Open a portal to their house, then," Megan said.

"Castle, actually," Mother replied as a rippling silver
mirror appeared in the doorway to Christel's office.

"Okay, here's the deal," Megan said, looking around
at the girls. "Paul is dead. Nobody is going to care
for you after this. If you're lucky, you'll only be
Changed. If you're unlucky you'll be turned over to
Reyes. Either way there are going to be some pointed
questions about this event."

"I can't believe you *killed* him," Christel shouted.
"Why?"

"Because I don't like being a slave," Megan replied.
"I'm not going to debate about it. It's done. And we're
leaving. Anyone who wants out, there's the door," she
added, pointing at the portal. "Anyone who wants to
wait for what Chansa and Celine will call 'mercy' can
stay." She looked around at the girls as none of them
moved. One of the babies started crying.

"Oh, for Pete's sake," she snarled. "I need to be
last. Who's going?"

"Me," Amber said. "Better anything than this life." She
walked to the doorway of silver and strode through.

That started a rush as almost all the women crowded
the doorway. Christel, however, stayed where she
was.

"Christel," Megan said, looking at her power gauge.
It was down in the yellow and dropping as thumps
indicated that the Changed were trying to break the

blocks on the door. "When they come through they're not going to be asking a lot of questions."

"I'm staying," Christel said, shaking her head. Her whole body was shaking for that matter.

Megan looked at her coldly then nodded her head.

"Okay," she replied, striding to the portal. "Good luck."

Jock McClure shook his head as Steffan, who was a nephew of some sort, threw a beef bone at young Jock. Young Jock responded by climbing onto the heavy oak table and hurling himself onto Steffan, the two of them rolling around in the rushes on the floor as dogs gathered around barking.

"I hate winter," he muttered, pulling his fur cloak around himself and picking up a mug of warmed mead. The long great hall of the castle was impossible to heat, and close as he was to the fireplace it still was bloody cold.

"The young bucks are getting restless," Armand Byrne said, nodding toward the brawlers. Armand had been a friend, and quite serious reenactor, before the Fall. When Jock had succeeded to the position of Laird McClure he had moved in to play "seneschal." After the Fall the two had made the roles real, managing to hammer together an alliance among others in the area that had been holding off New Destiny, with damned little help, for over two years. And winter was no respite; supplied from their bases in Ropasa the forces of New Destiny attacked year round. "Been a long one. Everyone's getting restless for that matter."

"And old bones don't care for it much either,"

McClure replied. He was a big man slightly shrunk by age, with long white hair that was pulled back by a gold cord. But his blue eyes were still bright as he watched the two youngsters rolling among the dogs and bones on the floor. "NO KNIVES!" he bellowed as young Jock fumbled at his belt. "Godfrey, break them up before that idiot son of mine makes more of a fool of himself."

Godfrey, who was easily the largest man in the room, plucked the knife from the boy's belt, then picked them both up and banged them together until they stopped struggling.

"No knives," McClure said. It was the reason that the swords were stacked against the wall; once two fighters got to battling they'd use anything to hand. He'd rather that the swords were in the armory but even in Dun McClure there was the chance of a sneak attack.

Such as if New Destiny formed a portal like the one that was opening up over the kitchen entrance.

"ATTACK!" Byrne bellowed, standing up so fast his heavy chair tumbled backwards. In no more than two seconds he had a longsword in his hand. But he was slow compared to Old Jock, who was halfway down the table with a massive battle-axe cocked at high port.

For a long moment nothing happened as fighter after fighter armed themselves and arrayed before the rippling silver mirror. Then there was a distortion and . . .

A very tall, and very beautiful, brunette female wearing a full body suit made of almost entirely transparent silk stepped into the room and immediately threw her arms around herself.

"It's *freezing* in here!" she snapped, looking around at the swords. "I really don't think you're going to need those," she added as she stepped to the side for another woman.

And another. And another. And another. All of them wearing halfway to nothing.

"Hullo there," Young Jock said to the brunette, lowering his sword so the point touched the ground. "I think we could be friends."

"Not unless you learn what the meaning of *bath* is," the brunette snapped.

"What the bloody hell is this?" Laird McClure asked in utter confusion as another woman stepped through, this one carrying an infant.

There was a gasp and a slap followed by a scream and a small woman launched herself across the gap to impact on Hugh Telford, who had wrapped his arms around a petite blonde. In a second, no more, Telford was on the ground, choking, from a blow that had appeared out of nowhere.

"You really don't want to do this," the brunette said as two of the men closed in on the smaller woman. She snap-kicked one in the knee and he tumbled over groaning, but Godfrey picked her up from behind and blocked her attempt to turn him into a soprano. "You really don't want to do this!"

"I want to know what the hell is *happening*!" Jock bellowed as the silver mirror rippled one more time and then collapsed leaving a good-looking, medium-height brunette, wearing nothing but a bikini, standing arms akimbo in the doorway to the kitchen.

"I'm what's happening," the girl said, pointing her hand and sending a lance of power that drove Godfrey into the wall. "My name is Megan Travante. I am a Key-holder. I just killed Paul Bowman to get his Key. And the next man who puts his hand on a woman in my presence will be sent to a very special and private version of Hell."

The women of the castle had been summoned and the girls and their children had been bundled off to warmer quarters. After that Megan and Jock McClure had retreated to his office, a much smaller room in the upper floors of the keep. He built up the fire as she wrapped a fur around herself.

"Mother told me you were in contact with the Freedom Coalition," Megan said.

"Aye," Jock replied, poking the fire to life and throwing on another billet of wood.

"I need to contact them and get us extracted," Megan said.

"Aye," Jock said, again.

"Is that all you're going to say?" Megan asked.

"It's a bit of a shock, lassie," McClure admitted. "We were expecting some of their Changed monsters to come through the portal, not a cluster of odalisques."

"Oda-whats?" Megan chuckled.

"Odalisques," McClure repeated. "Harem girls. So Paul had a harem?"

"He considered it a breeding group," Megan replied, sharply.

"And of course it had to be live cover," McClure said, taking a seat across from her. "I'll heat some mead if you'd like."

"I'd prefer tea," Megan said.

"Well, that we don't be havin'," McClure sighed. "Or clothes fer yuh for that matter. We might be able to scare up some blankets, but we don't be havin' the power looms that the UFS does; we've been fightin' too hard to make any. Can't you ken it, then?"

"I don't want to use the power," Megan admitted. "Laird McClure . . ."

"Call me Jock," McClure interjected. "People only call me 'Laird' when they're about to go to war with me."

"Jock, then," Megan said with a grin. "We won't tax you any longer than necessary. I'll contact Sheida and try to get her to let me teleport us out. We won't be here long."

"Might be longer than you think," Jock said. "The block they have is tight; it has to be. I'm not sure Sheida will drop it even for you."

"We . . . *I* can't stay here long. The rest of the Destiny councilors will be hunting me. If they throw their full weight against you . . ."

"Ack, they've been tryin' hard enough as it is," Jock said with a shrug. "They send their forces up into the highlands and we kill them. Or they land on the coast and we kill them. Or they sneak into a glen and set up a portal. And we kill them."

"You're not going to just be killing *them*," Megan replied.

"No," Jock said with a nod. "I *had* three sons. I've one now, lassie. I didn't say it was easy. I said we did it."

"If Chansa had the full backing of the Council he could have taken you at any time," Megan replied with a shrug. "If they know I'm here, they'll come for you. In force."

"Be a bit hard with most of their troops at sea," Jock noted. "Of course, we're by the sea, here. But I don't see them turning around their fleet just when it's on its way to Norau. And doing well, from what I hear."

"You hear a lot," Megan said with a frown.

"I've got big ears," McClure chuckled. "But I'll admit I hadn't heard of this harem. There's another girl here waiting for transport; your friends will be meeting her. She was in a brothel. Carried some important message apparently. Selkies picked it up then told her to come here. I'm liable to cause the Finn to rethink his bargain if this keeps up."

"What do you think I should do?" Megan asked.

"Ah, now it's questions is it?" McClure answered, nodding his head. "Not so much 'we must do this, we must do that.' I think you should be having a quiet chat with Sheida, lassie. And then getting your pretty little butt to someplace safer than Dun McClure. But until then, we'll fight for ye. They'll nigh pass us until the last McClure is dead and gone. Hang on a bit."

He stood up and went to the door, leaning out into the corridor.

"Get that heathen Baradur up here!" he bellowed into the hall.

"Baradur's one of the wee folk," he explained, walking back over to the fire and warming his hands. "I captured him in a battle with one of their clans. He's just been hanging around and eating my food ever since. I think I'll foist him on you."

The door opened shortly after and a small, heavily muscled young man entered the room. He was dressed in skins and furs and had a sallow, yellowish complexion, a bullet head with a topknot of black, lanky hair dangling from one side and a flat face with bright eyes half-hidden by epicanthic folds. Instead of the straight swords of the Gael he was armed with a long, back-curved sword on his left hip and a similar knife nearly the size of a sword on his right. He bowed to the laird and Megan, standing silently.

"Baradur, you've been eating my bread and salt for the last year," McClure growled. "And I'll have no more of it. I'm giving you over to the Key-holder for a servant. Serve her well or you'll have me to face!"

"Yes, Laird McClure," was all the man said. He had a strange accent, light on the ears.

"The wee folk are strange in their ways," McClure said, turning to Megan. "But they're bloody loyal. If he takes your bread and salt he'll die rather than let harm come to you."

"I have neither bread nor salt," Megan said, dryly.

"You can owe me," Baradur replied. He suddenly grinned showing a mouth full of bright, white teeth. "Although I'll also want silver, mistress."

"They're bloody mercenaries, really," McClure explained. "Good fighters for all they're small. Hard-headed, too. They don't fight for New Destiny, though. Oh, and they don't talk, so you can have a conversation around them and not worry about it."

"And I'm to take your word on that?" Megan said.

"Well, you'll have to, won't you?" McClure replied, gruffly. "But you'll find out. I'll give you some peace for now. Keep Baradur with you, though. I'm *fairly* sure the castle is secure, but I can't guarantee anything."

"Thank you," Megan said as he left the room. Baradur looked at her for a moment, then squatted, facing the door.

Megan took a breath and looked at the fire for a moment.

"Mother, please contact Sheida Ghorbani and ask her to send a projection."

She had counted to ten when the projection appeared. Sheida looked much older than the last time Megan had seen a projection of her, shortly after the Fall.

"So, Paul is truly dead," Sheida said, looking at the girl. She summoned a virtual chair and sat in it. "And you are the daughter of my friend Joel."

"My father is alive?" Megan asked, tears coming to her eyes. Even after the contact she hadn't been able to hope.

"Indeed, he's my head of intelligence," Sheida said. "We had a message about you only . . . a few days ago? It had some details of your situation. We had a very hard time deciding whether to let the agent contact you again."

"What did you decide?" Megan asked, honestly curious.

"To permit the contact," Sheida replied. "It was pragmatic, but, we felt, necessary. Besides, there were problems with stopping the contact even if we'd chosen to try. In the end we decided to use you as an agent, despite the risks. All our worries for naught," she added with a faint smile.

"I had a hard time deciding whether to kill Paul," Megan said. "I knew I could do some good as an agent. You've got no idea what I've learned. But my plans were so far advanced . . ." She paused and shook her head. "I . . . I really didn't want to kill him. But I *had* to!"

"Megan," Sheida said, sternly. "You did *well*. What you did was the best possible thing you could have done for Paul. I'm not sure that it's the best possible thing to have done for the *world*, but we can discuss that when we have you safe."

Megan nodded and shrugged. "Open up the teleport block and I'll bring the girls over now."

"No can do," Sheida sighed. "We're only able to hold it because of a single vote by the Finn. He's . . . too unpredictable to want to try the same route again. If I drop it for you, Norau will be vulnerable to penetration. We'll have to send a ship."

"The New Destiny fleet is at sea," Megan pointed out. "Somewhere not very far from here." She paused and gripped her hair. "I have *so much information* in my head! I don't know where to start."

"It will keep," Sheida said with a soothing tone.

"Not all of it," Megan said, suddenly looking into the distance. "There's a Destiny assassin on the *Richard*. He has orders to poison Duke Talbot and Admiral Chang. He might have done so already." She looked out the window of the room into the darkness beyond. "I'm not sure what timing he was supposed to use."

Sheida held up a finger and looked distant for a moment.

"I've sent an avatar to inform Edmund," Sheida said. "And I'll go ahead and track down the agent while I'm about it."

"The fleet has two targets," Megan continued. "The main combat fleet is to attack Blackbeard Base and kill the mer-women and take the children. The invasion fleet is aimed at Balmoran harbor. Jassinte is sending an army over the mountains to attack Hind and try to draw off some of the forces from the Assam reactor. I know the route they're taking. There are more assassins waiting for Edmund in Newfell. Celine has four new Change types they're holding back for the attack on Norau. There are Change acolytes with the fleet that—"

"Hold on, girl," Sheida said, waving her hand. "We'll do a full debrief as soon as we can. I'll send a ship from Edmund's fleet . . ."

"A carrier," Megan said, sharply. "I want a *carrier* from the fleet. With a full battle group."

"We're in the middle of a *battle*, Megan," Sheida said. "We need all the carriers we have. We lost too many in that idiotic battle off the Onay Isles."

"If I'm killed at sea, what happens to the Key?" Megan asked. "If it and I go into the water?"

"I'll damned well feed you power to keep you alive," Sheida promised, solemnly.

"New Destiny has a device that can drop personal protection fields," Megan countered.

"Impossible," Sheida snapped. "Mother would not permit it."

"She doesn't have protocols to prevent it," Megan said. "They're nannites that create a quantum field that the PPFs can't stabilize in. They only drop it for a few moments, but that's long enough for a knife or a sword to get through. Not to mention water."

"God, we do need to debrief you, don't we?" Sheida said. "Okay, a carrier. And a battle group. Edmund is going to go ballistic."

CHAPTER TWENTY-THREE

"You're insane!" Edmund snapped.

"Maybe, but Megan just saved your life," Sheida pointed out.

"He was going to use *cyanide*," Edmund snapped. "In my *coffee*. I hate almond in my coffee, it's nearly as barbaric as hazelnut. I would have smelled it. And I need *every* carrier, Sheida."

"The *Hazhir* is closest," Sheida said, definitely. "Detach it to pick up Megan and anyone else she wants transported. Do it *now*, Edmund. That's an order."

"Damnit!" Talbot snarled. "Okay, okay. Will do, my Queen. This is going to get people *killed*."

"Edmund, we have an additional Key," Sheida pointed out. "Which means no more depending upon the Finn for low-margin votes. That will keep people *alive*. Send the message. Or do you want me to?"

"You," Edmund admitted. "It will be faster and

less prone to intercept or confusion. I'm going to be busy anyway, trying to figure out how to survive with a third of my combat forces gone."

"Major Herrick," the messenger panted as she threw open Herzer's door. "Skipper wants you right away. She said to run."

"Look, knock or something," Herzer said, rolling out from under Bast.

"Sorry, sir," the female messenger said, going red and then pale and shutting the door hastily.

"Why me?" Herzer asked, throwing on his clothes. As he did he heard a cry of "All hands! Stand by to go about!"

"I don't know," Bast said, leaning her cheek on one fist and making a moue. "Hate all this military stuff. Do this. Do that. Go here. Go there. But you'd best run."

"Sorry," he said, as he tucked in his shirt. He leaned over and gave her a kiss, then hurried out the door.

He took the lower deck corridors, which were filled with running figures as the crew poured up on deck, and then realized that the messenger hadn't specified where the skipper *was*. He pounded down the officers' corridor and gestured with his chin at the skipper's door.

"Skipper in there?" he asked the marine sentry.

"Yes, sir," the marine replied. "You're to go right in."

Herzer knocked and entered the room at a bellowed: "Enter!"

"You sent for me, ma'am?" Herzer asked, stopping in shock at the sight of Sheida Ghorbani's projection. "Majesty?" he added, bowing.

"We've been diverted," Skipper Karcher said. "Her Majesty asked that you be present for the briefing. Your Majesty?"

"Call me Sheida for God's sake," Sheida said. "Paul Bowman is dead. The girl who killed him took his Key and escaped to the castle of the Clan McClure in Gael. She has requested that she be extracted by carrier. You're the closest."

"Good God," Herzer said.

"Sit, damnit," Skipper Karcher said. "You look like you're about to fall down. We're . . ." she did some mental estimation. "We're at least three days' sail from the west coast of Gael if the winds hold. And there's a Destiny carrier somewhere up there. They're probably closer."

"That's why I'm only telling you two," Sheida pointed out. "She also has information that New Destiny can overcome personal protection fields. I want to make this clear. She is to be protected. Use any means necessary. Get her to safety. She has some other women with her, I'm not sure how many. Pick them up as well as anyone else she wants transported. Protect her as you would me."

"Yes, ma'am," Skipper Karcher said. "Where are we picking her up?"

"Here," Sheida said, summoning a holographic map and pointing to an inlet on the west coast of Gael. "The area is near the battle lines with New Destiny. And if they get wind of where she is, they'll go for her with everything they have. This goes no further, understand?"

"Understood, ma'am," Herzer said.

"Have you already changed course?" Sheida asked.

"Before Herzer got here, ma'am," the skipper stated.

"Okay, here is some additional information," Sheida said with a note of distaste. "The girls are from Paul's ... harem. He considered it a 'breeding program' but the first term is closer to reality. Herzer, I know that you have background in rape trauma. This is going to be the same and ... different. I'm not sure what you'll be dealing with, but Megan is probably going to be a little odd at first. Deal with it."

"Bast is here, ma'am," Herzer pointed out. "She was one of the first ones to counsel Daneh. She's very good. She knows what she's doing in situations like that."

"Now that's the first *good* news I've had in a while," Sheida said with a tired smile. "Other than the fact that we have an additional Key. Well, that's the orders."

"Are we to sail directly to Norau from picking her up?" Karcher asked.

"I'm ... not sure," Sheida admitted. "Edmund really doesn't want to lose you. We'll have to decide that later. For now, pick her up then head in the general direction of Newfell Base. Oh, the invasion fleet is headed for Balmoran. I'm sending them a warning."

"Balmoran?" Herzer said. "Rachel is there."

"Oh, bloody hell," Sheida said, then disappeared.

"Oh, now I'm supposed to put on my ground commander hat?" Edmund said. "Evacuate the civilians."

"It's one of our biggest cities!" Sheida snapped.

"And it's big enough that it's indefensible," Edmund replied with a sigh. "If you won't evacuate, send messages to have them build breastworks around the whole thing, if they have time. If they *don't* then tell them to get the hell out of Dodge. I'll deal with the invasion as soon as I've dealt with the fleet. The ground forces are to stand pat and delay Paul's forces. My staff has the plans on that one. Second Legion's in place, First will move to block them from passing up the river. There are defensive positions already prepared. Some of that 'useless defense money' we've been pissing away."

"Edmund, we have to try to *hold* Balmoran," Sheida said. "That's important. There's too much invested in that town. We can't see it all destroyed."

"They won't have time to destroy it all," Edmund said. "Trust me on this. Burn quite a bit of it, yes. Maybe loot some if we don't trash their ships, yes. Destroy it all, no."

"Rachel's there," Sheida pointed out.

"I know," Edmund replied, his jaw flexing. "And she's a medico with the combat forces. She's not eligible for withdrawal."

"That's . . . rather cold," Sheida said.

"She's my only daughter," Edmund said, as cold as arctic ice. "I could have sent her back to Raven's Mill, where the townspeople know that a decent militia is a good idea. Where there are walls building. Where the cream of the Blood Lords would have been there to protect her. I sent her to Balmoran instead. That is for *me* to live with, Sheida. Understand?"

"Yes, I do," Sheida said, quietly. "How long until this is all over?"

"Years," Edmund said. "But if you mean this particular campaign?" He thought about it for a moment. "Seven days. It doesn't really start for two more."

"Doctor Ghorbani?"

Rachel looked up from the chart she was annotating and nodded at the duty nurse to wait a moment. The young man on the bed had a face that was twisted with pain from his broken leg. He had fallen from a scaffold and broken his femur. At least that was what the chart said. The only problem was that he was complaining of pains from his hip and lower leg as well. He was in a large cast and it was impossible to examine the rest of the area. Not that there was much she could have done for a broken hip, but the ankle or leg could have been set if the PA on duty had waited to fix the femur until he was conscious.

She noted that it might be necessary to rebreak the lower leg and then patted him on the shoulder.

"I'll give orders for an increase in pain medication," she said. "In the meantime just try to rest."

"Yes, ma'am," the boy said.

She nodded at the duty nurse and walked down to the end of the ward. "Yes?"

"We just got told that Balmoran is where the orcs are coming," the nurse said nervously.

"Well, I guess we'll have our work cut out for us," Rachel said as calmly as she could. "I've upped Robertson to ten milligrams of codeine; make sure that the other nurses check his chart before they administer it and get him another five milligrams now."

"Yes, Doctor," the nurse said.

"Our job is to fix people," Rachel noted. "Let the soldiers and sailors worry about where the damage is going to happen."

Megan looked at the walls for a while after breaking contact with Sheida, pinching her nose and furrowing her brow in thought.

"Baradur, do you know where the rest of the women are?" she asked.

"Yes, mistress," the bodyguard said.

"We need to go there."

Without a word the man stood up and opened the door, stepping through and checking the corridor. One of McClure's soldiers had been stationed outside the door and Baradur nodded at him as Megan stepped through.

"Where are the other women?" Megan asked the soldier.

"In the women's quarters by the kitchens," the soldier said. "The laird said that you were to stay in the turret, mistress."

"We're going down there," Megan replied. "You can lead."

"Mistress, the laird said . . ."

"Well, we're going down there," Megan replied, smiling thinly. "And *you* are going to lead. If the laird has a problem with it, he can bring it up with me."

"Yes, mistress," the soldier said, turning down the corridor.

He led her in the opposite direction from the main hall at which Megan looked over her shoulder and frowned quizzically at Baradur. The bodyguard just nodded and gestured down the hall.

She hadn't realized until this moment what a knife-edge she was riding. In the harem she had, more or less, understood the dangers. But here, in a the castle of a group of unknown, and unknowable, loyalties, she had to wonder just who she could trust. Even after reaching Norau she would have the same problems. Ownership of a Key gave the user a great deal of power, power that was desirable to just about anyone in this post-Fall world. She automatically had told the soldier to precede her but it wasn't until they were walking that she realized she didn't want him *behind* her. She had to wonder how much of that automatic paranoia was from her recent experiences and how much was from her father. And to wonder how much of it was valid. Their reception had been surprisingly friendly and the castle, despite the laird's own paranoia, seemed secure.

On the other hand, it was easier to follow the young man than to take directions if he was behind her.

They turned down a side corridor and entered another narrow spiral staircase. Baradur grabbed a torch just as they entered the black maw of the doorway so she could partially see where she was going. The stairwell could best be described as "dank" and she wondered at the amount of slime that was on the walls.

"Can I ask a question?" she said as she slipped the second time and bumped into the young man in front of her.

"Yes, of course, mistress."

"I've been in historical castles before; they were never this . . ."

"Worn?" the man laughed. "Mistress, there are nearly a hundred people packed inside these walls. That many people in an area like this leads to all sorts of nastiness. We've had people come down with *fungal* infections. And there's nothing we could do, even if we had the time, about stuff like this mold. Cleaning these steps would be a job for bleach. Do *you* know how to make bleach, mistress?"

"Yes, as a matter of fact," Megan chuckled, "I do. But I take your point. For that matter, I know some medicinal chemistry. I'm not sure if I *should* leave."

"Mistress, if you could help that would be great," the guard said, his voice curiously muffled. "But you need to get to somewhere decent as fast as possible. This is no place for a council member. You can do us much more good presenting our case to those bastards in Norau that don't lift a finger to help us. We've been fighting Paul's forces almost since the Fall and the only help *we've* gotten is from the Finn, who just told the New Destiny bastards that they can't use power."

He turned as they reached a mostly empty storeroom at the bottom and looked her in the eye.

"I don't know at what point the Finn will decide that we're not 'neutral,'" the young man said, shaking his head. "But I don't really care. When you've seen one of your best friends dying from not having a decent doctor it's hard to care about 'the big picture.' We need *help*, mistress, while there's anyone left to help."

"I'll do what I can," Megan said. "While I'm here and when I've gotten to Norau."

"Thank you, mistress," the young man said, gesturing to a door on the far side of the storeroom. "This way."

"How many people have you lost?" Megan asked as the soldier opened the door.

"I don't really know," he admitted. "More guys

trickle in from further up the highlands all the time. Right now we've got about thirty fighters here at the Clan and Innes has about a hundred. We had about eighty at one point. Some of them got killed, some drifted away. We don't hold a boy that's seen the war and decided it's not for him. He'll find someplace in the hills and make a farm and send us what he can. But if he hasn't the stomach to stand the orcs then I don't want him on my shoulder."

In the next room there were a few people sleeping, most of them women, girls really, two of them curled up with a young man about the age of the soldier. The others were curled up with each other, huddling under fewer blankets than there were bodies. They tiptoed through lightly, trying not to wake any of the sleepers.

The next room was well lit with torches along the walls and a dying fire in a large fireplace. From the utensils lining the walls, the large kettle in the fireplace and the tables, Megan suspected she had found the castle kitchens. And most of the girls from the harem were there. As she entered conversation stopped.

"I take it there's some problem?" she asked, looking at the faces. Shanea was standing with her arms folded next to an older woman Megan didn't recognize. Amber was on the other side of the woman with most of the girls Megan had brought arranged in a semicircle opposite the trio. Mirta was standing off to one side, watching. In addition to the "girls" and some women that, from their clothing and mostly angry expressions she suspected were native to the castle, there was a tall, incredibly tall, woman who appeared to have fully functional wings.

"Megan, it's bloody freezing in here and they tell us there aren't enough clothes or blankets to go around," Ashly said, angrily. She had her arms folded as well and Megan suddenly realized it was less a defensive stance than against the cold; she was still wearing only the brief clothing she had been wearing in the escape and she was shivering in the cold. Despite the fire that had, apparently, been burning in the fireplace, the room was bitterly cold. Megan realized that none of them were wearing more and she suddenly felt uncomfortable in the heavy fur robe that McClure had thrown over her shoulders.

"From what I've seen it's true," Megan said, taking off the robe. She immediately felt the biting cold of the room and regretted the gesture. But she didn't put the robe back on. "You should look in the next room."

"Mistress Travante, I'm Flora McClure," the older woman said, stepping forward with her hand out. The woman was small and slender to the point of emaciation. "Jock's wife. For some reason he didn't think we needed to be introduced," the woman added, acerbically.

"I suspect he's going to regret that," Megan said with a grin. "Look, Ashly, the rest of you, I had planned on going to Norau. That didn't work out. We're here and we're damned well not going back. If any of you think you'll be better off with the New Destiny legions, from what I hear they're no more than a half day's walk." She looked around at the girls and then snorted. "That's what I thought. We're here. Until we can get picked up we're going to have to make the best of it. Now, Flora, what can we *do* to help?"

"There's not much we can do, now, about clothing and blankets," Flora said, shaking her head. "We make sure each of the soldiers has a blanket and their cloak; they've often got to fight out in the wet and sleep out in it besides. But we only have the wool to make cloth with, and not much of that. We shear in the spring and what we get then is *it*. Most of it is woven by now and it's all in use. I've scrounged up a few blankets by taking them from other women; now they're without. I'll see what I can find in the way of clothing in the morning. That cloak you have Jock traded for and it's the only one like it in the castle; there aren't many fur-bearing animals up here in the highlands."

"We'll manage, Megan," Amber said. "We'll sleep in a pile with as many blankets as Flora can scrounge."

"This is going to kill my baby," Vera said.

Megan noted that the baby *had* been wrapped up in scraps of wool and shook her head. "Flora, can the pregnant women and the ones with children, at least, be put near a fire?"

"They can, but we can't keep it burning all night," Flora sighed. "We've got to cut the wood by hand, you know. And the wood gathering parties have to be protected from raids by the Changed. I was going to put them by the fireplace; it will stay warmer there longer. But we can't keep the fire burning." She paused and shrugged. "Most of the women sleep in here anyway; it's warmer than just about anywhere else."

"This is *warm*?" Ashly snapped.

"Yes, it is," Flora said, giving her a hard look. "Especially the stones right around the fire. It's a *privilege* to sleep by the fireplace in Castle McClure, missy. One that we're *ceding* to you, as guests. Just as we're not making you wash up from dinner, *tonight*. But *tomorrow* night, I don't care *who* your friends are, you're by God going to *help* or you'll be put outside the walls and find out what *real* hardship is."

There was a murmur of agreement from the women gathered behind her and Megan grasped Ashly's arm as the woman opened her mouth to retort.

"Ashly, a moment of your time?" Megan said, smiling in a friendly manner as her fingers closed on a nerve point in the woman's upper arm.

"Sure, Megan," Ashly said, grimacing.

Megan drew her aside far enough away that she *might* not be overheard.

"Ashly, we're dependent upon these people for the next few days, until a ship comes," Megan whispered, fiercely. "And they *don't* have any more to give. Bitching about it isn't going to get us anything but problems. And if you make enough problems I'll *let* them pitch you out in the snow. Do I make myself clear?"

"Yes, Megan, but listen to me," Ashly said, her face working as she tried to marshal her thoughts. "These people have been living in this for years. They're *used* to it. They don't like it but they can survive it. We're *not* used to it and I'm not sure we *can* survive it. There is such a thing as dying of hypothermia."

"Like she said, huddle up together," Megan replied. "I'll try to get you all close to the fire." She paused and then nodded at an inner thought. "I can expend *some* energy, enough to make sure that the babies and the pregnant women stay warm. If I can figure out a program to use. But *quit bitching*, okay? We've got to work the problem, not make new ones. And, tomorrow, we're obviously going to be put to work. Make sure that the other girls don't decide that's beneath them, clear?"

"Yes," Ashly sighed. "I almost said I wish I was back in the harem. But I don't. I didn't like being there, either, Megan."

"It will be better when we get to Norau," Megan promised, then frowned. "One question, are you having problems with the men?"

"Not since the scene in the hall," Ashly said. "I think they're petrified of you."

"What the girls want to do is up to them," Megan said. "But it's up to *them*. Let them make up their own minds. I doubt that Shanea would blink at sharing a blanket with one of the soldiers."

"I'm not so sure," Ashly said with a grin. "They really smell."

"I think we'll get used to it." Megan frowned. "I need to talk to Flora now. Work the problem, Ashly, don't be one."

"Got it."

"Flora," Megan said, walking back over to the group, "Ashly makes the valid point that we're not adjusted to this temperature. Nor are we dressed for it. I'm going to expend a small amount of power to make sure that none of them go into hypothermia. But we're going to *need* to get more supplies. Do any of the surrounding clans have spare material?"

"Not much," Flora said, frowning. "And I hadn't really thought about the fact that you're not used to it, although the clothing was pretty obvious." She made a grimace at that and Megan had to drown an angry reaction.

"We didn't *choose* how we dressed," Megan said, admitting that they *did* but not the general form. "What I was thinking is that I have a small amount of power that I can expend. I could probably do something for the other clans if they could come up with some blankets and clothes. Anything would be preferable to this," she added, gesturing at her own clothing.

"Agreed," Flora said, glancing at the soldier that had accompanied Megan to the kitchen who was discreetly eyeing the wide selection of female flesh on display. "If for no other reason than to keep the young bucks from rioting."

"That too," Megan said, frowning. "Given where we've just come from I'm going to put this as delicately as possible. Bed the babies and their mothers by the fireplace. The rest of you snuggle in as close as possible and use all the blankets that we can get. But if any of the girls want to share a blanket with one of the soldiers, I'm not going to raise any fuss. As long as it's the *girl's* choice."

"I won't mind," Shanea said, winking at Megan's escort.

"I'm on duty," the young man replied, blushing. "But . . . I get off in a couple of hours."

"Well, I don't know about getting off," Shanea said with a grin, "but we might see what can be arranged."

"Behave," Megan said, frowning. "It better be *clear* that it has to be *willing* bedding and I will have the balls of anyone that takes advantage."

"I don't think you have to worry about that," Flora said.

"I'm going to bed here," Amber said, her face

working. "I think I've had all of men I can handle for a while."

"That's settled then," Megan said, wiping her face. "Flora, is there somewhere we can talk? I know it's late . . ."

"No, not a problem," Flora said. "The rest of you get some sleep, early day tomorrow. Earlier than you're probably used to." She gestured at the cloak that Megan had set on one of the tables. "Take that."

"They can use it down here," Megan protested.

"Be damned," Flora said, definitely. "Take it—where we're going it's colder."

Megan put the cloak back on and then, trailed by Baradur and the soldier, followed Flora out of the kitchen and up more of the interminable stairs and down corridors until they reached a small room. It was set up as an office and it was pretty clear that it was Flora's sanctum.

"You two can wait out here," Flora said, gesturing at the corridor.

"Yes, mistress," Baradur said, taking up a position by the door.

"Thank you for intervening," Flora said, sitting in her chair and rubbing her face. "I don't know what would have happened if you hadn't. You make a good point that we're more used to the cold . . ."

"It is horrible isn't it?" Megan said. "It almost feels worse than being outside."

"It's the stone walls," Flora said, shrugging. "And the lack of heat. I should have handled it better but that Ashly . . ."

"Ashly is . . . Ashly," Megan said, shrugging. "She puts on airs like a queen."

"But you don't," Flora noted. "And you're the closest thing to it that Clan McClure has seen."

"All I am is a Key-holder," Megan protested. "I don't even know how to use it properly. I talk about doing healing, but I don't really know *how*."

"Well, the last bad injury we had died last week," Flora said. "But I'll send out runners to Innes tomorrow and find out if they have anything to trade. And anyone who needs healing. In the meantime you can be figuring out how to do it," she added with a faint smile. "With more mouths to feed and clothes to make from whatever cloth we can get, there's going to be work to do. I won't get any trouble out of your girls from it, will I?"

"Not much," Megan said. "As long as Ashly goes along, and she will or I'll tear a strip off of her. I tried to put Mirta in charge but she's not willing to put herself forward. Amber might, but she's . . . that's a long story. She's having a hard enough time putting her head back together I guess. And Christel stayed behind. I suspect that was a bad choice on her part." She frowned at a memory. "Who was that bird woman? Is she one of yours?"

"No," Flora admitted. "She turned up here just a couple of days ago. She's apparently a courier of some sort for the UFS. They couldn't pick her up so they told her to come here and wait for a ship. We *do* have some contact with the UFS. Not much, and not much in the way of help. But they've dropped off supplies before."

"I'll see what I can do about getting you more support when I get to Norau," Megan said, yawning. "I'm sorry."

"It's been a long day for all of us," Flora said. "And tomorrow's probably going to be longer. Go get some rest."

"I'll do that," Megan said. "Thanks for this talk. It helped." She looked thoughtful and then shrugged. "Getting all my news from Paul sometimes I felt like despairing; everything seemed to be falling New Destiny's way. I'm glad there are some people who aren't willing to just roll over for them, no matter how bad it gets."

"You're welcome," Flora chuckled. "We'll beat these New Destiny bastards yet."

CHAPTER TWENTY -FOUR

Megan patted the horse warily and nodded at it as it turned its head and snuffled at her. It already had a saddle and other bits attached. But getting up in the saddle was going to be difficult and she had no idea what to do after that. The horse turned again and blew into her hair.

"That's a good horse," she said, wiping at the moisture and then dodging as it lipped at her cloak. "Good . . . horse."

"Don't worry, mistress," one of the grooms said, coming over to help her. "Ever ridden a horse before?"

"No," Megan admitted.

"You know that thing about 'men are from Mars, women from Venus?'" the groom asked, cupping his hands. "Just grab on the bottom of the mane, there, mistress, and pull yourself up. Well, this here's a gelding, Broomy's his name. Stallions are from Mars, sure enough, most of them will take your arm off just for a joke. And mares, they're from Venus, except they're not constant by any measure. Sweet as honey one day and throwing you in the air the next. But geldings, well, geldings they're from Heaven, mistress. And Broomy's the heavenliest one of them all."

As he talked the groom had expertly heaved her onto the gelding's back and adjusted the stirrups for her shorter legs. Then he showed her how to hold the reins.

"You'll be following the others, mistress," the groom continued, walking the horse out of the three-corner shed and into the cloudy dawn. "Broomy will follow right along. You'll get the hang of it no time at all. The laird won't be going fast. Might trot and that takes a bit of getting used to. Just lift up in the stirrups and hang on the mane, then. Canter, now, canter's more comfortable than a trot but it can be scary. Seems fast to go so close to the ground and so far away if you get my drift."

"I'm afraid I will," Megan said as the other riders gathered. Most of them looked much more sure of themselves on horseback and all of them were armed. Megan suddenly realized that she didn't have as much as a belt knife and wasn't sure what they would say if she asked for a sword. Nor did she know what she would use it for. Her father had trained her in hand-to-hand combat, but he'd taught her nothing about projectile weapons or edged. For that matter, based on the motley collection of weapons McClure's best carried, she was pretty sure there weren't any to go around. Most of the group was armed with long spears that had the look of hasty craftsmanship. McClure had his big axe hanging from the saddle and a spear in his hand. His son bore a very long sword, immensely long with room for two hands on the pommel. He was a big guy but she wondered if he really could use something that size.

She counted the riders, fifteen, and realized that if the count the guard had given her the night before was right this was half the total fighting force of Clan McClure. If the castle was attacked in their absence it would be hard-pressed to hold the walls.

"Mistress," McClure said, kneeing his horse over by hers. "You stay in the middle. I know you're no rider but none of these boyos were before the Fall; you'll learn as they did. Just grab onto the mane if you feel yourself falling and keep pressure on your feet in the stirrups."

"What about Baradur?" she asked. He was standing by her horse. There wasn't a horse saddled for him, she noticed.

"Oh, I don't ride, mistress," the Chudai said. "I'll just trot along."

"He'll hold onto your saddle from time to time," McClure answered her unvoiced question. "Other than that he'll walk or trot along. It's their way. We'll take it at a walk as much as possible but we've a long ways to go."

"I'll keep up," Megan said, grimly determined to do just that. "And so will Baradur I guess. You just set the pace you think is best."

McClure didn't say anything, just looked at her solemnly, nodded and turned his horse for the gate to the castle.

He kept the horses, who were fractious and obviously anxious to get moving, at a walk as they rode out of the castle and down the slope to the glen below. Megan hadn't seen much of their surroundings and was surprised by the peaceful beauty of the scene. The glen below was heavily farmed, almost every square centimeter of flat ground plowed, some of it in winter wheat but most waiting for the spring to be used. It was covered in some sort of golden grass that bowed under a light snow cover. The mountains, hills really, rose sharp on every side. The glen was about six kilometers long, open at one end to the sea and narrowing down sharply at the far end, a faint path there ascended into the hills beyond. The castle was about two thirds of the way down the glen on the north side.

"That's where Chansa's forces hold," McClure said, gesturing to where the glen necked down and headed up into the highlands. "T' other side of yon hills is bandit country. We've a small fort up there that keeps an eye on them and a couple more," he gestured to the south, "up in yon highlands. Easiest way into the glen's through that pass, but they try to crawl up from the south from time to time as well. As well as landing down at the port."

"Seems that that would be the easiest way," she said, gesturing to the sea. There was a narrow tongue of water, covered by hills on both sides, that led out to the actual sea. She could see, as they turned into the hills to the north, the distant true ocean, tossed by wave and wind.

"They've got to sail up the loch, lassie," McClure pointed out. "We get four, sometimes six hours warning. We can set up for them in half that time and by the time they get here we've called in help from other clans. Since we're the only one with a decent port they send us help. We're still hoping for help from Norau but if we're without so much as a dock we don't think we'll get much."

"I see," Megan said, and grabbed at the mane as the horse scrambled up a narrow trail. The trail was paralleling a small stream that ran over mossy boulders towards the glen and was steep, half rocks and half thin soil. She had to concentrate on her riding as they passed through a defile and scrambled up a portion of fallen scree but she found that if she leaned upwards it was easier to stay on the horse. She was slowly finding her "seat" and didn't find riding nearly as hard as she expected. She did notice that the inside of her thighs were beginning to burn, though, and her legs, which she had thought were in pretty good shape, were starting to tire. As they reached the top of the hills, she wondered how long the trip would take.

Four hours later, feeling as if she had been put in a barrel and hammered up and down, they were sliding down the last of dozens of hills into a narrow glen. She had discovered what a trot was, and didn't like it. Fortunately, when they were going at the right pace Broomy had a gait called a "rack" which was much smoother. She'd also, when they hit the upper moorlands, discovered what a canter was. That was smoother, but as she had been warned, frightening. And exhilarating at the same time. She had had a hard time staying on the horse and as the rocks of the moorland, which was beautiful as far as she could notice, had flashed by she had wondered if she was going to end her adventure with her head dashed out on one of them. But just as she thought she was sure to go pitching headlong—her thigh muscles had long since turned to jelly and there was no way she could grip with her legs—McClure had slowed them back down to a walk as they reached another narrow defile.

As they had been going down the defile she felt as if there were eyes watching her and she noticed the riders, and their horses, were skittish.

"It's the wee folk, lassy," McClure had said, not bothering to look around. "They hold the true highlands. It's one of the reasons the orcs don't come over them."

"They live up here?" Megan asked, looking around at the apparently deserted landscape.

"Aye," Jock said, shrugging. "They say it's the only bit that's high enough to breathe. You'd think they lived on rocks but they run a few scrubby cattle and do a bit of hunting. And they trade, services, for one thing," he added, gesturing at Baradur. He had kept up the whole time, seeming to be barely tired by the trip. When they cantered, despite his statement that he did not ride, he had thrown himself up on the saddle behind her and, truth be told, kept her on the horse as much as anything.

"And they're not averse to a bit of banditry," McClure continued, darkly. "There's more than one reason that we've a group this large for the trip."

She looked down at her bodyguard who grinned without looking up.

"Lovely," she said, shaking her head.

The moorland had been the only reasonably flat portion of the journey. They had gone up and down for the entire rest of the four hours—the whole time seeing no signs of life except the rough track and, once, a covey of pheasant that had broken into the air as they passed—and she thought that if they didn't reach their destination soon she was going to have to ask for a rest.

But as they turned the shoulder of a hill she could see another castle, larger than McClure's, at the head of the glen.

"Innes?" she gasped, grasping at Broomy's mane as she slipped in the seat. Riding downhill, she had discovered, was much harder than uphill.

"Aye," McClure said.

"Big castle," Megan said. "Small glen."

"This is only one of six that Innes controls," McClure answered. "Two others are larger, one as large as Glen McClure. One of them's on the front lines with the orcs. But it's two ridges away from here. They lost one in the early days, took it back for a while, then lost it again. Be careful with Innes, lassie. He's a fine man but proud and he's a Stuart on his mother's side."

"What's that mean?"

"He's a descendant of Bonnie Charlie," McClure said, as if that answered the question.

"I'm still not following," Megan said, unsure if this was something that should be common knowledge.

"Charles the First," McClure said, shaking his head. "Arguably a man with a better claim to the throne of England than the ones that held it in the seventeenth century. King of the Scots, the Gael, for that matter. He wants to unite the Gael and retake Briton from Chansa. It'd be Culloden for sure was he to try. We can hold them in the Highlands, but get us down in the Lows and we'll be wheat to the scythe."

One of the group of soldiers began whistling, a haunting melody that caught at her mind. Others were singing low.

> *"Burned are our homes, exile and death,*
> *scattered the loyal men.*
> *"Yet e'er the sword, cool in the sheath,*
> *Charlie will come again."*

"What's that mean?" Megan asked, haunted by the words.

"It's called 'Isle of Skye,'" McClure said, shrugging. "From when Charlie was forced to flee for his life. For a long time the Scots thought that Charlie would return. He'd led a force down into Briton to reclaim the throne. Took a fair bit of land. Then he overextended himself. His force was trapped and slaughtered at Culloden Field. Then the Brits came in and emptied the glens, the first modern genocide, ethnocide really, in history. They killed every male that had anything to do with the uprising, forced all the farmers out, exiled half the population, enlisted the men in their armies and sent them overseas to die. The British Empire became one of the largest ever to rule on earth, but it was done with the Blood of the Gael. Three Charles lived in France as a government in exile, then they faded away."

"Does Innes sing 'Isle of Skye'?" Megan asked.

"No," McClure said, darkly. "'Isle of Skye' is about losing. The men of Innes sing the Bonnie Charlie song."

McClure grinned wickedly and nodded at a rider with a horn.

"Sound the horn, me bucko," he yelled.

> "O! Charlie is my darlin' my darlin' my
> darlin'
> "Charlie is my darlin' the young cava-
> lier!"

Malcolm Innes was tall and fair with blond hair that reached nearly to his waist, a chiseled chin and bright blue eyes. Looking at him Megan couldn't believe that there was anything in his head at all. But she found herself wrong.

"McClure thinks I'm mad," Malcolm said, gesturing with his chin at the older laird. They had retired to the local laird's office and sat by the fire sipping warmed mead as Megan's legs screamed in agony. Her feet were resting on the side of one of the largest dogs she had ever seen, nearly the size of a pony. Its shaggy fur was twined in her toes. This dog, along with a group of others, had followed them into the room and flopped down at her feet. She had propped them up when she saw the others do so. "That I've gone off my rocker with being a descendant of Charles the First. Don't tell me I'm wrong."

"You're not," McClure said, taking a sip of mead. "But it's a Gael madness and for that I forgive you."

"I don't think I can retake Briton," Innes said, grinning and leaning forward, tight as a spring as he presented his case. "Or set myself up as king. Yet. And I know I can't without the aid of Norau. But I *can* bring in the allegiance of ten clans, all of them blooded in war. I've more cavalry than anyone in the highlands. I've more supplies than anyone in the highlands. My men are better trained and better equipped because I can recycle them off the line. If Norau wants to retake Briton, and they'll *need* it as a jumping off point for an invasion of Ropasa, they'll need my help. And if they're on my side, I can bring in *all* the clans. This pretense of being Charlie's heir seems crazy, but like McClure said it's a *Gael* madness; the Highlands will follow a Stuart, especially if it means retaking the throne that was stolen from us."

"That was . . ." Megan did the math in her head. "What? Three *thousand* years ago give or take a few centuries?"

"Doesn't matter, lassie," McClure said, shrugging. "You heard the lads. This is mother's milk to the Gael."

"The term is 'cultural meme,'" Malcolm said, leaning back. "Memes hold on for remarkably long periods of time. Gael children were raised with the words murmured to them by their mothers, who had forgotten the meaning but liked the tune as a lullaby. You can find it anywhere that there was a strong strain of the Scots Gael, the southeast of Norau for example, or Anarchia before it was shifted. And here in the Highlands the strain is strong and deep. Hell, the theme of 'the king will return' permeates all Indo-European cultures. It's a philosophical basis for the Christ myth that existed long before he did or did not actually live. I can help Norau ride that meme to victory."

"And your price is the throne," Megan replied.

"It's a prize that I'll pay for," Malcolm said, leaning back. "With the strongest, and largest, allegiance they're going to get."

"Campbells won't like it," McClure said, grinning.

"'No dogs, tinkers or Campbells allowed,'" Malcolm said with a grin. "I can even swing the Campbells if Norau is behind me. And the Chudai will follow me; I've the blood of the British kings in me as well and they've been loyal followers of the Briton standard for so long it's nearly lost in history."

"Norau has its own legions," Megan pointed out. "They've never been defeated."

"There's no such thing as enough soldiers, lassie," McClure said. "Never."

"I'll give you what you need for now," Innes said, shrugging. "Some food from our stores, clothes for your people. What I want from you is to present my case to the leaders of Norau, Sheida and that war-leader of theirs, Edmund Talbot."

"Jock?" she said, looking at McClure.

"Aye, mistress," he said, formally. "They'll need the support here and Malcolm can give it. If the price is Briton, that's cheap enough."

"I'll establish a constitutional monarchy, of course," Malcolm said, shrugging. "Like Norau's. But I'll *rule*. My ancestors were here before there *were* Scots. We were here before the Romans, before the Saxons, before those Johnny-Come-Lately Normans. We've waited for thousands of years to reclaim what is *ours*. And the time is *now*."

Megan found herself arrested by the man's fanaticism. It seemed so . . . unworldly. He was talking about a defeat three thousand years before, and defeats thousands of years before that, as if it were only a minor setback. And, she realized, he was not alone. She thought of the soldiers that she had ridden with to the castle. They had sung the songs and, she could tell, believed in the—what was the term?—the *meme*. To the Gael the loss of their position, of their lands, was only a minor setback, something that, in time, would be righted.

And many of them thought that the time was now.

"I'll present it to anyone I can get to listen," she temporized.

"You're a Key-holder," Malcolm said, waving his hand as if that were a minor matter. "They'll listen. Edmund Talbot will listen. His real name is Charles, after all. And he's a Talbot. He'll understand. It may be a ghost, it may be a legend. But legends have won more wars than swords. And Charlie *will* ride again."

CHAPTER TWENTY-FIVE

"We're chasing a will-o'-wisp." Admiral Dario Sumstad slapped the railing and looked over at the ballista frigate that was maintaining close station. "I hate chasing ghosts."

"The UFS carrier has to be out here somewhere, sir," Captain Thahn Clussman said. The captain of the *Pierre Franc* watched the admiral warily but wasn't willing to let slip anything but willingness to follow orders.

"It might be," Sumstad said, turning away from the railing and pacing up and down the quarterdeck. He grimaced as a dragon landed overhead. "But Talbot is a tricky SOB. We know he moved the carriers south, but he could have run anywhere while we get further and further away from the Blackbeard group. Any word from the orcas?"

"No, sir," the captain reported. "No sign of UFS ships. No dragons spotted except ours. But they have run into mer and delphinos. They're having more and more trouble with them, as a matter of fact. The mer are using some sort of dart gun that is quite deadly."

"Put more ixchitl with the orcas," the admiral grunted. "I know it slows them down, but we have to keep down the losses in the damned orcas somehow."

"Yes, sir," the captain replied, walking over to the messenger station.

"Where are they?"

"We're currently here," Shar said to the assembled skippers and their dragon contingent commanders. They were using Edmund's quarters this time and it was crowded. "Two hundred kilometers northeast of Blackbeard."

"I thought it was getting warmer," one of the skippers quipped.

"New Destiny has split its combat forces into two groups," Chang continued, ignoring the comment. "The main group, with three carriers, is to our north and at last report continuing northward. The second group, two carriers, support ships and landing ships, are approaching Blackbeard from the north. As far as we can tell, they don't know we're here."

"Two on two," one of the dragon contingent commanders noted. "And they've got more dragons."

"They won't by tomorrow," Edmund said confidently.

"Can you tell us why, Admiral?" one of the skippers asked.

"No," Edmund replied. "But don't worry about the dragons."

"The first target is the ballista frigates," Shar said, lifting up the map and showing a diagram of ships. "You'll launch before dawn . . ."

It was two hours before dawn when the charge of quarters knocked on Gunny Rutherford's door and entered to wake him. He found the gunny, in full armor, kneeling in front of a candle-lit statue of a bull.

"Four hundred hours, Gunnery Sergeant," the CQ said.

The gunny stood up and looked at him with distant eyes, then nodded.

"It's a good day to die," he said, striding out of the room.

The CQ noticed an odd smell and, half against his will, walked over and looked at the bull. Its back appeared wet and when his fingers came away from it they were covered in blood.

"The New Destiny fleet is in sight coming down the Stream, sir." The messenger was braced to attention in front of the Blood Lord commander.

"Well, that appears to be that, Gunny," Captain Pherson said. Kenton Pherson was a pale-skinned twenty-six-year-old with light hazel eyes and blond, almost white, hair so fine that it was hard to discern on his uncovered head. He stood up and donned his helmet, buckling it down. "They say that god is on the side of the big battalions. Let's hope they're wrong."

"Well, sir, they also say that age and treachery beats youth and strength every time," Gunny Rutherford said. "Let's hope they're right."

"And what does that mean, Gunny?" the captain asked as they walked out into the first light of dawn.

"Well, sir, there are a few little fillips to the current situation you're not really aware of," Gunny replied as a man stepped into the torchlight outside the headquarters. He was of medium height with broad shoulders and huge forearms and triceps, wearing light-green leather armor, a metal cap and a short sword.

"And who are . . . Oh, Mr. Grameson," the captain said, recognizing the foreman of the workmen who had been sent to construct the mer-fortress. Pherson had tried to engage him in conversation a few times and had found him to be a surly and uncommunicative fellow.

"Actually, Captain, the name is D'Erle," the man said, smiling and holding out his glove-covered hand. "General Malcolm D'Erle, UFS Bow Corps."

Admiral Emile Arris watched the boats with Changed shock troops being loaded and looked over at the dragon-carrier captain.

"Signal the fleet to commence launching," he said.

The dragons started lifting off the starboard side of the carrier at once, flapping for altitude and then settling into figure eights. All of them were overloaded with fuel bombs and they couldn't glide very well.

He paced back and forth as the boats loaded in the gathering light, looking over at the troopships from time to time and waiting for their ready signal. When the last one came he waved at the signal team.

"Signal begin invasion," he called. "Hold the dragons

back until the ships are nearly to the shore," he added to the ship's captain. "I want them to arrive together."

"How long did it take you guys to get this together?" Captain Pherson asked as he watched the activity in the lagoon. "Sir," he added.

Large wood-and-leather bubbles, each at least ten meters across, were floating on the surface. As he watched, one started to sink from the lead weights being carefully placed around its circumference. It was stabilized on the way down by mer-women. Underneath were "legs" that held it off the bottom. Other merwomen were running lines from pumps scattered on the east side of the harbor. Once the shelters were constructed the attackers would first have to either take the pumps or clear the entrance before the mer could be threatened. The mer-children could in the meantime breathe the air in the bubbles.

"A few months," Malcolm admitted as the two bowmen continued to row around the scene of activity. Bubble after bubble was descending into the water and a large wood and metal porcupine arrangement was being constructed in the harbor's narrow entrance. "Obviously we were the 'workmen' constructing the fortress. It gave the boys some experience in really solid fortification work, I'll say that for it."

"Why aren't you up in Norau, sir?" Captain Pherson said, somewhat pointedly. "There's an invasion headed that way."

"Same reason you're not, son," Malcolm replied with a grin. "Edmund sent me here."

When they got back to the shore the remainder of the "workmen" were assembling premade shelters on the shore. They were constructed of plywood with leather covers that had a strange sheen to them.

"The leather is highly flame resistant," D'Erle explained. "And we have covers for the troops. They'll be hell to fight in, but better than burning to death."

"What about the archers?" the captain asked.

"Who did you think they were for?"

"Okay," the admiral said as the boats touched shore. "Order the dragons to attack *now*."

He could clearly see the battle from the dragon landing platform. The ranks of Blood Lords did not advance on the orcs unloading from the boats but instead awaited them in serried ranks on the crest of the hill. There were shelters set up on both sides and workmen still bustling around the battlefield even as the first orc ranks were formed.

But as the dragons winged over, the "workmen" dropped their tasks and ran to the shelters which had obviously been set up for them to be protected from the dragon fire. At the same time the Blood Lords lowered their shields and lifted silver coveralls from the ground until they were completely covered. As the dragons came in low in a sweeping pass over the defenseless Blood Lords, half of the "workers" popped out of the "shelters" with longbows in their hands. The dragons ran into a wall of arrows.

Each of the highly trained archers of the Bow Corps could send one arrow every two seconds for thirty minutes or one every five seconds for up to two hours. They were currently slightly out of shape, however, due to their construction duties, and the hundred and fifty bowmen contented themselves with only sending up a total of seven hundred carefully aimed cloth-yard shafts as the dragons passed overhead.

The bowmen were scattered to either side of the Blood Lord formation and they caught the dragons in a merciless crossfire. Some of the dragons were hit so badly that they fell out of the sky almost immediately while others managed to make it as far as the harbor, where mer-women waited with long pikes, before succumbing to the hideous fire. There were eighty dragons in the attack flight and forty of them were destroyed in the first volley, with most of the rest taking one round or another. But most released their loads of napalm, covering the Blood Lords, and the edge of the archers, in a rain of fire.

"Damn him," Admiral Arris cursed as the tattered remnants of his dragons staggered back into the air. Most of them had been hit and he saw more fall out of the sky even as the fires burned among the Blood Lords.

"They dropped their loads, though," Captain Lohnes pointed out. He gestured at the raging fires where the Blood Lords had stood. "The archers by themselves can't stop the Changed."

"Look," was all the admiral said. Striding out of the fire, their shields blazing, were the Blood Lords. Just then arrows began to fall on the Changed formation.

"Captain," Lieutenant Commander Strayer said. The XO of the *Wilhelm* was obviously agitated. "We're taking on water."

"What?" the captain said, rounding on his second in command. "Why?"

"There's a hole in the starboard hull," the XO replied as a petty officer came up and whispered in his ear. "There's another one formed to port, sir."

"Get a sail fothered over it," the captain snapped. He watched the Blood Lord formation move down the hill and then, with a shout, charge the still-forming Changed. The Changed broke ranks and charged themselves, the two groups meeting under a cloud of javelins as more arrows continued to fall on the battle.

"We're working on it, sir," the XO replied as the ship shuddered to the strike of a wave. "But . . ."

"How *much* water?" the admiral asked, looking at the ship and noting that it was riding extremely heavy.

"It's all through the lower deck, sir," the XO said, miserably. "It's getting ahead of the pumps. There might be more holes."

"Where the hell are they coming from?!" the captain shouted.

"Mer off the port bow!" the lookout called.

"Where the hell are the orcas!"

"Gunny, we will refuse the right flank," Captain Pherson said. The voice was muffled due to the silver firefighting suit he wore. But it was clear enough. "I believe they are attempting to slip out of our clutches."

"SECOND TRIARIII!" the gunny bellowed, lifting up the hood of the suit to be heard. "SIX PACES RIGHT . . . MOVE! A-HUT! A-HUT! A-HUT! A-HUT! A-HUT! A-HUT!"

At the shoreline the Changed that were left were

trying to scramble into their launches. Most of them had clawed out to sea, forgetting that in their armor there was no way that they could make it to the ships. A few had stripped off the armor but the Changed were heavy boned and heavily muscled, not to mention poor swimmers. Only those that made it to launches, and launches that had not been holed by descending cloth-yard shafts, were going to make it to the ships.

"We still can't do anything about *them*," the captain sighed.

"No, we can't, sir," the gunny replied as a ballista from one of the frigates whistled overhead towards the archers. The archers were in the process of changing over firers but most of them easily avoided the incoming ballista bolt. "But that don't mean they won't be done with."

"Dragons!" the lookout called. "Off the starboard bow!"

That was due east and into the still rising sun, but the admiral could barely make out the forms of dragons against the blaze.

"Ours?" Captain Lohnes asked, puzzled.

"No, I think not." The admiral sighed. "There's a carrier out there somewhere. Probably three. Damn that Talbot."

"What should we do, sir?" Fleet Captain Bouviet asked.

"Have the boats return for the second wave of Changed," the admiral said.

"Sir, with respect," Captain Lohnes replied. "I'm not sure I can effect repairs. We've lost more than half our dragons and the Changed are trying to land in the teeth of both bowmen and Blood Lords, not to mention their own dragons. And there's an unknown number of carriers after us while we're effectively locked in place. We should withdraw."

"The last admiral that tried to explain that sort of thing to Marshal Chansa is somewhere over there," the admiral replied, waving at the beach where the Changed were being slaughtered. "I choose not to withdraw."

"Age and treachery are wonderful things, sir," Gunny Rutherford said as the flight of dragons swept overhead and headed for the New Destiny task force. The anti-dragon frigate was to the west of the aircraft carrier so the dragons had to actually pass over the latter to reach their target. When they did the entire flight lined up and carefully passed over the frigate, dropping load after load of napalm onto its deck. Since they were dropping from out of range of the ballistas, many of the pots missed. But, then again, many of them hit. And not all the foam in the world could save a wooden ship from a deck covered in napalm. After they had dropped their loads they began landing at the base by the warehouses the "workmen" had been using.

"Don't tell me," the captain said. "Some of the workmen's 'solvents' are . . ."

"Reloads for the dragons, sir," the gunny replied with a nod. He pulled back the hood of his fire suit and lit a stogie on his still smoldering shield. "And more archers over there to cover them while they rearm. It's harder for them to take off and they can only carry two bombs. But they can recycle much faster. And we've got about three times the load of bombs a carrier can handle. And, of course, we don't sink if they get through."

"Was this the duke's plan from the beginning?" Captain Pherson asked, pulling back his own hood. One of the carriers appeared to be low in the water and was definitely showing signs of having a hard time turning its dragons around. The other was beginning to launch but even as the dragons staggered into the air, small, highly colored dragons dropped out of the sun onto them, firing darts that flashed silver in the sun. More dragons fell into the sea.

"Just a contingency plan, sir," the gunny said, taking a puff off of his stogie. "Just a contingency."

"Losing *Hazhir* has played merry hob with Stonewall," Talbot said. "It was only a contingency plan to start with. And now we're going to be playing catch-up to make our next rendezvous. Furthermore, we have to *destroy* the fleet here, since otherwise the dreadnoughts are going to run into heavy weather."

"Dreadnoughts?" Shar asked.

"I'm sending them down to pick up D'Erle and his men," Edmund said. "They're on their way, as a matter of fact. As soon as the Changed boats are patched up D'Erle and his men will prepare to embark. The dreadnoughts should be here by then. But instead of *Hazhir* screening them while we go take on the other task force, they'll have to run up the coast without any coverage, except some Silverdrake we'll fly off to them. Then we're going to have to head for the remnants of the combat fleet and finish them off."

❖   ❖   ❖

Admiral Arris stepped into the launch as the water rose over the bulwarks of the *Wilhelm*.

"Head for the *Tressam*," he said, watching the battle on the shore. The Changed were dropping out of the launches in the shallows, which were scarlet with blood, and charging up the beach to the line of waiting Blood Lords. There had been one attempt to change the landing area but there was really only one place to land and the Blood Lords and archers had it covered. As he watched most of the Changed fell in the shallows to a mass flight of arrows. The last few charged the Blood Lords but were cut down with hardly a dent in the Blood Lord lines. As soon as the charge was broken the Blood Lords conducted a well-drilled movement that brought new fighters to the front lines to rest those that had been handling the bulk of the fighting.

"Admiral," Fleet Captain Bouviet said, pointing towards the harbor. A flight of dragons had formed up and now vectored towards the fleet, heading for the *Tressam*.

The *Tressam* managed to get some dragons up—the small, fast wyverns had disappeared for the moment—and they tried to engage the oncoming flight of UFS wyverns. Some of the UFS beasts were, apparently, unladen and they turned to cut off the New Destiny dragons. There was a brief midair battle which had riders falling off into the water and a few dragons, he couldn't tell whose, following them down. But the main flight made it through and napalm rained all over his last carrier.

"Change directions," the admiral said. "Head for the nearest frigate. We're going to have to withdraw."

The UFS dragons, however, turned to the north.

"Are they withdrawing, too?" the Fleet Captain asked.

"More likely going back to their carriers," the admiral growled. "Which are going to dog our steps no matter what we do. Make for the frigate. Quickly!"

"I think that's about it, sir," Gunny Rutherford said. His armor was covered in blood as was the captain's; the last group of Changed had tried very hard to break out from the Blood Lord lines. "Six dead, fourteen wounded. Most of the wounded will survive."

"Gunny, is it just me or was this stupidly easy?" the captain asked. He didn't like losing people, but given that they had been outnumbered at least five to one that was a ridiculous total.

"It always is, sir," the gunny said, puffing up his stogie and tossing aside his battered and burned shield, "when you've got the right mix."

"The New Destiny fleet is fleeing to the south," Shar said. "Both carriers are on the bottom along with their anti-dragon frigates. All they have left are ballista frigates."

"Leave 'em," Edmund said. "Two dreadnoughts filled with archers can make hash of ballista frigates. How are the dragons holding up?"

"We lost about a dozen one way or another," Shar admitted. "Seven wounded that will be able to fly in a few days. All the Silverdrake made it back. And, you were right, the dreadnoughts are in sight to the north."

"Signal nine Silverdrake detached to the dreadnoughts; they have stalls set up for them. Then signal the fleet to make sail northeast. We've got more carriers to hunt."

He looked up at a knock on the door and yelled: "Enter!"

"Admiral Talbot," the messenger said. "Whale signal from *Hazhir*: Made rendezvous."

CHAPTER TWENTY-SIX

Megan had returned to the castle with a pack train of clothes and supplies, a slightly increased force courtesy of Malcolm Innes and a distinct distaste for riding and the society of the Gael. She was appalled by the speed with which the locals had reverted to a very sexually segregated, and repressive, society. It, quite frankly, infuriated her. Mirta, however, was much less upset by it.

They had been talking one evening after dinner when the kitchen had mostly been cleared and she and Megan had taken up stools by the fire. Baradur was perched in the corner, as always a silent observer. Since Jock had assigned him to her he had never been far away. He slept by the door of her room, tasted her food before she ate it and even checked the latrines when she had occasion to use them.

Mirta was, as ever, sewing. She had gotten some rough sections of wool and was making a better dress for herself when Megan burst out with her complaints.

"I like Jock McClure, I even like Malcolm for all his 'Gael madness,' but this . . . this . . . slave camp they run is ridiculous! Serfs in the fields, women kept out of the main room except to serve. It's *disgusting*."

"A bit," Mirta said, looking up for a moment, then going back to her sewing. "But it fits the society very well. Have you asked Jock or Flora about it?"

"No," Megan admitted. "Frankly, I don't want to piss him off."

"You might find it enlightening," Mirta said. "I doubt he recalls but I've met him before. He was one of the local dukes in the Society. Never quite made it to king, but he's a pretty dab hand with a claymore or battle-axe. Nice guy. I don't recognize Flora; he wasn't married back then. But he wasn't one of the very old-fashioned chauvinists you sometimes ran into in the Society. And a serious student of history. So, you have to ask yourself, why'd he change?"

"I don't know," Megan admitted. "Even in Ropasa it wasn't this bad. And from what I hear of Norau they've really maintained a very straightforward equality system. This is just so . . . medieval!"

"And there you put your finger upon it," Mirta pointed out, tying off a knot. "Let me ask you something: Why were women in preindustrial societies considered second-class citizens?"

"Because . . ." Megan paused and thought about it. "Because the men of the society kept them that way?"

"To an extent," Mirta replied. "To an extent. But you have to ask why it *started*. Did men and women wake up one morning and say: 'Okay, the guys are in charge?' Which came first, the chicken or the egg? More to the point, the human race went through a few hundred thousand year process of evolving a society where women were, almost *invariably*, chattel and second-class citizens. Even in most hunter-gatherer societies, despite the various tracts trying to disprove that unpleasant fact. Then, when technology started to dominate, women were suddenly empowered. What does that tell you?"

"That you know the answers and aren't willing to just give them," Megan said, frowning.

"The way to true understanding is to answer the question yourself," Mirta replied, smiling as she sewed.

"And the journey of a thousand miles often ends very badly," Megan said with a grin. "But I get your point; that the difference was technology. But I don't like the answer."

"Okay, let's take a look at the current situation," Mirta said. "Think in terms purely of economic value. The basis of the economy around here is small farming and sheep herding. What do small farmers do?"

"Plow and harvest?" Megan asked.

"Far more than that. But that will do. What do both require?"

"An ox?" Megan laughed, taking a sip of herbal tea then thinking about it. "I don't know, I've never done either."

"They require a good bit of upper body strength is the answer," the seamstress replied. "To keep a plow straight requires constant adjustment, which means pointing, and often lifting, a huge chunk of wood and metal. And the faster you can plow the more you can plow and the more likely you are to get your crops in the ground at the right time. Or at least *more* crops. Now, despite genetic tinkering, women are weaker than men in upper body strength. We also don't have the stamina for long-endurance, high-energy efforts that males do. Men can keep plowing or swinging a scythe long after women of equivalent condition and mass have dropped to the ground. Women are better in both, today, than males prior to genetic tinkering. But men are equivalently stronger. Sheep farming also requires a good bit of strength: You haven't lived until you've tried to shear a sheep. Lifting bales of fodder or wool, throwing a bull to make it a steer, cutting with a scythe, these are all things that men can do better than women. A farm can be run by one woman and two or three men, but the same farm would require *six or seven* women alone. And they require the equivalent food level of the males. The work that women do in the culture is important, but, frankly, anything they can do, except making babies, can be done by a man. Women get the jobs they do, caring for the hearth, cooking food, sewing, because they *cannot* do the jobs men do as well as men. By and large, as an average."

"I don't like that," Megan said. "I don't like it one bit."

"Don't like it all you'd like." Mirta sighed. "It's truth. Now in some societies, Ropasa to an extent and from what I've heard Norau to a greater extent, it's possible to mitigate the effects of the relative . . . worthlessness, and I chose that word precisely, of women. They have economically important jobs, clerks, managers, designers, that women can do as well as men. If they're permitted to. Ropasa was well on its way to forcing women out of such jobs, though. With Sheida as queen of Norau they're not going to start forcing women out very soon. I have no idea what it will be like in the long-run. But *here* it's different. They are on the ragged edge of survival; they don't *have* clerks and factory workers. And the most important people are *not* farmers or sheepshearers, but *fighters*, people who can hold a shield and swing a sword and stand up to the attack of Changed. To hold on to the land that they *do* have for farming and sheep raising.

"Now, there are a few women, even here, who could probably do the job. But, by and large, the men can do it better. I suspect there were a few women at the beginning who told everyone they were just as good as any man. And I suspect that most of them died on some battlefield or another. Men died, too, but not in the same numbers. Because men are pretty well designed for fighting and women just *aren't*. You could kill Paul because you used smarts and took him by surprise. Try to take on a male of equivalent strength, training and size in the middle of a battle and what will happen?"

"He'll kick my ass," Megan admitted, looking over at Baradur who was watching with calm and unreadable eyes. "I still don't like it."

"Again, don't like it all you want," Mirta grinned. "There's more and it's worse, but I'll let someone else cover that one. But that's *some* of the reasons that this group fell into 'traditional' roles so fast."

"How do you stop it?" Megan asked. "I don't want my granddaughters as drudges to some man!"

"You don't even have daughters, yet, dear," Mirta

pointed out. "Bit early to worry. But I know what you mean. Well, I'll be interested to see what Norau is like. I'm sure that Sheida has thought of this and if she hasn't I'm sure that Edmund will have brought it up. I know both of them, by the way, and they *will* remember old Mirta," she added with a chuckle. "Oh, the stories I could tell about those two!"

"You never told me you knew them," Megan said, cocking her head to the side. "When was this?"

"Long time ago, girlie," Mirta replied. "Back in the *old* days when they were just king and queen of the Society in Norau. They were *quite* the item for a while. Then Sheida made the mistake of introducing Edmund to her sister and that was all she wrote."

"How old *are* you?" Megan asked. The woman had always been reticent about her age. In the harem it had made sense; Paul tended to prefer young women and Mirta looked to be in her early twenties. And she could act like a teenager on cue.

"One hundred and forty-seven," Mirta replied. "Don't look it, do I?"

"Not a bit," Megan admitted. "And you're still fertile?"

"Didn't start ovulating until the Fall," Mirta pointed out, tying off a last knot and holding up the dress. "Better?"

"Very nice," Megan admitted. The seamstress had taken the basic shapeless dress and brought in the waistline, added material to the sleeves so they fell in a V, cut down the front and embroidered the edges. "Very nice."

"I can't wait to get decent fabrics again," Mirta said with a sigh. "It's the one thing I miss about the harem. But I could only make those dreadful lingerie outfits there. I'm looking forward to making *real* dresses again. Crinolines and ruffs and properly formed bodices!"

"How did you keep from getting pregnant with Paul?" Megan asked, not to be dissuaded.

"Always knew when to present myself and when to look uninteresting," Mirta said. "Kept track of days when I was fertile and avoided him then. Called the 'rhythm' method and it works remarkably well if you're careful. Not as well as tansy, I'll admit. I was glad when you started stocking that. But I could only filch the raw; I didn't dare grab your distillate. You know that stuff is lethal, right?"

"I tested it carefully," Megan admitted. "Stealing my herbs. You're a piece of work, you know that?"

"The one and only," Mirta said with a grin.

"And thanks for explaining the . . . social conditions to me. It makes it a bit easier to accept even if I don't like it."

"Oh, I don't like it either," Mirta said. "And I think it's going to be hard to change now that it's established. Especially given the fact that the economic conditions reinforce it. Get some power mills in here and it will improve. But until then . . ." She shrugged in resignation. "Well, it's late and your ship's supposed to arrive in the morning. I'd say get some rest."

"I think I will," Megan said. As she stood up Baradur stood up also and headed to the door to the corridor, stepping through and checking both ways before preceding her towards her room.

She watched the back of her bodyguard for a moment in puzzlement.

"Baradur, you were listening to the conversation I had with Mistress Mirta?"

"Yes, mistress," the bodyguard answered.

"Does your clan hold women to be second-class citizens?" she asked.

"No, mistress," he said, turning to look at her and grinning. "The women of the Chudai would never permit it!"

"Do they fight?" she asked.

"No, mistress, not unless our homes are attacked," the bodyguard said, turning back to watch the corridor. They entered a narrow stairway going up to the high turret that had been set aside for her use. "Then they fight very hard; no one fights like Chudai woman at doorstep. And they take care of the home. But we men are always fighting and so they must take care of the farm, too. And they have voice in council. My mother is headwoman of our village. There is head-man too, Barahadur Ju. He is war leader."

"Why do you think you do it that way?" Megan asked, walking carefully. The stairwell was unlighted and the stone steps were slippery.

"Has always been that way," Baradur replied. "Chudai are an old people. Always have been fighters. Women want male babies but a girl is accepted and loved. Women tell tales of old days when other tribes would kill girl babies as worthless. But not the Chudai. We came from far away, long ago. We were fighters for this land, for Briton and the kings and queens and the empress, all over the world. In time, there were no more wars and some of us settle here. But we kept our old ways, the way of the rifle and bow and kukri, the ways of our speech and the ways of our living. Now there are wars again, and the Chudai can live again." He turned to her and grinned again, the round face barely visible except his teeth. "Is very good times."

"Are you telling me you *prefer* this?" Megan asked, aghast.

"Prefer, mistress?" Baradur asked as they exited the stairwell. He checked the corridor beyond and then stopped, thinking. "If could change the world back, would. But Chudai are born to war. Baradur was born with kukri in hand coming out of mother's belly. Learned rifle, bow, kukri, sneak, from father. Can touch deer on its flank, so quiet move. Can kill one man in tent in sleep and leave others sleeping. Was *born* to live *this* life, mistress. Would change back, but not for Baradur, for all the other poor bastards born to other life."

"You are a very strange person, Baradur," Megan admitted as they reached her door.

"Everyone say that about Chudai, mistress," Baradur admitted with a grin. The bodyguard checked the room carefully, then came back out. "But nobody says we're easy to kill. Will live with that. Good night, mistress."

"Good night, Baradur," Megan said, entering the candle-lit room. "Long day tomorrow. Get some rest."

"Can I ask where we are this time, skipper?" Herzer said, coming up on the quarterdeck with a mug of coffee in his hand. The deck of the ship was bloody cold after the relative warmth below and he cupped the mug for its warmth.

"Thirty kilometers from the entrance to the loch or fjord or whatever it is," Skipper Karcher said, leading him over to the binnacle where a small light illumined the charts. "One hour until dawn; we'll be in sight just after. We may have to tack once to make the entrance clearly, but no more than that."

"What about launching dragons?" Herzer asked.

"Do we need them?" Karcher said with a shrug. "The invasion fleet is approaching Balmoran from last word; there shouldn't be any enemies around to speak of."

"There are dragons in Briton," Herzer pointed out. "I'd like to at least have Silverdrake up, if not more. Frankly . . . well ma'am, I'd suggest a full formation."

Karcher looked at him in the pallid light and frowned.

"Is that a request of my dragon contingent XO?" Karcher asked. "Or the representative of Admiral Talbot?"

"I think . . . that's the request of the representative of *Duke* Talbot," Herzer said after a moment's thought. "Whether it's for protection, or show, I'd like to have a full flight of dragons up. Ma'am."

"You got it," Karcher replied with a shrug. "Launch at dawn?"

"And send messages to the support ships to be prepared to launch their Silverdrake just afterward, ma'am," Herzer noted. "And more to the mer to give underwater coverage. I'll be on the first ship's boat in; Commander Gramlich will have the dragon contingent to herself."

"What about your girlfriend?" the skipper asked.

"I think that Bast should accompany me," Herzer said after a moment's thought. "I base that upon some of Her Majesty's comments."

"Agreed," Karcher replied. "Well, Major, make it so."

"Yes, ma'am."

Megan was shivering in the cold wind from the northeast as the small fleet sailed down the loch. The sails had been sighted at dawn off the entrance and the girls, along with a fair contingent from the castle, had hurried down to the stone dock that was Clan McClure's pretensions to a port.

It had turned out to be early—the ships were nowhere close to making anchor—and it had been a long cold wait. But the wait was almost over now. She saw ship's boats being lowered over the side of the carrier just as one of the girls behind her gasped.

Up out of the water seals were erupting. No, not seals, selkie, each with a metal crossbow on his back. They spread out along the beach that flanked the dock and took up formation, whipping their bows off their backs to cover the area. She didn't know how long they had been watching but she had noticed seal heads around since she'd arrived.

As she watched, the water began to boil with dolphin bodies, and the occasional pike-toting mer surfaced, looking around sternly, then settling back into the water. It was clear that someone was taking no chances in this landing; the land and water were covered.

As she thought that, she looked up. The ship coming to pick her up was, after all, a dragon-carrier. And, sure enough, right in the sun to the east was a flight of dragons. More dragons were dropping off the masts of the lesser ships, small, brightly colored dragons that ascended into the hazy sky with breathless speed. Suddenly it was as if the air was filled with dragons, spiraling in, their riders signaling to the carrier and the carrier signaling in turn.

All of this movement had distracted her from the approaching boats and she didn't look back at them until the lead boat scraped on the stone of the pier. Sailors scrambled up with lines but just as quickly a truly huge man in legion armor leapt to the pier, his hobnail boots striking sparks on the stone.

He was an imposing figure, well over two meters of metal and leather. His Roman-style helmet was buckled at the chin and the flaps covered his face except for a bit of nose and shadowed eyes. Little else could be seen of him between cloak, armor and kilt. The man strode over to where Megan waited, flanked by Laird McClure, and dropped to one knee, bowing his head.

"Mistress Travante, Major Herzer Herrick, UFS Ground Forces. I have been tasked by Queen Sheida to ensure your protection until we can bring you, and your people, to safety in Norau." As he said this he unbuckled his helmet and then looked up. "I am yours to command."

He looked up into Megan's eyes and she felt her heart literally stop, frozen by fiery green eyes.

"Bast, just this once, let me make the frigging entrance, okay?" Herzer growled. "It's my *job*."

"Okay, lover-boy," Bast said, hitting him on the

shoulder hard enough to be felt through the armor. "But you're just pawing the ground over actual harem girls to rescue and you know it."

"Key-holder," Herzer pointed out. "Council member by default. Meddle not in the affairs of wizards for they are subtle and quick to anger. This girl killed Paul Bowman; I'm not sure I'd *want* to date somebody that could do that."

"You do more than date me, boyo!" Bast pointed out.

"So why'd she have to do it?" Herzer said with a grin as he put on his helmet.

"Touché," Bast replied.

The women and Gael were all watching the dragons, as planned, although there was one fellow, a short, stocky, dark-skinned little bastard of a fighter by the look who was watching the approaching boats warily. Herzer jumped to the dock as fast as the sailors detailed to run the lines but his foot slipped on the slimy stone of the pier, causing a jet of sparks. He leaned forward and made it appear as if that was the standard way for a Blood Lord to arrive on a potentially hostile pier, then turned on his heel and marched to the awaiting group. Most of the women were dressed in clothes that were shapeless and simple but there was one in the group, a tall bird-woman apparently, who was naked except for a coating of down.

Herzer dragged his eyes from the bird-woman to the much less spectacular brunette who was wearing a chain from which a councilor's Key dangled. He dropped to one knee and recited his prepared lines.

"Mistress Travante, Major Herzer Herrick, UFS Ground Forces. I have been tasked by Queen Sheida to ensure your protection until we can bring you, and your people, to safety in Norau." He was unbuckling his helmet as he recited them and when he was done he looked up into her eyes. "I am yours to command."

The last words were strangled as he felt a jet of adrenaline dump into his system. The only time he'd felt this way was in battle, a tough one with enemies that had a serious chance of killing him. His skin was flushed and he knew he was, frankly, staring.

So *this* was what they meant by love at first sight.

When Bast saw the woman freeze, and heard Herzer stumble over his lines, she mentally sighed. Time to break in a new boy-toy. But she was continuing to scan the women that had accompanied the council member and let out a joyous cry at one face.

"Mirta!" she screamed.

Herzer shook his head as Bast yelled a name and bounded past him, picking up a woman who wasn't much taller than she.

"Apparently Bast has found a friend," he said, huskily, getting up off the slimy jetty. He turned to McClure, trying to remember his mission. "Laird McClure? In addition to picking up the women you have been sheltering we have supplies for you and your people. There are weapons, cloth and tools in the ships. If you have some people that can help them unload I'd appreciate it."

"Not as much as I appreciate the supplies," the laird said. "We'll get started at once."

"Herzer!" Bast said, dragging the woman forward. "You need to meet Mirta!"

"Good day, mistress," he said, casting a quick glance at the council member, Megan. He ran the name around in his head for a moment, trying not to append "Herrick" to it, and then took the small hand of Bast's friend. "Any friend of Bast's, et cetera. Nice to meet you."

"Not as nice as it is to meet you," Mirta replied, looking up at him with bright eyes. "I'm ready to get out of this gloomy land." She looked over at the laird in distress. "Not that I'm not grateful . . .".

"It's all right," McClure said. "Some take to the Highlands and some don't."

"If you don't mind," the bird-woman said, stepping forward. "I'd prefer to fly out to the ship. I don't like small boats and . . ." She shrugged, rustling her wings. "I don't fit well in them; I tend to reach for balance and . . ."

"That's fine," Herzer said. He looked up until he spotted a rider that was watching the group and signaled that the bird-woman was going to fly out. "Go ahead," he continued. "Mistress Travante . . ."

"Call me Megan, please," she said in a quiet tone.

"Megan, then," he continued, trying not to look her in the eye. "If you'd care to board the boat?" he asked, holding out his hand. As she took it he felt an electric shock pass through his body and he lowered her carefully into the waiting launch. The short man, obviously a bodyguard, followed her into the craft and Herzer held up his hand as others scrambled forward. "We can only take five. Bast . . ."

"I'll stay here with Mirta," Bast said, grinning. She winked at him and grinned wider. "Why don't you take *Megan* back and show her her quarters?"

"I'd like Shanea and Amber," Megan said, pointing at two of the other women.

"Bast, sort out the embark, will you?" Herzer said as he scrambled into the boat. "Make way. Head for the *Hazhir*."

Megan tried to sort out her feelings as they headed for the ship. She didn't believe in love at first sight, but her reaction couldn't be anything else. Well, maybe lust. Herzer was the most . . . masculine man she could remember ever meeting. It had taken her a long time to even notice that his left hand was missing, replaced by some sort of complex prosthetic. His face was also heavily scarred, one scar running from his ear to chin with another on the opposite cheek. And at some point his nose had been broken; it was slightly squashed. Despite that, he was handsome, very handsome. Too handsome. She had to get this under control.

"Major . . . Herrick was it?" Megan asked.

"Yes, ma'am," Herzer answered, then cleared his throat.

"I've heard the name before," Megan said, suddenly. "Paul hated you almost as much as he hated Duke Talbot."

Herzer suddenly grinned and she realized that he was far younger than he at first appeared, maybe her own age. She had taken him for nearly a hundred.

"You don't know how much that pleases me, ma'am," Herzer said, still grinning. "And may I congratulate you on your accomplishment?"

"It was . . . ugly," Megan said, shuddering at more than the wind off the water.

"Killing is," Herzer said gently, taking off his cloak and wrapping it around her. It was still warm from his body and was filled with his smell. She wrapped it more tightly around herself as much from the pure sensation as against the cold. For some reason she was no longer really feeling it. In fact, she felt like she was running a fever. God this was bad.

"I'd never killed anyone before," Megan said, leaning against him suddenly.

"Killing is a bit like sex," Herzer said, gently. "You always remember your first. After that it tends to blur a bit." He stopped and shook his head. "I'm sorry if . . ."

"I hope I never get to the point that it blurs," Megan said, leaning back and looking up at him. "But I'm glad that there are good people that can do the job when necessary."

"Good is a relative term, ma'am," he said with a shrug.

"I told you to call me Megan," Megan said watching his face. He was half turned away from her, watching the approaching ship.

"Good is a relative term . . . Megan," he repeated, working his jaw. "Most soldiers that are good at what they do are stone bastards. And I'll happily add myself, and Duke Edmund, to that category."

"Then for the time being you're my stone bastard," Megan said, suddenly laughing. "Thank you for coming to pick us up. What's with the dragons?"

"There are New Destiny forces nearby, ma . . . Megan," Herzer said, gesturing to the coxswain. "If it came to blows I wanted my dragons up. By the way, we should have loaded you last. That way you would be first to disembark. As it is, we're going to have to do some shuffling around."

"Your dragons?" Megan asked.

"Commander Gramlich's, actually," Herzer said, frowning at the bodies in the way of getting her to the front of the boat. "I'm the XO of the dragon contingent."

"I thought you were a Blood Lord?" Megan said as the boat pulled up alongside a floating platform. There was a short set of stairs up to the ship's main-deck and she could see a group of seamen formed up in a double line.

"Oh, I am," Herzer said, frowning. "But Blood Lord is a state of mind rather than a job description. Right now I'm the XO of the dragon contingent. Ma'am, would you mind if I got somewhat personal and just lifted you over the side? That's going to be the easi-est way to do this."

"That's fine," Megan said, standing up carefully in the rocking boat. Now that she had time to notice it at least part of her internal distress was nausea. She really hoped she wasn't going to throw up in front of everyone.

Herzer put his hand and prosthetic around her waist and lifted her as if she was a feather over the side of the boat and onto the small platform. As he did the bodyguard scrambled past some seamen and took up station behind her.

"Ladies, if you could exit at the front," Herzer said, gesturing to the dock.

CHAPTER TWENTY-SEVEN

Bast boarded the last boat out with Mirta and one of the other women. She slapped the seamstress on the arm and shook her head.

"I can't believe Paul Bowman would be stupid enough to take you for some sweet young thing," Bast said, grinning.

"I can play the game as well as you, ancient one," Mirta grinned back. "By the way, did you see Megan? She looked as if someone hit her between the eyes with an oar."

"Herzer was just as bad," Bast said, shaking her head. "It's like the first time Edmund saw Daneh. Sheida had just been killing time, but her sister, wooo-hoo! Going to have to break in new boy-toy."

"They're both trying so hard to play like nobody notices," the other girl said.

"Bast, this is Ashly," Mirta said, her mouth working.

"We've had our times, but right now we're in a state of armed truce."

"Mirta," Ashly said, shaking her head.

"Oh, can see this is going to be a lovely voyage," Bast said, chuckling. "If it comes down to cat-fights, though, putting money on Mirta."

"I've spent a lot of time building up a reputation for harmlessness," Mirta said, frowning. "I'm not sure I'm up to changing that now. So are we going straight to Norau?" she continued, looking over at Bast and ignoring Ashly.

"Don't know," Bast admitted. "Think not. Large battle going on. Invasion force reaches Norau . . . today, maybe tomorrow. Will need the carrier."

"So we're going from captivity to a battle?" Ashly snapped. "That's insane."

"Whole world insane," Bast said with a grin. "Did you not know?"

"This is just insane," Rachel muttered tiredly.

She still was the only doctor in the hospital and as the enemy fleet approached, the injury rate had just gone up. She had taken to sleeping on the ward rather than in the rather nice suite that had been set aside for her quarters; since she knew she was going to be called in just about every night it wasn't worth the fifty-meter walk.

In addition to the injury cases, the legion had been sending over their post-op patients. On one level it made sense; the hospital was far better quarters than a leaky tent. But, on the other hand, she didn't have the staff to handle the soldiers as well.

During the day, between one crisis and another,

she had been training her staff, most of the time, unfortunately, in practical exercises. The two PAs were barely adequate as nurses and the nursing staff was only up to simple instructions. She had finally had to open up the internal injury patient but by the time she did it was too late and the experience was nauseating. The nurses didn't even know the instruments or internal structure; expecting them to assist in a difficult operation was clearly a bad idea. But even with the best nursing staff there was no way she could have saved the patient. His spleen had been ruptured and there was damage to the liver. He'd survived the operation but he'd just . . . gone during recovery.

She'd set the two best of them to memorizing internal diagrams and had them assist on two "easier" operations, putting together comminuted fractures.

On a larger level she felt totally out of her depth. She was far superior in training and knowledge to the rest of the staff but she knew she was still a rank tyro. Every time before when she had a major question she had been able to fall back on her mother's enormous level of knowledge. Here it was only her.

Furthermore, she wasn't getting nearly enough sleep and neither was the staff. And now, with the invasion force only a day or so away, half the staff, including both PAs and one of her "trained" surgical nurses, had disappeared. It was just insane. There was no way to provide decent, or any, care under these conditions.

"None of them are in their quarters," Zahar said, shaking his head. "The whole town is evacuating; I don't see where I can blame them."

"I can," Rachel said, bitterly. "You don't just leave patients!"

"The word is that the legion won't be able to hold them," Zahar said, unhappily. "They're outnumbered almost four to one and there's too long of a line to hold. And who knows where the fleet is?"

"The fleet, which is under my father," Rachel noted, "is doing what it has to. I think you can be sure that Balmoran is in the forefront of his mind. And that, whatever it is doing, it is effective."

"Doctor Ghorbani," Keith said, sticking his head in the door to her office, "there's a patient from the legion on the way. Severe head injury. The legion physicians say they aren't qualified to handle it, so they sent him to you."

"This is just insane! What next?"

"What's going to happen next?" Edmund said, unhappily. The fleet was pitching through a heavy storm, groping northward for the remaining New Destiny carriers and hoping that the UFS fleet would find New Destiny before New Destiny found the *Hazhir*.

"Unfortunately, what is going to happen next is even worse winds," Shar said. "Reports from the back side of the storm are high winds from the northeast then a large high-pressure system."

"Which means *no* winds," Edmund said.

"Correct."

"Word on the *Hazhir*?"

"They're to the north of the storm, sailing eastward. Also to the north of the New Destiny fleet. They're trying to run the gap between the combat fleet and the invasion fleet. The dreadnoughts are to the east of the main storm and making decent time north to Balmoran. All we can do is ride it out and then get back in the game."

"Is there some way to work the edges of this?" Edmund asked. "Come around it and avoid the high pressure behind it?"

"We can sail inshore and follow the dreadnoughts," Shar mused.

"That would catch us between the land and the New Destiny fleet," Edmund pointed out. "With limited maneuvering room."

"True," Shar said. "To the east the storm apparently extends all the way to Briton; no getting around it that way."

"Head west," Edmund said. "We can't afford to be becalmed for two days. Especially *those* two days. We'll take the chance on getting caught in the vise."

"The legionnaire doesn't look very good, Doctor," Keith said from the door of Rachel's office. The orderly had been hanging around a good bit, she wasn't sure if it was because she wasn't panicking from the invasion or because he found her attractive and at the moment she didn't really care. She just wished he'd leave.

"No, he doesn't," Rachel replied, not looking up from the medical text she was reviewing.

"And he's not breathing very well," the orderly added.

"No, he wouldn't," Rachel said.

"What's wrong with him?" Keith asked, not deterred. "Besides having the side of his head stove in?"

"Subdural cerebral hematoma," Rachel said, sighing. The legionnaire had been struck, rather hard, by a post that was being set up in the Balmoran defenses. She knew she was going to have to do a trepan operation, basically open up his skull to relieve the pressure on the brain before it swelled to the point of necrosis. She'd *assisted* in a trepanning operation before, but she'd never actually *done* one and after losing her first major surgical patient she was not feeling particularly lucky.

"Subd . . . sub . . . what?"

"Call it 'brain bruise,'" Rachel snapped. "Look, Keith, I'm rather busy here . . ."

"Sorry, Doctor," the orderly said. "Who is going to assist you?"

"Ms. Katherine," Rachel replied.

"Uhmmm . . ."

"Don't tell me she's gone as well!"

"Doctor, I think it's just you, me and the administrator," the boy said, looking unhappy.

"Wh . . ." Rachel stopped and then looked at him and shook her head. "Why are *you* still here?"

"Nowhere else to go, miss," the orderly replied.

"Well, in that case, go scrub up," Rachel said. "You've just been promoted to nurse."

"Are we just going to sit in the cabin the whole trip?" Shanea asked.

Megan looked up from the light sculpture she was working on. She had been examining the extent of the power available to her, now that she actually had some free time. There wasn't much; enough for one teleport a day, assuming there was anywhere to teleport that

didn't have a block, and a very few other programs.
Not enough to ken or create anything worthwhile.
But enough for some slight telekinesis and to create
light sculptures. She was experimenting with them.
If she could create a real enough illusion it might
be worthwhile.

"I'm going to stay in here most of the time,"
Megan admitted. She looked over at the girl and
shrugged. "I think I sort of got used to being mired
in a room. Frankly, the great outdoors has gotten a
bit *too* great."

The ship was sailing westward under easy winds,
but she'd gone up on deck once and been surprised,
and displeased, with how uncomfortable even the light
breeze felt. It was cold, for one thing, and the vast
expanse of the ocean had actively frightened her.

For that matter, the attitude of the crew had
bothered her; they treated her like some sort of
goddess. Even Shanea and the other girls had been
treating her differently. Some of that, she knew, was
because of the brutal way that she had removed
Paul Bowman; apparently while she was picking up
the pregnant women some of the girls had looked in
and seen what happened to him. But, beyond that,
she was surrounded with the mystique of a council
member. The crew treated her as if she might make
them disappear, or be Changed into a toad, if they
bothered her in the slightest. The girls, either for the
same reasons or picking it up from the crew, were
beginning to treat her the same way. As if she'd turn
them into a toad or pour acid all over them.

There were only a few people who didn't seem
uncomfortable around her: Bast, Amber, Shanea and

Major Herrick. Bast was generally skylarking up in the rigging, Shanea and Amber generally visited her in the cabin and Major Herrick . . . She didn't really want to think about Major Herrick. And he seemed to feel the same way. At least he seemed to be actively avoiding her. Every time she had the officers to dinner in her cabin he had "other duties."

And, of course, there was Baradur. He was, as ever, sitting by the door to the cabin. As if the marine on the other side wasn't enough of a guard.

"You ought to at least go talk to Major Herrick," Shanea said. "I know you like him."

"Shanea . . ." Megan said, then sighed. "I do like him. But I think I've had enough men in my life lately."

"Only Paul," Shanea said, honestly perplexed. "I don't think Herzer would be like that. From what I've heard he's a pretty good guy in bed."

"Shanea!" Megan said then paused. "I really don't want to talk about it, okay?"

"Well, I'm going to go for a walk," Shanea said. "If you don't mind."

"I don't," Megan replied with a grin. "Just because I'm playing hermit, it doesn't mean you have to as well."

Herzer had just come up from the dragon deck when Shanea stepped onto the maindeck and he nodded at her.

"How are you this morning Miss Shanea?" he asked, formally.

"Oh, call me Shanea," the little blonde grinned. "And I'm fine. How are the dragons?"

"Doing well," Herzer said. "And the council-woman?"

"The councilwoman has decided to hide in her room for the rest of the voyage," Shanea said as Bast dropped from the rigging. "Hi, Bast!"

"Heya, Shanea," Bast said. "How's tricks?"

"Haven't pulled any lately," Shanea said, frowning. "Do you think I should?"

"Maybe after we get to shore," Herzer interjected, hurriedly. "Is Mistress Travante *okay*?"

"She just doesn't want to come up on deck," Shanea said with a shrug. "She just plays with light sculptures all day."

"Light and more," Bast noted. "I can feel the power wielding. I think she learns what she can do."

"Well, that's to the good," Herzer said.

"Why don't you go visit her?" Shanea asked. "I think she'd like that."

"I . . . don't think so," Herzer replied. "I . . . have to go talk to the captain. I hope to see you later."

"What time?" Shanea asked. "And shouldn't you ask Bast?"

"That wasn't . . . I need to go see the captain," Herzer said, giving her a two-fingered salute and retreating to the quarterdeck.

"What did I say?" Shanea said, turning to Bast.

"If I wasn't such a good judge of humans," Bast replied, "I'd think you were toying with the poor boy. As it is . . . I probably couldn't explain it. How's your head for heights?"

"Fine?"

"Good," Bast said, grabbing her arm, "I've something to show you in the rigging."

"I have something to tell you," Shanea said, as she mounted the ratlines.

"Aye?"

"I prefer boys for fun."

"Well, nobody would believe me but that *wasn't* what I wanted to show you."

"Captain," Herzer said touching his forelock. "Permission to come on the bridge?"

"Granted," the captain said with a grin.

"I heard there was a report of an orca pod," Herzer continued, glancing over at the chart. The charts had come back out as soon as Edmund's plans became apparent and he blanched when he looked at the updated positions. The *Hazhir* was sailing between the New Destiny combat fleet and the invasion fleet. They were apparently trying to slip through the gap and make it to Newfell Base. If either fleet noticed them the combined fleets could fall on them like wolves on a sheep.

On the other hand, this sheep had teeth made for more than shearing grass.

"Tricky, isn't it?" Karcher said, giving one of her catlike grins. "The worst bit is that we've got a high-pressure system bearing down on us; we're going to lose this wind in a bit. Then we'll be *becalmed* between both fleets. That's why I sent the mer and delphinos to check out the orcas; I didn't want them to know that there were any dragons around. Out here they could only mean a carrier."

Herzer opened his mouth and then closed it again.

"And, yes, I considered the possibility of an underwater attack," Karcher said with a grin. "But we're doing nearly forty klicks. A kraken would be hard pressed to keep up with us."

"If you don't mind, ma'am, I'd like to put a wyvern up prepped for launch," Herzer said. "Both a Powell and a Silverdrake. Just in case."

"No, it's a good idea," Karcher said. "See to it."

"Yes, ma'am."

"Come in," Megan said at the light knock.

"Heyo," Bast said, striding in and flopping on the cot that was one of the few places to sit in the room. "Been in here a long time."

"I'm more comfortable in here," Megan said, primly. "And I don't interfere with the working of the ship."

"And don't have to see the sky," Bast said. "Don't have to look at water stretching away on every side to the horizon, nearly infinite, what if something happen, what if ship sink, what happen then?"

"Bast . . ."

"People always say that, never work, even for council member," Bast said, her face solemn. "You know what makes people people?"

"No?" Megan said surprised at the apparent non sequitur.

"Interact with other people, mix in tumble of society," the elf said, doffing her sword and obviously preparing to stay a while. "Hermit only thinks own thoughts. Most of time bad thoughts. Think about fear of outside, think about fear of power, fear of failure, think about fear all the time. Fear reinforces fear."

"I was courageous enough to kill Paul Bowman," Megan said, hotly. "I just . . . don't like the sea."

"Too big," Bast said, nodding. "Swallow up as if

never exist. Understand. More fear there, though. Fear of self, methinks."

Bast waited as Megan played with a sculpture of a flower, muttering under her breath. Then the sculpture turned black and collapsed.

"I don't want to talk about it," Megan said with a shrug.

"Need to, though," Bast said, then waited again.

"Do you think you can outwait me?" Megan replied, gesturing up another sculpture. This one started as a face and seemed to morph itself into a skull as if against her will. She waved it away as well.

"Thousand years old," Bast said. "Gonna out*live* you much less outwait you."

Megan started to call up another structure then her hands dropped.

"Sometimes . . ." she said after a long pause and then stopped.

Bast pulled a stoppered flask from her belt and tossed it to Megan.

"Have a drink," Bast said. "Have two, then toss back. Going to need some myself."

"What is it?" Megan asked, sniffing at the opening. It was alcoholic, she could tell that much.

"Would make mysterious noises if real elf," Bast said. "Is Navy rum. Very high proof. Have big drink. Put hair on your chest."

"I don't want hair on my chest," Megan said, taking a swallow and coughing. "God that's rough!"

"Also burn hair off," Bast admitted. "Useful as paint thinner. Have another drink. Then start at beginning. Where meet Paul?"

So Megan started at the beginning. How Paul had

found her washing clothes. She had been a general maid for a local couple. She had many skills that would have gotten her better jobs but not in the small Gallic town she had washed up in after the Fall. At the time she was glad enough to get the table scraps while she tried to figure a way out of the hole. She had clawed her way to relative power in the harem and stood it when her time came with Paul. But it was not so much the rape, or the constant strain of maintaining her position in the harem while planning to kill Bowman, that had shaken her. It was the feelings that arose in her as the months and years went by. As the words, halting at first, began to spill out of her it seemed as if the ship must have hit a storm for all the waves out the window looked the same. Her tosses to Bast were going all over the cabin and she couldn't catch anymore. Finally she moved over to the cot and Bast sat at the end.

"I didn't want to love him," Megan said, almost pleaded. "And in the end, I didn't want to kill him either. I don't trust myself. I have this . . . weakness I found for servility. It disgusts me."

"But if had not found, would have gone mad or ended up like Amado," Bast pointed out, turning the flask upside down. "Blast, not a drop left."

"Mirta didn't," Megan pointed out.

"Bet you a dollar," Bast responded. "Could not fight and win. Could not lay out and succeed. Did the best you could, body and brain took over. Think you did very well, even ignoring killing Paul Bowman."

"Even ignoring falling in love with him?" Megan said, bitterly. "I just feel . . . broken. I feel as if there's no metal left in me."

"Yet held onto metal and killed Paul," Bast said. "Plenty of metal there. Fine and hard, harder than before your test."

"But what about this . . . instinct to servility?" Megan said. "Everybody wants something and I find myself wanting to please. I never felt that way before . . . this. And I really *loved* Paul." There were tears now to go with the cracked voice. "How do I trust myself? How do I trust my feelings about . . ."

"Herzer," Bast said with a grin. "Is okay, plain as day to everybody on ship with eyes. Herzer very easy man to love, trust me."

"But how do I know I didn't just glom onto the first reasonably presentable guy to show up?" Megan asked, bitterly. "Herzer is the first person I've seen who is . . . presentable."

"Malcolm Innes?" Bast asked.

"How do you know about him?" Megan said, thinking back. She'd mentioned him in passing but not described.

"Could write book," Bast chuckled. "Good looking fellow. Older than looks. Quite 'presentable.'"

"I couldn't live among the Gael," Megan shuddered. "I admire them. I even, sort of, understand why they live the way they do, the necessity of it that is. But I couldn't live there. Even as queen of the Gael or whatever. I'd end up ripping half their heads off."

"Not bad looking, though," Bast pointed out. "Feel the same way about him as you do Herzer?"

"No," Megan said in a small voice. "Besides, he was nuts."

"Wants to be king of Briton," Bast said, shrugging. "Lots of others in history with same madness. All

Gael mad. Should have met Boadicea, now there was a woman with a problem with servitude."

"Boadicea?" Megan said then frowned. "She was a *Celtic* queen in the time of the Romans. I'm sorry, Bast, but pull the other one, that was *way* before your time."

"Tell me if I lie," Bast said, her face straight, holding up two fingers as if in an oath. "Where you think *legend* of elves comes from? Point is, Malcolm may be crazy but it's regal madness. Plenty of women have fallen for it over the years. Eight wives of Henry for example, poor girls. Went to the slaughter like so many charging infantrymen in Somme and that's sort of the point. Women work one way, men another. Men charge the walls for the women, once more unto the breach and all that, women charge the men for the gene. If didn't fall for Malcolm, pretty, pretty Malcolm with as much power as anyone has these days, then aren't addicted to men, aren't addicted to servitude. So, feelings for Herzer are real feelings. Feelings to trust. Hell, not the first to fall for Herzer, I could tell some stories. But first that *Herzer* has fallen for."

"What about you?" Megan asked.

"I charge the walls *and* the gene," Bast replied with a merry chuckle.

"No feelings like you're inadequate?" Megan asked. "That, maybe it would be better if you just let the menfolk take charge?"

"Ain't human," Bast said, grinning. "Thousand years get tired of saying it. Elves are not humans. Don't have same wiring. Can play submissive game but not submissive at all. Humans talk about 'fight-flight.' Isn't binary, quaternary: fight, flight, bluff, submit. Every human is different pattern for different conditions, but *all* humans have all four to an extent. Elves don't. We have fight, flight and bluff. NO submit. All human interaction works on those four responses, including what you went through. You used bluff as much as anything with girls. With Paul you used submit. Had to. Now you fear it. Don't. Don't have to *use* it, most of the time, but is part of you. Watch it, don't fear it, know it. Going to be interesting with Herzer, though."

"Why?" Megan said, blearily. The rum had really started to kick in.

"Most prototypical heterosexual dominant you'll ever meet," Bast said with a wicked grin. "Knows it, now, controls it. Understands it and accepts it, now. But under 'heterosexual dominant' in the Net has picture of Herzer in armor."

"But what . . ." Megan gulped and wished there was more rum. "What if that's . . . okay?"

"Hmmm . . ." Bast said, nodding. "Bed and office two different things. For you has been the same and that's hard to handle. But with Herzer . . . you in position of authority and order him, off he goes like good little soldier. In bed . . . that's different. Just know that that's *you* and not *Paul*. Understand?"

"Understand," Megan said, yawning.

"Here," Bast said, handing her another flask. "Water. Otherwise gonna have spectacular hangover."

"Thank you," Megan said, taking a big drink and then lying back on the cot. "I'll think about what you said. When I wake up."

"And I'll see you out on deck," Bast said, buckling on her sword. "Tomorrow."

"Yes, ma'am," Megan giggled.

"Good dreams," Bast said, covering her with the sheet.

And they were good dreams. Megan couldn't remember them the next day but she did remember who was in them. And it hadn't been Paul Bowman for once.

CHAPTER TWENTY-EIGHT

"There's orcas out there," Tarree pulsed.

"Yeah, making a hell of a lot of noise, too," Elayna replied.

"They're pulling back towards their fleet," Tarree added. "Dragons." The New Destiny dragons had learned to attack the mer just as the UFS dragons went after orca.

"I know," Elayna said. "But why are they sounding? It's like they want us to know they're there."

"No sense," Herman whistled. The delphino pod leader was one of the senior delphinos, Jason's equivalent. And she knew him well enough to recognize that he was worried. "Trap feels."

"Agreed," Elayna said. "But we're not falling for it."

"Not for us trap," Herman suddenly shrilled. "Ship go!"

"Damn," Elayna snarled. "That's what feels wrong. They're trying to pull us away from the *ship*."

"Try not," Herman said, turning in his own body length and rapidly accelerating to the south. "Succeed did."

"I hate this damned motion," Joanna growled. The ship was becalmed, rocking in the waves.

"You'd hate it more if you'd seen the charts," Herzer replied.

"I heard," the commander replied. "But the combat fleet was still sailing south towards Edmund."

"Was," Herzer pointed out. "Without the mer for communications, we don't know what is happening."

"Tell me something I don't know, me boyo," the dragon said. "Nor do we know what's happening under our keel."

"Yeah, we would lose the mer just when we got . . ." He paused as he felt a tingling feeling go down his spine. He got up and looked around but there was nothing to cause the sudden feeling of dread. But he stepped towards the aft of the ship, walking slowly between the wyvern and then starting to run. He was going to look a fool if . . .

There was a sound of breaking glass and a shriek from the stern of the ship. From the captain's cabin.

"Quit bloody screaming!" Megan said as Baradur chopped at another of the hands that were scrabbling at the broken window. The hands were webbed and covered with fine scales for all they had five fingers. Megan dreaded seeing what they were attached to.

The marine guard plunged into the cabin, boarding pike to the fore, just as the first of the attackers made it past the wee-folk guard. The attackers were armored in scales with faces like frogs or fish but eyes alight with malevolent intelligence, they smelled of seaweed and rot. The first one over the broken out window sprang into the room on long, heavily muscled legs and tore the pike from the marine's hands, turning it upon its wielder and pinning him to the starboard bulkhead.

Baradur turned in a blur and chopped his kukri into the thing's arm, nearly severing it, and followed it up with a blow to the neck that left the thing decapitated on the deck. But in the time he had taken, two more had made it through the window.

Megan turned to bolt out the door, only to find the corridor packed with struggling sailors and the strange fish-men that had risen from the deep. She closed the door and leaned against it, trying to think what to do. Shanea, thank God, had quit screaming and was now holding onto her skirt. No help there.

Baradur was a blur, striking from side to side in the narrow quarters. The fish-men seemed to have only their long, hooked talons for weapons but they were using them well and the guard had taken many cuts. His foemen were piled at his feet but in a moment he was going to be overwhelmed.

Megan spoke a few syllables and pointed at one of the fish-men, stilling his heart and dropping him to the deck. She turned to another then another but even that minor use of power was draining and she could see her power-bar dropping into amber and then red as more and more of the creatures piled over the lintel. She could hear scrabbling at the door and leaned into it, holding it shut with her weight and her foot as the things pounded upon it. There were guttural screams

from beyond and a sound like melons being smashed
as the door was struck with the heaviest weight yet.
Her foot slid and a hand scrabbled around the door,
pulling at her sleeve.

Then Baradur, making a wild slash to the side, slipped
in the pool of blood that had built up on the floor and
fell, hard, slamming his head into the deck.

There was nothing between the girls and the attackers but slippery deck.

Megan pulled up a protection field and threw it
over both of them but, as she did, another of the
creatures pulled itself into the cabin. It was larger
than the others and bore a jeweled harness. It took
a small box from the harness and opened it, glaring
at the slight haze that surrounded her. It pulled a
pinch of dust from the box and with a guttural laugh
tossed it into the field.

Which blinked out of existence.

At the scream Herzer broke into a run, pounding
up the companionway and onto the maindeck which
was total chaos. Some sort of fish-men were clamber-
ing onto the ship from every direction. The startled
sailors and marines had barely started to fight back.
He paused and then turned as there was a thump on
the deck behind him.

"Go for the cabin," Bast said, drawing her saber.
"These are for me." She laughed and cut backhand,
taking the arm off of one of the fish-men and continuing in a circle that left another headless and a third
spilling his guts on the deck.

There were more of the fish-men in the corridor
to the captain's cabin, having apparently broken in

through one of the cabins to the side. There were several sailors already down in a welter of blood on the deck and one lone marine trying to hold the things back with his pike.

Herzer jerked the pike out of his hand, broke it off short and gave it back to him spread from one side of the corridor to the other.

"Hold it like that," he said, lifting the startled marine off his feet and charging forward.

The weight of the two drove the fish-men back until they were pinned in a struggling mass against the door of the captain's cabin. When they were, Herzer braced the marine with one hand and began stabbing over his shoulder, driving his short sword into the fish-men like the sting of a wasp, each blow a killing blow. Throat, mouth, chest, throat. As they choked out their life he pulled back on his ersatz battering ram letting the dead fall and driving forward to pin the living. The marine was raked again and again by the talons of the beasts but he held firm to the pike. Finally there was only one of the beasts who had his back to them, scrabbling through the half-open door. Herzer jerked the marine behind him, drove his sword into the creature's unprotected back and threw it over his shoulder as if it were no lighter than a cat. Then he slammed his weight into the door.

One of the things reached for her and she let him approach, shrinking away from the reaching arm until he was leaning forward, out of balance. Then one hand flicked up and grabbed his thumb. She wasn't sure, with the webbing, if a thumb twist would work but it did and the thing shrilled loudly as his thumb disjointed with an audible "pop." She ducked under the arm, lifting it in full control, grasped the wrist with her other hand and went through a complex twist that left her holding a dislocated arm. At that point she had total control of the target and she interposed the screaming fish-man between herself and its fellows.

Unfortunately, there were just too many of them and they crowded her as the shaman began muttering again. She concentrated and reached towards him with power but she was flat out, not even enough to squeeze a heart. She leaned forward, preparing to use her shield as a battering ram and . . . felt herself flying forward as an irresistible force smashed the door open. Suddenly Herzer was just *there*. He picked up the leader fish thing in one hand as he chopped another down and slammed the leader's head into the bulkhead above. Then he began slashing to either side.

The fish-men, who had thought they had won, rallied quickly and more began scrambling over the side. But there was no resisting the immense Blood Lord. Where Baradur's kukri had severed arms or heads the short sword of the Blood Lord cut torsos in twain. The deck, already wet with blood, began to fill with body parts. Then another marine came through the door bearing a broken pike and began using the shortened spear to one side. Last Baradur, shaking his head and weaving a bit, began slashing to the other. The three filled the room from side to side and nothing could break through them.

Megan shut the door to the cabin and bolted it, pulling Shanea, who had fainted, into a corner and just watched the slaughter. The things kept coming, it seemed for forever, as if they would never end, but the three had regained the window and held them there. Finally it was over. No more scaled hands scrabbled at the edges and the sounds of battle from the decks above had stopped.

She wiped futilely at the blood that covered her face and smiled as the Blood Lord turned from the window.

"Well, Major Herrick, I'm glad that I could finally get you to my cabin," she said, walking up to him and touching him on the face. "But you could have just knocked."

Herzer looked at her, searchingly, and then bent his head, slowly, and kissed her.

Rachel lifted the head injury up and tipped water into his mouth.

"Thank you," he said, weakly. "Where am I?"

"The Navy base hospital," she said. "How many fingers am I holding up?" she asked.

"Two," he replied.

"What's your name?"

"Kalil Barnhurst," the soldier said, wincing at the pain in his head. "Priv . . . no corporal, I just got promoted. Serial number 25-3-5-01."

"Good," she said, running a pin down his side.

"Ouch. That hurt."

"Be glad it did," Rachel said with a smile.

"You a nurse?" he asked, leaning back. He raised his hand to his head and winced again. "What happened?"

"From what I was told, a large pole hit you in the head," Rachel replied. "And, no, I'm your surgeon.

But all the nurses have left. The New Destiny fleet seems to have run them off."

"Shit," the young man said, looking around wildly. "Are they here?"

"Not yet," Rachel assured him. "And I'm sure that the legion will hold them."

"We're not *planning* on holding the hospital," the legionnaire said acerbically. "We're going to be lucky if we can hold onto the camp. You've got to get out of here!"

"I've got more patients to take care of," Rachel said, standing up. "And even with the ones that could be moved and not have it kill them, I don't have the people to move them."

"You do now," a voice said from the door to the ward.

"Who are you?" Rachel asked the officer in the doorway. He had some resemblance to Herzer but it was mostly the legionnaire armor and the way he wore it, as if fifty pounds of metal were just a normal uniform. But she also vaguely recognized him from somewhere.

"Sergeant Pedersen!" the soldier said, happily if weakly.

"Note the tabs, Kalil," the newcomer replied, gesturing at his shoulder.

"When did they make you a lieutenant, sir?" Kalil asked.

"About three hours ago," the lieutenant said, walking over and holding out his hand to Rachel. "Doctor Ghorbani, Lieutenant Bue Pedersen . . ."

"Now I know where I know you from," Rachel said. "You're from Raven's Mill."

"Yes, we've seen each other around but I wasn't sure you'd remember me."

"You're one of Herzer's friends," she continued.

"More like buddies," the lieutenant grinned. "We're not close or anything. Point is I've brung a detail to load up the wounded and move them to the camp. It's not as nice as the hospital but it's a damned sight safer."

"There are several . . ." She paused and then gestured at the door to the ward. "We need to discuss this outside."

She led him to the deserted nurse's station and shook her head. "Most of them can be moved if you've got carts. But some of them, and Kalil is one, are probably going to be killed by severe movement."

"I'm surprised he's alive at all," Bue admitted. "I saw the accident; I thought he was a goner for sure. You're definitely your mother's daughter."

"The point is," she said, ignoring the praise, "that he's being held together by spit and glue. I had to remove part of his skull and replace it with a plate. If he's on a bumpy cart down to the camp, and then exposed to all the infections that are standard in camp conditions, he's never going to make it."

"He's not going to make it here, either," Pedersen pointed out. "New Destiny doesn't bother with niceties like keeping wounded prisoners alive. If they're not fit enough for Change they go in a common grave. You hope they slit your throat before they toss you in. And it's pretty reliably rumored that all of them don't get graves; the Changed will eat anything. There's a local power network from the solar nannites; can't you summon some healing and fix him at least to the point he can be moved?"

"Drained," Rachel said, shaking her head. "This time of year it doesn't pick up much power and I've drained what little there is. Including for the repair on your soldier's skull." She didn't add that if she hadn't drained it when the bleeding got really bad he would definitely have died. Without the long-lost dissolving sutures she'd had to drain the field to repair the cranial vascular system.

"We'll have to take the chance," Bue said. "They're not going to survive here."

"How long until the New Destiny forces get here?" she asked, rubbing her face in weariness.

"No more than two days. We think they're going to land on the south end of the peninsula and invest the fort. But they'll send out columns around it. One of those is bound to come here. And by then you won't be able to get in the fort. You'll have to retreat inland. I don't know what's up there to go to; there's another legion on the way but they're not expected for two weeks. Tarson and Harzburg are the closest towns and they're pretty wild if you know what I mean. We're still not sure which way Harzburg is going to jump."

"They're part of the Union," Rachel protested.

"Nominally," Bue said. "But the mayor of Harzburg has declared that he'll make Harzburg an open city if they get that far. That's not what I call a ringing endorsement."

"They're insane, New Destiny won't care a flip if it's an 'open city.' They'll still sack it."

"No shit," Pedersen said then grimaced. "Sorry."

"I've heard it before," Rachel grinned. "Look, after you evacuate those that I think can be moved, leave me two carts. If it comes to it we'll load the rest on those and head for Tarson."

"Why Tarson?" the lieutenant asked. "They already went to New Destiny once."

"From what Herzer said I'll take my chances with them over Harzburg," Rachel replied. "And with a couple more days Kalil, at least, will be closer to the point that he might survive the journey."

"Okay, Doctor," Pedersen said, uncomfortably. "But watch your ass."

"I will," Rachel said. "And I'll watch your people as well." She paused and shook her head. "I hope you don't mind if I say that I wish Herzer was here?"

"Nope," Bue said, shrugging. "So do I."

Herzer found Megan in the bow of the ship, looking out over the ocean, Baradur, a bandage around his head, crouched by the butt of the bowsprit.

The *Hazhir* had finally caught a breeze and was scudding along over light seas, headed southwest with every sail set that the ship could handle.

"I thought you didn't like open spaces," Herzer said, walking up quietly.

"Oh, my God," Megan said, grabbing at her chest as she spun around. "You scared the shit out of me."

"In that case, you need to keep better situational awareness," Herzer said, smiling faintly.

"You sound exactly like my father," Megan said, sourly, then grinned. "But I'm *glad* you sound like my father." She turned back and looked out over the waves again, shivering faintly in the cold wind. "I don't. But I have to get used to it. Again. Being cooped up in the harem . . . all I wanted was to see the outside world again. Even that moldy old castle McClure was better. I didn't even mind the ride through the moors. But . . . this . . ." She shuddered and turned away from the view.

"Being at sea isn't for everyone," Herzer said, shrugging. "It's another reason that some wyvern riders can't handle sea duty. If you think it's immense from down here, you ought to try up there." He looked at her for a moment, then shrugged out of his cloak, and started to wrap it around her.

"I don't need coddling, Herzer," she said, tartly, waving it away.

"You're cold," Herzer replied. "And you don't have my body mass. Hell, what I'm wearing is three times as warm as what you're wearing and I'm *used* to being cold. Take it."

"Yes, sir," Megan said, smiling faintly as he tossed it on her shoulders. She closed her eyes and shivered again at the brush of his hand and arm. "We have to talk," she added, quietly.

"That we do," Herzer admitted.

"I'm . . . strongly attracted to you, Herzer Herrick," Megan said, turning back to look out over the waves. She wasn't really seeing them and at the moment it was a better place to look than into his face. "But . . . I was attracted to Paul. I don't *trust* myself when it comes to being attracted to men. Do you understand that?"

"Yes," Herzer said, stepping forward to stand beside her. He kept a respectable distance between them, however.

"I was . . . with Paul for a long time," Megan continued, carefully. "Many times. I did *not* like it. At first. Later . . . I came to enjoy his company. I fell in love with him, Herzer, and I had to kill him. That was hard. Very hard. And knowing . . . feeling how *wrong* it was to fall in love with . . ." She stopped and shook her head.

"Your rapist," Herzer said, clearly.

"Thank you for pointing that out," she replied, angrily.

"It's called psychological trauma," Herzer said. "There are those that think that you don't have to talk about it. Strong people will just 'get over it.' 'Talking about it just makes it worse.' Bullshit. Everyone who lives through psychological trauma, who *really* lives through it, finds a way to talk about it. Hell, that's half the purpose for debriefings. It's the reason for 'trooper blasts.' That's *why* when the fleet got its ass handed to it the first time, the duke made sure there was one hell of a party when they came in. People get hammered and they *talk*. You get some of it out of your soul by sharing the pain with others, even if they're people who have had the same pain. There are dark things that happen in people's heads. *Everyone* who has been in a traumatic situation has them. One of the main reasons to talk about it, especially with people who know what you have been through, have been in the same situation or have studied the reactions, is to learn that *others* have the same dark things." He sighed and shrugged.

"I'm gonna tell you a little parable," he said, glancing at her.

"Am I going to like the story?" Megan said, smiling faintly.

"No," Herzer assured her. "Once upon a time there was a young man who went for soldier . . ."

"That would be you?" she asked, jokingly.

"No, not me," Herzer said. "That will be obvious in a bit. Anyway, he joined the Blood Lords figuring it would be better than cutting wood the rest of his life. And he did pretty well. He didn't do so well that he rose really high, but he was a pretty good soldier. Maybe too good. Always in the thick of it. Lots of combat, even when it was scarce. Always wanted to be out on the line. Then, one day, he got sent off to train some militia who were having bandit problems. He had a real . . . thing for bandits. Anyway, the militia, with his help, managed to trap the bandits." Herzer paused and frowned. "Under *certain* conditions, legally, such persons can be given a summary field trial and executed. My . . . friend didn't do even that. He had them tied up, lined up and then he slit their throats."

"Ugh," Megan said. "You're right, I don't like the story."

"The militia was a little shaken and they tried to hush it up but it got back to the UFS authorities who, after an investigation, gave him a choice: full court-martial or resign. He resigned."

"They didn't try him?" Megan said, surprised.

"No, they didn't," Herzer replied. "Despite the fact that I recommended it and so did Edmund. You see, my friend had a problem; he enjoyed killing too much. That was *why* he was always in the thick of it. He'd gotten addicted to the . . . sense of *power* that comes from taking a human life. That is one of those things that doesn't get talked about *nearly* enough. That, horrible as combat is, there's a . . . rush to surviving it and a positive sense of . . . godlike power when you take another life. There are lots of people that say they don't enjoy any aspect of combat. Most of them, the ones that keep going back, are liars."

"You feel it, too," Megan said, quietly.

"I feel it," Herzer replied. "That's part of *my* dark side, one part. But I don't *like* that dark side and I sure as hell don't nurture it. But my point is that *you* are going to come out of what you went through with a dark side. Your own. You'll think that that side is something different. That there are things in there you don't want to share because *nobody* could feel the way that you do. But that's not true. Others have the same thoughts, the same shameful thoughts, and feelings. And by *talking* to people who understand, who have been through the same things and have studied them and understand them, you can come to understand them, too."

"Those people are few and far between," Megan said, turning to look at him. She stared at the profile for a moment and then frowned. "I'm . . . sort of surprised that you're an expert."

"I'm not on rape trauma," Herzer replied, continuing to look out at the ocean. "But *combat* is psychological trauma. One of the classes I teach is how to reduce post-combat stress, otherwise you lose too many troops to it. One way or another."

"One of the soldiers at the castle was talking about that," Megan said, frowning again. "But he didn't put it that way. Just that some of the soldiers couldn't handle the fighting . . ."

"We put a lot more effort into training than Clan McClure does," Herzer said, turning his head to glance at her, then looking back at the ocean. "One of the purposes is to weed out the soldiers that won't be able to handle the *mental* strain. But even the ones that make it through standard training have problems. Either they lose the edge, lose the ability, to fight or . . . they go the other way. Losing them is a logistic and economic failure, one we can't afford. Spending a certain amount of time and money on making sure they can make it through more than two battles is worth it. So we do. Debriefs, unit counseling, individual counseling at unit level, trooper blasts, they all play a part. Humans are social creatures; we manage our pain by *sharing* it in one way or another. You wouldn't *believe* the sorts of practical jokes that combat soldiers play on each other. That's a way of bonding and sharing the pain as much as anything else."

"I don't have anyone to share it with," Megan said, softly.

"Bast is the only expert we have available on rape trauma," Herzer said, shrugging. "Daneh, Edmund's wife, is probably the person you could talk to best, but she's not here. Bast is. And you've been avoiding her."

"You know why," Megan said, turning away.

"Yes," Herzer said, glancing at her again. "And you don't need to."

"So you say," Megan replied, bitterly.

"Bast and I . . ." Herzer said, then paused. "I was about to say 'we go back a long time.' But we don't, only a few years. Very . . . hard years but not so long, really, *especially* not to Bast. She has already *told* me that I'm lost to her."

"Are you still sleeping with her?" Megan asked.

"Yes," Herzer replied. "We've been sharing my bed. It's barely large enough, but we're used to that. Oh, you mean *sex*?" he asked, as if it was a surprise. "In that case, no."

"What?" Megan said, looking at him again.

"No," he said, turning to look at her. "I won't say it hasn't been *tempting*, but I knew it would matter to you. So did Bast. So . . . we took a reprieve." He paused and grinned. "Frankly, I needed to build my strength back up anyway."

"You didn't need to do that for *me*," Megan said, angrily.

"Did I not?" Herzer replied, tightly. "Megan, I have the, unfortunate, reputation of being a tomcat. I'll admit that I'm not serially monogamous. Bast is, but I'm not. She's fine with that. But the point is that I don't fully understand women, but I understand them well enough. And I understand that there's . . . something going on between us. If I said 'Oh, well, we carried on regardless' then that would, at the very least, hurt your feelings, would it not?"

"Yes," she admitted.

"Giving up fooling around for a few days is not going to kill me," Herzer replied. "I had to forego it for a year and a half one time because of the nature of a mission. And you are *important* to me. More important than any woman I've ever met . . ." He paused and shrugged. "Well, any woman that matters for this discussion. And you're not fully healed, maybe never will be. I'm not stupid enough to think that I can jump right in your bed. Or that it will be easy even once we . . . get over this . . ."

"Yes," she said, smiling faintly. "This. You're not, at all, what I expected you to be, Herzer Herrick."

"Oh?" he said, frowning.

"As I said, your name had come up. The Blood Lord's Blood Lord. The most dangerous soldier the UFS has is another way of saying it. That mission you were talking about. Was that Harzburg?"

"Yes," Herzer said, surprised. "It was."

"You'll be happy to know that you pissed people off at the *highest* level," Megan said, grinning. "What I *didn't* expect was a philosopher."

"That I'm not," Herzer argued.

"Well, then, a good field psychologist," Megan replied, shrugging. "Someone who cares about the feelings of others. And understands them, which is stranger. A warrior, a killer, that was expected. Not this." She stepped across the intervening gap and put her arm through his, leaning her head on his arm. "Someone I could love."

"Oh," Herzer replied, standing as still as if a bird had come to land on his outstretched finger.

"I think it's okay if you put your arms around me," Megan said after a moment.

"Speaking of a good field psychologist," Herzer said, stretching out the arm she was holding and wrapping her into his side.

"Someone who has a girlfriend I *really* don't want to piss off, come to think of it," Megan said after a long moment's silent communication.

"Bast has already let me go," Herzer replied. "She told me so, bluntly. If it makes you feel any better, she's in *your* corner. She apparently didn't care for Paul long before this war. Anybody who . . . removed him would be okay in her eyes. Well, almost anyone."

"What about us?" Megan asked, still not moving away from his side.

"She's fine with 'us,'" Herzer said. "She looks likes a teenager and sometimes she *acts* like one but she's *old*, Megan. Ancient. She has had more . . . boy-toys in her time than it's possible to count. *Edmund* was one, once upon a time."

"Good taste," Megan said, smiling secretly.

"Well, I hope so," Herzer replied. "I'm . . . not perfect, Megan. I have many, *many* flaws and many things about myself I don't like. From the point of view of 'us' I have some . . . issues which are going to be right pains in the ass for both of us. But Bast isn't one of them."

"What issues?" she asked, leaning back and looking up at him. From any distance he was a big guy. This close up he was just . . . immense.

"That's . . . one of those things *I* have a hard time talking about," Herzer replied, grimacing. "Especially since I don't want to lose you. I don't want to . . . drive you away. Let's get to know each other a little better before we talk about *my* problems, okay?"

She looked up at him again and then pulled out from under his arm, slightly, keeping her own arm on his waist, so that she could face him.

"Noooo . . ." she said, quizzically. "I don't think you would drive me away. But I think it's something we need to talk about if it's worrying you that much." She watched his profile for a moment as his jaw flexed and frowned. "You won't drive me away, Herzer. We'll work through it, one way or another. I promise you." She felt him starting to move away and her fingers tangled into the back of his tunic. "Don't even *think* of trying to walk away from me, Herzer Herrick. You can get some space if you feel like you need it, but don't you dare walk away."

Herzer looked down at her for just a moment then looked out over the water again.

"Let's just say I have some of the same problems Paul did," he ground out, his jaw flexing. "I just understand them a hell of a lot better. I'm a sexual dominant."

"Oh," Megan said, her eyes widening. She felt a flutter she'd almost forgotten existed and rigidly suppressed it. "That's it? I was afraid you were gay or something."

"It's a problem, Megan," Herzer said, looking down at her for a long moment and then back out at the water. "I'm experienced enough in general to only let it show with . . . ladies that have similar interests. Bast is *anything* but a sub but we do play the games. In fact, she was the one that got me over my . . . horror at it. And other things. I can play neutral but in a long-term relationship . . . it's going to be an issue. Even if you *think* you're interested, or are willing to *be* experimental, you're certainly not ready for it now and may not *ever* be. And it's something that we'll have to watch *carefully* because of your experiences."

"What if someone . . ." Megan paused and shrugged. "What if I was interested in that sort of thing *before* my experiences?"

"Doesn't really matter," Herzer replied. "Trust me. What you went through is going to have altered your responses no matter what. I've had more than one . . . girlfriend. Okay, lover. I've had more than one lover who was raped in the post-Fall period. Most of them were neutrals, a few were subs. All of them had major land mines that I had to tiptoe around. I don't *mind* tiptoeing around the land mines, but if you think you don't have them, you're nuts."

"No, I know I do," Megan said, quietly.

"And when you trip a land mine like that," Herzer continued, "the scarring is worse, in a way, than the original damage. Because of the addition of failed trust. Just miscuing, usually, but it comes across as failed trust. Especially since . . ." He paused and shook his head. "This conversation is going in some strange directions."

"Keep going," Megan said. "Especially since what?"

"Especially because of the nature of the dom-sub relationship," Herzer said. "You know what I mean by dom-sub, in general, right?"

"Yes," Megan said, making a moue. "Give me a little credit, okay?"

"You just think you do," Herzer said, frowning. "One of the aspects of the relationship is . . . probing mines. Pressing boundaries is the way it's usually explained. The sub will get more from the play if you press at the boundaries. So does the dom, but I'll skip that for now. But if you press the boundary too hard, or too far, it pushes the sub out of enjoyment and into fear and horror territory. *Anything* can do that and the dom has to be *really* careful to avoid it. With a woman who has been . . . has had scarring sexual experiences in the past, the reaction is that much greater." He looked down at her and frowned, shaking his head. "I'm terrified of hitting your mines, Megan. I really am. I don't want to lose you. I'm afraid to even touch you. I don't know what will trip you. *You* don't even know what will trip you. And, let me add, when you get your full powers as a councilor, I really *don't* want to be turned into a frog!"

"I won't turn you into a frog, Herzer," Megan said, sliding back under his arm and snuggling into his side. "Maybe a newt. But a pretty one. With red spots."

"Oh, thanks," Herzer replied, grinning.

"The newt king," Megan said. "King of the Newts."

"Just what I need."

"You really are different than I'd expected," Megan said, leaning into him. "I'm glad that my love at first sight made sense. And I do trust you. We'll have problems, I don't know any couple that doesn't. But we'll work them out. Okay?"

"Okay," Herzer said. "I'm glad. Love at first sight, huh?"

"Pretty much," she replied. "I guess I'm just a sucker for big guys in armor."

"You just like my dragon."

CHAPTER TWENTY-NINE

"Prepare for air-ops!"

"Enemy flight off the port-quarter!"

"Well, Shar, it begins," Edmund said, stepping out from under the dragon platform to look off to the east. The anti-dragon dreadnought had automatically changed course and now was coming into line on parallel course to the carrier, close alongside. Close enough that he knew the helmsmen on both ships had to be sweating.

"Better than three to one odds," Chang commented as the first of the Silverdrake dropped off the crosstrees and climbed for altitude to engage the oncoming dragons.

"I don't count that many," Edmund replied squinting against the light. "I think some of them are going for the dreadnoughts."

"That ought to be interesting."

✧　　✧　　✧

"UFS dreadnoughts at two o'clock," one of the riders signaled.

"They're carrying troops," Captain D'Allaird yelled to his second in command. "No anti-dragon frigates covering them."

"Some of those damned Silverdrake, though," Lieutenant Ringle signaled, pointing to the smaller dragons that were bearing down on them.

"Second division, go for the Drakes," D'Allaird signaled. "The rest, bear on the dreadnoughts. Close in, they're not rigged for anti-dragon defense."

"You think they'd have gotten word," Gunny Rutherford said, shaking his head as the dragons lost height and lined up for the close drop on the dreadnought.

"Every Cannae requires a Varius," General D'Erle chuckled. "Or, more appropriately, every Agincourt requires the French. Prepare to receive dragons!"

"Message from *Corvallis*, sir," the messenger said. His face was blackened with soot from the fires that had just been put out. The main-sails were going to have to be replaced but other than that the ship was fit to fight.

"*Corvallis* reports fires out," Shar said, passing the message form to Edmund. "That firefighting system of Evan's is a life-saver."

"But they also report that their dragons had to turn back from the attack on the fleet," Edmund growled. "And they lost nearly half their dragons."

"I hope we do better."

Sergeant Fink had wanted to be a dragon-rider from the first time she saw them. She had a normal fear of heights, she wasn't insane, but dragons were the only thing in this Fallen world that gave any of the powers that had been lost. She had enjoyed high-floating, a form of hang-gliding, before the Fall. And she'd even thought about getting a wyvern or doing a full-flight mod. But that was before the Fall.

She'd joined the Navy because they told her that she could apply for dragon-riding. And she had but she hadn't been accepted. Too many applicants. So she'd done her job and bided her time until, by luck as much as anything, she made it in. Now she spent as much time as she could riding. Some of the riders had gotten a bit burned out and there weren't many that would take even the slow, boring, reconnaissance flights. But she would, any flight she could.

So now she was up, on a pleasant day, slightly overcast with high cirrus clouds. Winds were pretty solid but that just made the gliding easier. She had about another hour and a half to go before she was relieved, lying on the back of her dragon, banking occasionally to keep the fleet in sight while still staying as far out as she could to the southwest. Somewhere out there was the New Destiny fleet. With luck, she'd spot it before either she or her own ship was spotted.

Charoo rumbled in his chest and turned slightly to the south and she spotted what the dragon had. Regular splashes and the wide V of wakes. She turned and looked behind her and, sure enough, she was right into the sun from the New Destiny fleet. There was little or no chance that she had been spotted. She looked for their own security dragons but didn't see any.

"Okay, we've got 'em," she muttered to the dragon, banking it back to the north. "Let's see if the lookouts are paying attention."

She withdrew a curious mirror from a pouch on her harness and put the back to her eye. The mirror had a clear spot in the middle with a metal grid buried in the glass. The bright sun caused a small intensely bright reflection to form in the grid. By laying the reflection over the distant ships she could be sure the reflection of the main mirror was pointed at them. As soon as she had it aligned, she started angling the mirror so that it was reflecting towards them and then away, careful to avoid pointing at the New Destiny fleet.

"Commander Gramlich?" Captain Karcher said, dropping through the overhead and landing lightly.

"Ma'am?" the dragon said, getting to her feet.

"We're about to start air-ops," the captain said. "Be damned if I'm going to sit this one out. The New Destiny fleet is in range to attack. I've put out a mer team as a turning point. Get your damned wyverns in the air."

"Yes, ma'am!"

"Take the Powells and head for the New Destiny fleet," Karcher said, springing back through the hatch. "I've got another job for Vickie."

"I thought we were staying out of it!" Megan said.

"*Corvallis* and the *Richard* are outnumbered," Herzer replied, calmly, as he finished putting on his leathers. "We're in range. We can't just let them carry the whole fight."

"What if we're attacked while you're gone?" she asked, angrily. The shambles from the fight still wasn't cleared from her quarters and, ignoring the suggestion of the captain, she had installed herself in Herzer's. Bast was still sharing the quarters but despite the crowding the elf seemed actually pleased that she was here. So was Megan, until this stupid plan had come up. "For that matter, you could be killed!"

"Megan," Herzer said, gently. "I'm a soldier. Sometimes I ride a dragon, sometimes I swing a sword. I . . . hope that we have something special between us. But you're going to have to accept that one of the problems of being my friend is that I go out to try to kill other people. And they try to kill me. It's my job and I'm good at it. You're going to have to decide if that's what you want in a . . . friend."

"I know that," Megan said. "I even like it, except when you're going out to get yourself killed." She reached up and touched his face, then kissed him. She'd meant for it to be a light, chaste, kiss, but she suddenly found herself holding him tight. Finally she pulled away brushing at his face again. "Get out there, Herzer. Go get me a carrier."

"Yes, ma'am." He grinned, then picked up his helmet and left the compartment.

"*Corvallis* is sinking," Shar said, sadly. "Edmund, I think we have to retire."

"Damn if I will," Edmund said, shaking his head. The second flight of dragons from the New Destiny flight had been lighter than the first; they were hurting them. But with the *Corvallis* out of the fight both flights would concentrate on the *Richard*. "Angle in closer. If we can't get them with the dragons then we'll damned well board the bastards."

"We lost *how* many dragons?" Admiral Trieste shouted.

"The dreadnoughts are filled with archers," his chief of staff said. "We only got five back, those that were engaging the Silverdrake. And they lost three of those to the Drakes. The rest of the flight is . . . gone. They flew right into the trap. It looks to be at least a battalion, maybe a regiment, of longbowmen."

"Where are the dreadnoughts now?" the admiral asked.

"They're sailing towards us," the chief of staff said with a grimace. "Depending on the winds they'll be here in an hour. I'm not sure we can face them with anything we have."

"Forget the dreadnoughts," Trieste said. "Go for the carrier. And point us away from those damned archers."

"Wyvern off the port bow!" the lookout called.

"At least sixty," Chang said.

"Looks like the gamble didn't pay off this time, Shar," Edmund admitted. The UFS dragons were in the air already but he wasn't sure they'd have anywhere to land. They'd recovered a few of the *Corvallis* Powells and they had been added to the strike force. But that wouldn't help their carrier.

"The ballista frigate will get some," Shar said. Maybe one in five from past experience, which wouldn't be enough, he didn't have to add. "But the Drakes are worn out."

"More dragons to stern," the aft lookout called. "It looks like *Drakes*!"

"Son of a bitch," Edmund said. "Damn that Karcher!"

"You think they're from the *Hazhir*?" Shar asked.

"Have to be," Edmund growled. "Which means *Hazhir* is completely uncovered."

Shar watched as the flight of Drakes descended upon the New Destiny dragons. From the angle they had come right down out of the sun and they dropped at least a dozen before the New Destiny flight broke up. The Drakes flew right through the formation and then banked back, taking up a rear position and firing at the flight from behind. More dragons dropped but the flight bore into the carrier nonetheless. They still had to run the gauntlet of the anti-dragon frigate and as that ship opened up the Drakes hastily banked off, heading for other ships in the fleet to land and rest.

The reduced New Destiny force—a bare twenty had made it through the hail of fire from the ballista frigate—lined up on the carrier and dropped their loads. One by one the bundles of fire rained on the deck, covering the carrier in fire.

Edmund covered himself with his cloak, then threw it off as the napalm splashed on it. Some more had landed on his leg and he grimaced in pain as he covered it with foam from an extinguisher. Sailors had been covered with the stuff and he saw several jump over the side in unspeakable agony. He gritted his teeth at his own burns and looked around, shaking his head.

"Abandon ship," he growled. "This thing is done for."

"Agreed, Admiral," the captain said, giving the orders.

"I'll transfer my flag to the *Shuiki*," Edmund

continued, limping to the side to see if there was a whole boat. "Save everyone that you can."

"There are only two carriers left," Joanna bellowed. Unlike the UFS, New Destiny had their fleet bunched up. "Go for the carriers; ignore the damned anti-dragon frigates."

Herzer gestured to the south where another flight of dragons had just appeared out of the haze. It was apparent that they were carrying a full ordnance load. If they were New Destiny dragons they would have unloaded already.

"Suggest we concentrate on one carrier and leave the other for them," he signaled.

"Agreed," Joanna bellowed. "Go for the nearer carrier."

Herzer looked over at Sergeant Fink and signaled "Stay on my tail." The young rider looked scared but she nodded.

He lined up behind Joanna and headed for the nearer carrier. The sun was setting in the west and they had maneuvered to have it at their backs; they should be dropping right out of the sun on the fleet. Hopefully they would have the element of surprise.

The southerly group, however, was apparently sighted early and one of the ballista frigates changed course to get between it and the southerly carrier. The dragons came in low, determined to destroy the carrier, and the slaughter was terrific. Herzer could see dragon after dragon falling into the water to no apparent effect. There were three ships firing up at the wildly maneuvering dragons and the few that made it through missed the carrier completely.

"Change of plan again," Joanna bellowed. "Herzer, take first and second division and attack the south carrier. Get the damned thing. Burn the bastards."

"Will do," he yelled, signaling for the formation to split. They were still high but as they passed over the edge of the fleet he put the group into a stoop, angling to the rear of the southern carrier.

It was apparent that the fleet had finally spotted the formation but it was too late for them to maneuver. Before the ballista frigates could even begin to turn, Herzer's force had lined up on the carrier. It hauled its wind and started a turn, trying to tack away from the dragons, but Herzer was having none of it. He lined up on the maindeck and dropped his force lower, getting in so close he was afraid they'd tangle themselves in the rigging. He saw a crossbowman on the mast lining him up and could have sworn he heard the click of the bow being triggered. Where the bolt went he had no idea and by then it was too late anyway. He'd dropped his load and watched it track in smooth and true onto the deck. One, two, three bombs, right down the middle, beautiful wide splash. The carrier immediately triggered its firefighting apparatus but, one by one, the dragons dropped their loads of fire, many of the pots hitting the masts and shattering to spread their fire over the sails. All the foam in the world wasn't going to put that fire out.

He banked away and turned to the north where the other carrier was on fire, seriously roasting, as well. Looking over his shoulder he saw that it appeared that the carrier was done for and, what was more, they'd taken no casualties at all.

"That's just flipping amazing," he muttered. He

checked his mount but the wyvern was flying well and no bolts seemed to be sticking out of anywhere. Then he noticed a sharp pain in his rear. He looked back and shook his head in anger as the pain really hit.

"Damn," he muttered, grimacing against the burn of the bolt sticking out like a flag. "I *would* take one in the ass."

"*Hazhir* reports attacking the New Destiny fleet," Shar said, looking up from the signal he'd been handed. "They got both remaining carriers."

"That's confirmed?" Edmund asked.

"Confirmed," Shar assured him.

"Casualties from *Hazhir*?" Edmund asked.

"Essentially zero," the admiral said. "They had two wyverns injured and a rider. Other than that nothing. They're prepared to continue operations against the fleet and requesting orders."

"Damn it's nice having capable subordinates," Edmund said, shaking his head. "Forget the rest of the fleet; there's nothing there worth fighting for. Break off the attack. Signal the dreadnoughts and the fleet to assemble and turn for Balmoran. We're not done yet."

"General Magalong?" Bue said, saluting the officer behind the desk. "New Destiny landing fleet approaching from the south. Just sighted southwest of the point."

"Very well," the general said. Cierra Magalong was a political appointee but he'd been through the Blood Lord training, even at his age, and had attended the abbreviated Raven's Mill War College. He was as prepared as almost anyone for the war that was coming. But he had very limited actual combat experience and *nobody*, not even Talbot to his knowledge, had any experience on war of this level.

Second Legion had six thousand legionnaires and just under three thousand supplementary combat forces, engineers, provosts and the like. In addition there were four thousand support personnel with basic training as spear holders but essentially useless in a fight. And he had twice the normal perimeter to protect.

He had been given the mission of holding the core of Balmoran, primarily to protect the nascent metal- and woodworking industries for which the town was famous. To do this he had assembled a slightly enlarged camp around the most important foundries and emptied the dockside godowns into it. If he could hold out, and he had more than enough supplies to do so, he'd eventually be relieved. In the meantime, New Destiny was going to find the Second Legion a remarkable pain in its rear area.

"Send the order to fire the docks," Magalong said to one of the runners stationed in the office. "Pull back the outposts and tell the Naval base to evacuate."

"I spoke to the surgeon at the base yesterday, sir," Bue said. "She was reluctant to evacuate the remaining wounded because she feared they'd die if they were moved."

"Well, tell her to fish or cut bait," Magalong snarled. "And get her ass into the camp."

"Captain Cicali, I really don't *care* what you think," Conner said, smiling thinly. "My mission has priority over your ship. Get it in there."

The small fleet of fast schooners had swung wide to the west of the New Destiny fleet and was now approaching the Balmoran peninsula well to the north of the town. So far, it appeared to have remained unobserved. Or, if it was observed, it had probably been dismissed as a reconnaissance mission.

"I understand, Mr. Conner," the captain said, unhappily. "But you've got to understand. There are *shoals* up here. If we go tearing in at max speed, it's not just going to ground my ship. It's liable to *sink* us. And you and your . . . people." The captain glanced at the hulking monster behind Conner and gulped. "Then your mission will have failed *anyway*."

"Get us in as fast as possible," Conner said, after a moment's thought. "And as close to the south end of the base as possible. If you can't make it through the shoals, we'll go to the boats. Just *do* it."

"Yes, sir," the captain said, one ear on the leadsman. "I need to reduce speed, though. *Slightly*."

"Whatever," Conner said, watching the distant shore. "As long as you get us to the base before it evacuates."

"Miss!" Keith yelled from the lobby. "Dr. Ghorbani!"

"Here, Keith," Rachel said, emerging from the last occupied ward. "What?"

"There are ships coming, Miss!" Keith said, grabbing her arm. "We've got to go!"

"We've got wounded to move," Rachel said, dragging her arm away.

"No *time*!" the orderly said, desperately. "They're at the wharves! They didn't fire them in time. They're coming *now*."

"Here?" Rachel said, angrily. "Why *here*? They were supposed to attack the *town*."

"They're here, miss," Keith said, pulling at her again. "Come on. We have to go."

Faintly, but not far away, Rachel heard the banging of metal. It sounded like a small smithy but she recognized the sound having heard it before. Then there was a scream, not far away at all.

"Go hitch up the carts, Keith," she said, her mouth dry. "We'll . . ."

"I don't think we have time, Miss," Keith argued, shaking his head.

"Do what I say!" Rachel snapped as the door to the clinic opened.

The man who walked through the door was tall, with fair hair, wearing a gray robe that was embroidered with silver. On the hem of the robe were symbols Rachel didn't recognize. The robe had a few spots on it, dark black in the light from the windows. But Rachel had no question what the spots were from. If she had any question, the monstrous, blood-covered *thing* that followed the man into the lobby answered them.

It was at least two meters tall and broad in proportion, with a face that was both bestial and, in a horrible way, beautiful. It had protruding canine fangs that interlocked from top and bottom, black lanky hair and mad, red eyes. But the face itself, the high cheekbones and forehead, the aquiline nose, struck a cord with her and she found herself searching it in horror.

"Elf?" she whispered.

"One of my mistress's toys," the man said, walking up to her with his hands folded behind his back. "Just one of her things. As, I suppose, am I," he concluded, looming over her. Rachel found herself mesmerized by his gray eyes.

"Dr. Rachel Ghorbani, I presume?"

"What the hell are you doing here?" Rachel asked.

"Looking for you, of course," the man said, smiling. "There are some people who think you might be useful. We'll have to see, won't we?"

Rachel looked around but there was clearly no escape.

"The hell . . ." she muttered just as there was a yowl from the landing. She turned around and raised a hand as Azure strutted forward, tail raised and bristling. She had seen the cat come home with full-grown bob-cats in its jaws, but the group of orcs and especially the elf would mean the death of a pet she had had since childhood. "No!"

The orcs had all drawn their swords and were looking at the puma-sized house cat nervously. The elf-thing slowly drew its own sword and pointed the tip at the hissing cat.

"Graaa," the thing snarled, crouching and following the moves of the cat with focused intensity.

Azure was crouched, tail lashing, ready to spring, but the cat's eyes were locked on the elf's as if it knew that the thing was the only real threat. Azure's rear paws scratched at the floor, searching for purchase, and his tail thrashed again. He shifted his hindquarters, then turned his head to the side with a yowl.

"Sraaa," the elf replied, the tip of his sword swinging back and forth lightly.

Azure took another look, then sat up, licked his shoulder in disinterest, turned and trotted up the steps.

"Azure?" Rachel said, her eyes wide. She wasn't sure whether to be relieved at the fact that her pet was going to survive or crushed at the desertion.

"Well, now that that's out of the way," the man said, taking her by the arm, "let's go see what use we can put you to."

"Sir," the messenger said, sticking her head in the door. "Duke Edmund is arriving." She'd knocked this time.

"Great," Herzer growled, wincing as Bast rubbed more unguent into the wound. "Has Commander Gramlich been informed?"

"Yes, sir," the messenger replied, glancing at the councilwoman. Megan was sitting at Herzer's desk, frowning.

"Any word on the situation at Balmoran?" Herzer asked.

"No, sir," the messenger replied. "But we got the word that we're the last carrier. Duke Edmund is transferring his flag here."

"He can have my cabin," Megan said, one cheek twitching up in a grin. "Happily." It still had bloodstains on the floor; they were soaked in deep enough that the wood would have to be replaced.

"The captain would like you there to greet him if . . . you're recovered from your wounds, sir," the messenger continued. "And she asked me to ask the councilwoman if she was willing as well."

"Oh, definitely," Megan said, smiling thinly. "I look forward to meeting the redoubtable Edmund Talbot."

CHAPTER THIRTY

"Duke Edmund," Captain Karcher said, dropping her salute as the pipes dwindled away.

"Captain, glad I was right in choosing you," Edmund said, gripping her hand.

"We were lucky, milord," Karcher replied, shrugging.

"Luck favors the prepared, Captain," Talbot said.

"My XO, Commander Sassan," the captain said, ignoring the implied compliment.

"Pleasure to meet you, Commander Sassan," Edmund said, shaking the major's hand.

"Major Herrick you, of course, know."

"Herzer," Edmund said, grinning then noting the way he was standing. "Catch one?"

"In the ass, milord," Herzer replied.

"Happens," Edmund said, chuckling. "Embarrassing, though. Hey, Joanna."

"You owe me *quite* a combat bonus, Eddie," Joanna

replied. "My wing took out both remaining carriers. Based upon clause fourteen, sub-section b . . ."

"Submit a bill," the duke said, shaking his head.

"And this is Councilwoman Megan Travante," Karcher said, ignoring the interplay.

"Mistress Travante," Edmund said, gently, noting how close she was standing to Herzer. "I know your father and I have the honor, I think, of calling him a friend. I am glad beyond measure that you are with us again."

"Thank you, Duke Edmund," Megan said, curtseying.

"Mistress," Edmund said, grinning slightly, "while you're not a member of the aristocracy, you are of much higher status than I. You don't curtsey to me, I bow to you," he added and did so.

"That . . . is going to take some getting used to," Megan said, fingering the chain around her neck. "I would like to introduce my . . . retainer, Baradur."

Edmund peered at the wee folk for a moment and then said something in quick, liquid tones.

The guard frowned for a moment and then replied, puzzled.

"The language has shifted," Edmund said, frowning. "But where did you come from?"

"The wee folk are among the tribes of the Highlands," Megan said, surprised. "You know of them?"

"Not from the Highlands," Edmund replied, rubbing his beard. "But I recognize them. Old memory, very old people. Good soldiers, the best. There were some in Anarchia as well. I'd give my right arm for a battalion of them. And on that note, we need to talk. Mistress, if I could have a moment of your time. Herzer, Joanna, which means the wyvern bay, damnit.

Shar, get the fleet squared away on the course we agreed upon and then come join us."

"Yes, sir," the admiral said.

"Mistress?"

"This way," Megan replied, gesturing towards the wyvern bay.

"What we have here is a grade A cluster f . . . a grade A cluster," Edmund said as soon as chairs had been secured for the bay. Joanna was curled at one end with Bast lounged on her and the rest were gathered in a semicircle. "New Destiny landed on the north end of the peninsula, inside of it, and have put in a fortified camp cutting off Balmoran. They also have control of the waters around it but only until we get there. However, they're installing portals and can supply through them . . ."

"I thought that porting into Norau was impossible," Megan said, frowning. "It certainly was for me."

"Force majeure," Bast said, shaking her head. "Who hold land own land. Very old protocol, but protocol still."

"Correct," Edmund said. "They hold the land, now, they have sufficient forces in place that we cannot immediately throw them off, and have water access to it. Ergo, under the damned protocols, they can port into it. Even destroying their fleet won't change that. We have to beat them on the ground."

"Fortified camp?" Herzer said, frowning. "That will be hard."

"Indeed it will," Edmund replied. "And they took the Naval base and most of its stores. That's where they're resupplying from, now."

"Rachel?" Herzer asked.

"Unknown," Edmund replied, his face hard.

"If they've captured Rachel . . ."

"It doesn't matter," Edmund said. "This is not about rescuing Rachel, Herzer, get that straight. It's about breaking New Destiny's invasion."

"Rachel is your daughter . . ."

"I know that very well, Herzer," Edmund replied, tightly. "But this is not about special privileges for my daughter. She takes her chances just like every other combatant . . ."

"I was *about* to say," Herzer said, cutting him off, "that as such, she has access to information that New Destiny wants to know. Yes, I care if Rachel lives or dies, but I suspect that if New Destiny knows that she is there, they're more interested in what they can *squeeze* from her. Recapturing Rachel, therefore, certainly has an *allowable* level of necessity to it, Duke Edmund."

"Edmund," Joanna said, "Herzer has a point. You might be so close to the situation it's a point you're ignoring to avoid the special privilege issue."

"We don't know where she *is*," Edmund ground out. "We don't know if she's among the refugees from the peninsula. Or if New Destiny has already ported her back to Ropasa. If they have, she is *gone*. And this meeting is not about where Rachel is. It's about how to throw New Destiny off the peninsula." He looked at the others and nodded. "Very well. The bow corps is on the dreadnoughts about a day behind us . . ."

"I have five remaining wounded," Rachel said, trying to ignore the blood-spattered monster following Conner. Not to mention Conner who, if anything, terrified her more. "I am aware that you normally kill your enemy's wounded and I cannot prevent that. However, if you leave them be, I will willingly work on your own wounded. If you kill them, you can still force me to do so. But I will do a much better job as a willing doctor than as an unwilling one."

"Show me," Conner said, gesturing courteously towards the wards. "I promise on my honor as an acolyte of the Lady Celine I will not have them killed."

Rachel tightened her face and led the way into the ward. At the sight of the blood-spattered elf the two conscious wounded drew up, aware that with no weapons there was little they could do.

Conner strode over to Kalil, looking at him with his head cocked to the side and then extending a hand and muttering. Kalil flinched back but all that happened was that an enlarged hologram of his skull appeared in the air. Conner looked at it, rubbing his chin thoughtfully.

"So much power," Rachel whispered, leaning forward to examine the hologram.

"We have power in New Destiny," Conner said. "You can have power, if you are willing. A plate?"

"Subdural cerebral hematoma," Rachel sighed, ignoring the implied offer. "I didn't have enough power to do internal repairs; I had to relieve the pressure."

"It's very good work," Conner replied.

"You're a doctor?" Rachel asked.

"Of sorts," Conner said. "With power, not this sort of work. But we have techniques that you don't, or are unwilling to use." He continued down the line of wounded, examining each of them. At the last one, an abdominal injury, he stopped and shrugged.

"This one is dying anyway," he said.

"You *don't* discuss a patient's condition in *front* of them," Rachel snapped.

"Well, he's unconscious, isn't he?" Conner replied, ignoring her. "Would you like to save him?"

"Of course," Rachel said, angrily. "But *I* don't have the power."

"That is what you think," Conner said, smiling at her in a maddening way. He whispered under his breath and the soldier began to glow. "There. There is the power you need."

"I can't *sap* a wounded man for the power to *heal* him!" Rachel snapped.

"Oh, you must not take too much," Conner admitted. "But there is power in plenty here. He is not so far gone." He touched her shoulder and whispered again. "There. Take it. And heal. You can take it from him. You can take it from others. You can take it from yourself. Everywhere, there is power to be had."

Rachel *felt* the link and used it to bring up a diagnostic holo, one that she had rarely been able to use. Power was apparently power and her own protocols worked with it. The soldier had been struck by a cart. The legs and ribs were easy enough to repair, or at least splint, but the swollen abdomen had shown extensive internal injuries and without a skilled team she had been reluctant to open him up. Now she could *see* the extent of the damage. There was no way she could draw enough power from him to even repair the ruptured spleen, but . . . she tapped into herself, drawing her own nervous energy, and began to effect what repairs she could.

"Silly," Conner snapped as her knees sagged. "Very

silly. Draw from *him*, not yourself or you'll never be able to do anything."

"I've stopped up the worst," Rachel said, weakly. "I can do the rest later, when I'm recovered. I won't be *you!*"

"Then watch how *I* heal them!" Conner roared, spinning her across the room to the elf and extending a hand. He began to chant and light formed around all of the wounded.

"What are you doing?" Rachel asked, desperately. "Stop it!" she yelled as, one by one, the wounded began to shriek, encased in balls of light. Then the shrieking changed tones to hoarse bellows and when the light was gone five orcs were sitting up in the beds, snarling at one another and shouting curses at the Changed elf. They cowered away from Conner when he glanced at them, though.

"I promised I wouldn't *kill* them," Conner said, maliciously. "Take her away."

"Bloody hell," General Magalong said, quietly, as the cohort closed ranks again to make it through the gate. "Get the ballistas ready, we've got to get them some room."

New Destiny had taken the Fleet base and established a large fortified camp on the north end of the peninsula. Even with all their forces they couldn't cut the peninsula entirely, but they could do so for all intents and they had. He had sent the cohort, one of three, out to probe the defenses. He was getting back less than two thirds.

Besides the orcs that made up the bulk of the New Destiny forces there were massive creatures scattered among them. Orcs could rarely break the shield-line of a well handled cohort but these things had simply smashed into the line, soaking up the sword and spear damage to open holes that the orcs poured into. Three times the cohort had nearly been broken before they retreated. The things weren't particularly smart or fast but they were immensely large and powerful; he had seen one pick up a trooper in either hand, while their fellows hacked at its legs, and throw them through the air.

Another of the things made its way through the orcs, charging clumsily at the line of legionnaires. The general smiled faintly as the line didn't even bend, just kept up its steady backward motion, the troopers facing the thing like battling automatons. There wasn't any percentage in turning to flee, that would just open up a bigger hole for the orcs to attack.

This time, though, they were close enough for support and three ballistas fired at the thing. Two of them missed, one pinning a pair of orcs to the ground in the front lines and another falling deep. But the third hit it on the shoulder, spinning it around and off its feet, the shoulder nearly severed. Despite the enormous wound, the thing got back to its feet, but it never even made it to the legionnaire line, falling and crushing an orc as it finally bled out.

The legionnaires continued to shrink their formation, closing their gaps as they filed into the camp. As they closed with the walls, defenders began pitching pots of burning napalm at the orcs, slowing them up and keeping them from pressing on the legionnaires. More ballista bolts fell as well and bolts from some of the crossbowmen. Finally, a massed company threw their pilums and the last of the legionnaires marched stolidly through the gates, which closed behind them.

The New Destiny forces pressed forward as well but the rest of the legion was already manning the walls and the attack was repulsed with bloody losses, the legionnaires poking the orcs from above with their pilums and groups of them using them to pincushion the larger monsters. After about fifteen minutes of that horns rang from the far camp and the New Destiny forces retreated, leaving a windrow of their dead under the UFS lines to stink up the morning.

New Destiny was already starting siege operations against his lines as well. Attack trenches and parallels were going in, the earth being moved by more Changed and a few local humans who had been unlucky enough to be captured. The cohort's primary mission had been an attack against those. One that had not been successful.

For that matter, he wondered at the preparations. New Destiny *could* simply swarm him. If they threw enough bodies. There had been ten thousand, at least, in the invasion fleet. More would be coming in through portals. They *had* to be worried about time and they couldn't move until he was reduced. So why were they starting an elaborate siege?

"Send for Lieutenant Pedersen," the general said. "I want his thoughts."

Rachel stepped back from the casualty as she finished suturing the artery.

"He's going to be in pain when he wakes up," she said, lifting one eyelid with a blood-covered hand and checking the dilation of the pupil. "I'll write out an order for morphine. No more and no less, understand?" she said to the orderly. The man nodded at her, frightened, and called for stretcher bearers to move the officer out.

Rachel had only been working on humans. The Changed were so numerous, and of so little relative worth or so it seemed, that only their human officers were given treatment for wounds. Changed either survived them or died.

Rachel turned on the spigot and ran her hands and forearms under the water. The one good thing about this camp was that New Destiny had installed running water in the hospital. On the other hand, it was cold and getting blood off with cold water was a pain.

She turned her head at a flicker in her peripheral vision, frowning at Conner who, as always, was followed by his monstrous elf-thing.

"Pity you couldn't save the leg," Conner said, glancing at the casualty.

"I said you weren't going to get my best work if you pissed me off," Rachel replied, coldly, turning her back and ignoring him. He wanted to see her suffer. He could kill her, he could rape her, but she was damned if he was going to see her sweat.

There was another flicker in her peripheral vision and a distinctive "swish-thunk." She spun around and the Changed was just about done wiping his sword. The New Destiny officer's head had not even had time to roll off the blood-spattered surgery table. It did, as she watched, and struck the ground with a sound like a broken melon.

"You SON OF A *BITCH!*" she screamed, picking up a scalpel and throwing it at him as hard as she could.

Conner leaned slightly to the side to let the wandering missile pass and smiled maliciously as the elf-thing caught it in midair and stepped forward.

"No, Roc," Conner said, holding his hand up and laughing. "Let her get it out."

"Do *not* waste my *time*!" Rachel snapped. "Do whatever you're going to do to me. Torture me, rape me, kill me, whatever. But *don't* waste my time!"

"But that," Conner said, gesturing at the headless corpse. "That *was* a waste of your time. We have no need of crippled officers. One more mouth to feed."

"You people are too much," Rachel said, turning back to the sink and scrubbing her hands furiously. She grabbed a towel and gestured at him, half angrily and half in amazement. "You're a fucking *idiot*, do you know that? Not just a fruitcake, that goes without saying, but an *idiot*!"

"Why am I an idiot?" Conner said, calmly, tilting his head to the side as if her opinion was of enormous interest to him.

"Do you know who Herzer Herrick is?" Rachel said, throwing the towel in a basket and taking off her apron for a new one.

"Oh, yes, paramour of yours, isn't he?" Conner replied, smiling.

"No," Rachel said. "Your oh-so-puissant intelligence is *off* on that score. But would you say he's *useless* to the UFS?"

"No," Conner replied. "Quite useful, actually."

"And did you know he was missing a hand?" Rachel asked, gently.

"Yes," Conner replied.

"IS HE ANY LESS USEFUL WITH ONE HAND?"

Rachel shouted, throwing her hands up and then pointing at the corpse. "Do you know *anything* about that person?"

"Other than the fact that he has no head," Conner said. "no."

"So you don't have *any* idea if he might have been of use to you," Rachel said, throwing her hands up. "He might have been a *whiz* at logistics! A *master* of sorting out intelligence and finding that *one* clue that wins the battle! But *you* don't know! And now, you never will! Because you cut his *head* off! A tisket, a tasket, a head in a basket! *That* is why you're an idiot, not to mention a FRUITCAKE."

"Miss Ghorbani, you suffer under a misapprehension," Conner said, smiling faintly. "The misapprehension is that anyone in New Destiny *cares*. Oh, not about your *opinion*, that, as you said, goes without saying. No, rather about the fate of one individual, no matter *how* potentially able. Are you familiar with the saying 'Quantity has a quality of its own'?"

"Stalin," Rachel said. "My father loves to rave about its stupidity. He especially cites the *reality* of Zhukov."

"Who is Zhukov?" Conner asked. "For that matter, who is Stalin?"

"You *see*?!" Rachel snapped. "You're an *idiot*. You're quoting things you don't even know the genesis of! You don't know the *reality* surrounding them *or* to what it *directly* related! It wasn't a *general* quote it was about a *particular weapon*! And if you're going to apply it to *people*, the *falsehood* of the statement is directly associated with the original person who said it!"

"So . . . who is Zhukov?" Conner said, politely.

"Ack! I'm not here to teach you ancient history," Rachel snarled. "I've got more butchery to perform. I suppose you'd *prefer* that I concentrate on those who aren't *too* far gone and won't need a lot of recovery?"

"Yes," Conner replied. "More or less. You're not going to tell me who Zhukov is, are you?"

"Go look it up!" Rachel snapped.

"Russian general," the elf-thing said, sibilantly. "Commanded the Siberian Army during the early stages of the Phase Two of the First Planetary War. Later commander of the whole army. Possibly saved Russia. That is arguable."

"If Zhukov hadn't mobilized his Siberians, Moscow would have fallen," Rachel snapped.

"Russia had lost Moscow before," the elf-thing replied. "It destroyed Napoleon."

"Completely different situation," Rachel said. "Even with the partisans, the Germans had the logistics to hold it through the winter, easily. And by the end of the winter, they would have held Murmansk as well and taken Stalingrad. The only thing that kept them from doing that was Zhukov."

"They didn't have sufficient security for their supply lines," the elf argued.

"Excuse me," Conner said.

"They could draw them, were drawing them, from units from Eastern Europe," Rachel said, shaking her head. "No, it was the Siberians . . ."

"EXCUSE ME!" Conner shouted. "What in the *hell* are you talking about?"

"The Russian Winter Campaign of 1942," the elf-thing replied.

"That tells me *so* much!" Conner snapped.

"What are you?" Rachel said, looking at the elf-thing.

"I am Roc," the elf-thing replied.

"I said what not who," Rachel said, thoughtfully.

"What am I?" Roc asked Conner.

"You're my bodyguard," Conner snapped.

"I'm a bodyguard," the elf-thing said, turning back to Rachel.

"Like hell," Rachel said, musingly. "You're one hell of a violation of protocols is what you are. I assume the Lady hasn't found out, yet. Pity. Be interesting when she finally opens Elfheim back up. She flipped her *lid* when they made the wood-elf prototypes. She's going to find a new meaning of mad when she finds out about this . . . thing."

"That is besides the point . . ." Conner said, showing the first real signs of anger.

"Not in your case," Rachel said, happily. "Just knowing you're anywhere *near* one of these things is going to make you a *special* treat for the Lady. She's had thousands of years of experience in coming up with nasty things to do to people. I'm sure she'll pull them *all* out for anyone associated with . . . that," she finished, pointing at the elf. "And why the hell is he a *bodyguard* when he's the first thing I've found in this crowd that *doesn't* have his head screwed into his ass? At least he knows who Zhukov is."

"That is not your concern," Conner said, his mouth tightening.

"Hey, Roc," Rachel said, grinning. "You really ought to take over, you know? At least you have a clue."

"Roc is not going to 'take over,'" Conner said, smoothing his features. "He is fully controlled."

"Like hell," Rachel said, frowning. "Hey, Roc, what do you think about Bedford Forrest?"

"He was a fine cavalry general," the elf-thing replied. "He had the *gaslan*."

"Elf word, damn," Rachel said, wonderingly. "They're not preprogrammed. The data on Zhukov *could* have been but why preprogram elvish . . . ? This isn't a construct, is it?" she added, horrified.

"That is enough," Conner said, raising his hand. "One more word and you will find out *how* controlled Roc is."

Rachel opened her mouth and then closed it with a clop. But she stepped forward, nonetheless, right up to the thing, staring it in the eye. It stank. Not human body odor, something like the smell of the orc Changed but much worse and included in it was the smell of the rotting blood in its harness. But she stayed there, for a moment, peering into his eyes, trying to find any spark of what he had once been. All she could see was that there was a world of fury behind those eyes. She reached up, gently, touched it on the face and then turned away.

"I've got more butchery to do," she said, her voice catching. "But I guess I'm not the first, huh?"

"Just get back to work," Conner said, gesturing the thing to proceed him.

"Goodbye, Roc," Rachel said, softly, stepping over to the sink and starting to wash her hands again. "Whoever you were."

CHAPTER THIRTY-ONE

"What do you think, Lieutenant?" General Magalong said, looking out the window at the retiring New Destiny forces. Their first salient was already a hundred meters from the New Destiny fort and they appeared to be preparing the first parallel.

"I think we've got us a fight on our hands, sir," Pedersen said. He was standing at parade rest in front of the general's desk.

"I think so as well," the general said, turning away from the window and waving to a chair. "Sit, Lieutenant, before you keel over."

"That wasn't that hard a fight, sir," Pedersen said, but he sat anyway, sliding forward to keep most of the mess off the chair; he was still rather bloody.

"Those big . . . things . . ." the general said.

"I think the general consensus term is ogres, sir," Pedersen said, grinning slightly. "Too . . . clumsy for trolls."

"Ogres and trolls, oh my," the general replied.

"Yes, sir," Pedersen said with a nod. "They're slow and clumsy but hard to fight. Very long reach. Might be better attacking them with a pike wall. Longbowmen will do a number on them, though, at least at any range under a hundred meters. Heavy crossbows as well. I don't think they're a carefully thought out construct; they seem to be just a human design . . . increased. That's why they're so clumsy; humans aren't designed to be five meters tall and as broad and heavy as they are. I think . . . if we have some pikes made up with a sharpened edge that stretches back about two meters . . . Then assign a particular unit to drill with them. Intersperse them in the regular forces to respond when one of the ogres attacks. That should handle it. They just caught us off-guard."

"Ogres and orcs and I saw at least two different types of Changed working on the parallels," the general mused.

"Yes, sir," Pedersen replied. "As long as they don't come out with a corps of orc composite bowmen I'll be happy, sir."

"Not much to be happy about, Lieutenant," the general said, nervously. "Why are they *here*? Why are they using standard siege techniques instead of swarming us?"

"That . . . is a good question, sir," Pedersen said, frowning. "Waiting for something?"

"The rest of the fleet to arrive?" the general asked. "First Legion?"

"Possibly," Bue said, musingly. "And, possibly, they don't have all the troops in the *world*, sir. They may *have* to conserve them. We're not the only group they are fighting."

"I'm more worried about some sort of a trap," the general said. "They haven't done a number of things I would expect. No attempts at porting into the town. Port in here, set up a port on *this* side and we have trouble. No dragons. Just standard siege works. I don't trust it."

"Doctor Ghorbani," Conner said, brightly, stepping in the small tent she had been assigned. "Come with me, won't you?"

"You've got that 'I know something bad that you don't and I want to gloat' look on your face, Conner," Rachel said, frowning but getting up from her camp-bed.

"You know me so well," Conner said, dryly.

"Hey, Roc," Rachel said, looking up at the elf-thing. *"Adelas tomall."*

"Do not speak to Roc," Conner said, sharply, waving at her and muttering a word.

A wave of pain so strong it, for a moment, made her knees sag, washed over Rachel. Then it was gone.

"Okay, okay," she gasped. "I get the point. No talking to the elf-thing. Damn. He was the only person in this camp that had a brain."

"Come with me," Conner said, striding down the line of tents. "So, here we are, peacefully carrying out siege operations against a town we don't particularly need."

"So I noticed," Rachel said. "And soaking up casualties doing it."

"Doesn't it seem silly?" Conner said, getting back some of his sunny disposition.

"Yes," Rachel replied. "It does."

"Well, I hope it's not *too* obvious," Conner said as they came to a tent. A Changed was exiting, a new one from the looks of it, and hissed at them for a moment until it noticed Conner's robes. Then it backed away, fawningly.

"So you're making more Changed?" Rachel asked, her stomach dropping.

"I hope that anyone observing thinks that," Conner replied, sweeping back the door of the tent. "But, no, we're not. Behold."

Within was a large frame made of some sort of silvery metal and a portal. He gestured her into the tent and then waved for her to follow through the portal.

When she reached the far side her stomach dropped. The portal was set up in the door of a castle in a large valley. And the floor of the valley was *covered* in tents. Changed were everywhere, most of them in semiorderly groups.

"There are eleven of these portals," Conner said, smiling. "Each of them with a force of about seven to ten thousand Changed on the far side. They have been drilling on entering the portals and the gates of the camp are . . . large for a reason. Your father thinks we don't know that he is on the way with archers. With Blood Lords. With another full legion. But we do, oh we do," Conner said, quietly smiling. "And a little bird has whispered in the right ear that we have *you* as well. In the camp. Alive. Unharmed. Mostly."

"My father will . . . not come for me," Rachel said, bleakly.

"Oh, I think he will," Conner replied. "Besides, he

has to defeat us, doesn't he? Your father always leads from the center of his main force. First Legion has assembled to the northeast of us and will come down from there, deploying near the head of the peninsula. The bowmen are at least a day further away but they will land near Wilamon and march overland, fast, arriving just in the nick of time and deploying to the north. Dragons will attack from sunward. Did I mention the anti-dragon ballistas? Edmund will feint that he only has one cohort to draw us out. We'll 'take the bait.' Then he'll attack us with the main force of the legion while the bowmen press us from the flank. We'll retreat, run, back to the fort. They will pursue. And when they do . . ."

"You bastard," Rachel said, imagining it in her mind's eye. Her father often said that one of the main mistakes that was made again and again in military history was failure to adequately follow up a broken enemy. He drove routs as hard as he possibly could.

"And when he comes, when they all come, we will have them trapped. And we'll destroy the closest two legions and then, Miss Ghorbani, the war will be all but over."

In the woods a shadow moved, ever so slightly, then settled again. A white head lifted to sniff the air, yowled faintly, then settled back to its vigil.

"Archers will debark here, at Wilamon," Edmund's chief of staff for *land* forces said. "They will march overland at a rapid pace and assemble on the reverse slope of this hill . . ."

Edmund nodded as the briefing went on. The

archers were in for a hard night's travel but, weather permitting, they'd arrive in enough time for a bite to eat before the main battle. If the enemy moved the way he anticipated, they would slay them. The group of Blood Lords Gunny had brought with him would do for close support if the orcs broke towards the archers. Between the Blood Lords and their stakes, the archers would be fine.

And he still hadn't told anyone about Fell Deeds.

The battle should go about as well as any battle he'd ever planned. Things would go wrong, but nothing they couldn't handle.

So, why was his stomach on fire?

"That is the outline of the ground phase. Questions?" the chief of staff asked.

"I have one," Herzer said. He was in the briefing representing Joanna and the remaining dragon wings. "I know I'm the air guy for this one, but I've got an issue with the ground plan," he said, looking at Edmund then the intelligence officer. "You say there's only ten thousand in the camp. That's what they landed with. Why haven't they reinforced with portals?"

"We don't know," the intel officer admitted. "There have been teleports, but we can't tell the difference between them and portals. The number of ports has been . . . high. But they have *not* reinforced by portal and, yes, that has us worried."

"Duke Edmund?" Herzer said, widening his eyes.

"What would you have us do, Major Herrick?" Edmund asked, softly.

"Not what they expect," Herzer replied. "These movements are the minimum that *I* would expect, given our logistics and movement constraints. But, going in cold like this, the word 'corncob' comes to mind. I also note that there is no indication of anti-dragon defenses. That seems . . . well nigh to impossible."

"These are questions that we're not going to take up at this time," Edmund said, softly again. "Continue with the briefing. Major Herrick, I'll see you afterwards."

"You've got a concussion," Rachel said, holding a candle up to reflect off the ocular mirror over her eye. The left pupil dilated normally as did the right. "You need three days, probably no more, of rest in a quiet tent. Is that going to be a problem?"

"No," the officer growled, pulling on his shirt. "Not the way this damned siege is going."

"Fine, we're done," Rachel said, backing up and rotating the mirror up.

"You should come by," the New Destiny officer said, reaching out to touch her red hair. "You'd enjoy yourself."

"I'd rather fuck a Changed," Rachel replied, coldly. "Get out."

"That can be arranged as well," the officer snarled, reaching for her.

"First of all, if you get your blood pressure up having sex, don't blame me for the headache you'll get," Rachel said, avoiding the grab. "And as to the rest, you'll have to take it up with Mr. Conner."

The officer paused at that and then shrugged. "There will be later."

"I'm sure," Rachel replied. "Now get the hell out of my hospital."

She ducked through the flap of the tent and walked

to the rear. The back of the main examining tent was by the east wall and there was a broad avenue between it and the wall. Since it was only used to move troops during an attack or a drill, it was a relatively quiet and out of the way spot for her to try to get her head back together.

The two Changed assigned to watch her followed her out. They were remarkably docile for Changed but that was Conner's doing. As long as she stayed in the hospital area and didn't try to talk to anyone but patients, they left her completely alone.

She looked up and nodded. The UFS fleet had to be near because there was a dragon up watching the camp nearly every day. It was right towards the sun but that suited her just fine. She ducked her head and twiddled the reflector back over her eye then looked back up at the dragon. It was a chance but she didn't think the Changed were smart enough to know what she was doing. They had been instructed not to let her *talk* to people, not to prevent her from *signaling*.

"Herzer," Edmund said as the major came through the door. His eyes widened in surprise as the Blood Lord was followed by Megan Travante. "Mistress Travante. I asked to see Herzer, however."

"Am I unwelcome?" Megan said sitting down in one of the chairs. She glanced at the floor and saw that the bloodstains still hadn't been removed.

"No," Edmund said after a moment. He picked up a pair of stapled together message sheets and flipped them to Herzer. "From one of your dragons keeping an eye on the camp. You were right."

Herzer looked at the sheet and frowned. The top was broken words, the bottom an attempt at translation.

"Eleven gates in tent," Herzer read. "Trap for legion and archers. Seventy to one hundred thousand Changed. Feigned retreat. Conner in charge. Buggly." He looked up at Edmund and frowned. "Buggly?"

"I used to call Rachel my little buggly-wuggly," Edmund said, frowning at the desktop. "Not the sort of thing you would expect them to extract in questioning."

"And not the sort of thing they'd tell us," Herzer said, waving the paper. "That it's a trap. But you suspected that, didn't you?"

"Yes," Edmund replied, still looking at the desktop. "And even my intended counter to it won't work against the full force. Unless . . ." He leaned back and rubbed at his chin, closing his eyes. "A hundred thousand. How fast for them all to emerge? Figure two abreast through ten portals with the eleventh for special weapons and groups. How fast are they *emerging?*"

"Figure twenty per second," Herzer said. "Close enough. But, sir, we can't *let* them come out!"

"This is the bulk of the New Destiny army," Edmund pointed out. "If we can break them, here . . ."

"Will all due respect your Dukeship," Herzer said, tossing the paper back down. "We can't face a *fraction* of that force!"

"Yes we can," Edmund said, his eyes flaring open. "Don't kid yourself. It's all in the timing and we can do timing; they can't."

"Timing is all well and good . . ." Herzer said.

"How long to construct a fortified camp?" Edmund asked.

"Two hours," Herzer replied, automatically.

"Not a full camp, just the beginnings," Edmund said. "Stakes and one trench."

"Say . . . forty-five minutes," Herzer said. "Why the catechism?"

"I think we can get that down to fifteen," Edmund replied. "Okay, the first force comes out. There's a brief clash. They run back towards camp. What happens then?"

"We pursue, the main force comes out of the portals and we get our head handed to us," Herzer said, sighing. "They'll probably start coming out in the middle of the battle. The retreating forces will be diverted *around* the camp to the side gates and the main force will sally through the north gate."

"How long?" Edmund asked. "For the main force to reach the archers?"

"Say . . . fifteen, twenty minutes?" Herzer asked. "Why?"

"We don't pursue," Edmund replied. "Or, rather, the whole force doesn't. We go to the archers' hill."

"And construct a camp?" Herzer said, aghast. "No *time*, sir!"

"There's enough," Edmund said. "We'll have the archers and some people we'll link up with them start on it. The Blood Lords with them can get it pegged out at least, start on the parapet. Then when the rest get there . . ."

"They just have to settle down and dig," Herzer said. "Fast. But, sir, there are a *hundred thousand* of them, against *six* thousand. Even in a camp that's long odds!"

"No, against *twelve* thousand," Edmund said, poking

at the table top. "Caught between *two* fortified camps. *Two* legions. Besides, it's only going to be about fifty thousand, tops."

"Sir," Herzer said, frowning, "Balmoran is too far away to directly affect the main force. They'll be concentrated, we'll be dispersed. And they have a fortified camp in the middle . . ."

"Oh, I forgot that part," Edmund admitted. "They won't have their camp. We will."

"And how have you been spending your time, Miss Ghorbani?" Conner asked as Rachel was led into his tent.

"Sewing up your more *useable* officers that forgot to duck," Rachel replied. "How's the siege going?"

"Slowly, slowly," Conner answered. "Unfavorable winds slowing down the fleet, don't you know. Can't rush things too much. But they should be here in the morning. Since I'd *hate* for you to miss the show, I think your duties as a doctor are about done. You'll be staying . . . closer to me. Won't that be *fun*?"

"I dunno, do I have to talk to you or can I just play with Roc?" she asked, grinning. "I bet he plays chess."

"I have . . . spoken to Roc about his interactions with you," Conner said, smiling thinly. "There will *be* no more interaction. Understood?"

"Of course," Rachel replied, sadly. "Hate to break the elf out of the monster, wouldn't we?"

"That would be . . . quite impossible," Conner said. "There is nothing left of what you would call the 'elf.' Yes, as you've surmised, it is a modified elf. And there will be more, many more."

"Only so many on earth," Rachel said, musingly. "And they can't reproduce . . ."

"There are ways and ways," Conner replied. "There *will* be more. Not that it will matter to you, of course."

"Of course," Rachel said, twitching one cheek. "Although, one of my fondest dreams is being the one that tells the Lady about it."

"Forget those dreams," Conner said, bluntly. "As soon as your father takes the bait, you'll be going back to Ropasa. Where . . . something different awaits."

"More or less what I expected," Rachel sighed. "So, in the meantime, what?"

"Well, as a matter of fact, I *do* play chess," Conner said, pulling out a board. "Care for a game?"

"I can't imagine you playing chess," Rachel said, frowning as she sat down. "There's no way to cheat."

"Conner is, as far as I've been able to determine, my opposite number with New Destiny," Travante said. He and Sheida were present as avatars for a meeting with Edmund, Shar, Megan and Herzer. "He is . . . not a general. Probably a criminal before the Fall and now something like the head of their intelligence corps and assassination arranger. It was he, undoubtedly, that set the assassins on you, Duke Edmund."

"So what is he doing in charge of this?" Edmund asked.

"The New Destiny force is commanded by General Kossin," Travante said. "I would suspect that Conner is something on the order of a control or a political agent, sent to . . . watch the proceedings rather than directly command. And if part of the plan was to capture your daughter, he would probably have had some charge in that."

"I'm getting increasingly angry and frustrated with the degree of penetration New Destiny has managed," Sheida said, shaking her head. "They knew where Edmund was and they knew where *Rachel* was. We've determined that there is a leak here, at a very high level. We've even determined who it is . . ."

"Don't tell us," Edmund said.

"I wasn't going to," Sheida replied, frowning and looking over at Joel. "I probably shouldn't have even mentioned that much."

"But since you have . . ." Joel said, "we've . . . cocooned the known source. From now on New Destiny will get only what we want them to get. From that source, at least. There are other suspects, here and elsewhere. But the time for housecleaning is . . . not yet."

"Agreed," Edmund said, frowning. "But we *need* to clean house. Soon. Certainly before any counterattack."

"We have to deal with *this* attack, Edmund," Sheida reproved. "Not worry about future plans."

"Actually, I've already got a staff *working* on future plans," Edmund replied. "You have to start the planning at least this early. However, yes, we have to deal with *this* attack first. And we will."

"You're confident of that?" Joel asked. "The . . . correlation of forces is suboptimal."

"Let's just say that . . . I'm sure that tomorrow will be a day of many fell deeds," Edmund said, smiling tightly. "If that's all . . ."

"I think so," Sheida said, frowning. "Good luck, Edmund. You've never failed me before . . ."

"This won't break the string," Edmund assured her.

"Since I'm here," Joel said, coughing and clearing his throat. "I don't suppose I could have a moment alone with my daughter?"

"I'm headed for my cabin," Edmund said, standing up and gesturing at the door. "Mistress Travante is free to have the room as long as she wishes."

Sheida nodded to the two of them and vanished as Edmund, Shar and Herzer left the room. Herzer looked over his shoulder as he left and Megan smiled at him. He grinned back and closed the door.

"I'm . . . very glad to see you well," Joel said, his voice catching slightly. He cleared his throat and sighed. "Very glad."

"Just as glad as I was when Herzer told me you were alive," Megan replied, grinning. Then she paused and frowned. "Any word on mother?"

"No, unfortunately," Joel said. "She's in a New Destiny held portion of the Briton Isles. I haven't asked agents to go poking around for her, obviously. Far too dangerous for her. And them. One of Edmund's plans that he alluded to will involve the recapture of the Briton Isles, first. Then we might be able to find her. If she was home."

"But we're here," Megan said, brightly if brittlely.

"Yes," Joel said, sighing. "I don't want anything to happen to you, now. Once you close with the coast we can portal you to Chian . . ."

"I think . . . I should stay here," Megan said. "At least until the battle is done. If it goes bad, I can always port out. And . . . well I'd rather stay here, for now."

"I noticed that you seem . . . close to Major Herrick," Joel said. "I don't suppose that has anything to do with it?"

"You mean my boyfriend?" Megan replied, grinning. "Dad, if you don't have agents on the boats, I'd be very surprised. And where the councilwoman is sleeping would be part of their reports."

"As is her attachment to a young Blood Lord officer," Joel said, nodding. "One that . . . spends a great deal of time trying to get himself killed."

"He's very good at *not* getting killed, as well," Megan replied. "And as he pointed out to me, that's his job. I want him to come back, but I think I'd love him less if he *wasn't* what he is. He'll make it; I have to believe that. And despite what your reports might say we're *not* having sex. Too soon for me, something he understands. He's a very *unusual* young soldier."

"Yes," Joel said, dryly. "I've seen *those* reports as well. How is Bast taking it?"

"She's sleeping in the same cabin," Megan chuckled. "She's been good company. Herzer has suggested, a couple of times, that I . . . discuss things with her. About . . . what happened to me. I've talked to her some but not as much as either would prefer. I know I have to talk about it but . . . Bast is the wrong person for me. I'll find a counselor after we get this battle settled. I promise."

"Good," Joel said. "Something else I can relieve my mind of. You've made me very proud of you, Megan. I was proud of you before, naturally; any father with a fine daughter is. But what you have been through, how you handled it, how you are handling the burden thrust upon you now, all of them make me very proud. Your mother would be proud as well. Will be when she hears about it."

"Thank you," Megan said, her face clouding. "I won't say that any of it was easy."

"Very few things that are easy are worth the time it takes to do them, Megan," Joel said. "What you did was *hard*. And you did it well. What you are doing now is *hard* and you are doing it well. That is *why* I'm proud of you."

"I'll keep that in mind," Megan said, making a face.

"Now, go assure your friend that you've had a *nice* chat with your Poppa," Joel said. "He looked as if he wasn't sure."

"I will," Megan said, standing up and cocking her head at the avatar. "I can't kiss you good night but . . ." She put her fingers to her lips and threw him a kiss. "Good night, Poppa."

"Good night, Megan," Joel said. "Be well."

"I shall."

CHAPTER THIRTY-TWO

"Ensign," Edmund said as Van Krief came in the cabin. "Feeling a bit left behind on the tide of events?"

"A bit, sir," Van Krief said, sitting down nervously as Edmund waved to the cot.

"Well, you're not anymore," Edmund said, tossing her a dispatch envelope. Unusually, it was still unsealed. "Read that."

Van Krief opened the envelope and extracted the three sheets within. She read the first sheet, her face a somber mask, then turned to the second on which was included a map and the last, which was a signals supplement. When she was done she looked up.

"Comments?" Edmund asked.

"Bold, sir," was all she said.

"Necessary," Edmund replied. "Magalong has to *move*. He's done well in the defense but he is going to have to move like lightning. You're taking that dispatch to make that clear and to make clear *why*. You know why, right?"

"Yes, sir," Van Krief said. "Sir, I'll make sure he understands."

"But only Magalong," Edmund said. "Keep this very close. If it gets out, we're all up a creek. And don't go and wrap those around some cigars. Understood?"

"Yes, sir," Van Krief replied.

"Dragon leaving in thirty minutes. You're on it."

"Yes, sir."

And then there was one.

"Sheida," Edmund said, sighing. "Sorry to bother you again."

"I'm three hours behind you, Edmund," the queen said, smiling. "And you're never a bother. But *you* should be getting some sleep."

"Agreed," Edmund said. "I think the reason Alexander conquered half the world was that he was *young* enough. But this won't wait. What I've left out of most of my orders is the real battle. And for that I need two portals."

He explained for a moment and then had Sheida pull up a schematic of the battlefield so she could understand.

"Bold," Sheida said. "To the point of rashness. You risk our two most experienced legions, a major town, the loss of the coast."

"A hundred thousand orcs will *mean* the loss of the coast," Edmund pointed out. "If we get half the pieces moved correctly, the *right* half, we'll have mouse-trapped most of Chansa's forces. At least a goodly chunk. I don't care *how* many people they have in Ropasa, they've got to keep some supporting their forces. Ergo there's only so many they can use as soldiers. And we'll have winnowed them down heavily. It's a chance I've been waiting for, one of the prerequisites of taking Ropasa in our lifetime."

"And if we take Ropasa, they'll be squeezed down to . . . Northern Frika and some holdings in Sind."

"Exactly, and the northern wildernesses. And few major power sources after which *you* can take care of the rest. That's if we *can't* capture some of the Key-holders. But we've got to destroy their forces, winnow them down at least, with minimal loss to us. And we can do it. Here."

"And you need . . ."

"Two portals," Edmund said. "Surely you have the power for those?"

"Power, yes," Sheida frowned. "Just one problem. I've agreed to limit portal creation to Key-holders only. When we first started making them, there were . . . security issues. And too much power use. It's a voted-on protocol. I can't break it."

"Who's free?" Edmund asked. "Send them to Raven's Mill."

"I suppose Elnora, not that she's going to be . . . *willing*," Sheida said, wincing.

"Megan?" Edmund suggested. The other UFS Key-holder was an academic and a specialist in domestic affairs. Hardly the person he'd prefer handling a critical military task.

"I'd . . . rather wait," Sheida replied. "I want to get more of a feel for her. I trust her on one level, she's Joel's daughter after all. On another her . . . experiences are going to have affected her. I don't want to thrust too much on her at first."

"Very well," Edmund said, shrugging. "If you could send Elnora to Raven's Mill, then, to prepare."

"I shall," Sheida said, sighing. "It's never easy, is it?"

"Nope."

Prior to the Fall, Elnora Sill had been an academic, specializing in the history of "Women's Issues." Like everyone else on earth, it had been a hobby rather than a vocation but one that she followed with intensity.

After the Fall, and after the initial scramble for simple survival, she had been selected by Sheida Ghorbani as one of several counselors on specific post-Fall problems. Besides issues directly related to the rise of women from virtual serfs to equals in society, Elnora was widely versed in surrounding disciplines. From Elnora's perspective, the rise of women was, essentially, one of technology and economics. Therefore she had to be versed in both disciplines to ensure the validity of her models.

As time went on she became a closer and closer counselor of the queen on a variety of issues. Their thematic positions meshed very well and while Sheida was widely read and highly knowledgeable, like any good manager she did not consider herself an *expert* on every subject.

When the previous Key-holder had succumbed to the dangers of Dream, a highly advanced form of virtual reality, Sheida had asked Elnora if she would accept the Key. After much painful thought, Elnora accepted. On one level it would increase the likelihood that her theories would become policy, not to mention giving greater automatic status to women in the United Free States and, hopefully, their allies. On another level it would make it hard for her to continue her studies, especially studies of the changes that had occurred in female status post-Fall.

She had continued as an advisor, and now implementer, of Sheida's policies. She had concentrated, however, on domestic issues. Her knowledge of anything military, other than that the war was going on and generally where battles were taking place, was limited. The one area where she had been very hands off was the subject of women in military forces. The military had been fair and evenhanded on the subject, in her opinion, simply requiring that females meet the same standards as males. The fact that many females were *unable* to do so—it took a very odd female indeed to survive Blood Lord training for example—was besides the point. The military created the chance, it was up to women to take it if they so desired. Equality of *opportunity* not *outcome* was one point where she and Sheida agreed entirely.

So she was somewhat surprised to be asked to undertake an, essentially, military mission.

"I can do it," Elnora temporized. "But I have no experience in military matters, Sheida."

Unlike Sheida, who maintained her reign from her beleaguered home in the Western Range, Elnora maintained a small office near the capitol in Solous. She had been going over notes from the day's meetings when Sheida had contacted her and the interruption was not to her liking, either in manner or content.

"All you have to do is go to Raven's Mill and set

up the portal," Sheida said. "Your contact on that end is General Lanzillo, who has been briefed that you are arriving. The timing on portal generation is tight, but we'll have communications on it. All you have to do is stand by until the portal has to be generated, generate it and then you're done."

"I have meetings . . ." Elnora said, frowning and brushing her light brown hair out of her eyes.

"Elnora," Sheida said, gently, "there is a time and a place for everything. What we have been working on is of vast importance. In the long term. But at *this* time the most important thing we have to consider is whether we can prevent New Destiny from taking our eastern cities so that we can *keep* working on those policies. You can't work on civilization if the barbarians are *inside* the gates."

"Intellectually, I'm aware of that," Elnora said, grimacing. "However, much as I *admire* the military, of course, at a distance . . ."

"You're not *comfortable* with them," Sheida said, smiling slightly. "I understand. However, in this case . . ."

"I'll do it," Elnora said. "When should I leave?"

"Unfortunately, as soon as possible," Sheida said. "We need to ensure that everything is prepared."

"Right away?" Elnora said, gasping. "But I'll have to instruct my aides . . ."

"Elnora," Sheida said, firmly, "go to Chin. Contact General Lanzillo. Put in a portal to Raven's Mill through one of the inactive gates. Go to Raven's Mill. Ensure that you're ready for the rest when you get there. Please."

"Very well, Sheida," Elnora said, standing up and nodding. "If that's all?"

"Have fun?" Sheida asked. "Think of it as research. Studying the myrmidon in its natural habitat."

"Mr. Chambers?" Elnora said, frowning slightly. "Sorry to bother you."

Chambers looked up at the avatar and then stood up. He had been working late in his office in the War Department and he carefully controlled the start at seeing the Key-holder in the room.

"Mistress Sill," he said, bowing from the waist.

"Oh, posh, Mr. Chambers," Elnora said, waving a hand. "I don't need that. But I do need a bit of advice . . ."

Harry Chambers had been an agent of New Destiny for nearly three years. He hadn't *intended* to become an agent; it had just sort of . . . happened. A touch of bitterness and a bit of hubris had caused him to talk about things he shouldn't have talked about. Small things. Then a little stroking, some favors granted and before he knew it he'd turned over *real* information, the sort that could get you hanged. After that, one thing had led to another.

If you're two hundred years old and even half bright, it was hard in the middle of the night to lie to yourself. He'd been manipulated, sure, but he'd *let* himself be manipulated. What had the UFS done for him? What had Sheida and Edmund done for him? Edmund had damned near cut his leg off in the moments after the Fall. Sure, they'd been sparring and who knew that the personal protection fields were going to fall *just then*. But it had still been a damaging wound. He still limped from it, even healed.

Sure, it should be "completely healed" and unnoticeable. But *he* could still feel the blade slicing into his quad. For a person who had always considered his body his best asset, that sort of wound was *mentally* crippling. And Sheida, the bitch, when Tanisha gave up her Key, who did it go to? Did it go to her closest aide? No, it went to a woman, an academic, somebody who didn't know what was happening in the world without a ten-thousand-word briefing.

And he'd passed information *right under their noses*. Gotten them back for all the things they'd done to him. And New Destiny had money, lots of money, for the sorts of information he passed. No way to spend it, not yet, but there would be. He had a sack full of gems ready for a quick exit. Hit a couple of portals, get to the exterior of the teleport shield and he was golden.

He'd been considering taking just such an exit lately. He'd been Sheida's aide since right after the Fall. But just last month he'd been "promoted" to a war department undersecretary position, a liaison to the House of Lords. Technically he should be getting even better information than before; he could call on any information available in the war department. But some of the information he had been sent . . . didn't make sense. Didn't quite fit other information he was sure about.

If he was being fed *dis*information, it meant that someone suspected him.

Sheida had become . . . cooler as well. And there were rumors, rather well-placed ones, that an intelligence service had been formed. Oh, there was already the Intelligence Coordination Committee, but this other service didn't even have a name. "The Group" was the name most often associated with it, the head of it just known as "T." There was a confidential budget, a rising one, but that was all he had heard about it.

He knew for a fact that the Intelligence Coordination Committee did not suspect him. But this other "Group" might. In which case, he should bolt.

The problem was, now he saw what used to be called a "main chance."

"The problem is," the stupid woman babbled, "Sheida's sent me off like I'm some soldier of hers but without even *that* much briefing. I don't know any of these people."

"I know General Lanzillo," Harry said, soothingly. "A good man, a good academic. He's the local area commander but since most of what he handles is schools, he was chosen for his experience in military history and military sciences. He is a bit ... uhm ... gruff ..."

"The problem is that Sheida is expecting me to handle some of the military aspects as well," Elnora said, frowning. "I don't know a battalion from a legion. This has to be held *very* closely you understand. I really need ..."

"I'm free at the moment," Harry said, smiling. "And ... used to this sort of harum scarum military operation. I can leave a message that I've been called away on Council business. That won't be questioned. If you would like me to accompany you and help ... ?"

"That would be wonderful."

Rachel fingered the blade in the candlelight. It was somewhat like a long knife, a surgical blade designed for deep cutting in amputations. Good dwarven surgical steel, it was sharper than any dagger, with a razor-sharp point. She had made a scabbard for it under the noses of her guards, the guards now surrounding her tent, and slipped it into her bosom while in the latrine. It was her court of last resort.

The battle would probably start around dawn. By noon her father would have probably beaten the New Destiny forces, given what she had communicated. But win or lose, Conner would be able to take her back to Ropasa. And she wasn't going to let that happen.

She placed the point of the scalpel at the top of her neck, just under the skull. She'd considered several options but all of the rest depended upon bleeding, something that could be fixed relatively quickly. No matter how good Conner was, he was going to be hard-pressed to revive her with a severed third vertebra. It was an interesting question in neural transmission and muscle flexion. Could she cut her spine before the signals to her arms became scrambled. A modern physician certainly had the *strength* to cut their own spine. But was it possible?

She thought she would probably find out tomorrow.

She pressed the scalpel in a bit harder and flinched as she felt the fine tip cut into her skin. She could find out now.

She withdrew it from her thick hair, a problem that she'd already considered, and wiped the tip off on a cloth. Then she slid it back into the scabbard and down into her bosom.

Tomorrow would be soon enough. As the thief said, maybe the pig would sing. As long as she was still on this side of the portal, there was hope.

✧   ✧   ✧

"Too many things to go wrong, boss," Herzer said as Edmund mounted the wyvern.

"If some go right, we're no worse than we'd be otherwise," Edmund said. "If most go right, we'll be better. If none of them go right, we're up a creek."

"Well, we'll be there," Herzer said, saluting. "Good luck."

"Same to you," Edmund replied, then tapped the wyvern-rider on the shoulder. The dragon hopped onto the catapult and was launched into the sky, the leader of the UFS now headed to join the First Legion.

Herzer went down into the wyvern bay, which was crowded with extra dragons, and passed through it to the flight ready room. The riders were crowded too; it was standing room only on the last dragon-carrier in the UFS fleet. The riders were joking, the sound was good but . . . strained. Many of them were from carriers that were burned, sunken, wrecks. And all of them had been at sea for too long in the crowded ships. They also felt the tension of the day that had yet to dawn. Everyone knew that throwing the enemy back was important. None of them, besides Herzer and Joanna, knew how important.

"Settle down," Herzer said, stepping up in front of a plywood-covered map board. "Everyone know the mission?" They'd had the initial brief the night before so there was a scattered chorus on the varied theme of yes.

"Sergeant Fink?" Herzer said, pointing at the junior rider.

"We take off in . . ." Fink looked at the bulkhead-mounted clock and gulped, "one hour. Assemble off

Wilamon Point. Wait for first engagement then, on signal from Commander Gramlich, split into two echelons and bombard the New Destiny field force. Return by divisions and continue sorties until exhaustion or defeat of the New Destiny force. In the event of retreat on the part of our own forces, we cover the retreat."

"Very good," Herzer said, nodding and looking around the room. "Everybody got that?"

"Yes, Major," one of the riders from the *Richard* said. "It's easy enough."

"And known throughout the ship, right?" Herzer said. "Meg . . . Mistress Travante swept this room for technologicals before this meeting. All the corridors around us are being secured by marines, unobtrusively. Why? Because everything that Sergeant Fink just said is . . . let us call it a lie. This is your real mission brief . . ."

"First call!" the sergeant bellowed, pounding on the doors. "Boots and saddles!" He continued down the corridor, pounding on the door of each of the Blood Lords that were stationed at Raven's Mill. He was charge of quarters and it was time to face the bright new day. In another hour he'd be off-duty for twenty-four hours, after having been on-duty for the same, and he intended to be deep in the arms of Morpheus in two.

Behind the sergeant the platoon sergeants of the Blood Lord battalion spread out, passing the word they'd just been given.

"Drop the PT uniform," the triari said, shaking his head. "Full armor and weapons. Draw starts in fifteen minutes."

"What the hell?" the private said, dropping the light cosilk uniform back in his footlocker and pulling out a field uniform. "Why?"

"The damned general's called a surprise inspection for 0800 hours. There's time for chow at least . . ."

Malcolm D'Erle was dogged. There was no other way to describe it. His feet were burning, his chest was on fire and he was dog weary.

The archer corps had debarked at Wilamon on schedule and, after collecting some sketchy transport, had headed for the battlefield. It was sixty-five kilometers by road from Wilamon to the hilltop they were intending to use and they had a bare fourteen hours to make the movement. They'd marched in a standard series of quick march and double-time with breaks every hour. But the breaks seemed shorter and shorter as the time went on. The transport was mostly carrying water and the general had passed brutal messages on intake and usage of same. Food could wait. Rest could wait. The only thing that mattered was getting the majority of the archers, in some half-living condition, to the hill, on time.

And they'd made it. It was two hours before dawn when a group of green-clad, longbow-toting Rangers stepped out into the road and waved a bullseye lantern at the archer corps.

"Looking for General D'Erle," the lead Ranger said.

"Here," Malcolm gasped as the group was brought to a reasonably quiet halt. He could hear the archers falling out by the wayside but that could wait.

"Lieutenant Aihara, Fifth Rangers," the Ranger said,

his voice pitched to carry but soft. Not a whisper, that could be heard at a greater distance. "We've been scouting the New Destiny force for the last two days. We have your approach lines marked out and had wagons brought down with food from Tarson. No fires, obviously, but the food is bread loaves and meat. Casks of water and some wine if you wish to issue it. Chow line's set up."

"Lieutenant," the general chuckled, "you are a sight for god-damned sore eyes."

"Sir," another figure said, coming out of the gloom. "I'm Ensign Destrang, General Talbot's aide."

"Yes, Ensign?" the general said, raising an eye at a dress uniform covered in greenery.

"I need a quiet word with you, sir," the ensign replied, softly. "Soon. I have a dispatch from General Talbot and supplementary orders."

"Let me get this clusterfisk under control," D'Erle said, frowning and looking over his shoulder at the collapsed archers. "Then we'll talk."

CHAPTER THIRTY-THREE

"I can put this on myself, you know," Herzer said, extending his arms backwards.

"Us to do," Bast replied. "Hold open, Megan."

The ancient Romans had put an enormous amount of thought and practical research into making field armor that a soldier could wear day in and day out and Edmund Talbot had seen few reasons to ignore them. The loricated legionnaire armor was made of overlapping steel plates, lorica, that were effectively thin steel bands held together by small fittings on the inside. They were bent to go around a human body and open on the front. There they were tied with leather bindings. They had to be bent back to be put on, but other than that the armor could be donned like a coat and was, for armor, remarkably comfortable and cool.

Herzer had already donned the cosilk undershirt, with wide half sleeves to prevent chafing from the edge of the lorica, the steel-faced leather kilt and the thick cosilk scarf that wrapped around his neck and folded across his chest. The latter was to prevent the armor from digging into the neck and also acted as a slight protective collar against rebounds.

Herzer tied the front of the armor as Bast and Megan put on his shin, knee and thigh guards. Then he held his arms out, smiling faintly, so they could attach the bracers. On his right, his only, hand he slipped on a leather glove backed with steel inserts on the outside. Last, Megan placed his helmet on his head. The original Blood Lord helmet had been a barbute, a solid helmet of steel with a thin "T" on the front for breathing and sight. Recently, the legions had gone to the original Roman design. It was far more comfortable and gave much greater vision in battle. Of course, the face was essentially unprotected, but nothing was perfect.

He looked at the two of them standing side by side, the childlike beauty of the ancient elf with her long, curly, blue-black hair and cat-pupiled green eyes standing next to the much more subtle beauty of the councilwoman and shook his head.

"Do I get to keep both of you?" he asked, holding out his arms.

"Friends are," Bast said, accepting and joining in the group hug. "Friends will stay. All and always."

"I won't kick her out of bed, mind you," Megan said, trying to smile.

"Will help with armor?" Bast asked Megan.

"What armor?" Herzer said, frowning.

"Going with," Bast replied, slipping out of her bikini top and bottom. "Hard fight have. Back will cover. Ride Joanna. Won't mind."

"It *is* going to be a hard fight," Herzer said, frowning harder. "A bloody *shambles* fight. You're as good as anyone in the world, better than me, but you're going to need *armor* and I don't know any in this ship . . ." He stopped as the elf produced a square of fabric the size of a handkerchief from her apparently bottomless pouch. She started unfolding it. And unfolding it. When it was *fully* unfolded the deck of the compartment could be seen through a long, grayish bodysuit.

"Hard to put on," Bast said, sitting down on the deck and shoving one leg in. "Megan to help?"

"What is that?" Herzer asked. He always tended to get a bit . . . horny before a fight. Just one of his many demons. And the sight of the elf writhing on the floor putting on that . . . cat-suit combat-nightie, was a bit more than he was prepared to handle.

"Carbon nanotube," Bast grunted, shoving an arm into a sleeve that ended in an integral glove. "Not very stretchy. Think have gained weight."

"Carbon . . . what?" Herzer asked as Bast got up and stretched, hard, finally getting all her digits into place.

"Carbon nanotube," Bast said, posing with her arms in the air. She looked from one blank face to the other and then pouted. "Diamond? Girl's best friend?"

"You mean that's a *suit* of carbon nanotube?" Megan said, aghast.

"Yeah," Bast said, simply, pirouetting in place so the zipper at the back was presented to Megan. "Zip me?"

"That's the stuff that they used to put in tourney armor to make sure *nothing* could get through it, right?" Herzer said.

"And in wyvern wings." Megan nodded, zipping up the back. "That's why they're impenetrable."

Bast folded up her hair in a quick bun and slipped a cover over her head. Like the rest of the suit it was nearly invisible.

"What do you think?" she asked, posing again and then turning in place.

The suit was essentially transparent except in carefully selected . . . *mildly* opaque spots.

"Put your eyes back in your head, Herzer," Megan said, dryly. "Besides, you've *seen* it."

"But this is . . . different," Herzer said, wonderingly. The suit glittered faintly in the lamplight and he remembered what Bast had said about diamonds. That was, essentially, what the suit was, a flexible covering of solid diamond.

"Third floor," Megan said, chuckling, "combat lingerie . . ."

The elf ignored the byplay and picked up her bow and saber.

"Ready?" she asked Herzer.

"Sure," Herzer replied, bemusedly. "Why don't you *always* wear that?"

"Doesn't breathe very well," Bast said, frowning. "Gets hot. Hard to take off in case want fun." Her eyes grew distant and she frowned, then looked at Megan and reached out to stroke her face. "Say no goodbyes, yet."

"Why?" Megan asked, tilting her face to the side.

"Is not time," Bast replied, frowning. "*Gaslan* is . . . shifting . . ."

❖   ❖   ❖

"Message from station one-three-seven, Mr. J," the messenger said, handing over a sealed envelope.

"Thank you," Joel said as the messenger left. He slit the envelope open and frowned at the contents. One cheek twitched for a moment and then he stepped quickly into his secretary's anteroom and opened up a speaking tube.

"Communications," a voice said when he whistled into it.

"Operational Immediate to all stations . . ." he said.

Brice Cruz had been a Blood Lord when most of the pussies going through the chow line hadn't heard the name.

Sure, he'd had his problems. Been up the ranks, been down the ranks. But kicking him out of the corps over a few miserable bandits had really pissed him off. At first. Herzer had been the one to bring him the news. He'd known Herzer since right after the Fall, when they were both apprentices in Raven's Mill. And he knew that Herzer would go to bat for him.

So when *Herzer* had told him that *Herzer's* recommendation had been a full court-martial, well, he had to think.

He'd spent a good bit of the next year thinking. Besides starving there wasn't much else to do. Gunny Rutherford had recited a poem one time, something about Black Sheep. One of the lines was about "slipping down the ladder, rung by rung." That was his life in a nutshell. When you're too dangerous to be a soldier, and too honorable to be a bandit and a lousy farmer, there wasn't much going but "slipping down the ladder, rung by rung." The only thing that kept him from thinking about it was what wine and beer he could afford working as a wandering laborer.

They'd found him in a miserable slop of a tavern, drunk as an owl on bad wine and near half dead. They'd sobered him up and then started asking questions. After a while, he realized that if the answers were wrong, he wasn't walking out of the hut they'd taken him to. But the answers were right. And so he'd been given a new job. It wasn't as good as being a Blood Lord and really getting it stuck in. But, and this was the key point, they'd promised him that if he was a good boy and played by the rules, he'd occasionally get to kill people. The flip side being that if he fisked with them, even once, he'd be visited by unpleasant gentlemen with similar abilities and then there would be no more Brice Cruz.

He'd thought they were crazy when they put him back in Raven's Mill. But it was remarkable what a change of hair and skin color along with a few things you could do with a face could do. Nobody had twigged. And, after all, he knew the town and the Blood Lord Academy inside and out. He'd been there before half the buildings were built. Had *built* a third of them.

He'd taken a job in the kitchens and done a professionally middling job. Never so good that he could get promoted, never so bad that he got fired. And he kept his ears open. From time to time he passed on bits of information that he'd picked up. Nothing much, Raven's Mill in a lot of ways was a backwater.

This morning was unusual, though. The commandant had called for a surprise inspection. And he'd heard one of the headquarters guards that was coming off duty saying that Councilwoman Sill and some undersecretary from the War Department were in the building. Just a surprise inspection wasn't too odd; the commandant was a right bastard about them. But put it together with the visit, though, and something was happening.

He glanced at the clock and looked out the window. Right on time.

"Spell me," he grunted to one of the assistant cooks. "I had too much coffee."

He stepped out back to the latrines and opened up the door to the third stall.

"Clearly we need better facilities," he said to no one in particular.

"It's clear," a voice answered from the next stall.

"Councilwoman Sill and an undersecretary from the War Department are at headquarters," Cruz said, conversationally. "And there's a surprise inspection. Maybe dog and pony show for them. Lots of tenseness going around."

"I heard half of that already," his control said in a hard voice. "And we have a problem."

"What's that?" Cruz asked, buttoning up his pants.

"You've got a mission," the control said. "One that you have to take right now. Can you get in the headquarters?"

"Yeah," Cruz replied. "If I *really* have to."

"You *really* have to," the control said, tightly. "It's game time."

"In the *headquarters*?" Cruz said, trying to keep his voice down.

"In the headquarters," the control replied. "Now. There is exactly no time."

"I can't get *out*," Cruz said, quietly but angrily.

"Let us handle that," the control replied. "Just do it."

"Fine one to talk!" Cruz snarled. "You won't be looking down a platoon of swords!"

"It doesn't matter," the control replied. "This is game time. You took the salt. There is one way out of this organization and that is feet first. You can do it of old age or . . . other ways. But if you try to run, you'll just die tired."

"Son of a bitch," Cruz said, quietly. "Fisk it. Everybody dies sometime. Who's the target?"

"Do you understand your orders, General?" Edmund asked, watching First Legion file out of its fortified camp. They were leaving a half cohort to hold the walls; if everything went to hell, they could always fall back on it. The rest of them were marching silently to the south, towards the battle.

"Yes, sir," General Lepheimer said. The legion commander was another political appointee but one that Edmund would have chosen himself. The UFS, the world, had precisely *no* military officers at the Fall. They were still trying to train a professional corps. But Lepheimer was a long term student of military history and his tactics, in simulated battles, map exercises and the few small skirmishes he had engaged in, had been sound.

Lepheimer chuckled dryly in the darkness and looked over at the duke.

"When I told my boys it was going to be a battle to tell their grandchildren about, I didn't realize how right I was."

"Well, if we have grandchildren to tell, it will be because of what they do today," Edmund said.

As he said it the pipes of the legion began to swirl and the battle hymn of the Blood Lords was roared from six thousand throats.

> *Axes flash, broadsword swing,*
> *Shining armour's piercing ring*
> *Horses run with polished shield,*
> *Fight Those Bastards till They Yield*
> *Midnight mare and blood red roan,*
> *Fight to Keep this Land Your Own*
> *Sound the horn and call the cry,*
> *How Many of Them Can We Make Die!*

"Blood to our blood, General," Lepheimer said, saluting. "We'll get it done."

> *Follow orders as you're told,*
> *Make their yellow blood run cold*
> *Fight until you die and drop*
> *A force like ours is hard to stop*
> *Lose your mind to stress and pain*
> *Fight till you're no longer sane,*
> *Let not one damned cur pass by,*
> *How Many of Them Can We Make Die!*

"Breakfast for the general," Cruz said, waving the tray in front of the two guards' faces so they could smell it clearly.

"Secure room," the left-hand guard said. "Nobody goes in."

"Blast," Cruz replied. "If I don't get this to him quick I'm in trouble." He held the tray out to the left-hand guard. "Hold this for me."

"What?" the guard said, automatically taking it. As he did Cruz swung a roundhouse punch into his face with his right hand and followed it up with a left to the right-hand guard. What looked like light gloves against the morning cold had steel inserts and lead palms for weight. It still hurt.

"Good thing they changed the helmets," Cruz muttered, shaking his hands to get feeling back in them. "Never could have done that with a barbute."

He palmed a dagger, then slipped the latch on the soundproofed door.

The room beyond was about ten meters long and occupied mostly by a large conference table. Harry Chambers was standing at the far end, holding a long dagger in his hand. Elnora Sill was sitting in the end chair, facing the door. Her head was tipped back revealing the gash in her neck that went almost to her spine. General Lanzillo was on the floor with a dagger in his back.

"Good," Cruz said, closing the door and bolting it from the inside. "You managed it. Have you contacted higher, yet?"

"What?" Harry said, reaching down and pulling the necklace that held Elnora's key from around her neck. "No."

"Do it, quick," Cruz said, going over to the general. "Good thrust. Nice technique. In the future, though, do the kidney first. It paralyzes them."

"Who are you?" Harry said, clearly flustered.

"Your *backup*," Cruz snapped. "You don't think you'd be sent on a mission with no backup do you?"

"But I didn't *tell* anyone . . ."

"What? You think we don't watch you?" Cruz

replied, shaking his head and going over to check Elnora. "Call Conner. We've got to get out of here." He reached down to touch the councilwoman's neck and then punched back, driving the dagger into Harry's stomach then ripping down. He twisted it as he withdrew and then punched the Undersecretary For House Relations in the face, hard.

"Fucking *traitor*," he said, kicking the dagger out of the man's nerveless fingers.

He picked up the key and turned to the door, opening it just as one of the response guards was running at it with his shoulder. The guard sprawled on the floor and then bounded back up, sword in hand, swearing at the bodies in the room.

"I am an agent of the UFS Counterintelligence Service," Cruz said, arms outstretched, holding up the key in one hand and the dagger in the other. "This was an authorized termination . . ."

"Herzer," Sheida said, appearing in the air as the major was getting ready to mount his wyvern.

"Your Majesty," Herzer replied, startled. He slid back to the deck and bowed.

"No *time*, Herzer," Sheida snapped. "Where's Megan?"

"Here," Megan said, stepping away from the mast where she'd been keeping out of the way.

"We need to talk, *fast*," Sheida said. "Somewhere secure. Where?"

Herzer thought about that and shrugged. "Landing platform. Wind's from for'ard, it will carry our voices away."

Herzer and Megan hurried up the companionway

as Sheida wafted behind them. Captain Karcher bounded up to the landing platform and Sheida waved her hand.

"Make sure we're not overheard," Sheida said, calmly but definitely.

"Yes, Your Majesty," Karcher said, bounding back down to the quarterdeck and clearing the rear. She took the wheel herself, the only position that might overhear.

"Elnora Sill is dead," Sheida said, rapidly. "Assassinated. We retained her key, thank God. But someone has to activate the portals."

"Oh," Megan said. "A council member."

"I'd go myself," Sheida said, nodding, "but there would be . . . complications . . ."

"I'll go, of course," Megan said. "We have the two for the front here. If I have the authority?"

"You do," Sheida replied. "I'll port you to Raven's Mill . . ."

"This is outside the blocks, Your Majesty," Herzer pointed out.

"Damn!" Sheida snapped. "Damn, damn . . ."

"I wouldn't have taken the port anyway, Your Majesty," Megan said, softly. "I'll go on Joanna."

"Like hell you will!" Herzer said. "It's going to be a madhouse!"

"There will be you, Joanna and Bast to protect me," Megan said, defiantly. "And that *is* what I'm going to do."

"Joanna can carry you to inside the blocks," Sheida said. "From there you port to Raven's Mill. That's *safer*, Miss Travante."

"Too bad," Megan said. "I'm going."

"No, you're *not*," Herzer said.

"We don't have time to argue," Megan replied, smiling. "Get moving, Major."

"She's right," Sheida said. "We don't have time to argue. And Travantes are stubborn as the day is long." She sighed and shook her head. "Get going, you two. Herzer . . . keep her alive."

"I will, Your Majesty," Herzer said, wishing he could be sure of it.

"Don't worry," Megan replied, sadly. "*I've* got a personal protection field. You don't."

"Go," Sheida said, vanishing.

"Not even a good luck," Herzer groused, climbing back down to the maindeck. He grabbed Megan's hand and they threaded their way through the cluster of crewmen who were arming the dragons. Taking her hand was a necessity as much as anything; the crews were highly drilled and moved in a synchronous fashion. Someone with no experience moving among them was as likely as not to be run over by a group carrying highly volatile bombs.

They made their way to Joanna, with Bast already seated on her neck, and Herzer picked Megan up, tossing her onto the dragon.

"New passenger, Commander," Herzer said, angrily.

"What?" Joanna replied, turning her neck. "Why?"

"Change of plan," Herzer said, running away through the organized chaos. "She'll explain."

CHAPTER THIRTY-FOUR

"UP THE GEESE!" the archers shouted as the first flight of arrows sleeted into the orc formation.

Edmund was watching the progress of the battle from a platform at the rear of the legion lines. As expected, the New Destiny forces reacted poorly to the sudden appearance of the archers.

The legionnaires had been holding the line for nearly an hour, but they were taking relatively few losses while piling up a ton of bodies in front of them. The legionnaires were arranged in a checker-board formation, rather than shield to shield, the first rank taking the brunt of the fighting, the second rank taking the few who made it past and the third only handling "leakers." As he watched, the lines shifted and reformed, bringing forward the second rank to take up the battle while the front rank retired, in stages, to be the third. This was one of the secrets that made the legion so effective, the ability to continuously replace

their front-ranked fighters with fresh troops and wear
the front rank of their enemy down.

Legions in history had never been supported by a
longbow corps, but the combination was a natural. One
of the two weaknesses of the Roman army had been
its reliance on auxiliaries for projectile weapons and
the relative weakness of those. Mostly they had used
Balearic slingers. A sling was a deadly weapon against
unarmored troops but it was relatively short-ranged
and of limited utility against any force in armor.

Longbows, on the other hand, were accurate to three
hundred meters and could pierce almost any armor at
two. With the legions pinning the New Destiny force
in place, the archers were having a good killing. As
he watched, wave after wave of cloth-yard shafts fell
among the orcs, slaughtering them in droves. One of
the big "ogres" they had been warned about made its
way through the press but before it could even reach
the legion lines it began sprouting feathers. Only the
feathers were visible, and not many of those, as the
arrows punched deep into its flesh. It fell well short
of the legionnaire lines, crushing two orcs under it.

It probably wouldn't have mattered, anyway, because
a platoon of pike bearers had rushed to the spot
opposite its path, prepared to make their way to the
second rank and either fend it off or kill it.

Everything was going precisely to plan except one.

"Where in the hell are the dragons?" Edmund
growled, pulling out a pocket-watch. The newfangled/
oldfangled things were hideously expensive, but more
than worth it when timing was crucial. He looked at
the time and put the watch away.

"Late?" General Lepheimer asked.

"Ten minutes," Edmund replied, sourly. He saw a trickle of orcs falling away on the left flank. Now would be the time to order a charge. But . . . it wasn't *time* yet! Or, rather, it was but he wasn't *ready*!

"Damnit, Herzer," he muttered. "Where are you?"

There was a light wind from the north and Azure suddenly sat up, sniffing the air, his mouth open in a grimace to catch the slightest of scents. After a moment he dropped back to his belly and began slithering forward, purring faintly. He had the scent of the Great One of his human's household. And where the Great One went, enemies fell before him.

It was payback time.

General Magalong shook his head as he lowered the binoculars. He could see the orcs starting to stream back and the archers on the hillside. But look to the east as he might, he could see no sign of dragons.

"Where are they?" he asked Ensign Van Krief angrily.

"They'll be here, sir," Van Krief said. "Now's the time."

"There was supposed to be a signal!" Magalong replied. "The *dragons* were supposed to signal!"

"We don't have time, sir," the ensign said. "They're breaking *now*. We have to move *now* to be in position."

Magalong looked one more time to the east, shielding his eyes and squinting against the sun, then sneezed thunderously. Then he turned to one of his aides and shrugged.

"Open the gates."

✦   ✦   ✦

"Okay, let me get this straight," Colonel Heiskanen said. "You're a counterintelligence agent. And all those bodies are . . . ?"

"Colonel, I just do what I'm ordered," Cruz replied. His arms were tied behind him and Heiskanen dangled the key in his own hand. "I was ordered to protect the councilwoman, if possible, and terminate Undersecretary Chambers with extreme prejudice. Since *he* killed the councilwoman, and the general, I'd say I had reason. Don't you?"

"So what's the deal with the big posts?" Heiskanen asked, pointing to the empty portals.

"I have no idea," Cruz said, looking over at the assembled Blood Lord battalion sadly. "I'd say, though, that you're about to go somewhere."

"The last time you were here, officially, we were trying to decide whether to court-martial your ass," Heiskanen replied, angrily. "And now you tell me you're a *counterintelligence agent*? A counterintelligence *assassin*?"

"Colonel, with all due respect, that's something for my superiors and your superiors to work out," Cruz said. "Your job, right now, is to communicate with *somebody* who knows what the *councilwoman's* orders were. Because I don't. And, sir, I'd do it damned fast if I were you."

"Listen up, legion!" Magalong shouted from the back of his horse. The legion had exited the walls thrown up around the center of Balmoran and now was deployed in open order on the fields in front. "On my orders you will *double-time* to the enemy encampment! First

Cohort Bravo will refuse the left flank. Third Cohort Charlie will refuse the right. Everyone *else* will assault through the south gate! It's *supposed* to be open! If it's *not* we're going to take it anyway!"

He spun the horse in place and waved forward.

"Quick time . . . March!"

The legion stepped forward at the repeated commands and Magalong nodded at the bugler. "Sound for double-time."

As the bugle rang over the formation the legionnaires raised their pilums and began to trot.

"BLOOD AND STEEL!"

"FINALLY!" Edmund shouted, looking up to the east. "Go, go, GO! Signaler, break right!"

"God damn, we're late," Herzer shouted.

"Not my fault!" Joanna yelled back. "On my mark . . . BREAK!"

"Ah, perfect," Conner said as the orcs began running for the camp. The legion was following at a slower pace, not keeping in contact or breaking to pursue, which was unfortunate but wouldn't really matter. By the time the second force was through the gates they'd be out of position to be supported by the archers. He looked behind him and smiled as the tide of orcs started spilling out of the portals. They had been drilled carefully. Walk to the portals and then run down the corridors to the north gate. He felt the gate under him creak and smiled as the first of them started spilling onto the field. The retreating orcs had also been drilled. If they came for the main gate they'd be slaughtered like pigs. Go for the sides. And they were, splitting into two streams, the one to the east gate larger by far since it was closer. The main force approaching the legion was masked by the ones in retreat. They might be noticed by the archers, but it was unlikely that even Edmund Talbot . . .

"Dragons!" one of the sentries yelled, pointing to the east.

"Ah," Conner said, looking over at Rachel. "And now your vaunted dragons turn up. A day late and more than a credit short." He turned to look out over the retreating host and grinned. "And they'll come in and drop their load of fire over the poor retreating orcs, then fly back to their ships. By the time they are turned around, the legion and your elite bow corps will be slaughtered and we'll have our anti-dragon defenses up and waiting."

"General," a messenger panted, coming up the stairs out of breath. "Balmoran . . ."

"What?" General Kossin said. "What about Balmoran?"

"They've sortied, sir," the messenger said as the orcs pounded by below.

"A forlorn hope?" the general asked. "A cohort?"

"All of them, sir," the messenger said, desperately. "It's the whole legion!"

"I don't have the forces left to repel that," the general said, angrily. "Unless . . . move the reserve company to the south gate," he continued to one of his aides then turned to the others that were hovering around. "Move *all* forces to the south gate. Hold them off. We'll deal with them when the rest are through the gates . . ."

"Spoiler attack," Conner said, lightly. "You've more than enough forces to hold them off." He glanced up at the dragons and frowned. "They should be turning . . ."

Rachel finally quit looking out over the field and looked up at the dragons, squinting against the sun. He was right, they *should* be turning to attack the original force. Unless . . . they were going to attack the portal force. She was no tactician; she left that up to her father. But she knew something Conner didn't and it was a balm to her bruised soul.

"Things not going exactly as you planned, Conner?" she asked, sweetly.

"They rarely do," Conner said, still watching the approaching dragons. "That is the reason for leaders . . . They're not attacking the orcs," he said as the dragons split into four echelons and entered a dive. "They're attacking *us*!"

"The legion's moving," General Kossin said, angrily. He glanced up at the dragons, determined that none were headed for their position and then ignored them.

"They're supposed to!" Conner shouted as the first echelon dropped a sheet of napalm over the east gate. The gates were covered with leather against just such an attack as were the towers to either side, but he could see burning orcs abandoning their positions.

"No, they're moving *left*," the general ground out. "Towards the archer hill."

"What?" Conner said. "What? Impossible!"

"No plan survives contact with the enemy, Conner," Rachel said, sweetly. "That's why they call them the enemy."

"No!" the New Destiny agent said as he saw what the attacking great dragon was carrying. "Noooo!"

"Right about there, I think," Joanna bellowed, dropping the two open portals in the camp's main boulevard and flaring out to land. She kept her wings and tail extended as she landed and spun in place, clearing out a quarter acre of land in the process. There were some defenders in the area; they stood as much chance against her as the tents that were smashed to the ground.

Herzer flared out his wyvern just north of the portals and then slid off the side, slapping it on the haunch with his sword even as he blocked an attack with his shield.

"Get out of here you silly thing," he shouted, gutting the attacking orc and kicking him away. The wyvern got the message, took three awkward hops and was airborne.

Herzer saw Bast interpose herself between a squad of orcs and the wooden portals and he ran to do the same to the north. As expected the tide of orcs that were coming out of the New Destiny portals had been carefully drilled. They were to the north of the UFS portals, and running away. None of them so much as glanced behind and the few officers that tried to stem the tide and get them turned around were bowled over. The only orcs they had to contend with were the remaining defenders in the camp. Those that weren't either headed for the south gate or immolated in one of the attacks.

Megan had already slid off the greater dragon and was running for them. He checked to make sure nobody was targeting her and then went to work.

Even "relatively few" defenders were far more than the UFS had for this strike. Orcs were coming at them from every side and he closed with the portals to keep them off the, relatively, fragile beams and especially away from Megan.

Bast was doing the same on the other side but the majority of the work was being handled by Joanna. Her tail flashed back and forth, hard and fast like a giant crocodile, and any orc unlucky enough to be caught by it was tossed through the air like a grain of rice. Her wings batted as well and the concussion from them was enough to stun any of the orcs.

One of the big ogres came charging from the south and she hopped over some stunned orcs to engage it. The ogre, for a change, was carrying a huge club. She dodged a clumsy swing and bit the ogre on the head, crushing the massive skull in her teeth.

"Pthack!" she spit. "Damn they taste bad!"

Megan ran through the chaos, jumping over guide-ropes from flattened tents and dodging bits of debris until she reached the open frames of the portals. Then she placed one hand on either frame.

"Mother!" she called. "Do you hear me?"

"Yes, Miss Travante," a voice said out of the air.

"There are two portals prepared at Raven's Mill," Megan panted. "There should be some Blood Lords waiting. Do you know which ones I'm talking about?"

"Yes, Miss Travante," the voice said.

"Establish link here," Megan said. "Code Beta Fourteen. Power Authorization One-Nine-Four-Five."

The portals blinked to life and Megan jumped between them, out of the way of the tide of elite

Blood Lords that would be pouring out any second . . . any . . . second . . .

She waved her hands as if to shoo them through. Waved them again.

"HERZER!"

Herzer spun in place at the scream and looked to see what had happened to her. But Megan was fine.

"What?" he shouted, taking a blow on his armor and dropping his shield to crush the orc's foot. Then he slid his sword into its neck and turned back. "What?"

"NO BLOOD LORDS!" Megan shouted, dancing from foot to foot. "Where are the Blood Lords!? There was *supposed* to be a tide of *Blood Lords*!"

"Shit," Herzer said under his breath. "Joanna! Cover this side!" he yelled, spitting another orc and dashing to the gate.

He stuck his head through and shook it at the sight that greeted him. The whole battalion was standing at parade rest while the colonel was haranguing someone in a cook's uniform. He cleared his throat.

"Colonel?" he said, urgently.

"Major *Herrick*?" Colonel Heiskanen said.

"Yes, sir," Herzer replied, desperately, waving a blood-spattered sword to point behind him. "Did we forget something, sir?" he asked in a mad voice. "The *battle*? The orcs? A *camp to capture*?"

"What orcs?" Heiskanen shouted. "What camp? What the *hell is going on*?"

Herzer froze at that and then stepped through the gate. There was, precisely, no time to explain and the plan had gone straight to hell. Oh, well.

He looked at the assembled ranks for a brief moment and then raised his sword over his head.

"BLOOD LORDS!" he shouted. "BLOOD TO OUR BLOOD, STEEL TO OUR STEEL." He spun in place and pointed through the portals. "FOLLOW ME!"

Megan picked up a broken tent pole and fended off the orc that was menacing her, backing towards Bast. Of course, that wasn't a great option, either. Bast was surrounded by orcs. They were dying, fast, but it didn't mean one of them wouldn't get in a blow on Megan.

"Oh, shit," she said. "Am I dumb or what? Mother, Personal Protection Field, please, Authorization Beta-Charlie."

As the PPF came live the pole was cut off short. She dropped it and stuck her thumbs in her ears, waggling her fingers at the orc.

"Nah, nah," she taunted. "You can't get me!"

The orc raised its sword and let out a hoarse bellow of fury, darting forward just in time to be bowled over by an armored wave.

Herzer smashed into an orc and tossed him aside where he was trampled by the flood of Blood Lords coming through the east gate.

"Portals," Herzer shouted, turning to face the groups that were running through and gesturing over his back. "Knock 'em down! Knock 'em down! Knock 'em down! Portals, portals, portals! Knock 'em down! Knock 'em down! Knock 'em down!"

Blood Lords were highly drilled but they were also taught to *think*. Where the tide of orcs was appearing was apparent and the groups spread out, heading for the portals. Others, though, thought of other things and turned aside, spreading a perimeter around their own portals to defend them.

Joanna, seeing that the plan was finally working, headed for the furthest portal to the east. It was just north of the east gate and after she'd flicked it, and its fellow, over with her tail, she headed for that. More Blood Lords moved to follow her.

"Major Herrick," Colonel Heiskanen said as he made his way through the pandemonium around the gate. "What is going on?"

"Sir, there is no time for explanation," Herzer said, grabbing a passing officer. "Lieutenant Julicher, grab your platoon and as many others as you can. Head for the south gate," Herzer said, pointing. "Get it open. Second Legion is coming through at a double-time."

"Yes, sir," the lieutenant said, and immediately began bellowing for his triari sergeant.

"Joanna!" Herzer bellowed.

"Yo!" Joanna yelled, swinging her tail around and knocking a couple of orcs over.

"Get to Megan and Bast!" Herzer shouted. "Let the troops get the gates. Make sure Megan is okay!"

"Got it!"

"Lieutenant Sosinsky," Herzer said, grabbing one of the officers just emerging from the west portal. "West gate. Take your platoon, as much of it as you can find. Take it and hold it until relieved."

"Yes, sir," the lieutenant said, dashing in that direction.

"Take your *platoon*, I said!" Herzer shouted. "Sergeant Turzak! Get the platoon and *try* to keep that young idiot alive!"

"Yes, sir!"

"That's a *fisk* load of orcs!" Colonel Heiskanen said. "Captain Wallo!"

"Leave 'em alone, sir!" Herzer shouted. "Let them run out the gate! Get the portals knocked over! Then close the gates when they're *out*!"

"*That's* what this is about!" Heiskanen said, looking around. "Then they'll be—"

"Out there and we'll be in here with Second Legion, sir," Herzer said. "No sweat."

"No sweat, you said!" Gunny Rutherford yelled.

"Oh, shut up!" Edmund yelled back, braining an orc with his hammer.

They were on the front lines of the legion, helping to hold back the first spray of orcs from the main force while half the First Legion did a world record job of constructing a parapet behind them. As promised the lines had been marked out and everything to hand but the timing had turned out to be . . . a little tricky.

"I should be going swimming about now!" Gunny Rutherford yelled, slamming his shield into an orc and then gutting it from the side. "Making my sacrifice to the Bull God! Maybe having a haircut or picking out which mermaid wench to try to have half-breed babies with!"

"You know you love this shit, you old coot!" Edmund shouted, blocking a blow with his shield and then slamming the hammer into the orc's unprotected knee. They always forgot to guard the legs.

"We're about done here, sir!" General Lepheimer yelled from the parapet.

"Well then get the damned archers to give us some

fisking *space!*" Edmund shouted just as he heard a grunt from Gunny.

He leapt to the side and brained the orc that had his sword raised for a killing blow over the fallen noncom. Gunny was still breathing but he had a gash the size of a forearm in his side, the heavy blow from the orc having smashed the loricated plate in. Ribs were visible. Gunny Rutherford wasn't the only legionnaire down and the shield wall was well and truly broken, just scattered legionnaires left in front of the parapet trying to stem what seemed like all the orcs in the world.

Edmund let out a curse and activated his armor. He'd been saving the charge for desperate times and these seemed desperate enough. It began to glow blue and he felt the fatigue wash away as nannites scoured his body of toxins, enhancing his strength and speed. Not as good as the old days, when he'd first met the gunny and they'd been young idiots trying to bring some order to the shambles that was Anarchia. But good enough.

The general waved the archers forward to the parapet and looked over, searching for the UFS commander. It took him a moment to find him in the pile of bodies. Edmund was a *blur*. He appeared to have Gunny Rutherford over his back and was wading through the orcs as if they weren't there, headed for the right-hand bastion.

"Ropes!" the general yelled, pointing to the remaining legionnaires. Some of them had gotten some movement room, if only because Edmund had killed everything in front of them. "Archers!"

❖   ❖   ❖

The portals were metal set in concrete blocks. They were well stabilized but six or eight Blood Lords could generally push one down.

Lieutenant Sivula stepped back and brushed his hands together, just as there was a thump from underneath the fallen portal.

"That's gotta hurt," he said, wincing. For the orcs that had been running through the portals, it had to be like running face first into a brick wall. However, the blocks left a certain amount of space underneath and he could see hands starting to scrabble around the edges. "Ah, weel, now, that's not on," he muttered drawing his sword and stabbing under the gate. He was rewarded with a howl and smiled. "Sorry!"

CHAPTER THIRTY-FIVE

"Oh . . . shit," Conner said as the last portal was tipped over. He could see figures swarming over the south wall, where the orcs, attacked from in front and behind, were running around uselessly. Speaking of useless, the last of the main force was just about through the north gate and they were being followed by a line of legionnaires. He could picture what was going to happen in his mind's eye. They'd take the gate, shut it, and then the New Destiny force would be trapped on the *outside*, caught between two legions.

"Indirect approach," Rachel said. "Strike where your enemy is vulnerable. Gotta hand it to Daddy. If you don't, he'll take it anyway."

"Right," Conner said, his face firming. "We're out of here."

"What?" General Kossin snapped. "Just like that?"

"Just like that," Conner said. "You can handle the rest. You've still got more forces than the legionnaires.

But Miss Ghorbani and I are *out* of here. Roc. Bring
her."

Rachel stumbled forward at a hard shove and looked
over her shoulder at the elf-thing.

"I'm going, I'm going," she muttered, following
Conner down the stairs. His tent was in the northeast quadrant, which was still free of UFS forces.
She looked around, desperately, but he was careful
to avoid the Blood Lords headed for the gate. He
had his back to her but she could *see* the glitter of a
personal protection field. She touched her chest and
grimaced, looking to the west where she knew safety
lay. Only a few meters. Only a few.

"Don't," Roc growled, touching her in the back.
"Go."

She looked down one of the streets of tents and
saw a familiar figure trotting to the north.

"HERZER!"

For the next step, Herzer had to *see*. He'd headed
for the north gate, which he could see Blood Lords
fighting for. There weren't many defenders and as he
watched the gates started to swing shut. From up on
the command tower he'd be able to see how the rest
of the battle was going. Down here it was total chaos,
but a chaos that Colonel Heiskanen could handle, not
to mention General Magalong. But what happened
next would be the key.

He was about sixty yards from the gate when he
heard his name shouted to the right.

"Rachel?"

"Great," Conner said, shaking his head. "The heroic rescuer. Roc. Take him." Conner waved to drop his personal protection field and grabbed Rachel by the wrist. "Come on, bitch."

"Herzer!" Rachel shouted, digging at the steel-like vise around her wrist. "Elf, Herzer! ELF!"

The . . . thing charging him was a *demon* and it was *fast*. He raised his shield to block the first lightning blow and the sword of the thing nearly clove it in half. He darted in, thinking that with that much extension it would be off-balance but the blow that hit him came out of nowhere, knocking him to his knees. He rolled backwards and up, managing to get his prosthetic up and catch the sword in it with a shock that ran down his arm and through his whole body. But the hand wasn't steel, it was adamantine, and it gripped the sword for a moment, binding it, as the thing yanked at it, nearly yanking him off his feet. He tried to dodge under the sword and get his own weapon in play but the thing had far too much length of arm for that to work. Finally it got its weapon free and he backed away, watching Rachel being dragged towards a tent, helpless to save her as he'd been helpless to save her mother.

The thing looked at him for a moment, cocking its head to the side and then raised the sword for a blow he knew he could neither dodge nor block.

"Not so," Bast said, striking from the thing's unprotected side.

The monster moved faster than the eye could see, but the blow from the light saber still opened up a gash on its ribs, cutting through the mail that armored it like tinfoil. The thing leapt backward again, considering its new foe.

"Go to Rachel," Bast said. "This one is mine."

Herzer didn't even nod, just started running.

"Quit struggling, bitch!" Conner shouted, dragging Rachel closer and grabbing her by the hair, then slapping her on the side of the head.

Rachel saw stars for a moment and then shook her head, trying to clear it. Suddenly, Conner had her in a chokehold and a knife had appeared in his hand.

"Take one step closer and she dies."

Herzer tossed the sword in the air, weighing his chances. The man was much larger than Rachel and although he was trying to use her as a shield there was a fair amount in the open. And Herzer was _pretty_ good at throwing a sword. _Pretty_ good.

"Don't try it," the man said. "You're not that good. I know."

"You're . . . Conner," Herzer said, quietly. Rachel's face was frightened but set, her hands clasped to her breast.

"Yes, and that means you know I won't hesitate to kill her," Conner replied. "Take one step closer and she dies right in front of your eyes."

"Take one step back and I'll take the chance," Herzer said. "I won't have her disappear."

"We're _both_ going to disappear," Conner laughed. "I can port out at any time."

"_If_ you could teleport, you would have already," Herzer replied, pointedly not watching Rachel. "Leave her and you can go free."

"No chance," Conner said, stepping back and dragging at Rachel.

"Conner," Herzer said, conversationally. "There's something you really need to know."

"What?" Conner said, suspiciously.

"I'm not the one you should be afraid of," Herzer said, gesturing with the sword over Conner's shoulder.

"Don't give me that," Conner said, taking a step back. "That's the oldest trick in the . . ."

Rachel felt herself thrown forward as sixty kilos of enraged housecat landed on the agent's back. Conner let out a scream and stabbed backwards with his knife but Rachel was nearly as fast. The scalpel came out and stabbed downward with the precision of a wasp killing a spider. It withdrew from his leg in a fountain of arterial blood.

"That was your femoral artery," she said in a light tone. "And femoral nerve, which is why you're experiencing so much pain at the moment." She stepped forward and looked at the staggering agent for a moment, and then drove the scalpel into his stomach and upward.

"That will have gotten your liver along with various blood vessels," she added, conversationally, as the agent finally fell to his knees and then face, the cat continuing to rake his back with hind-claws. Azure finally shifted the grip of his jaws and closed them on the agent's neck with a snap of something breaking.

"That would have been your trachea," Rachel added calmly. "So in my professional medical opinion, you're going to die of lack of respiration before you *bleed* to death."

❖   ❖   ❖

When the prey was finally still Azure lifted his muzzle from the agent's neck and mewed at his human.

"Good kitty," Rachel said, rubbing him on the bottom of his bloody jowls. "*Good* kitty . . ."

"This is a bit hot," General Lepheimer said, looking down at the mass of orcs that were swarming First Legion's hastily formed parapet.

"Yes, it is," Edmund said, pulling out his watch and then looking up at the sun. "Wouldn't you say it's just before noon?"

"About that," the First Legion commander replied. "I mean, there's quite a lot of them."

"Yes, there are," Edmund replied. The main mass of the orcs from the portal had hit the parapet like a wave and the rest had joined in since trying to attack their own former defenses didn't seem to be working. If there was any control over the battle on the New Destiny side it was not apparent.

"The archers are getting tired," Lepheimer pointed out. "And we're rather severely outnumbered."

"That we are," Edmund agreed.

"And they're pressing around to the right flank," General Lepheimer continued, pointing towards the end of the ridge where orcs could be seen spreading out and heading up the grass covered hill.

"Yep," Edmund said.

"General, why are you so . . . calm about that?"

"Hold it," Edmund said, glancing to the east then taking off his helmet. He lay down on the parapet and pressed his ear against the wood then smiled. "Oh, well," he said, standing back up and brushing off his armor, "close enough for government work."

"What?" Lepheimer asked as he handed back the helmet.

"You hear it?" Edmund said, smiling.

"No?" the general said, clearly out of his depth. Then over the sound of the battle he *did* hear it. Or, rather, feel it. A rumbling in the ground. "What the hell is that?"

"That," Edmund said, turning and pointing to the right flank.

Over the hill a tide of horsemen appeared, long lances shining in the sun. They didn't even stop their canter, simply dressed ranks on the move, locked in knee to knee and sped into a gallop as the long lances lowered to the attack and a great cry rose from six thousand throats.

"KENTIA!"

"Make signal to both legions," Edmund said, buckling his helmet. "Advance to attack."

EPILOGUE

"How long has this been going on?" Edmund asked, as Bast and the big . . . thing separated.

"Couple of hours," Herzer said.

"You know there's a battle going on, right?" Edmund asked.

"Couldn't be that important if you're here," Herzer pointed out. "Hey, Kane, glad you could join in the fun."

"Fun," Kane said. "I just rode damned near two thousand *klicks*. I'm not sure I can dismount."

"Well, it's the journey that counts, right?" Herzer said.

"Gunny Rutherford bought it," Edmund said as Bast flashed in and out, stinging the thing and opening up another rent in its tattered armor.

"I'm sorry," Herzer said, quietly.

"Holding the line while the parapet was being finished."

"It's how he would have wanted to go," Herzer said with a shrug. The elf-thing managed to tag Bast, hard and she backed away, favoring her arm.

"Bullshit," Edmund growled. "He wanted to die from a stroke while lying in a hammock being fellated by a sixteen-year-old redhead named Tracy."

Herzer thought about that for a long time and then looked at Edmund for the first time since he'd arrived.

"Why *Tracy*?" he asked.

"I have no idea," Edmund replied. "He was pretty drunk when he told me that. But it's the sort of thing that sticks in your mind. And I never worked up the balls to ask him. I wish now that I had."

The two combatants separated and Herzer held out his hand. One of the watching Blood Lords slapped a water bottle in it and he tossed it to the elf-thing. Edmund had noticed the pile of them and wondered about it.

"Very . . . something," Edmund said. "Noble, I guess. Stupid, maybe."

"Bast insisted," Herzer replied. Bast had accepted a bottle from Rachel and drained it, tossing it aside and checking over her sword. The elf-thing's was heavily notched but hers was unblemished.

"So, how long is this going to go on?" Megan said, walking up and slipping her hand under Herzer's arm.

"Bast said something about stopping at nightfall," Herzer replied. "Get some rest and food and start again in the morning."

"So what's it to be?" Megan asked, aghast. "Two immortals locked in an epic battle until the end of time?"

"Unless one of them gives up," Herzer said, shrugging.

"Nope, not on," Edmund said. "That thing got a name?"

"Roc," Herzer replied.

"Roc," Edmund said, holding up a hand as he walked past it over to Bast. "Hang on a bit, we've got to pow-wow. Hey, Bast," Edmund continued. "Nice suit."

"Edmund," Bast said, nodding at him and rubbing her left arm. "The battle went well?"

"The usual problems," Edmund said, shrugging. "Bast, we've got other things to do."

"I don't," Bast said.

"No, but we can't simply set aside part of the camp as an arena," Edmund replied. "Are you going to win this, soon?"

"*If* I were a true elf, yes," Bast said, frowning. "He has not the *gaslan*. Of all the things they have done to him, separating him from the *gaslan* is probably the worst. To create a fighting machine and take away its greatest strength . . . madness!"

"That would be Celine," Edmund sighed. "*Gaslan*?"

"Elf thing," Bast said, shrugging. "Hard to translate. To know of the way of battle. To know the myriad ways that battle may go and to choose among them for the one most right. You have it, a little. So does Herzer, I sensed it in him from the beginning. All elves have it, much. True elf would have won by now. But I have not the mass. I can touch him, but not penetrate. He can, sometimes, touch me. But rarely and then I have the armor."

"You've certainly carved him," Edmund said, looking at the rents in the armor and the blood that covered the thing.

"To laugh," Bast said, merrily. "Fast heal do elves. Fast heal do . . . those," she added, pointing at Roc. "No, must penetrate and cannot, until one of us tires much. May be him, may be me. Not today. Tomorrow. Afternoon. Maybe day after."

"Nah, ain't gonna go that way," Edmund said, shaking his head. "Sorry." He turned to the monster. "Roc?"

The thing, which had been glaring at the Blood Lords, looked at him and nodded.

"In about ten minutes, I'm going to have about a hundred archers here," Edmund said. "Now, the rest of these people are all noble about this stuff. I'm not. I don't think you are, either. You'll probably catch some arrows and deflect others, but in the end we're going to fill you as full of arrows as an armory. Understand?"

"Yes," the beast answered.

"You can surrender and we'll find a nice little fortress for you to haunt, or you can die. Your choice."

Roc fingered his sword for a moment and then pointed it to the ground. He stepped forward, provoking a rustle from the watching Blood Lords, and then took a knee, his head bowed.

"That one," he said, pointing at Bast. "To that one will I give my life. She is worthy."

Bast walked over to him, keeping carefully to the off side of the sword and slipped her saber under his chin.

"Look at me," she said. "*Adano*."

The beast looked up at her with hate-filled eyes.

"Who binds you?" she asked.

"I am bound to the name of my lady, Celine," the beast answered, angrily.

"You were bound to another name, once," she said, offering her hand and bringing the beast to his feet. She barely came to his waist. "I swear that you can be bound to Her again," she added, placing her left hand on his chest. "*Aso mua, shato moas latan.*"

And they vanished.

"What just happened?" Herzer said. "Did they port?"

"Mother?" Megan said. "Was that a teleport?"

"Dimension shift," the voice answered.

"Elfheim is closed," Edmund said. "Where did they *go*?"

"Mother?" Megan asked. "Where did they go?"

"I am not programmed to track dimension shifts," the voice replied. "But *shato moas latan* translates to 'that which is lost.' In a very ancient vernacular, humans would call it . . . Shangri-la. . . ."

APPENDIX

Paul Bowman, Leader of New Destiny, Minister for Ropasa (Deceased)

1. Chansa Mulengela, Minister for Frika, Marshal of the Great Army
2. Celine Reinshafen, Minister for Ephresia, Chief of Research and Development
3. Lupe Ugatu (Vice Minjie Jiaqi), Governor of Hindi (in dispute)
4. Reyes Cho, Minister for Soam (in dispute)
5. Jassinte Arizzi, Minister for Chin (in dispute)
6. Demon, lone actor

FREEDOM COALITION KEY-HOLDERS:

1. Sheida Ghorbani, Her Majesty of the United Free States, Chairman of the Freedom Coalition
2. Ungphapkorn, Lord of Soam
3. Ishtar, Counselor of Taurania and the Stanis States
4. Aikawa Gouvois, Emperor of Chin
5. Elnora Sill
6. Megan Samantha Travante

NEUTRAL:

The Finn

NOTABLE HAREM GIRLS:

Christel Meazell: Senior female in the seraglio, pre-Fall paramour of Paul Bowman

Jean Meazell-Bowman: Christel and Paul's son

Shanea Burgey

Meredith "Amber" Tillou: pre-Fall paramour of Paul Bowman

Ashly Wenman

Karie Szymonic

Mirta Krupansky

Velva Focke

Vita Kolemainen

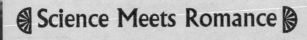